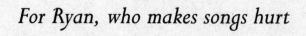

For Ryan, who makes songs hurt

Teen Killers in Love

A Novel

LILY SPARKS

CROOKED LANE

NEW YORK

This is a work of fiction. All of the names, characters, organizations, places and events portrayed in this novel are either products of the author's imagination or are used fictitiously. Any resemblance to real or actual events, locales, or persons, living or dead, is entirely coincidental.

Published in the United States by Crooked Lane Books, an imprint of The Quick Brown Fox & Company LLC.

Crooked Lane Books and its logo are trademarks of The Quick Brown Fox & Company LLC.

Library of Congress Catalog-in-Publication data available upon request.

ISBN (hardcover): 978-1-63910-076-7
ISBN (ebook): 978-1-63910-077-4

Cover design by Alvin Epps

Printed in the United States.

www.crookedlanebooks.com

Crooked Lane Books
34 West 27th St., 10th Floor
New York, NY 10001

First Edition: August 2022

10 9 8 7 6 5 4 3 2 1

Teen Killers in Love

Also available by Lily Sparks

Teen Killers Club

Chapter One

John Doe

If I were in love with a killer, I would never admit it. Not that I'm in love with Erik, obviously. I have one hell of a crush, sure. But what's a crush that's never confessed? Just a secret you can't keep from yourself. Nothing at all, really.

I've been trying not to stare at Erik, the camper with the highest body count in the Teen Killers Club, since he fell asleep a few hours ago on this shabby little bus headed toward my hometown. But I haven't been this close to him since back in the loft of the Star Barn, when he cut out the kill switch camp was using to track me, after he killed Angel Childs. Then he held back the cult members long enough for me and Javier to go free. And for the worst night of my life, I thought I would never see him again.

But here he is right next to me, lips slightly parted as he breathes, so I keep staring and staring. Like if I could stare for long enough, I could get used to him.

With his eyes closed he looks cruel, like one of those invincibly hot guys who's been welcomed in every room they walked into. But awake, he's never completely easy in his skin. His mind is constantly whirring, body tensed like some chase is about to begin, his nails bitten down to the quick on both beautiful hands. His hair, once long, is singed all the way to his scalp in places now; the rest looks like he cut it away in a hurry, uneven whorls and cowlicks standing out in places like a broken halo. His hoody is black, which helps hide the streaks of soot. His eyes, when they were open, were frighteningly green and ringed by broken veins.

"I was dodging police and tracking you and Jav all night," he'd told me in the few hours he was able to stay awake, voice just above a whisper. "We'll probably be on the run again before dark. His kill switch was still trackable when he took you to the bus depot, so it won't take them long to deduce which bus you're on. If we start pulling over, wake me up."

The truck downshifts onto an off-ramp, and before I can wake Erik, a fine crease stabs between his thick eyebrows, and his eyes twitch open.

"Already?" he says in a scratchy voice, leaning forward and blinking. We both catch a sign that reads "Santa Maria 20 miles," sliding by the window. He stretches his neck, cracks his knuckles, then turns bright eyes on me. "This isn't good. You have everything in case we need to run?"

He means the key we found searching Jaw's room, the guy who I thought had killed my best friend Rose and framed me for it. The key to the security deposit box that holds the evidence Jaw has been using to blackmail the real killer: Rose's mom, Janeane. If we can get up to Ledmonton and retrieve that evidence, I can use it to clear my name.

"Run where?" I drop my voice and gesture toward the gas station, the lone mark of civilization in a sea of golden grass hills and their violet shadows. "We're in the middle of nowhere."

"Time for a pit stop!" the driver answers someone sitting closer to the front. "Grab some food, use the facilities—"

Did I imagine it, or did the driver glance at us in his rearview mirror? I look to Erik. His face is perfectly calm, but he gives me a small nod like he saw it too, and we both take our backpacks with us down the center aisle.

Across the parking lot, against the dim blue sky going pink at the edges, is a violently green and yellow neon sign that reads "CACTUS BURGER."

"Might as well get something to eat," Erik says, opening the door for me, "though this is not where I wanted to take you on our first date."

"This is *not* a date," I sputter.

"Exactly. I refuse to tell our grandkids our first date was at a *Cactus Burger*." Erik eyes the slippery yellow walls and orange tile floor with distaste. "So this will be strictly dinner and making out."

My heart throbs and I swallow a nervous laugh as we join the line curling around a low dividing bar, hardly daring to look at him after a joke like that, and totally unable to process him in this setting. It's impossible that Erik's slightly too broad shoulders and tensed, crackling energy could exist in the same space as a bank of broken ketchup dispensers and baskets of hot sauce packets. But there he is, just behind me, eyebrows shooting up when our eyes meet, like he expects me to ask something. No, just staring until I believe you're real—sorry.

When I turn to scan the menu above the counter, Erik's arms go around me, and I startle, whipping around with a heart hammering at the contact. Our faces are now just inches apart. His clothes smell like smoke, but he smells like the air after it rains.

"Shouldn't we be keeping a low profile?" I almost squeak.

His eyes this close are mesmerizing, his right pupil torn all the way down in a slit, like a cat's. He puts his mouth right next to my ear.

"Look around. No one's looking at us now."

A bearded man in a Carhartt cap right behind us seems to be memorizing the specials; the guy next in line is earnestly considering his own shoes. No one wants to be the creep staring at the teen couple.

"This is just good strategy," Erik whispers. "May I?"

I nod, heart thrashing in my chest, and he hitches me onto the rail across from him, so I'm half balanced on the bar but mostly leaning against him, his arms still around my waist. There's a smile in his deep voice. "And I know a way we can hide both our faces at the same time."

"Good strategy . . ." I manage to say, and my restraint dissolves. My arms circle his neck and his perfect mouth covers mine. The dingy yellow walls become a golden haze, the kitchen's microwaves weaving a delicate techno melody as he pulls me into him, and I'm back there again. That place I go when we kiss, that place where everything becomes overwhelmingly real and completely a dream at the same time.

And I know I need to pull away. Erik is an apex manipulator. He made a bet back at camp that he could get me to fall in love with him. And he's far more likely to try to win a bet than be overcome by real feelings. A guy who's a player is scary enough; what happens when that player is also a serial killer? What happens to the girl who falls for his game? Until I know what the hell happened to Erik's ten victims, every moment in this dream world just makes me a bigger idiot. Not to mention the scandal of the Cactus Burger. I *know* this.

And yet I cannot stop.

It's Erik who pulls away first. I look up, breathless, and see his eyes fixed above and behind me, on the TV mounted above the soda machines.

WANTED, the screen reads, and below it are our mugshots, side by side. My hair was blue then, his long, but that's clearly us, stiff-faced and hollow-eyed. SIGNAL DEERE under my face, ERIK DOE under his.

"We need to go," Erik says.

"Next in line!" The cashier snaps, face gray under their yellow visor. I'm debating if we should turn and run through the crowded line behind us when the doors sweep open again, and I hear the muffled crackle of a walkie-talkie. Someone is waiting outside the Cactus Burger, someone with a walkie-talkie. Highway patrol? I don't look back; I freeze in place, and then Erik catches me up in his arms.

Carrying me like we're newlyweds stepping over our first threshold, he walks to the register, sets me on the long counter and whispers in my ear, *"Drive-thru window."*

The cashier makes a noise like a seal as I step down on her side of the counter and run for the kitchen, Erik springing over the Formica after me. We swerve past shelves of hot lamps, sinks of sizzling oil, and spigots of soft serve, almost slamming into a reedy guy with a hairnet and caulking gun of sour cream.

"Take what you want, man!" he yells, gloved hands up. "I ain't dyin' for Cactus Burger!"

Erik steers me hard left, toward another guy with a headset and eyes like saucers, pushing him out of my way so I can dive headfirst through the tiny take-out window.

The lady at the wheel of the car pulled up in front of me has a tray of drinks in her lap and one hand extended for her food as I twist my shoulders through. The instant our eyes connect she screams, *"Oh hell no!"* and flies forward. The next car pulls up, trap music so loud the hot hood of the ancient Taurus shivers as I set my hands down on it and start crawling.

"Whoa whoa whoa!" The horn blares below me, and I almost lose my balance. "Get off my hood, bitch!" the driver yells.

Then he lets out an incoherent cry as Erik throws open his door and tosses him across the pavement. I get into the passenger seat as Erik climbs behind the wheel. It stinks like weed inside, which might be why the driver is now leaned up against the brick wall of the Cactus Burger, laughing hysterically and yelling, "That's my car, though!"

We briefly stall, Erik grinding the shift knob into first, before we speed away.

Blue and red lights bounce cross the chrome body of the Greyhound bus ahead, highway patrol cars parked at either end. Erik swerves past them and speeds toward the snow cone–pink and red of sunset, almost drowned behind a bank of dark clouds growing on the horizon.

"There's already an APB on us." Erik sighs, taking the on-ramp onto the freeway, "Well, at least we can still have dinner. Here." He hands me a greasy bag. "See if there's anything vegetarian."

Despite my rollercoaster nausea from the last five minutes, and despite knowing full well he is, was, and always will be an apex manipulator, I'm touched he remembered.

"You want me to type a location into the GPS?" I fish a cracked but glowing screen from my footwell. "The guy's phone is still in here."

"The nearest railyard. There were cameras in the drive-thru—we'll have to ditch the car soon."

I set the location and prop it up in the cupholder, then open the Cactus Burger bag. There are three huge cups of fries and three burgers.

"Erik *Doe*?" I say, handing him an unwrapped burger once we're at speed. "Is that why you said I wouldn't believe what your last name is? Because I'm Deere and you're Doe?"

"Doe isn't my real last name." He wolfs down the food, eyes fixed on the road. "It's a pseudonym. Like John Doe."

"So how do they know your first name?" I'm already halfway through a cup of fries.

"Speaking of first names, where does Signal come from?"

"Nice try changing the subject!" I laugh. Then a thick raindrop hits the windshield, and he swears. I turn on my knees in the front seat and dig around in the messy back seat for an umbrella, a plastic bag, anything that will protect us, since we'll be on foot soon.

"What *is* your last name?" I call back, rooting around in what seem to be piles of dirty laundry, but then I touch waterproof fabric: a rain jacket and a nylon baseball cap. Nice.

"Erik?" I catch his expression in the rearview, eyes as hollow as they were in his mugshot, and then twirling red and blue lights swoop past in the other direction.

"Signal, please put on your seat belt," he says calmly.

I turn and flatten myself against the passenger seat.

"Is this a weird time to tell you I've never driven manual before?" Erik says. I turn to him, eyes wide, and he laughs out loud.

"You're kidding," I say, relieved.

"No, not kidding"—he smiles—"but how hard can it be? I've gotten us this far."

"Okay, okay, um—we're going to shift to a higher gear. Do you have your foot on the clutch?"

"*That's* what that is," he says, and I grab the stick shift and guide it into gear while talking him through the transition, and then he accelerates hard, threading precisely between the cars between us and our exit.

Ten minutes pass on the clock, but it feels like an eternity, the sky closing in lower and lower overhead, and rain washing over the windshield, until Erik turns off the exit and slips under an overpass, the arch on the other side just a sheet of silver rain caught in the streetlight, and I help him park.

We get out beside a row of tents sheltering under the overpass. Erik insists I take the rain jacket, pulling the hood up over my head before putting on a denim jacket and the nylon baseball hat. He leaves the keys in the ignition and the doors open.

"Wait!" I run over and set the bag of uneaten food next to the closest tent before running back to him. He hugs me to him then, planting a kiss on top of my head with such intensity it throws me off.

"What was the strategy on that one?" I laugh, but he's already scanning the road ahead. The intersection is clear. We run out of the echoing dark of the overpass, rain chasing us faster and faster down the block.

* * *

"On three," Erik says as the train approaches and its whistle cuts through the rain.

We've been crouched behind a beach dune just past the trestle bridge long enough I'm shuddering from cold, and he's wetter than I am, which is saying something. He's insisted on wearing both backpacks for the jump, but otherwise seems to take it for granted I can do this.

I wish I had his confidence.

I watch, rather than hear him, count to three as the train rushes by, and when the last car is in sight we dash across the sand. He lunges for the ladder beside the open sliding door and grabs for me. For a terrifying moment my hand slips down his wet wrist, then some long-dormant muscle activates in my core and my foot gains the lower rung as he grabs my collar and hauls me into him. I cling to his wet jacket, refusing to imagine how my body will jounce along the ground if I fall. Erik guides my hands to the cold rungs of the ladder bolted to the freight car, hanging from it himself by one arm, like he's windsurfing. Once I'm secure, he throws his head back and a passing streetlight stamps his smile in white on the darkness, a smile of radiant joy, as his hat flies free of his shorn head. Then he easily leaps around the doorframe and disappears into the freighter. After several tense moments, I throw myself after him, sprawling out across the rough particle floor and almost weeping with relief.

The freight car is empty, aside from bits of straw and a wood palette rattling in the corner, the sliding doors of the container open on both sides. Erik sheds our backpacks and settles down beside me, warm fingers locking with mine as he helps me sit up, pulling me close against him. We lean into each other and stare out at the ocean alongside the train, a heaving darkness under a purple sky tie-dyed with black clouds.

"All in all," Erik says, "a good day."

"There's an APB out on us now," I say, teeth chattering. "There are hundreds of miles between us and the security deposit box, and if we're taken into custody before we get it—two Class A fugitives—"

"Yes," Erik says calmly, "but on the other hand, we're alive. We've got transportation and an oceanside view."

"That's true"—I squeeze his hand—"and those were really good French fries."

He looks down at me, and I can sense his smile. "And at last," he says, "I get to be alone with you."

He's lucky I don't tumble out of the freight car, the words hit me so hard. I keep staring out at the ocean, heart jerking in my chest, knowing if I look up, we'll kiss. And I can't do that again because I don't trust myself to stop.

There are many reasons to get a girl alone, and they all involve things I'm not ready to do. Like . . . die.

"And at last," I say quietly, "you can tell me about your number."

The hidden ocean rolls in the silence between us.

"When you were with Javier," Erik says, "he told you about the guy he killed, yes?"

"Yeah."

"And you were cool with it, right?"

"I don't know if I was *cool with it*"—I tuck wet hair behind my ear—"but I could *understand*." I stumble over my words, still shaking, cold all the way to my bones. "Because it didn't come from, like . . . it wasn't in cold blood or something. He's not *evil*. He wasn't going out killing people for the fun of it or something."

"For the *fun of it*," he says, voice flat. "Is that what you think I did?"

I try not to think of his face across from Angel Childs.

"What—are you *scared* of me?" He starts to laugh, then registers my expression. "You're scared of me," he says after a pause.

I look up at him, begging him to understand what I can't deny. Erik is the only person who believed I didn't kill Rose; he understands more of what I've been through than anyone else; and he saved my life. But all I can say for sure about Erik is that the thought of losing him again scares me to death.

"I barely know you, Erik. But I want to."

"No, you want to judge me," he says with an angry smile. "You want me to offer up my life story so you can decide whether or not you're allowed to like me. Well, I'll save you the time: you're not. I'm not *not* evil." His smile gets harder. "So now what? Can you turn your feelings off, just like that? What are you, Signal, some kind of *psychopath*?"

"I thought you were all about telling the truth." I look up at him. "At camp you said I never asked your side. Now I'm asking. And you won't answer?"

"Nope," he says lightly. "I made that offer when you had a kill switch and couldn't run away from me."

I let out a horrified laugh. "Erik, what the hell did you do?"

"Knowing me won't make you like me more." He stares out into the dark, then adds dryly, "And I have my bet to win."

I should take this as a warning. And maybe I would if I hadn't grieved for him all last night, spent sleepless hours begging God to let him still be alive somehow. But I did, and he's here, and my hand won't let go of his.

Many dark beats of track pass under us before he asks, "You really want to know?"

"Yes."

"Okay then." He drops my hand, gets to his feet, and crosses the rocking freight car to the other door.

"Seriously?" I half shout, trying to be heard over the lurching heartbeat of the track, the wind rushing all around us. I don't think he hears, leaning against the edge of the door, hazy lights cutting him out and dark swallowing him again and again as we shoot by car dealerships and stretches of hillside, all-night diners and overpasses.

"What're you doing?" I call across the car.

"Looking for a jump-off point."

You're leaving? I almost blurt, but swallow the words and say instead: "Shouldn't we take the train as far north as we can? Try to get to Ledmonton faster?"

"I need to take you to my house first." He turns his head over his shoulder so I can hear, but doesn't look at me. "It's on the way."

"Your *house*?" The container floor tilts like the deck of a ship as I stand and cross toward him. "Your house with, like, your family in it?"

"They don't live there anymore."

The way he says it makes me colder.

"But it'll help me explain."

"Explain what?"

"My last name. And everything else." He turns back to me as we pass a glowing car dealership, and his eyebrows shoot upward. "Your lips are *blue*!" He immediately pulls his wet jacket off, throws it on the floor, then yanks the black hoodie he's wearing over his head. He holds it out to me, still dry and hot from his body. "Put this on."

"Then *you'll* be cold." All he has underneath is a thin thermal.

"I'll be fine." He rolls his eyes like I should know he can't feel cold. But *of course* he can. His outstretched hand is red with it. So I take the hoodie and put it on, but when he sits down again, I sit close beside him. He looks at me, startled, and I hold out one side of the waterproof jacket I'm wearing.

"We can share this."

"Good strategy," he says, voice hoarse at the edges. Then he pulls me into his lap, hugging me against him, my back pressing so tight against his chest he could count the notches in my spine. He has to feel my heart throbbing this close; hopefully it's masked by how hard I'm shivering. He sets his chin on my shoulder, the warm shape of his ear pressing against my neck, my head melts back against his, and the shivering stops. But my heart still rattles me harder than the track. I never would have thought it was possible to feel this much holding still.

* * *

I must doze off, because Erik wakes me, tugging gently on my shoulder.

"We have to jump in five," he says. Outside, the world is flying by, but the rain has stopped. Erik crosses the container. "Try to land in sand."

I nod, grinding the heels of my hands into my eyes, but when I get to the door and stand beside him, the beach seems so far below. Erik hangs out the side of the train, scanning the track and gripping the doorframe so muscles rise along his forearm. The cars ahead of us start to curve away from the shore, an iron scythe snaking around a bluff and into a narrow tunnel ahead. He looks back at me:

"On three?"

Oh. That's so soon. But I nod quickly.

"One. Two—"

The crash of the ocean drowns three as he launches himself wide of the train, hitting the beach in a rooster tail of pale sand. I jump down a beat after him, going limp, slight bend in my knees, a pose learned from falling off the obstacle course at camp on a daily basis. The momentum sends me tumbling like a rag doll, cold sand in my eyelashes, my lips, my hair.

Erik helps me to my feet as the train disappears into the tunnel. It's just us and the full moon on the beach.

"We have to climb a few stairs," Erik says, "but it's not far after that."

Moonlight carves the winding wooden staircases out of the cliffs above us, soaring what seem hundreds of feet into the dark. The black ocean shatters to gray shards on the rocks below as our footsteps ring up the narrow planks. When we reach the top, there's a chain link fence with a sign: "PRIVATE PROPERTY: STAY OUT."

Erik disappears over it before I've finished reading the sign. I take a moment, panting, bent over, hands on my knees, before I haul myself over the top and land with a moan of effort.

"Weakl—"

"*Don't*"—I gasp—"you dare. Call me. Weakling."

He takes my hand and leads me around a dry fountain in an overgrown garden. We're in the backyard of someone's house? No, not a house. Even in the dark, I can tell that's a mansion in front of us, the wingspan of an ultra-modern pitched roof black against the stars. Erik fishes up a rock from a garden of them at the edge of a broad deck and throws it into the back door with a reverberant smash. Then he opens the door, leans in, and enters a security code on a panel before throwing it open for me.

"Please, come in, come in. Make yourself at home!" he says. "The living room is down to your left, past the pillars. I'll get some wood from the pile."

Past the *pillars*. Cool.

I walk through the door and start down a narrow marble hall the length of a football field, the house unfurling around me, soaring white walls and black skylights. The furniture is hidden under heavy drop sheets and dwarfed by the vaulted ceilings; it feels like we've snuck into a museum. Two raw marble pillars at the end of the hall lead down into a dim room enclosed entirely by minimalist French doors, and I stare out at the dark ocean horizon, hovering beside the shape of a covered couch, until he comes in.

Erik sets an armful of wood on the hearth and opens the flue with a metallic shriek. Then he turns and throws off the drop sheet behind me, revealing a low cognac leather sofa, longer than my bed back at the trailer park, before disappearing again. I nervously perch at the edge of it.

He comes back with a glass full of water, smiling. "Water's still on. Electricity's not, as you may have noticed."

"This is your house?"

"Was," he says, and a match springs to life in his hands. A moment later its grown into a cheerful blaze in the gigantic black granite fireplace, lining his features with gold. Above the mantel is a framed photo portrait of a handsome family: mom, dad, a teenage boy who isn't Erik, and a kid who unmistakably *is*, at maybe age twelve.

"My last name," Erik says, staring into the fire, "is Wylie-Stanton."

"Wylie-Stanton?" I almost laugh. "What, like the test?" The Wylie-Stanton test is why I went to camp in the first place. It analyzes your data and designates your potential to cause harm to society along a lettered spectrum. If you test as a Class D, you're harmless. If you test as a Class A, you're irredeemable.

"Yes. Exactly like the test. My mom and dad, like I told you, were a forensic psychologist and a—"

"Computer programmer," I finish. "I remember. You told me on our night hike."

"My parents developed the Wylie-Stanton. And they based it on me," Erik says. "I am the original Class A all others are measured against."

Chapter Two

Proof

My glass of water falls to the floor.

"I'm so—so sorry, I—"

It doesn't break, but as I lean down to get it, the floor sinks away from me. When I sit back up, the room swings around us queasily. Black filings, like the first day on the obstacle course, wash over my vision.

"Signal?" Erik sounds very far away.

Cold sweat breaks out across my face. I blink fast, but the filings keep coming, everything is going dark. I knead my eyes with my fingers, panic washing over me.

"Signal, what's wrong?"

I stare up through the narrowing darkness to the door. I have to get away from him before I pass out. I need to shut myself up somewhere and figure out what it means that he's the ultimate Class A, that he's not *not* evil, that maybe there is no explanation for his ten, no misunderstanding, maybe not even regret. I shoot to my feet, but the blackness tightens and blinds me, sparkles of light evaporating behind my eyes as my overheated brain forcibly disconnects from reality.

My knees buckle, but before I fall, my feet are swept out from under me. I'm cradled by the smell of rain, the muscles and cords of his shoulder standing out under my cheek. But all I can see is darkness as he carries me away from the heat of the fire, into the echoing marble hall, and then somewhere dark, and then down.

Down, down we go, down endless stairs, down to what feels like the center of the earth, somewhere still and silent and cold. There's a snapping sound, like a flag in high wind, then my shoes are pulled away, and softness and warmth cocoon me. But I can see nothing in this elemental dark, not until I leave consciousness completely, and my nightmares paint with terrible colors the other Erik, the bloody-mouthed Erik across from Angel Childs, the Erik I have tried so hard to unsee.

* * *

It's still black when I wake up, with no idea where I am. But I'm holding a flashlight, one of the heavy-duty square ones with a handle, hugged to my chest like a teddy bear. I find the switch, and a big bubble of pale light slides over blue and white nautical-print wallpaper across from me. There's a cherrywood desk too, a closet door, a bookcase. And right above the bed, a two-page photo plate cut from some old art book and tacked to the wall. It's Michelangelo's sculpture of the Virgin Mary holding a dying Jesus on her lap. I squint at the description: the *Piéta*.

Erik's room. This must be Erik's room. I'm still in his hoodie too, and everything else I had on except my still-wet sneakers, which are tangled in the drop sheets heaped below the bed. I squirm my feet back into them as I inspect his bookshelves: a lot of nonfiction. History, travelogues, and true crime, surprise, surprise. A few Sherlocks. A couple large martial arts trophies are hidden almost out of view, placed at the ends of his shelves to keep the books from spilling out.

There's also a shelf with just framed pictures. A seven-year-old Erik scaling a climbing wall and another picture of him, a little older, climbing a red canyon with no ropes. A picture of him at ten or so in a life vest, with a gray-haired man on a boat. The gray-haired man is a carbon copy of Erik, down to the torn pupil; but whereas Erik has coloboma in one eye, the older man has it in both.

I'm about to go over to the desk, when I remember his taunt in Jaw's house: *"You clearly have no idea how to search a guy's room."*

I turn around and tilt Erik's mattress off the frame, like it's the hood of a car. And there, on the slats of the bed, is an old red-and-white Mead composition notebook, squashed flat as a dried flower, and on its cover, in all-caps Sharpie, is written:

ERIK WYLIE-STANTON
ACCOUNTABILITY JOURNAL

I seize this little gem and get back under the covers with the flashlight immediately. The first page has questions written out in black fine-point Sharpie, with the even lettering of a precise adult. The answers are in blue ballpoint, and scrawled by a much younger hand:

If someone hurt you, how would you feel?
Hurt
How can somebody that hurt someone else become accountable?
Write in a journal, I guess
Why is it important to be accountable if you hurt someone?
So you can go back to school and see your friends again
What advice do you have for somebody who physically hurts others?
Don't get caught
Finish the statement "I sometimes find it hard to tell the truth when . . ."
I sometimes find it hard to tell the truth when no one believes it's the truth anyway

Ever the smart-ass. But whoever was writing in Sharpie is not amused. Their answer, at the bottom of the page:

Erik, if you want to go back to school, you need to take these exercises, and why we're doing them, a great deal more seriously. Your glibness about what happened in August is deeply troubling to both me and your father,

and devastating for your brother. Skye would be well within his rights to press charges, and it's only because I believe so strongly in your capacity for growth that I have convinced him not to. So I need you, Erik, in the following pages, to *truthfully* describe the incident with your brother, and why it was wrong—

A light tapping on the door makes me jump.

"Yes?"

"There's lunch upstairs," Erik says, his deep voice muffled by the door.

Lunch? How long have I been out?

"Okay! Be right there!" I shove the notebook between the wall and the mattress as his steps retreat upward. I grab some toiletry items from my backpack and open the bedroom door onto a tall, steep staircase. Another door hangs open at the top of the stairs, letting daylight bounce down to me. When I climb to the top, I notice the handle locks from the outside. And I'm struck, moving down the echoing hall of his family's palatial house, passing door after door of empty rooms, that they would keep Erik in a windowless basement.

A mirror flashes from one of the doorways along the hall, and I duck inside a bathroom, bracing myself before meeting my own eyes in the mirror and facing the worst. No breakouts, that's a relief. But I look . . . dewy.

"That's one way to put it," I imagine Rose saying, rolling her eyes at me. *"Is that your forehead or a slice of real New York pizza?"*

I take a few pumps of whatever is in the porcelain soap dispenser on the marble counter, wash my face with cold water, then blindly grope around for a towel. There's not even a drop sheet. I end up blotting my face with the fabric shower curtain before pulling out the lip gloss, concealer, and eyeliner I'd tucked into my pocket.

"Are you trying to look cute *for a* serial killer?*"* I imagine Rose saying. *"Ugh. Like, that's a* thing, *I guess. There are some lonely little freaks out there, right? Both the Menendez brothers got married in jail. But,*

while you know I love a bad boy . . . a full blown, locked-in-the-basement psychopath? Hard pass, Signal. Hard *pass."*

I blink at myself in the mirror. Rose—or at least, my internalized composite memory of Rose—has a point. Erik told me last night he is empirically the most dangerous person in the world. The only sane, self-respecting reaction I can have now is to march into the kitchen and announce it's time to part ways. I don't need a babysitter, I can get up to Ledmonton on my own, without spending days and days in dark ravines and deserted houses alone with the "ultimate Class A." Just the fact I'm not running out the back door right now is proof I'm falling for his act. I'm flattering myself that his motives are kind.

As unthinkably painful as the idea of leaving is, it will only be more painful by the end of today. The only rational thing to do is cut things off now, while I still can.

But I can put on some eyeliner to say goodbye. That's just basic self-respect.

* * *

Erik is in the kitchen, at a tabletop propane grill set up on the huge granite kitchen island. Smoke trails out a window forced open by bougainvillea vines that're taking over the kitchen: violently magenta flowers spill into and up out of the sink, climb along the walls, curl around the crystal knobs on the cabinets and shelves, giving the late afternoon sunlight a rosy glow. Erik, haloed in pink, moves red peppers and pineapple around the grill. Three Hello Fresh crates litter the counter beside him.

"You stole a bunch of meal kits?"

"I had to find a vegetarian one." He shrugs, then points with his tongs to the table. "You can start on the macaroni and cheese."

I almost stop short, staring at the two settings laid out across from each other on the fully set dining table. He's put out placemats, two sizes of plates, coffee mugs, and glass goblets. Even *tea lights.* And yes, some delicious mac and cheese.

"You made this on a grill?" I say, pulling back one of the heavy wood chairs and taking a seat.

"I did a lot of grill cooking at camp. Not Naramauke—this other program I went to. It was called Higher Paths. It was a hike-in camp for, uh, 'troubled youth.'"

"What's a hike-in camp?"

"You go off the grid and hike deep into the forest for several weeks. No phones, no electricity, and you're hiking all day, every day. Setting up camp, breaking down camp, carrying all your stuff, and making your own food. There are lots of talk circles and therapy language, but I don't know. I liked it. I went on one every summer after I started homeschooling." He's been talking too fast, like he's racing to fit everything in, but now he pauses. "And we can get into that, if you can hear about my past without collapsing in shock."

"Maybe let me eat something first."

"Right." He nods, a small crease cutting between his eyebrows as he shuffles the food on the grill. Then he abruptly stops and turns to me. "No. You know what? I need to explain something."

"You don't need to—"

"Yes, I do. You fainted before I'd hardly told you anything."

"There's more?" I mutter as he comes around the counter and pulls out the chair across from me.

He's showered recently. His hair is still wet, the collar of his white T-shirt clinging to the line of his neck. He was so relaxed when I first came in, but now his broad shoulders are high and his eyes lit up with urgency. He's trying to get ahead of something. Like he knows I'm about to tell him I need to leave.

"You said you want to know me? Well, I'm the original Class A. All Class As share some aspect of my psychological profile because my parents developed the algorithm to find other kids like me." He says it so coolly. "The plan was to catch them early, when they could still be rehabilitated. The way my mom was trying to fix me."

"Okay."

"But all the other Class As—the people like me—that they found were, uh, not very 'fixable.' Selfish, manipulative, psychopathic—"

"*All* the other Class As? What about Nobody?" I snap. "And Jada and Dennis and—"

"Exactly! This is my point, Signal." He smiles, his dimple flashing. "Camp was the first time I met Class As who were cool. And also I met *you*."

"Also?" I raise an eyebrow. "Oh, so I'm not cool?"

"No." He shakes his head, dimple going deeper. "Being cool is mostly good acting. You'll never be cool, you're too earnest. But you are *good*, Signal. The first good Class A I've ever met." His eyes soften. "Any algorithm that puts *you* in the same category as *me* is worthless. So when we clear your name, it will expose the system for the total sham it is. End the Wylie-Stanton. End camp. And make the Director answer for what he's done."

I fall back in my chair, stunned.

I'd asked myself many times why Erik was so invested in solving Rose's murder. Why he came back to help me search Jaw's room after his kill switch was out. Why he'd risked his life to save me. And here is the answer: to end the misuse of his parents' algorithm, the Wylie-Stanton. Which makes sense, more sense than what *I'd* assumed, certainly. Just the thought of what those assumptions had been makes my face go hot.

"Why didn't you just tell me?" I ask at last.

"I needed to talk through the case and make sure we could prove you were wrongfully convicted, for one thing." He shrugs, "Gut feelings don't overturn verdicts."

I bend my face toward my plate. Birdsong and waves fill the sunny silence as I struggle to master myself.

This is a fight worth fighting. To end the increasingly prohibitive laws against Class As, to end camp, to keep our friends from going on more missions. There's no question of me leaving him now, not with so much on the line.

But I'm also terrified at how close I came . . . to *what*, exactly?

To thinking he liked me, when he never did. He needed to solve my case and got bored hanging out with me, so he made his little bet to entertain himself. And I almost fell for it.

"Erik, I'm completely with you on this. There's nothing I want more than to end the Wylie-Stanton. I'll do whatever it takes—go anywhere, testify to anything." I take a deep breath. "But while we're working on this, I need you to stop with the emotional manipulation."

"Emotional manipulation?" He laughs. "What are you talking about?"

"You know what I'm talking about. Like—like acting like we were kissing yesterday—"

"Acting? Who was acting? We kissed. We'd be kissing right now except you'd probably faint again."

"There will be no more kissing. Or flirting. Or bringing up that stupid bet—"

"You bring it up more than I do."

"Um, no. I had totally forgotten about it, until you got on the bus and announced you'd won."

"I did win." He crosses his arms over his chest. "You just won't admit it."

I shake my head. "You're so *arrogant*."

"I'm not arrogant; I'm perceptive. And you're projecting—"

"Let's not start with the therapy talk."

"Excuse me, but you accused me of emotionally manipulating you, which is not a nice thing to be accused of. I've done nothing but be honest with you. I haven't manipulated you into anything. I'm sure it's scary for you to have such *naughty feelings* for me, but—"

"I don't have feelings for you."

"Cool. Can you try looking me in the eyes when you say that?"

I shake my head and mutter curses under my breath as he pushes: "Any time today is fine. Unless you need a cold glass of water. Or a cold shower?"

I fight to unclench my jaw and finally meet his relentless stare, focusing on his torn eye. Something like a shiver makes its way up my neck.

"I don't have feelings for you," I tell him.

"Then why are you so scared you'll lose my 'stupid bet'?"

His beautiful smile gets wider the longer the silence between us stretches. I fight not to squirm in my chair, knowing every atom of my discomfort is registering with him, and break off the stare first, defeated.

"What are you even trying to win?"

"Say the magic words and find out," he says, and I shoot up from my chair so fast the heavy wood screeches against the tile.

"I'd rather cut my tongue out."

"Why?" He laughs. "What the hell, Signal—what did I ever do to you?"

My mouth open and shuts. There's nothing I can say that won't indict me. All he's done is believe I was innocent and help set me free. I took it personally, I read into it, and now I'm mad at him. *I'm* the arrogant jerk here, the victim of my own grandiose fantasies. Except—

"Why did you have Dennis test your kill switch first?"

His smile drops. "Excuse me?"

"When I asked our camp's computer genius to hack my kill switch before our missions, he said it might kill me. I told him to do it anyway. But then, according to Javier, you told Dennis to test *yours* first—"

"Is that a bad thing?"

"No. But I want to know why. Why did you ask Dennis to do it?"

Erik blinks at me. He starts to answer, then stops himself. High spots of color rise in his cheeks. "Javier told you about that? What a *gossip*."

I lean over the table.

"And that was before you knew if you could clear my name. You didn't even know for sure I was innocent! You risked having your kill switch set off for what? For a *hunch*?"

"Not a hunch." Erik leans forward in his chair and stabs the tabletop with his finger. "I knew you were innocent as soon as I saw you, never mind the fact you almost puked cutting up a *mannequin*—"

"Gut feelings don't overturn verdicts, Erik. Answer the question."

"Or *what*?" Now his chair screeches back, and he rises to his full height across from me, forcing me to look up at him. "You don't get to interrogate me. If I choose to risk my own life, to protect the proof *I* need to get what *I* want—"

"But you didn't have any proof!" I'm getting too heated, and it's contagious: his chest rises and falls faster the more I talk. "Dennis turned off your kill switch before you stepped foot in Jaw's room. Before you found the lunchbox or the necklace or the security deposit box key. You didn't have any evidence to protect!"

"I'm not talking about the evidence in Jaw's room," his eyes are wide and glowing green with morning light. "That's not my proof—that's for everybody else! I'm talking about you; you yourself are my proof—"

"Proof of *what*?"

"That there's good in me!" he says, then stops short. Like he's as surprised by the words as I am. He grabs for the long hair that isn't there, ducking his head and breaking eye contact. "You tested as a Class A. So, somewhere in me, there is something good like you. There has to be." He meets my eyes then. "You're the proof."

That does it.

The plates rattle as I put one knee and then the other up on the table and grab the collar of his shirt. He meets me in a kiss that feels more like proof something inside me is really bad.

His heart is racing against my chest as my fingers dig into the thin cotton across his back, and then his head lowers hungrily from my mouth to my neck, mugs rolling and goblets crashing onto the floor around us in explosions of glass. All my resolve is going to pieces, shattering against the silent testament of his hands, that he wants to touch me as much as I want to touch him. And I know, *I know* I'll pay for this. But yesterday I thought he was dead, and now he's here, and I am more alive than I've ever been. I'll pay for this. I'll pay anything.

Then someone pounds on the door.

I freeze at once, but it takes a split second longer for Erik to pull his mouth from below my jaw, his arms still gripping me as we both listen:

Bang, bang, bang!

"Police?" I whisper.

He releases me with a swear, then climbs down the table without rattling a dish, catching one of the mugs I send rolling as I follow him down to the floor.

As he hurries down the hall ahead of me, there's a flash in his hand, the blade of a kitchen knife held close to his side. When did he grab that? What is he thinking? If it's police, they'll have guns.

"Open up!" a rough voice yells through the door.

Erik turns the knife in his hand.

"*Erik! Signal!* I know you're in there!"

"Wait!" I grab his shoulder, and he stares down at me with eyes I barely know. "Erik, wait. That voice—"

I get in front of him and throw open the door.

"Nobody!" I cry as she collapses into my arms.

Chapter Three
Grand Theft Auto

She falls forward, her beautiful face so drawn and pale, her coat soaked through, like she never got out of last night's rain. But before I can hug her, Erik pulls me away and behind him.

"How did you find us? Did camp send you?" He brandishes the knife at Nobody, who is now clutching onto a high travertine table at the side of the hall for support. From the tension in her figure as she glares back at him, I know she's calculating how to get his knife.

"No." I shake my head, stepping between them. "We're not doing this. Absolutely not." I stand in front of Nobody, my arms outstretched protectively, and frown at Erik.

"Oh, great," he snaps. "Stand with your back to her so she can wrap her hands around your neck and choke you out—brilliant move."

"Well, if she does, won't my face be red. But better that than to stand here and watch you two turn on each other."

He's not even listening, too busy watching Nobody over my shoulder, so I soften my voice:

"Please, Erik."

I don't think I've ever said his name so gently. And his eyes flick back to me, even though the rest of him is tensed for a fight.

"It's not enough to have good in you somewhere, okay? You have to choose it. If this is going to work, I need proof that you can choose it."

And I'm not even sure what I mean by "this"—clearing my name? Me sticking around? Or something else. I think I meant something else. But whatever this is, it keeps his eyes on mine, and he lets the knife drift down to his side.

"Camp didn't send me here." Nobody says. And with some effort, she turns and claws damp white hair from the back of her neck. "I don't have their switch in me. See?" At the top of her spine is an angry red gouge.

"We need to clean that up." I wince. "It looks infected—"

"We knew about the switch," Erik says, the veins of his knife hand still standing out on the inside of his wrist, like the strings on a violin. "What I want to know is how you found us."

"Dennis gave me your address," Nobody says. "Saw the smoke from the street, figured it was you two. I need a place to lay low. They're after me same as they're after you."

"Who? The police?" I ask.

"No. Us. The 'Teen Killers Club.' Like he said." Her voice is bitter. "Camp didn't send me, but one of them's going to get the job. Much as I hate to back this bald asshole up, if I'd been Jada? You'd be dead right now, Signal."

My stomach goes cold.

"Bald? Wow!" Erik reaches up to his recently cropped hair as if to check that it's still there. "No need to get personal. Come on. All I did was pull a knife on you."

"Yeah, and if I'd slept the last couple days, your ass would be a pile of ribbons right now."

"You go ahead and tell yourself that." He grins, tucking the knife in the back of his pants. I duck under her shoulder then, throwing her long, lanky arm around the back of my neck, and she sags against me. He catches her other arm, and we ease her away from the foyer. Nobody's head falls back as she takes in the marble hallway, the soaring stairs and atrium beyond.

"Why's there a hot air balloon in here?" she asks.

"It's a sloop sail," Erik says, "from a regatta our family's boat placed in a couple years ago."

"Right." Nobody cuts me a look. "Nice hideout."

"Not anymore," Erik says. "Everyone at camp will have the address by now, if I know our Director."

"You don't mean—" My throat sticks. "You think he'll torture Dennis? Get him to tell where Nobody went?"

"Hopefully Dennis just tells him whatever he asks." Erik frowns. "Because I'm pretty sure camp has my address on file. I wonder who'll find us first? Javier would've started closest, but they'll let him get back first for questioning, I bet."

"Questioning." Of course. They'll interrogate Javier about Star Barn. Hopefully he tells them whatever they want, too.

"My money's on Jada," Erik goes on lightly as we guide Nobody through the kitchen door. "What do you think, Signal?"

"I can't believe they'd really hurt us."

"It's not up to them," Nobody scowls at the mess on the floor as we steer her into a chair, glass goblet and coffee mug shards crunching underfoot. "You two fight or something?"

"Or something." Erik glances up at me. I refuse to meet his eyes, and focus on Nobody:

"So Kurt and Jada came for you and Dennis?"

"Yeah, but Jada's heart wasn't in it. And Kurt's a *mess*."

Kurt had just lost his brother, Troy, before we went out on missions. And Troy and Jada had just started a relationship. They had both gone through missions while grieving, before they were ordered to go hunt down their friends.

"Camp wanted Dennis back, so he could code and whatnot. Me, I was just a straight hit. They didn't make them chase me far. Guess camp figures I'll get myself killed fast enough on my own."

My stomach flips over. "Kurt and Jada tried to *kill you*?"

Nobody shrugs. "They didn't try *that* hard."

Erik pats her on the shoulder and she frowns at him. "Do you want steak and if so how do you like it?"

"Hell yes, I do." Her face lights up. "Rare, for the love of the Lord."

I straighten up the table as Erik gets her a big glass of water and lays a massive piece of red cow muscle on the grill. Nobody downs the water in one long tilt, stringy white hair falling back from her pale face, and finishes with a gasp. When she sets down the glass, I notice there's dried blood under her fingernails. Hopefully from cutting her own neck and not someone else's. But I don't ask.

"So you came all the way here from Los Angeles to stay at an empty house?" Erik asks.

"I'm heading North anyway. Got something from Dennis for a friend of his."

She pulls a baggie out of her inside coat pocket. Inside is a wad of candy bar wrappers rubber banded together. She carefully unwraps them to reveal a matte black thumb drive.

"Gave it to me before Jada and Kurt showed up. Said if things went bad, to get in touch with a guy called Aarush. See if he can turn the rest of the switches off." She wads it carefully back into the wrappers again. "I'm s'posed to meet him at the San Francisco Opera House tomorrow night." Her voice gets lower in her throat, embarrassed. "But I ran out of money."

"No worries," Erik says, sliding two steaks onto plates. "One of my dad's safes still had cash in it."

"And we can go with you!" I say, and reach across the table to squeeze her forearm, "We're going North too—we can all travel together."

"You want to travel with me?" She frowns.

"Yeah, duh!" I laugh. "It'll be fun."

"Well. Okay then." She smiles. "Why're you two heading North?"

Erik looks at me expectantly, but I can't help remembering how Javier reacted when I told him I was innocent. Maybe it's better to sort of ease into that.

"It's kind of a long story," I tell her, "but we're hoping if we play our cards right, we can put an end to camp and maybe get the Director behind bars."

Nobody's face doesn't move except for her eyebrows, which go way, way up. She doesn't so much as blink until Erik sets a steak swimming in translucent red juice in front of her.

"Well!" she says at last, picking up her knife and fork, "meat, money, and a plan. What more do we need?"

* * *

I shiver in the basement, fresh out of the shower and dripping all over Erik's room, hurriedly rooting around in my backpack for clean clothes. Erik is upstairs, packing anything he thinks we'll need; Nobody is showering in the master bathroom.

Once I've got jeans and the giant USC hoodie on, I pull the desk chair in front of the door and retrieve the composition notebook from between the bed and the wall, turning back to where I'd left off: Erik's scrawling thirteen-year-old handwriting describing what he did to his brother.

> *What happened with Skye is what I said.*
>
> *He kept saying I didn't know what I saw, but I did.*
>
> *So I had to show him I was serious, that he had to leave Alice alone.*
>
> *I put a trip wire across the bike path the night before and went out early in the morning to wait in the tree. When he went out for his morning ride, the bike went out from under him, and he was stunned enough I had time to drop down on him.*
>
> *I showed him the box cutter and told him I was serious and he needed to leave her alone.*
>
> *He laughed and told me I was an f-ing freak and punched me hard, so we started fighting.*
>
> *He's bigger than me. So I didn't hold back.*
>
> *I didn't realize how bad it was until I stopped. I'm not happy about him having scars.*
>
> *But he wasn't taking me seriously.*

The Sharpie returned at the bottom of the page:

Erik, I know you are a very intelligent young man. You're aware if you claim your premeditated attack on your brother was on another's behalf, the consequences won't be as severe. But I have spoken with Alice, Skye, and Dr. Ledrick extensively. You made false allegations against your brother to put yourself in a more favorable light. That is NOT being accountable.

You need to take responsibility for your actions. Only then can we move forward.

I SAW THEM
I SAW THEM
I SAW THEM

It went on for three pages like that, the letters scrawled bigger and deeper each time. There were a few blank pages before the next entry, and his handwriting was much neater in the few lines, though the pen dug deep here as well, as though writing it cost a great deal of effort.

I accept that I attacked my brother, Skye, out of jealousy. And I must have been curious on some level if I could get away with hurting him. I masked my actions with altruistic motives.

I am very sorry for hurting my brother and for being the kind of person who enjoys hurting and deceiving people.

Please, can I come back home now?

Or at least call?

Mom, please will you just talk to me

I shut the notebook there, overcome. And this is why I can't trust myself anymore: what's upset me isn't the description of how Erik attacked his own brother. It's the line begging his mom to talk to him.

Why am I immediately certain Erik *was* telling the truth about Alice and that his mom was in denial? Am I so far gone that I will sit here and convince myself I could know Erik better than his *own mother*?

I put the notebook in my backpack and stagger upstairs and back through the pillars to where I fainted last night, the large black fireplace in the white room under the portrait of Erik's family.

Last night all I noticed was that the other guy wasn't Erik. Now in daylight, a couple things hit me: Skye is the male version of their mom, who is gorgeous. Skye basically looks like an angel who's been training for the Olympics: absolutely jacked, with an open, sunny smile. Beside him the twelve-year-old Erik, ducking his head to hide his torn eye behind his long bangs, looks almost anemic. Erik doesn't particularly look like his dad either. He seems to have come fully formed as a reincarnation of the old guy—his grandfather, I'm guessing?—from the photograph in his bedroom.

I climb the open gallery staircase that circles the boat sail, up to the bedrooms on the third floor. Its red, green, and blue stripes glow like a massive stained-glass window from the sunshine pouring in the skylight overhead. It's a singular decoration, something indisputably of another world. I think of the yearly debate with my mom over where to put our fake Christmas tree: completely behind the TV or slightly in front of it? You could pull this sail over the trailer I grew up in, and both ends would still touch the ground.

Up on the third story, I hear the shower running through the first door I pass, the master bedroom. The next room is smaller, I step inside and look out onto the ocean through high, thin windows, a tangle of tree branches just below them. Walking back out into the hall, I notice block letter stickers on the door across the gallery, like stickers you'd put on a mailbox, reading "SWS."

Skye Wylie-Stanton.

The large room is stripped bare: no photos, no books, no desk. The wallpaper has the same blue and white print as Erik's. A poster of a Gran Turismo Sport video game clings to the wall, but under the drop cloth the bedframe doesn't even have a mattress.

What would I even expect to find in here? What am I trying to learn about Skye?

"Whether or not he's still alive," Rose's voice hisses. *"Duh."*

There's a sharp pain in my temple as the thoughts rush in all at once: Where is Erik's family? His parents designed an algorithm to find more kids like him to help. Well, things certainly took a turn with that plan. So where are they now? Did Erik have something to do with why this house is now empty?

Why am I so afraid to even ask?

I could go confront him right now. But if he is some super-genius manipulator, and knows I have the notebook, he could wrap some story around what's inside. If I *don't* tell him I have it, but get him to talk about the past, I can match what he says against the notebook. See if he tells me the truth. And if he doesn't, then . . .

The door goes flying open.

"What're you doing in here?" Nobody stares down at me, in her towel.

"Oh . . . snooping, I guess."

"Find any clothes?"

"No—but I have stuff in my bag you could wear. And it's all your size since we switched missions . . ."

"Great," she says, and I chuck my grimy backpack onto the middle of the empty four-poster. She scrounges through and, with a look of pure disgust, pulls out the hippie jeans I was given for my mission at Owl's Nest. She steps into them, scowling. As she dresses, it's clear her burn scars extend only just past her elbows, like nightmarish evening gloves. The rest of her is as perfect as her face. Yet her arms are the only part of her body she doesn't hide; though she has left her face uncovered so far around me and Erik, which feels like a compliment. Like she trusts me with it.

Nobody pulls out Erik's sooty hoodie, sniffs it, then winces back. *"Smoke."*

I take it from her quickly. "That's dirty—Erik was wearing it in Ojai."

"Erik came to Ojai?" She tilts her head. "Before or after Javier took off?"

"Before," I say—and then, off her knowing expression, "It's complicated."

The side of her mouth jerks. "I knew you liked him."

But her smile drops at whatever face I'm doing.

"Did he hurt you?" she says, in a tone like she'll go down and snap his neck if I say yes. Which, knowing her, she very well might.

"No! No," I say quickly, "he saved my life." And I tell her, in fits and rambles, about the last couple days. About how Erik helped solve my former best friend's murder, and Javier saw us kissing, and Erik had Dennis test his kill switch first. About Angel Childs giving me a chance to stab him and how I couldn't. How Erik had saved me, and how I thought he'd been lost in the fire.

"Well," she says when I finish, "that explains his new haircut."

"You're not mad I didn't actually kill my one?"

"Hell no." She frowns. "That was my only problem with you. Now we can be friends."

Ouch. "I thought we were friends."

"Well, now I know you didn't behead your last buddy, it's official."

My laugh comes out like a sob, and I sink down beside her onto the slats of the covered bed.

"So you're with Erik now?" she asks.

"I have no idea."

"He likes you."

"He wants me to think so," I say, "for sure. Back at camp, he bet that he could get me to fall in love with him. And that's the first thing he said when I saw him again; that he'd won. Then this morning he tells me to say 'the magic words,' and it's like . . ." I stare down at the floor. "Like it's all just some game to him."

Nobody puts a hand on my shoulder. "It's called being straight," she says, and when I laugh, she doesn't crack a smile: "Relationships are always a game to guys. They don't stop playing around until you beat them. Make him say it first."

"Is that even possible? This is *Erik* we're talking about. I'm not sure he has feelings."

She laughs then, and I nervously dart over to the door to make sure he's not out in the hall listening or something. The third story is empty, so I return to the bed and lie facedown beside her, the drop sheet rough against my face, my stomach in knots.

"I mean, I'm not trying to dunk on him—it seriously concerns me."

"You think he's a psychopath?"

"I don't *know*!" I admit. "He's helped me so much, and more than that, he *gets* me. Like, he gets what I'm thinking and my sense of humor more than anyone. But there's this *other* Erik"—I see him walking through the smoke, his mouth bloody, his hand outstretched to me—"that I can never understand. So that's the debate, between my heart and my head: How can he be both? What if the 'good' Erik is just an act?"

"Forget it then," she says simply. I turn on my side and look up at her, startled. Her face is calm and almost smug. "Not worth the risk."

I stammer, trying to articulate some denial, and she rolls her eyes. "That's the right answer, but it won't help. There's no debate, Signal. Your heart wants what it wants, your head just covers for it. And in my experience, what the heart usually wants is to ruin your damn life."

"In your experience?" I give her a tell-me-more look. "Your girlfriend ruined your life?"

"In the best way." She smiles a bittersweet smile. "Far as Erik goes, I bet you could beat his ass." Nobody stands, then pulls me up to my feet. "And if he tries to hurt you, I'll put him in the ground."

* * *

After dark, we shoulder our things and walk down to "town": three manicured streets in sight of the beach, gas lamp–style streetlights haloed by marine fog.

"Get him to use both hands," Erik tells Nobody. She gives him a dark look before splitting away from us. Just in case anyone is paying attention, we want to approach the pub from opposite ends of the street.

Despite the cold damp air, the floor-to-ceiling windows of the Sea Weasel pub stand wide open, live music and half-drunk twenty somethings leaking into the fog, hazy figures slouching over cigarettes and phones. Erik and I are a block away when a deep male voice behind us cries:

"Guys! Wait up!"

Erik's arm goes around me, and he seems to deliberately slow down, even as the footsteps ring out faster behind us.

"Guys!"

They could've sent Javier. He was closest, after all, wasn't he?

"Guys!"

I glance behind us. A tall figure, silhouetted in a white haze from oncoming headlights, races toward us. He has close-cropped hair and broad shoulders, and my heart wrings with a sickeningly hard beat just as a tipsy couple emerges from the mist in front of us:

"Tony! Is that our Uber?"

"Look," Erik says gently, rubbing my shoulder, "Nobody's already found a mark."

Down the block, directly under a streetlight, Nobody glows like an angel. A lanky guy in a fedora hat hangs from her gaze like it's a nail through his forehead.

". . . so this way?" She waves her hands up the street, scars hidden by pulled-down sweater sleeves.

"No, your other left—" He chuckles and pockets his phone so he can mirror her, gesturing with both hands in the opposite direction.

"Let's go." Erik says, and half collapses against me. I make a show of supporting him, and we shuffle behind Nobody's mark. Then I trip and Erik stumbles into him, hard.

"Whoa! So sorry!" I pull a queasy-looking Erik away from the fedora guy and offer an apologetic smile.

Fedora guy glances at Nobody before he manages to smile back. "No worries."

When we get around the corner, Erik covertly checks the phone he just stole.

"Uber will be here in five minutes. Red Scion. Ride is Mark, driver is Dathan," Erik says, "We should cut through the bar, get further up the street to catch it."

I follow him into the crowded pub through one of the tall, open windows, and wave for Nobody's attention as we pass in front of her. Fedora guy has his back to me. I make a face to alert her that he's reaching back for where his phone should be, and Nobody playfully punches his shoulder. He leans in toward her, flirty, and she cuts me a burning look: *How much longer?*

I hold up five fingers, then Erik stops so abruptly, I practically bounce off him.

A bleary-eyed girl blocks us, kohl smeared up one temple and a paper "Bride-to-Be" tiara tipping over the other.

"Where do I know you from, dude?" she shouts over the too-loud live music.

"You don't."

"Krissy, where do we know him from?"

Two drunken friends flank her then. They smile at Erik without acknowledging my existence.

"Oh, wait, he's on TV, right?"

"I feel like I saw him *just last night*—what were we watching?"

"Are you an actor?"

Erik waves the phone. "Our ride's here," he says, and shoulders past them.

"I'm getting married, by the way!" the bride-to-be calls, *"Last chance to stop me!"*

"How long until they realize where they saw you?" I whisper, when someone grabs my shoulder.

I spin around, and Nobody puts her hands up. "He knows," she says. "He's looking for you two."

Erik curses, just as a watercolor wash of white blooms at the very end of the street, and two beams of blurry light rush toward us. We hurry toward the headlights, breaking into a run as we get close, Erik all but leaping in front of the car in his efforts to flag it down.

"Hey!" A male yell, thin in the heavy night air. *"Hey! You two!"*

Nobody and I throw ourselves into a back seat sick with vanilla air freshener, the driver turning down booming pop music and glaring at us.

"Thought this ride was for one?" the driver says. "Which of you is Mark?"

"It's my brother's profile." Erik gets in beside me, voice artfully bored.

Just past the driver's face, through the windshield, I can see the figure of fedora guy materializing out of the fog.

"He said he'd added riders and changed the destination to my dad's place, but . . . I can text him to make sure."

The driver tilts his phone holder, refreshes his screen. Once. Twice.

The fedora guy leaps over the sidewalk curb. His hat flies off his head, but he doesn't stop to retrieve it.

"Look man," the driver sighs, "you really shouldn't be sharing family profiles, but it went through okay, so . . ." He eases his foot off the brake while rerouting his map, and looks up just in time to see the fedora guy throw himself at the passenger door, hand slipping off the handle. Dathan snaps the power lock with a curse, honks and swerves away hard.

"These drunks need to watch what they're doing! In this fog?" Dathan shakes his head, "Sorry about that."

I turn and see the hatless guy melt into the fog. I could sob with relief.

"No worries, Dathan," Erik says. "How's your night been?"

"Not too bad." There's only the crinkle of the wrapped candies in the console and slosh of water bottles in the net pockets at our knees for a long moment. Then Ariana Grande's voice fills the silence again, and Erik and Nobody lean back in their seats.

I sit forward. Our driver keeps tapping his phone. His eyes meet mine in the rearview mirror. Pinpoints of sweat dot his forehead.

"You can get on the highway from here," Erik says as the entrance to an onramp flashes past. Dathan says nothing. "Or up here, just turn left, up here," Erik says louder.

But Dathan flies by that exit too, taking a main road off the highway. He tilts the phone sharply toward him, and I catch a flash of blue hair.

Our mugshots.

I lean back and whisper to Erik:

"He knows who we are."

Erik turns to Nobody, starts whispering to her. She makes a sharp hiss.

I've got to stop this car before they do something we all regret.

"Dathan?" I shoot forward, intentionally blocking as much of him as I can with my body. "Hey. Could you pull over here? I think I'm going to throw up."

He doesn't answer.

"I'm going to seriously barf all over your car, okay? Pull over!"

"Go ahead," Dathan's hand fumbles across his screen. "They can clean it up at the police station!"

A tinny voice from the phone: "Nine-one-one operator. What is your emergency?"

"Yes, hello! My name is Dathan Metzger, and I got that couple from the Cactus Burger in the back of my car right now! Can you track this phone and send the nearest—"

The rest of his words are cut off by Nobody's arm wrapping around his windpipe, and Erik joins her in hauling him backward, the white beams of the headlights curving the wrong way across the foggy two-lane road.

Chapter Four

Dead Load

"No!" I throw myself over Dathan's flailing legs and grab for the wheel, yellow and white lines sliding wildly under the hood. As I scramble over the console, desperate to get my feet on the pedals, Dathan's sneaker connects with my ribs hard enough to kick a scream loose.

And then Dathan *howls.*

"You touch her again and I take your eye," Erik says in a voice I barely recognize as I guide the car back into our lane and start groping for the window button.

"Erik, *no—*"

"Darryl? Darryl, stay with me." The 911 operator is still on the line. "We have your location. Assistance is on its way—"

I throw the phone onto the highway, pieces flying up and rattling against the car like ocean spray as I veer onto the nearest exit, an access road that follows the train tracks. Dathan thrashes furiously in the back seat. They've bound him with the center seat belt.

"No!" I whip around, *"Do. Not. Hurt. Him."*

"He's trying to kill us!" Nobody says.

"*We stole his*—you know what? I'm not arguing about this." I pull off too fast, skidding across the gravel shoulder and almost rolling into the scrubby grass, braking with a jolt. Nobody starts calmly explaining that we need to keep moving, police could arrive any minute, but I cut her off.

"We will not hurt anyone," I tell them coldly. "We're better than that." I stare Erik down in the rearview until he looks up from Dathan's panicked face and into my eyes. "We're letting him go," I continue, "and rating him five stars."

"Fine," Erik says, voice thick, and shakes his head like he's trying to wake himself up. Then, to Nobody: "Could you come 'round this side and leave your door open, please?"

She glares at me, then him, then launches herself out of the back seat, slamming the door a few times before leaving it open to register her absolute fury. As she crosses through the red taillights, Erik holds up the fedora guy's stolen phone so I can see it in the rearview, and taps the last star.

"And a big tip too," I say.

"But *Signal*"—Erik suppresses a smile—"that'd be *stealing*."

I shoot him a look, and as he shifts the phone to his other hand, Dathan twists his head free enough to speak.

"I'm going to rip your damn heads off!" Dathan says. "Class A freaks! I hope they throw all your asses in jail for a thousand years!"

"We were in jail," Erik says coolly, "but they let us out to train us how to kill people. At a place called Camp Naramauke. That's Nay-Ra-Maw-Kay, Dathan. In the Cascades. Be sure and put that in your police statement."

Nobody opens the door beside him, and they silently negotiate how to guide the still-trussed Dathan across the seat and through the open door. Erik slides a kitchen knife from inside his hoodie. Its gleam pierces the dark as he lowers it to Dathan's chest.

"Be ready to go when we say. Toward the tracks," Erik tells me as Dathan chokes back a sob.

"What are you—"

With one stroke, the kitchen knife slices through the seat belt binding Dathan, and he's loose. Dathan's thick arm swings up, clutching and clawing for Erik, but Nobody blocks him, and the two of them manage to push him along the slick back seat and through the open back door before he's gotten too many hits in. He screams the whole time that he's going to kill us all, we're not taking his car, and Erik yells to me:

"Drive!"

But I know Dathan is partly in the back seat, partly trying to crawl back inside. Terrified, I lift off on the brake and wheel forward just enough to scare him fully out and onto the ground, but he swiftly gets up again and starts running alongside us, then lunges for the swinging back passenger door.

"Go!" Nobody hollers as Dathan's fingertips screech across the inside of the glass, and I hit the gas just enough that he loses his grip and belly flops onto the ground. Nobody slams the door shut, cursing at me to move already, but I linger until I see Dathan stagger back on his feet. Then, at last, I peel out.

* * *

Erik navigates me through a dizzying series of access roads that cut north and west until we're several miles up the coast, and when the streetlights thin to darkness, he directs me up a narrower unpaved road, the car straining up the steep cliffs until we gain a ridge overlooking the dark ocean. Tiny lights from airplanes and oil freighters draw the lines of the delicate net of civilization, and we wait several minutes after the last set of headlights has faded around the far cliffs before we get out. Below the ridge is a deep ravine. Nobody figures out how to put the car in neutral, and we all three push it over the deep trench between the ridge and the road, a crunch of fender and shriek of tree echoing below us.

"You think it's going to blow up?" I ask as we stand at the edge of the ravine, listening to the cooling motor tick down below.

Erik shrugs. "Maybe?"

"Hell no!" Nobody snaps, glaring at Erik. "Don't you know anything about cars?"

"I know they bore me to tears." He stares at the fedora guy's stolen phone and then jerks his chin toward the highway. "We need to cross that road."

We scramble down the hillside and dart across the empty highway, then climb up to a trail that threads the edge of the cliffs, the ocean air like the taste of tears at the back of my throat.

Nobody shivers, hair a cloud in the damp wind. "Where are we?"

Erik stares into the bubble of pale blue light from the phone. "Around Pedro Point, in Pacifica."

"We should get another car." By "get" she means hijack, of course.

"Too risky." Erik shakes his head. "They'll have picked up Dathan by now. They'll be looking for us."

"You're an accomplice of the 'Cactus Burger couple.'" I smile. "Sorry."

She gives me a dark look.

"I don't know how he recognized us so fast," I go on, and as the trail gains the top of the cliff, I lower my head against the wind. "You think we were on the local news or something?"

"Yes. So we should skip San Francisco," Erik says. Then, to Nobody, "Can you contact Dennis' friend? Get him to meet you somewhere less busy?" A beat: "Nobody?"

We both turn to see her standing still, in the middle of the path, several steps behind us.

"I will be at the Opera House tomorrow night," Nobody declares. "I will claim my tickets by eight."

"We can't just waltz through a densely populated area right now." Erik's jaw flares in the light of the stolen phone screen. "It's too risky."

"Risky?" She laughs. "What do you call both of us getting our asses beat so a witness could walk free? 'Cause I'd call that risky."

He stares back at her, and then the phone screen goes out and they're just silhouettes against the queasy gray sky when she says, "We both know we should've killed that driver."

I curl into myself, cold stealing into my bones, wishing for once the tide was louder as she goes on.

"So don't take risks to impress Signal and then try and tell me where I can't go."

"If Signal goes into San Francisco and gets arrested, that's it," Erik says. "We'll never have another chance to clear her name."

"Yeah? You clear Signal's name, and then what? I'm still guilty. So are you. One way or another, you and me, we're going back. To camp, to jail, to hell. I don't know. But I got a few things I need to do first. So maybe we just part ways here."

"Have a nice life." Erik holds out the stolen phone. "There's a BART station a couple miles north. I suggest ditching the phone after you memorize the map."

"We can't split up," I tell Erik, then turn to Nobody. "And we can't kill people willy-nilly up and down the California coast either, okay? They're looking for the Cactus Burger *couple*. Or three teens together. But if we go separately into San Francisco—on different trains or whatever—we could get lost in the crowd. Like three needles in a haystack, right?" Erik and Nobody gauge each other's reaction, and I go on excitedly. "We could even try and change how we look to disguise ourselves, like we did at camp. Then meet back up at the Opera House!" I look back and forth between them. "Right? Right?"

"Did you . . ." Erik turns to me. "Did you just say 'kill people willy-nilly'?"

Nobody shoves his shoulder to get his attention. "We got the money to get spruced up?"

"Yes. Everything short of facial surgery we can cover."

"Fine." Nobody pulls back her arm, and the stolen phone goes sailing into the night, a blue spark that goes dark before it hits the ocean. Then she pushes past the two of us, continuing up the trail in long strides.

"So what's the big deal with the Opera House?" I call, chasing after her.

"They're doing *Swan Lake*."

"A classic," Erik says with a what-the-hell face at me.

"It is?" she asks absently.

Erik stifles a laugh and takes my hand, sending a thrill down my arm like I've struck my funny bone.

"Doing okay?" he asks.

"Fine, totally fine." I'm freezing and exhausted, but what else is new.

Erik, with an exasperated sigh, slings his backpack around to his chest and then kneels so quickly in my path I almost fall across his back. "Up here, Weakling. Let's go," he commands, patting his shoulders.

When I protest, he backs into me, arms going around the tops of my legs, and I throw my arm around his shoulders before I fall backward, giggling. He stands and then charges forward, barreling down the narrow cliffside path, flying past Nobody.

"BEEP, BEEP!" he yells, sliding and slipping along the pebbled path but never close to losing his balance. He gets to a peak in the trail and whirls us in a circle right at the edge. Ocean and land, ocean and land twirling around us, my arms tight around his chest, laughing so hard I can't breathe. My head falls back, and the stars wheel around us; my head falls forward, and the hot muscles of his neck fit against my cold cheek like I was made for him. I close my eyes, and ghost circles of starlight are burned into my eyelids.

He stops abruptly, his attention caught by a patch of ocean lit up way ahead, a sheet of bright utilitarian light turning the black waves below a deep, cold green.

"What have we here?" he says, moving up the hill, not even out of breath.

The construction site ahead will one day be an ocean-front mansion. But for now, it's just the dead load, more lines than house: three floors under a slanting roof, a few particle-board walls around a curving spine of central staircase. There are piles of lumber and scrap and a chain link fence with green netting veiling us from the road. Nobody says she's going to go water a tree; I climb up the staircase that curves through three floors of air, the expanse of the ocean and stars laid out before me forever as I reach the very top.

Erik has beaten me here by climbing up the struts. He sits, back to me, legs swinging off the edge of the third-story floor, his shape blacker than the water and starlit sky. I sit next to him, letting my legs hang beside his, and he takes my hand without speaking. And I know I should pull away, but I lean a little closer to him instead, heart pounding out of time with the slow crash of the tide below us, glassy depths of gray illuminated by the motion light below.

"Just so we're clear," he says, a little shiver in his voice, "this is not our first date, Signal. There will be walls at the place I take you on our first date."

"What happens to you after we clear my name?"

"I haven't thought about it much," Erik says, "but once I know you're okay, I'll have to disappear."

The waves roll below us for a moment as I squint at him through the dark.

"Just until the world knows camp exists and our Director is behind bars. A few years, tops," he adds.

"You're just trying to make me cry again."

"I have *never* tried to make you cry."

"You wouldn't just *disappear*."

"I could come visit?" He cocks his head to look at me. "Be your own personal ghost. I'm not going to pull a Javier, that's for sure. Try and push you away for your own good or whatever. Consider yourself warned." He stares, hard. "I will take as much of you as I can get."

I sigh and lay my head against his shoulder so he can't see me tear up. He leans down toward me.

"Would you meet me?" There's a smile in his voice now. "After we clear your name. And I have to disappear. Then one night, you're up late in your dorm . . ."

"My *dorm*? Wow, did I get into a nice college?"

"You're up late in your Harvard dorm, studying for your library science degree, texting some Class D jackass when, knock knock knock . . ." I'm laughing now, but I can feel him searching my face. "If I found your window, would you let me in?"

My answer should be: What about those ten? But the line of childish handwriting in his journal swims through my head: *"Would you just talk to me please."*

I nod slowly. "I'll always talk to you, Erik. About anything."

He crushes me to him then, hugs me so tight I feel his deep sigh wring the muscles of his side.

"Signal," Erik says, "I didn't kill ten people."

My heart lurches with hope, but as the silence lengthens, a prickle creeps up my neck.

"How many, then?"

"I don't know."

"Like . . . you don't remember?"

"Like I *don't know*. Who really died, who killed themselves, what even happened . . ." In the gray haze behind the motion light, his expression seems genuinely bewildered. He stares into the water crashing below us without focusing. "I've never had to put it in words before. And you have no reason to believe me."

"You were the first person to believe me. Whatever you can tell me, I want to hear."

"Okay. Okay." He takes my hand, then looks at me sharply. "Your hand is like *ice*. Come on, let's get out of this wind."

I follow him to the corner of the two standing walls. He pulls a bedroll from his backpack and lays it out over the particle-board floor, and we sit leaning up against the wall, huddled for warmth, staring into the velvet abyss of night sky and ocean.

"Where to start . . ." he says; then, in a rush: "My mom wasn't just a forensic psychologist. She was head of the department at Stanford. She consulted for the FBI. She was brilliant."

She *was*.

"So, she caught the warning signs in me early."

"Warning signs? What, you mean like . . . hurting animals, or something?"

"You're referring to the Macdonald triad." He frowns. "Bed-wetting, arson, and animal cruelty. When all three traits present in childhood, it can indicate psychopathy. Yeah, no, I didn't have any of those. I like animals, hate fire, and had absolutely no bed-wetting issues." He looks at me, suppressing a smile. "I can't make you many promises, but I promise you'll never catch me cracking out the rubber sheets."

"What were your warning signs, then?"

"I reminded her of someone in our family who was . . . the reason she got into forensic psychology, apparently. He was abusive and psychotic and unhinged," he said. "I had a psychiatrist by age five, Dr. Ledrick. Also highly respected, though sure as hell not by me." He clears his throat, "And everything was alright, or in stasis at least. Until I hit puberty."

"Then what happened?"

"Adolescence is rough for most people, right." He shrugs, biting at his nails. "I would get bored and act out in class. I would sneak out at night. And then there was an incident with my brother. I told you about it once, on our night hike." His eyes flash to me and away. "It almost made her give up on me."

He had told me he attacked "an emotionally abusive narcissist." He hadn't said it was his own brother. But I'm glad he's telling me now; the story checks out against the journal at least.

"After that everything changed. Which was fair," Erik stares out at the ocean. "A lot of other moms would've given up. Or pressed charges." His eyes are flat. "But she gave up her career to homeschool me. Told me it would be her life's work to turn me into a good person."

I frown at the phrase. He looks up, noticing the tiny gesture, so I smooth my expression and squeeze his hand. "Go on."

"The hike-in camp helped. But even there, I had difficulty 'relating.' We'd get around the old fire circle for group, and they'd all be confessing to, like, internet addictions. And there I was with intrusive thoughts about jamming my thumbs through my brother's eye sockets."

He says it so casually I shudder.

"That's what kicked off her and my dad designing the Wylie-Stanton. My mom wanted to start a rehabilitation program for kids as messed up as me—"

"You *aren't* messed up."

"Maybe reserve judgment on that point until the end of the story."

"Erik." I turn to him. "Your parents told you that you were *messed up*?"

"No, never." He holds my gaze. "Have you ever wondered why the Wylie-Stanton gives criminals an 'A,' and normal people a 'D'? It's scoring each psychological profile based on how close it comes to mine. I'm the 'A plus.'" He smiles a cutting smile. "You can imagine what a self-esteem boost that is."

I take a deep breath. I don't let go of his hand.

"Dr. Ledrick thought the algorithm was a great idea. He even went and pitched it to some connections he had, secured a research grant. Then they had enough money to . . . I want to say *vivisect* me, but the more accurate word is *quantify*. Everything about me that could be put into numbers was. I went through months of lie detector tests, cognitive evaluations, the PCL-R of course—that's the Psychopathy Checklist–Revised—and an MRI brain scan, my dad ran analytics on my search history, that was . . . interesting." He lets out a sigh. "And then, right as they finished the algorithm, my family was in a car accident."

He slides further against the wall, just his broad shoulders propped up, eyes fixed on something I can't see, gripping my hand. It takes him a long moment before he says, his voice very deep, "My parents died instantly." Then he swallows. "My brother's hip was destroyed; he was in traction for months. Dr. Ledrick took me to the funeral, and after the burial he says, 'Your brother is too young to manage you. He's signing your conservatorship over to me.'"

His fingers are very tight around mine, his face expressionless.

"I didn't even *fight it*," he says almost to himself, then looks right in my eyes. "So. Signal. This is where we start counting bodies."

As he describes it, I can picture it so clearly: Dr. Ledrick's outpatient facility, not a chrome and glass lab, but something more like an old folks' home. Speckled linoleum floors perpetually gritty from bleach, scuffed mauve walls, the scent of microwaved food leaking from under heavy rubber trays. There were windows on the first floor only; fluorescent lights on the upper stories froze his months there into one long, cold noon.

"It wasn't as rough as camp," Erik says. "I had hot water and internet. Friends could sign in to see me, I could sign out to see them—at first. But then the pills started." He pauses. "Have you ever taken Adderall?"

I shake my head.

"And you don't seem like the cocaine type . . ." He squints at me, and I manage a weak smile. "You know when you drink way, way too much coffee?"

"I never got into coffee."

"Of course not," he says, the corner of his mouth jerking. "How about an all-nighter? You've stayed up all night before?"

"Oh yes. Many times."

"Okay. You know how right when dawn comes, you're kind of shaky and seeing things at the edge of your vision, but also vaguely euphoric? The pills were that, but times ten thousand. And they made me stronger. I could move faster, think faster. But while being like . . . just . . . ever so slightly out of my mind?"

It's hard to imagine a version of him stronger or faster than he is now, let alone a version of him out of his mind. But it was this version of Erik, at just seventeen, which walked into the first "confrontation experiment."

He describes a room like a dance studio: white cement, wood floor, a massive mirror taking up one wall. Dr. Ledrick told him he'd be going to Class A group therapy. Inside the room was a ring of folding chairs, but only two guys: one in his twenties, the other in his forties. Both wore prison jumpsuits. The younger one didn't look up when Erik came in, but both went completely still; an anticipatory awareness that put Erik on edge. He turned to Dr. Ledrick to see the door being slammed in his face. The handle was immobile when he tried it, locked from outside.

The man in his forties stood up and walked toward him.

"He was acting like the tough guy in a bad movie." Erik says, staring into the dark.

But the younger guy stayed in his seat, staring through the floor. He didn't seem to want to watch what was about to happen, his hands balled up around something.

When Erik turned to hit the emergency call button by the door, the big guy slammed him up against the wall and pulled out a knife. Erik, hyper from the pills, wrestled loose, grabbed a folding chair, and knocked the knife out of his hands. Both scrambled for the weapon, Erik got to it first, warned the guy off. When he rushed Erik anyway, Erik planted it in the center of the man's leg. Or tried to.

"It was a stage prop, not a real knife. It didn't even cut the fabric. But he still fell to the floor, grabbing his leg and screaming," Erik tells me. Unnerved, he pressed the knife into his own arm, heard the squeak of a concealed spring as the blade disappeared inside the handle. A moment later, an orderly came in and escorted the man out, handling him as though he'd been injured. The orderly refused to answer Erik's shouted questions. Just locked the door again.

The younger guy was still staring at the floor, face beaded with sweat. Erik called out to him, then approached warily. The moment he was within arm's length, the young guy looked up.

"They said if we fight, I can go," he said.

And then he sprang at Erik, a second knife flashing in his hand.

"Everything I know about fighting has its roots in how badly that guy kicked my ass." Erik laughs. By the end, he had Erik pinned to the floor by his neck, and was about to bring the weapon down, when the door opened again. As the guy looked up, Erik wrenched the second prop knife away from him and put it in the center of his chest. But this time, the blade did not retract. It buried itself in living muscle, scraped against bone, and the younger guy looked down into Erik's eyes as dark blood seeped through the back of his even white teeth.

Erik holds up one finger.

"But you thought it was a prop!" I cry. "You didn't *mean* to kill him."

"I don't know if the person I killed would appreciate that distinction," Erik says, grabbing for where his long hair should be. "And why did I fight so hard to win if I truly believed it was a prop? Why not just let him stab me? No. I knew. Instinctually, I knew."

"That doesn't mean you're . . ." I flounder for a word. "That wasn't murder, Erik."

"Whatever it was, after that I wasn't just a patient. I was a prisoner."

Based on Dr. Ledrick's assessment, Erik was judged incompetent to attend trial and ordered fifteen months of treatment under Dr. Ledrick. Paranoid of what Ledrick would try next, he refused to leave his room. So, the next experiment came to him: a bed was moved in across from his, a stranger close to his age introduced as his new roommate.

"He was a paranoid schizophrenic," Erik says, rubbing at his eyes. "Sweet guy. Scared of me, but not aggressive until they started pilling him up. On I want to say night five, I woke up and had a syringe right up against my neck. I had no idea what was in it. So I started talking to him."

Erik holds up a second finger.

"You talked him into . . . into killing himself?"

"I talked him into putting the needle into his own neck."

"But . . . *how*?"

"Some people are like a keypad with three numbers worn down. You know where to hit, it's just a matter of in what order and how many times."

I blink at him, and he looks down, the crease deepening between his eyebrows. "They got him out of there very quickly. So maybe they saved him. I don't know—I don't know what was in the syringe. But they came in fast enough they had to have been watching us the whole time."

"That's self-defense, Erik."

"Yeah, well, it *really* impressed Dr. Ledrick. After that came more roommates, roommates who would always mysteriously get access to weapons. Or I'd get restrained in some way, usually zip-tied to the bed. So I'd have no choice but talking my way out of it."

"Meaning . . . talk your roommate into suicide."

He nods, still not looking at me. For a long moment we listen to the unhurried roll of the tide.

"How many 'roommates' did you have?"

"Ten in eight months." But he only holds up four more fingers. "The first five, before they started restraining me, I'd break something on them—a thumb, a collarbone—to get them taken away before things came to a head. The last one, I made him jab himself with a syringe, and he went into convulsions and was dragged out. But the next day, they had to bring me to the first floor for a suture, and I know—I *know*—I saw him through a window, in the parking lot. Alive."

"Maybe they were all placeboes, then? Maybe it was saline in the syringes, the way the first knife was a prop?"

"Maybe?" Erik sounds unconvinced.

"And you tried to protect them. By—breaking their bones or whatever. It's not like you *enjoyed* killing people!"

He won't look at me.

"Right?" My voice wobbles.

"There is a certain . . . satisfaction . . . in any expertise." He still won't look at me. "I have dreams sometimes where I find out all of them are still alive, that I never hurt anyone. But I also have dreams where I wake up across from a fresh new roommate and get to start . . . chiseling away at them."

Get to.

His gaze is locked on the ocean at our feet. "I'm not *not* evil, Signal. I never will be."

"But you were on pills—"

"Is there a pill that could make *anyone* a killer? Can there be chemical forms of a soul? I don't think so. I wish there were. I could take a new one every day and be as good as you." He finally looks at me, with a smile so beautiful it hurts, then drops his head again, "The pills just set loose what was already in me."

"They also could have made you hallucinate is my point, Erik. Dr. Ledrick had a staff. I can't believe all of them would look the other way while you killed random people. Someone would have reported Dr. Ledrick to—to somebody!"

"Oh, one of the nurses did report him." Erik bites at his nails. "This one nurse, who would actually talk to me. I told her about my mom, about the experiments. She told me she was going to talk to someone over Dr. Ledrick, and I really thought, like, a SWAT team would come in the next day and break me out. But she didn't come in the next day. Or the next. Finally, I ask one of the orderlies, 'Where's Nakira?'" He swallows, hard. "He told me I knew damn well where she was." He holds up another trembling finger. "She'd killed herself, he said. So, what happened there?" Erik's face is painful to look at. "Did Ledrick fire her? Scare her off? Did he *have her killed*? Staff went to a memorial service, people *grieved* for her. To this day, I have no idea what happened to her. But that was the last time I asked anyone for help."

There's hot itchiness behind my eyes as my head sinks onto my arm, just beside his. I will myself not to cry at his voice, the hollowness of it.

"Not that any of the staff had been exactly chatty, but after that no one would talk to me at all. So I put all my focus into getting out. I memorized the schedule of every orderly and security guard. Every camera location, I tested for blind spots. And finally, someone called in sick, their schedule had a gap, and I made my attempt. I stole one of the ambulances and almost got out of the parking lot. But I hadn't counted on the exterior security guards being armed. One shot took out my rear tire. Another went wide. Killed a janitor going home from his night shift."

He raises another finger and stares at his hands, black against the stars.

"That's all of them. I *think* that's all of them. I am almost certain that's all of them. And Angel Childs." He tallies his fingers uncertainly, then shoves his hands under his elbows.

"So how did you end up in camp?" I ask.

"Dr. Ledrick gave me a talking-to after the escape attempt. Through a speaker." He grins, enjoying the words. "And behind a *double-sided shatterproof mirror.* He knew he was next, of course. That I would never stop trying to escape until he was dead, and I had killed him." Erik shrugs. "A week later, I was at camp."

"Wait." I blink. "Dr. Ledrick knows about camp?"

"Oh yes." Erik looks at me. "He's our Director."

Chapter Five
The Library

My jaw is hanging open when he turns to face me.

"You were *tortured* by the *Director*?"

"You believe me."

My heart could break at the relief in his voice.

"Why wouldn't I believe you?" I can't hold off anymore—I have to wipe away the tears streaming down my face. "I was at camp. I saw what he did to Troy."

I hadn't realized how cold I was until he pulls me against him, and I lose it. I cry into his shoulder, overwhelmed. I don't know what scares me more, the idea he could be lying or my cold certainty he's telling the truth.

"I'm sorry," I whisper against his neck, warm against my marble-cold face. "I'm sorry, I'm sorry, I'm sorry."

"*I'm* sorry. I didn't realize you'd take it so hard. It's sort of sweet," he says. "The best Class A crying for the worst one."

"Don't say that," I stutter. "You're not the worst anything."

"Sure I am. Anyway, I always liked to think we were opposites, back at camp."

"What? Why?"

"They attract."

I let out a teary laugh, and then someone is kicking our feet apart; I look up to see Nobody looming over us in the dark.

"It's too cold to sleep alone. Move over," she announces.

Before Erik can refuse, she throws herself between us, spreading her long arms in a yawn. "I'm *beat*," she says, then turns to me and mouths: *"Slow. Down."*

"I wasn't, we weren't—" I trail off, mortified, hoping Erik hasn't picked up on our chaperone's intentions. Finding us wrapped around each other on the ground has given her a very wrong impression, but I can't explain it without him overhearing, so I turn on my side and watch the tiny lights of a plane drift like unanchored stars. Nobody, beside me, smells strongly of the soap from Erik's house; flowery and expensive. I lie half on the slick sleeping bag and half on the rough particle board, the single sleeping bag far too narrow for three, going over what Erik's told me. I'm so lost in my thoughts, it takes a moment to register that they're talking with each other, and I start picking out their words from the tide.

". . . you saw *Swan Lake* before?" Nobody asks.

"Yeah. When I was a kid."

"Do you remember what it was about?"

"Hmm." Erik yawns. "There's a prince who falls in love with a swan, but then a wizard makes him cheat on her with another swan."

Nobody makes a disgusted noise. "Sounds terrible."

"It's very symbolic. The subtext is like, the prince promises to love this woman who lives every day as a white swan; but then he's drawn to her double, the black swan. They're symbols for what you *should* want, versus what you just *do* want. A super-ego-versus-id kind of thing." A beat as he yawns again. Then: "Tchaikovsky was gay when that was, uh, illegal, so. Self-hating genius makes great art. More news at eleven."

"How does it end?"

"Everybody dies."

"Even *the swans*?"

"One of the swans goes down hard when she finds out about him cheating—"

Nobody's creaky little laugh makes me smile despite myself.

"What? This is serious art, Nobody," Erik says indignantly. "And I watched it happen with these two eyes, okay, *through my own tears.*"

"It's a soap opera about birds!" She is shaking with laughter next to me.

"It's a *beloved classic,*" Erik says. "People generally go see it for the music."

"The music is good?"

"It's *great.*"

"Yeah, but I bet you have weird taste in music," Nobody says, and Erik laughs.

"Maybe. I'm a single repeater."

"What's that?" I ask.

"When I like a song, I listen to it over and over and over."

"Everyone does that." Nobody sniffs.

"Maybe it's a Class A thing," Erik says. "How about you, Signal? Single repeater?"

"No," I say. "But I haven't heard *Swan Lake* yet."

* * *

Birds wake us while it's still dark, seagulls crying for the coming sun, the ocean gray as slate under a concrete sky. We clear out fast, shivering and damp with dew, and head back to the trail, divvying up the food we have in our packs, heads down in baseball caps on the off chance we pass some early morning jogger.

I will take the first bus stop; Erik and Nobody will walk on to the next one and get on only after my bus has passed.

"See you at the Opera House," Nobody says. "Seven thirty sharp."

Erik puts a thick stack of hundred-dollar bills in my hand. "This is two thousand dollars."

"Erik, what the hell!"

"Don't spend it all in one place now." He leans in and kisses my cheek, a pang of excitement at the contact multiplying as he smiles at me, his dimple catching the early morning sun. "See you later."

By the time I'm done dividing the money into discreet portions throughout the backpack, the bus is coming down the empty highway, brushed with the first blush of dawn. It's going to be a long ride from here to the BART and then into the city.

Good thing I have some compelling reading material.

* * *

How are you working on your empathy?
Dr. Ledrick got clearance for me to volunteer on the suicide hotline at the facility. Under supervision, I answer calls from eight to twelve PM, four nights a week. Listening to people's problems and trying to gauge how they feel has been fascinating.
What areas could you improve?
Two girls I know from the yacht club are claiming I am their boyfriend all of a sudden. I need to be more clear with girls I get involved with that I am not available for long-term romantic relationships.
What are your greatest goals right now?
To find a new psychiatrist. And to find someone to talk to who is not a psychiatrist at all.
Who is someone you admire for how they treat others?
Grandpa Wylie gives sick gifts and tells great jokes and doesn't let Skye get away with anything. I wish I lived with him.

This got the first black Sharpie answer I'd seen in pages:

No, Erik. Believe me, you don't. We are "no contact" with Grandpa for reasons you are well aware of.

The black Sharpie response showed up only one more time while I read, after the response to the question:

Describe a time you showed empathy.

The answer has been blacked out completely. I tilt the page to see the words embossed by younger Erik's forceful scrawl:

When Alice gave me her Michelangelo book. I knew then it was only a matter of time.

That matter is resolved, Erik.

You are not putting me through this again.

I am trying to help you but that's only possible if there's a part of you that can take accountability. There are people who simply do not have that capability, like your grandfather. I need you to show me you are not like him.

* * *

I close the notebook and look up at the towering pink columns around me at the Palace of Fine Arts. Shapely statues luxuriate at the top of them, smiling down at me through trailing green fronds, but no one else seems to notice me alone on my bench at the edge of the pond. Joggers and nannies and tourists don't give me a second glance. I'd always heard of San Francisco as being rainy and gray, but the sunshine today is perfect. It turns the bay the color of the cloudless blue sky above and lines everything it touches with the palest yellow shine.

My hat is pulled low, and my face has been hidden in Erik's diary the last couple hours, waiting for the hair salons to open. But the sun is intense enough it must be past ten, so I pack up and start uphill, not sure where I'm going but enjoying the freedom to get lost. I've never walked around with so much money, or in such a big city. Somehow walking in a crowd where no one knows each other makes me feel like I'm not alone.

After turning down a few random streets, I spot a salon door, a girl with green hair just turning the closed sign over. She leads me to a chair where another girl with a stud under her lip combs through my shoulder-length hair with a bored expression.

"Well, what're you thinking?" She yawns. "Layers?"

"I want to look completely different," I say. "Do whatever you want—just make me look as different as possible." I pause, then add, "And ideally, like, better."

The stylist looks stunned. "Whatever *I* want? Are you sure?"

Once I've managed to convince her I'm serious, she wakes up considerably, grabbing my hair and moving it around my head with an intense expression.

"What's going on with the color?" she asks warily. "You used box dye recently, right?"

"Less than a week ago." I had to dye my hair before going out on a mission. We had all been made over so we'd be less conspicuous when we went after our targets, that seasick day after the Director came to camp. The memory stings like a sore throat. The moment comes back in full color: Troy leaping up from where we lay on the ground, to defend Jada after the Director kicked her sleeping bag. The way his eyes filled with red when the Director pointed his fob at him and set off his kill switch.

"Well, I'm thinking we treat the box dye as your filler and dye over it darker. You okay with going darker?"

"Whatever you want," I tell her honestly.

She trades her comb for a razor and goes in. Minutes later I have bangs, heavy fringe that ends right across my eyebrows, and my hair falls just a little past my chin. She then covers my entire head in rich black dye, and I page through a crinkled magazine while it sinks in, though I'm not really registering words or images. I'm thinking of the other makeovers from that day, of my friends back at camp.

Jada, who'd always gravitated toward the pinkest shirts and sharpest knives, had gone on her mission in all black; kitted out like a club kid in creepers and illusion tights and goth makeup, to take out the manager of an underground music club. A makeover was more her thing than anyone else's, but she was so deep in grief over Troy she wasn't really there for it.

And Kurt, Troy's brother. Always the sweeter and shyer of the two tall, athletic twins, when Troy would crack everyone up, Kurt would always laugh the hardest, beaming at him like he was magic. I don't even remember what he wore to his mission, because I could hardly bear to look at his face; he was in so much pain, taking on his target all alone.

I'd been so lucky to have Javier as my partner for our mission. Javier, for his makeover, had had the tear tattoo by his eye and the tattoo memorializing his brother covered up to better fit the profile of a preppy USC student. He'd been so supportive, even after Erik showed up and we . . . no—I. I kissed Erik, and Javier saw and then he'd . . . he'd helped me escape camp. Told the Director I died in the fire at the Star Barn.

What would they do to him, now it was obvious he lied? My stomach clenches up at the thought. Of course, he could say he didn't know I survived. I certainly had thought we'd really lost Erik. Still, a guilty flush of heat sweeps up my neck, and I try and beam a thought into Javier's head: Whatever they want to know, tell them. Save yourself.

I almost laugh then. Save himself, at camp, with a kill switch in his neck. There's no saving anyone at Naramauke. They will send them out again and again and again. A makeover each time, different depending on the mission. But the real transformation will be on the inside. Hardening themselves to take out each target, until there is nothing of them left. And then they'll be kicked out and killed off by the next generation of campers.

"Time's up!" the stylist says, tapping my hand like she's tried to get my attention a few times, and she eases me over to the sink.

By the time she's done washing out the color, she's getting very excited. She turns the chair away from the mirror as she styles me, giddy about the coming reveal. And it is shocking when I face the mirror at last: a stranger stares back at me, all big eyes under her dark bangs, and I smile. Even the smile looks better, somehow.

"You like it?"

"I can hardly tell it's me," I say. "It's perfect."

People turn to stare as I leave the salon. I don't think I've ever felt this gorgeous or unfamiliar to myself.

I practically sashay four streets over to the thrift store the hairstylist recommended, stopping halfway to wolf down a vegan BLT.

The thrift store is nothing like my beloved Ledmonton Salvation Army. It's one of those heavily curated places where nothing is cheap. But I find a black puffer coat long enough to double as a sleeping bag, and a slightly worn pair of black high-top Vans to replace the plimsolls currently going to pieces on my feet. And then I actually gasp when a floor-sweeping black tulle gown with a boned bodice appears in the middle of a clearance rack. Someone put new staff on pricing: it's designer, and so expertly cut it should be behind glass.

The cashier does a double take when she scans it. "This is a *find*," she says, very seriously, like maybe she won't let me buy it, then pauses. "And I love your hair." And she slides it across the counter to me, like my hair has proved I'll appreciate it.

"Thanks." I smile, throwing the bag over my shoulder, and glance up at the TV above her just in time to meet my own hollow eyes. My mugshot, with Erik's beside it, flashes before cutting to footage of us making out in Cactus Burger. Then the broadcast cuts to live footage of Dathan's red Scion being towed out of the ravine. Scrolling below it:

"MANHUNT ACROSS NORCAL FOR FUGITIVE TEENS."

I need to go. I need to go *right now*.

"Hey! Hey! Your change?"

I'm already running out the door, out onto the crowded sidewalk, knocking hard into someone's shoulder and rushing past without apology, my head ducked down. Everyone's staring at me like before, but it's sinister now, every nod from some random guy makes me flinch as I pull my baseball cap back on.

I hurry down a side street, buy a pair of oversized sunglasses and a hideous, dad-brand sunhat, then disappear down the first empty alley I can find and crouch behind a dumpster. With shaking fingers, I fish out the key to the security deposit box, the one we found in Jaw's room, and fasten it to the strap of my bra, in case I have to drop my backpack to run. I move all my larger bills directly into my clothes pockets and put on the puffer coat, resigning myself to carrying around the thrift store bag with my dress in it. Maybe that will help the disguise. After all, what kind of idiot goes shopping during their own manhunt, right? A *manhunt*.

Does Nobody know yet? Is Erik okay? I have no way to reach either of them. I just need to play it cool and find a place to hide in the middle of San Francisco for the next three hours. I drift back out into the street, skin almost itching at how many people are around me. A coffee shop? There might be a TV. Back to the park? But it's so busy, everyone in town eager to soak up the sun.

And then I see a sign for the library up ahead and almost break into a run.

* * *

The caliber of the San Francisco Library is truly unprecedented in my experience. Airy and modern inside, floor after floor of stacks opening up to a vast swirling skylight. For a moment my head falls back, struck at the enormity of it, but I catch myself before I take off my sunglasses. There are no TVs in sight here, but I'm still getting looks.

"Yeah, because people aren't used to seeing a teenage bag lady, Signal," Rose's voice hisses in my head. I *am* wearing an ankle-length puffer coat, bulging backpack, a sunhat, and sunglasses indoors, and standing in line for the free internet station. The quick looks from the people around me aren't suspicion—they're concern. Thanks, weird, internalized Rose voice.

"Any time, bitch!"

A seat opens up across a computer, and I thankfully hide behind its flatscreen monitor.

I double-check how to get to the War Memorial Opera House—luckily it's just up the street. Then I google Dr. Ledrick and scroll through what the search engine returns until I see an entry for a consulting professor at Stanford and click to his page, chest tightening in the blink before his photo loads.

The Director's hollow eyes stare back at me from my screen, nailing me in place.

"So your man was telling the truth last night," Rose's voice says in my head. *"Does that make him less scary . . . or more?"*

I immediately back out of the picture, goose bumps rising on my arms even in my puffer coat sleeves as I go down the list of web results. Every source on Dr. Ledrick is glowing. The same man who I saw kill Troy and who tortured Erik is indisputably a leading authority in mental health for adolescents. He's lauded for "salvaging" the Wylie-Stanton algorithm after the death of its creators and for his work with troubled youth, and buried deep in his Wikipedia there's a single line about his involvement in neurochemical testing for the army.

Surely the man who casually killed Troy moments after kicking Jada in the gut has some history of violence. I search "Dr. Ledrick" and "murder" and see a link pop up to Armchair.org, the true crime message board Erik introduced me to.

The back of my throat goes sour as I click the link.

"WHO MURDERED THE WYLIE-STANTONS?"

Power. Privilege. Hidden secrets. The Wylie-Stanton family was picture-perfect California royalty until a trip to the family lake house ended in bloodshed along the highway.

A high-speed impact along the cliffside wall of the remote mountain highway left two people dead and one fighting for his life.

But was this some freak accident?

A hit-and-run?

Or, as the Mt. Shasta community has insisted ever since, something even more sinister?

"Pinholes in All the Right Places"

A month after the tragedy, local mechanic Gregory Spotts, who oversaw recovery of the Wylie-Stanton's vehicle, allegedly told the owner of a local bar that the brake lines of the 2018 Mercedes-Benz GLK had been tampered with.

"'Pinholes in all the right places' was his verbatim quote," the bartender claimed in a Facebook post that has since been taken down.

When police later asked Spotts for an official statement, however, he refused. Spotts has since sold his shop and left Mt. Shasta. Did Spotts just have a few too many one night?

Or did someone take steps to silence him?

The Suspects

What makes this case interesting is how few people had access to the car in the one night the Wylie-Stantons spent at the secluded Wylie estate, and all of them were trusted friends or actual family of the passengers in the vehicle, Monica, Todd, and their college-age son, Skye:

Erik Wylie-Stanton, their disturbed younger son

Curtis Wylie, Monica's father, head of CurtPro Pharmaceuticals, and classic car collector

Alice Vazquez, senior at Laney College, Oakland

Owen Heo, Todd's personal assistant

Dr. Ledrick, Erik's longtime psychiatrist and Monica and Todd's business partner.

I click through the links to the pictures of each suspect, all except Skye, whose link is broken.

Curtis Wylie I recognize as Erik's older double from the photo back in his room. The picture links to the CurtPro Pharmaceuticals "founder" page.

The picture of Erik is a grainy image taken from a distance. I wonder if it was chosen because of the way the light catches his cat eye, giving his smile an almost demonic energy.

Alice's picture looks like it's taken from a college brochure. She's standing in what looks like an auto shop; a caption reads "Publicity photo, Machine Technology Lab, Laney College." She's smiling like she has to, but a pair of safety glasses hides the expression of her eyes, and her body is swallowed up by a giant hooded sweatshirt.

Owen Heo's picture is from the "meet the team" page of his current tech job; he sits at a conference table, wearing designer glasses frames and a self-conscious smile.

I force myself to click on Dr. Ledrick's image, and there is our Director, across from Erik's parents at some kind of benefit dinner.

An impatient cough from someone in line brings me back to the present. I've gone way past my fifteen minutes of internet time, so I send the rest of the article to print, grab the stack of pages that spit out from the printer, and barrel back to the stacks to read the rest.

Family Holiday Gone Wrong

When the Wylie-Stanton family and Owen Heo entered the gated Wylie compound and followed its wooded drive to Curtis Wylie's stunning lakeside mansion, they were expecting something like a family reunion; it was Monica's first visit to her father's estate in four years. Owen was also looking forward to meeting Dr. Ledrick, who was joining them at the house with news about the beta version of an algorithm that would later become the Wylie-Stanton Index Classification.

Curtis Wylie was best known in the small community of Mt. Shasta for funding the annual Christmas parade and always closing out the celebrations by appearing, dressed as Santa, in one of his classic cars. The former chief executive of CurtPro Pharmaceuticals had a storied collection of vintage vehicles, which he housed in a stand-alone garage that he religiously locked down after dark. The keys to the garage were kept in a secret location in Mr. Wylie's office.

The garage was visible from the terrace, where Owen and Todd were working for most of the visit, so anyone who went in during the day would have been noticed.

Since the family cut their visit short and made the fatal drive back down the next day, there was only one night for someone in the house to have gained access to the vehicle.

In the wake of the rumors, Owen detailed the visit in his personal blog, which he soon after deleted (he was widely criticized for its "inappropriate tone"). However, Armchair.org community members gathered screenshots and have assembled the rough time line below:

- 1:00 PM arrival. The family parked their car in the garage before going up to the house, which Owen described as "what you might get if Walt had demanded a 'Hunting Land' at Disney World." They were met on the deck by Curtis and Alice Garza, which immediately changed the mood. Again according to Owen: "Monica gave Erik a look like she was ready to slap the smile right off his face."
- 2:00 PM lunch on the terrace. Owen remembers it as strangely tense: "Erik was always a bit of a brat but managed to bring it to a whole new level, and his mom was not having it." Skye tried to make small talk, asking about Alice's mother and her senior year at college.
- 3:10 Dr. Ledrick arrived and parked his vehicle in the garage.
- 3:30–4:00 Todd and Owen worked on the terrace after lunch. Alice ran down the steps to the lawn shortly after they started working, appearing, in Owen's words, "completely freaked out."
- Skye spoke with his grandfather in his office; Skye had recently gotten an apprenticeship with a professional stunt driver in LA, but according to Owen, his parents did not approve: "they were like, we did not just pay Stanford all that tuition for you to go play zoom-zoom like you're five." Apparently, however, Skye won his grandfather's support, as their conversation ended with Skye taking out a '60 Porsche Spyder onto the open drive to wax and detail.
- Elsewhere, Owen bore reluctant witness to a fight between Monica, Dr. Ledrick, and Erik: "It was easily the most awkward forty-five minutes of my life, trying to code

with my boss while his wife and her business partner bitched out his son in literally the next room."

- 4:15 After the argument, Erik ran through the terrace and down to the lawn. Owen saw him and Alice walking by the lake shortly after, and described them as having "some kind of heart-to-heart."
- 6:00 Dinner was brought out, but "family time was definitely canceled," according to Owen. The tense clan split up to eat. Skye ate with his mother and Dr. Ledrick in the kitchen, Todd and Owen ate on the terrace while working, and were joined by Alice, who "seemed wildly uncomfortable."

  Erik and his grandfather, Curtis, ate lunch together in Curtis's office.
- 7:00 Owen went to retrieve his phone charger from the Wylie-Stanton's Mercedes. Finding the garage locked, he went to Curtis's office and interrupted an intense conversation with Erik to ask for the key, which Curtis removed from its hidden drawer.
- 7:10 On his way out of the garage, Owen ran into Curtis again. He was giving Dr. Ledrick a tour of his car collection. Curtis asked Owen to return the key to his office, reminding him of the drawer in the desk where it was kept.
- 7:30 When Owen returned to the terrace, Todd announced they were done with work for the night. Monica was also on the deck and, in Owen's words, "smoking like it was going to bring her sanity back." She told Owen that they would be leaving the next day, not staying the entire weekend.
- 7:45 Owen, trying to locate his guest room, accidentally walked in on Skye "making out" with Alice in the library. Owen apologized and "turned on my heel, trying to get the hell out of there." He was surprised when Alice followed him out and offered to show him to his guest room, which was next to her own.

Alice asked him if he'd "noticed any streetlights on the mountain roads on the way up," but Owen could not remember if he had.

- 8:00 Owen video-chatted with a friend.
- 9:15 Owen went to the deck to retrieve his charger and saw Dr. Ledrick pacing by the lake with Monica, having an intense discussion about a camping excursion. Owen paused to listen, because "if they were going to try and drag me along on another family 'vacation' they were going to need to pay me overtime." But after hearing Monica "shut down" Dr. Ledrick's proposal, he returned, relieved, to his room.
- 10:30 A crash downstairs made Owen step out into the gallery that overlooked the living room. There, another family argument was coming to a head, with everyone but Alice seemingly involved. Erik was refusing to return home with his parents the next day, insisting he would rather "live at his grandpa's mountain house in the middle of nowhere."
- 11:00 According to a later police statement given by Skye, he and Dr. Ledrick began a conversation in the living room at this time that lasted a couple of hours.
- 2:00 AM Unable to sleep, Owen went out on his room's balcony to smoke, when a motion light snapped on over the lawn. Erik was walking Alice, her clothes "as wet as if she'd fallen in," over to a car waiting in the drive, which Owen had not seen before. He assumed Erik had allowed it access through the gate. Erik did not approach the car, and no one came out of it. Alice got inside and left the estate without saying goodbye, and "her clothes, suitcase, toiletries, even her phone" were left behind.
- By 8:00 AM the next day, Monica was packed and ready to leave. When Erik could not be found, Monica and

Todd decided to drive back down with Skye, and Curtis could bring Erik down whenever he returned to the house. Sensing that Monica was "not thrilled" about this arrangement, Owen offered to stay behind and drive Erik home that night, an offer that almost certainly saved his life.

- 9:00 Owen was tasked with packing up Alice's room. He found a letter to Erik in a sealed envelope, which he put out on the terrace table. He also found her phone. "The screen was unlocked when I picked it up, and the last text popped up. It was from someone named Marco and read, 'If I see him I'll kill him.'"
- 10:30 When Erik at last returned to the house, Owen saw him read and then destroy the letter.
- 11:30 Highway patrol officers contacted Curtis about the collision. Skye was airlifted to a hospital, where Owen drove Dr. Ledrick, Curtis, and Erik.
- Skye said in his statement to police that he did not remember what happened immediately before the crash.
- Dr. Ledrick, who shortly after took custody of Erik from Skye, refused to let police question his patient alone.
- A month after the crash, mechanic Gregory Spotts said in the hearing of several bar patrons that the Wylie-Stanton's brake lines had been tampered with. When police approached him about officially making a statement, he refused. Shortly after, Spotts sold his shop and left Mt. Shasta.
- Erik was made a full-time patient at a private mental health facility shortly afterward.

So, Armchair Detectives . . . *"whodunnit?"*
Users, submit your theories below!

COMMENTS (7)

BigBootyBrenda: Who is this Marco guy making threats against Erik? Could he have run in and cut the brakes?

JackOfAllTrades73: What people don't understand is that it's almost impossible to cut the brake lines of a modern car. It's an '80s movie trope. You can't just cut some lines and send someone over a cliff. For the family to get as far as they did, without a warning light turning on or the brake pedal going soft, would require a gradual letting of fluid and someone shutting down the computerized warning system.

> **CC_CUBA:** Which is why the mechanic who recovered the car said "pinholes in all the right places" maybe?
>
> > **JackOfAllTrades73:** I'm not saying it's not possible, only that whoever did it knew exactly what they were doing & had to have had at least a few hours alone with the car.
> >
> > > **CC_CUBA:** Gotcha. My question is why didn't the mechanic tell the police?
> > >
> > > > **Lets_Get_Em:** Everyone in Mt. Shasta will tell you, Spotts was leveraged up to his eyeballs on his shop. Someone paid it off to shut him up about the brake lines. The police filed the accident as an "unspecified vehicular malfunction," and to this day it's considered an accident, not a murder.

AgathaCrispy: Psycho little brother did it, end of story.

* * *

I've been curled up into a ball the whole time I've been reading, jaw clenched, stomach churning. Now I let the pages fall and lean against the stack of books behind me, relief flooding me with a physical pins-and-needles sensation.

Although the time line was brutal, it's convinced me of one thing: Erik did not kill his parents. I've seen firsthand he knows nothing about cars, and the brother who wanted to press charges at thirteen would hardly have covered up multiple murders for him.

But that leaves the question: Who *did* kill the Wylie-Stantons?

"The library will be closing in half an hour," a soft voice intones over the PA.

That can't be right, they close at . . . I do a double take at the clock.

7:25.

I'm already late to meet Nobody and Erik.

Chapter Six

The Opera House

I stand at the top of the stairs leading down to the lobby of the War Memorial Opera House. The crowd below me would be intimidating, even if I weren't afraid of direct eye contact; all the men in suits, the women in jewel-tone gowns. The air thrums with expensive perfume and mannered chatter, enclosed by a vaulted ceiling honeycombed with gold rosettes. I still smell like the pink soap in the library bathroom that I took a sink shower with.

Checking my bags went smoothly, at least. The checker was swamped and barely looked at me. Now, I try to scan the crowd while hiding my face, hoping I see one of them soon. Because if they're not here, then that means . . .

There's a white flash of hair over a perfect face; it's Nobody, her hair cut short like a man's, but with a swooping bang she can tilt over her face. When our eyes lock, hers go wide, and she waves at me.

Erik looks in the direction she's waving, but he looks past me at first. Then slowly his eyes travel back, face struck by dawning recognition. They're both in black tie; to which Erik has added a gray bomber hat—the kind with the flaps you can secure under the chin, like old pilots used to wear. But he reaches up to take it off as I walk toward them, staring like he's still not sure who I am.

"I almost didn't recognize you! Your hair looks amazing!" I tell Nobody. She looks like a model just in her shabby streetclothes, but in her tailored black suit she looks like she could walk the red carpet at the Oscars. She takes my hand and makes me do a spin.

"You did *good*," Nobody says approvingly.

Erik is still staring at me.

"Thanks for the new haircut." I smile at him.

He keeps staring, then: "Don't mention it."

"I told the hair stylist to make me look as different as possible."

"I don't know that it makes you look *different*," he says. "You just look more like yourself."

A musical chime sounds through the lobby, and the crowd surges for the huge arched doors into the theater.

"Here we go!" Nobody hands me a ticket as we're swept toward the ushers with scanning guns, and then up a dizzy series of stairs to the nosebleeds. I don't think you can be any farther away from the show than we are, almost the back row of the top balcony, with a vertigo-inducing view of the entire orchestra pit and stage. I sit between Erik and Nobody, Nobody excitedly leafing through her program, Erik still staring at me.

"We were on TV," I tell him quietly.

"I saw!" His smile is mocking, and he indicates the hat in his lap. "That's when my ears got cold."

"Do you think anyone here . . .?"

"No." He shakes his head, so confident my shoulders lighten. "The lights are about to go down, anyway. Watch—it's cool."

He points to the massive chandelier above us, a sunburst shape in a vault of sky blue, that bathes the auditorium with a moony white glow. First one light, then the next, and then the next goes out, faster and faster, like dominoes falling in a spiral cascade, the light seemingly chasing itself out of existence as an excited hush falls over the audience. And then, in the sparkling dark, as the first piercing notes of the overture rise from the orchestra, Erik takes my hand and leans in toward me.

"This," he whispers, "this is our first date."

I slide my fingers through his as the audience breaks into applause, and the massive curtain lifts.

Dancers as small and dainty as porcelain figurines flit through milky pools of spotlight, and Nobody leans forward until she's practically hanging out of her seat. And when the dancer playing the prince is approached by the only black ballerina in the company, offering him a comically oversized goblet, Nobody claps her hands over her head like it's a monster truck rally.

I'm about to gently shush her, when she turns to me and says, "That's my girlfriend!"

I lean forward, watching the ballerina with renewed interest, then find her photo in the program: Amy Johnson, age nineteen. I almost point out the photo to Nobody, but she's riveted to the stage, so I focus on the dancers as well.

They're all getting very excited about a crossbow. The guy playing the prince is holding it aloft and leaping in circles, when Erik lifts my hand from the armrest between us. I hold very still as his breath brushes the inside of my wrist, along the roadmap of blue veins at the base of my palm. Then he kisses me, right there, right where you take the pulse; a hot, leisurely kiss that makes me sway in my seat like the first tilt of a Ferris wheel. It feels like the music is coming out of my bones.

"Hey," Nobody whispers, "Aarush is supposed to meet me before intermission in the lobby, but my girlfriend still hasn't done her solo—"

"We'll go," I say quickly. I stand, hand still in Erik's, and pull him after me.

I lead him down the steep stairs between the rows of balcony seats, and though I'm unable to look back at him, I could swear I hear him laughing under his breath.

The moment we're out of the dark of the balcony and in the muted light of the hall, I turn to face him, backing against the wall, my hands on his wrists, pulling him after me.

"Yes?" he says, like it's a question. "Did you want to speak with me?"

"No," I tell him, shaking. I lean forward then and press my lips just below his ear. My lips trace the ridge of his jaw, the line of his throat, the lift of his chin, all the places I have stared at for so long, until at last, *he's* the one overwhelmed. His smile deepens against my cheek, and then I feel him react. My mind fills with a remembered video: a lit match touching gasoline in super-slow motion, the pure primeval force restrained to a point of hypnotic beauty. His hands are like this, slow-motion fire consuming me with deliberate gentleness, and he dedicates his mouth to my throat with such thoughtful intensity I lose my breath. We slide against the wall, the music surrounding us, in a simple contest of who can make the other one feel more.

There's a discreet cough, an usher in a white coat gliding past us toward the balcony, and Erik pulls himself upright, offering me his arm. We stagger down the stairs back to the gold and marble lobby, walking like we've just traded a boat for land.

The lobby is empty except for the music, changed by the distance and the vaulted arch of the ceiling. Erik stops and holds out his hand.

"Shall we dance?"

"I *really* can't dance."

"That's okay, it's just an excuse."

"An excuse for what?"

He shrugs. "To be closer to you." And then he takes my hand and sends me twirling out from one arm, so my black skirt sweeps in a circle across the white marble floor, and snaps me back in so close I'm sure we're about to kiss again. But he steps to the side, back very straight, chin lifted high. I try to "follow" and tread hard on his foot.

"You *really* can't dance." He laughs, holding me tighter, and somehow, it's the funniest thing I've ever heard. I collapse against him, laughing, and a moment later his arm goes to the small of my back, our hands clasp and elbows extend, and we try again. We keep it simple this time, making slow, waltzy circles around the lobby, the soaring columns and frosted glass globes of the golden lamps spinning around us like an old-fashioned carousel.

"It's a shame you're missing *Swan Lake*," he says.

"We can still hear the music out here. And that's the draw, right?" I smile. "Although, I don't know. I have a theory on that."

"Let's hear it."

"Well . . . the white swan and the black swan are both played by the same ballerina, right? And that's always how it's done, right?"

"Almost always, yes."

"And that's what everyone was talking about in the lobby. Kind of placing their bets on how well the same dancer could play the good girl and the bad girl. Or they'd compare other dancers who really nailed both sides. So maybe that's why a soap opera about birds is this big beloved classic. Because one dancer is the hero and the villain at the same time."

"Sure," Erik says. "It shows off their range."

"But more than that. Like you said, it's symbolic. Maybe it's reassuring to see someone can embody two extremes. Because then it feels like more of a choice for everyone," I finish awkwardly, "whether to be the white swan or the black swan."

"Is it a choice?" He frowns thoughtfully. "You can't choose your nature."

"But the *dancer* does," I point out. "The dancer ends the show as Odette, after having this interlude as a triumphant, dark version of herself. She knows what it's like to give in to her darker impulses, but still chooses to be good. And that's what counts, the *choice*, right? Like, does goodness even count if it's just your innate programming?"

"Yes," Erik says. "Absolutely yes. There's not enough good in the world to get picky about where it comes from." His eyes are steady on mine as he goes on, "But if we follow your theory, that *Swan Lake* presents the ultimate triumph of the dancer's better nature, what does it mean that it costs her the Prince and her own life? Don't you think that's . . ." His words trail off as I spin back across the floor, landing just short of his chest, and smile up at him.

"Yes?"

He shakes his head like he honestly can't remember.

"Don't I think that's . . .?" I prompt.

"Hot. Insanely hot." His arm goes around my waist, and then he scans the lobby impatiently. "There's got to be some kind of private lounge or telephone booth or something around here—"

"And miss the music?" I tease.

"Honestly, I think the music sounded best in the stairwell. *Incredible* acoustics."

"Incredible," I agree. "But we're supposed to meet that guy in the lobby."

"Oh, right." His dimples flash. "That whole ending the Wylie-Stanton thing. You distracted me."

"Yeah, with my fascinating *Swan Lake* theories."

"It is fascinating, and I think you're onto something," he says, twirling me out again, "but your theory isn't about the ballet. It's about yourself." I turn back toward him, more slowly now, his gaze heavy enough I can practically feel it on my skin. "You're drawn to your dark side, which, according to all the available data, is me." I land in front of him, and he looks down at me, his eyes hard. "But you're confident your better sense will prevail."

"You're not my dark side, Erik."

"Yes, I am. That's what this is. Two oppositely charged magnets," he says, his hand fitting into the small of my back: "Click." But he doesn't spin me away from him. Instead, his warm hand glides up my exposed spine, and I go completely still as beautiful shivers ripple out from the contact. His hand moves up along my shoulder, then gently brushes along the line of my neck to my face, his thumb following the contour of my jaw. He stares the whole time so hard, like he's trying to learn each inch by heart. I'm frozen in place, but I'd swear the room is spinning.

"Is it like that for you too?" he asks at last.

"Like what?"

"This, like . . ." His brow furrows. "*Relief.*"

Something in my chest twists.

"Like I was the last person in the longest game of hide-and-seek, and then you found me."

I'm about to answer him with something soft and stupid, but catch myself in time.

"Wow." I laugh. "Nice line."

He steps back from me then, ducking his head away and laughing too, though it doesn't sound like his laugh. I catch his hand and push my fingers through his again before he can retreat further, and he goes still except for his breath. I could swear he's breathing harder, like he feels this as much as I do.

Is the only way to find out for sure, as Nobody said, to beat him at his own game?

"You know, I've been meaning to ask"—I keep my voice light—"what do I get, if I win the bet instead of you?"

"Win it how?"

"Like if I get *you* to confess *your* feelings first."

Erik still hasn't met my gaze since I laughed at him, but now his eyes rise to mine, flat and cruel.

"Oh, come on, Signal," he says. "You and I both know I don't have feelings."

My heart jerks at the words. Then I recognize them: they're my own, something I said to him at camp. Unconsciously, he's hit the intonations the same way I did, like he's heard it a thousand times. Maybe he has. It's funny, the words that get stuck in our heads, the ones that dig in the deepest.

I reach up and touch the edge of his cheek, the raised curve just past the corner of his eye. His jaw flares and his eyelids drop, like he's trying to absorb all the sensation as I trace the curve of his solemn face, all the way to the turn of his chin, as though my finger were a tear. When my finger stops his eyes open so slowly, and they're shining. Some strange new power surges through me, like I'm holding his heart in my hand. Like he has a heart, after all.

"Poor baby," I say softly. "Come on. Let's make it interesting. What does the winner get if the other person says the magic words first?"

"Everything," he says. "But only if they mean it."

"If you're going to keep throwing these lines at me, we need to work on your delivery."

Erik lets out a genuine laugh. "Fine. That time I *was* trying to be smooth, but honestly you deserved it."

"Yeah, well, the effort showed. Your delivery the first time was way more natural. Next time, maybe go a little angstier. Like, bite your lip and sigh."

"Show me?" he says innocently, lowering his mouth closer to mine. "Bite my lip?"

A giddy laugh bursts out of me, when a thunderous clap makes us both wheel around. The main doors into the lobby burst open as a tall guy in a motorcycle jacket and neon-green baseball cap hurries toward us. Erik moves reflexively in front of me.

"Signal?" the guy hisses. "Erik?"

Erik's face is impossible to read as he nods to the stranger.

"I'm Aarush," the guy says, scanning the lobby. "Where's Nobody? We should go. Right now."

I could swear I see red and blue light bounce off the street as the door falls shut behind him.

"We should get our stuff," I say quickly, getting the ticket for my bag, but Erik keeps his hand on my arm.

"It's intermission in five minutes," he says. "Why not wait for the crowd as cover?"

Aarush shakes his head. "I've been listening to a scanner. I got here maybe ten minutes ahead of the police. We have to go out the back."

Erik takes my bag ticket. I grab my skirts up in both hands and sprint up the marble stairs.

* * *

When I get back to our balcony seats, Nobody is watching her girlfriend rise en pointe, one leg fully extended. She holds for one beat, then the audience bursts into applause. Nobody looks up at me then, eyes streaming, but her smile drops at my expression, and she launches herself out of her seat.

We meet Aarush and Erik, with our bags, at the door to the balcony. Aarush strides straight through the nearest fire door, the red and gold of the Opera House bursting like a bubble as we run along a narrow concrete hall and down a series of shivering metal staircases.

"Hey! *Hey!* You can't be down here!" someone calls.

"Go, go, GO!" Aarush's feet drum the stairs behind me as we plunge down another story, landing in an echoing basement.

"This way, this way—" A squeak of fire doors, then wind and cold and traffic sounds wash over us. We're out in some weird back unloading area, and he's sprinting for a massive BMW SUV. Aarush throws our bags in the back seat, then cracks open the trunk.

"Get in!"

A look passes between the three of us.

"Why can't we have doors?" Erik asks.

"They were setting up checkpoints on the bridge on my way here. Between that and the curfew, they aren't going to let four teens traveling alone out of the city right now."

Curfew? I'm about to ask what he means, but Nobody is already getting into the trunk. Erik helps me up, then curls around the other side of me, and Aarush throws a moving blanket over us before slamming the door down, the lock clicking into place. A moment later, the engine starts below us.

"Nobody," I hiss, "where is he taking us? I thought you just had to give him a thumb drive."

"Yeah, me too," she whispers back.

"You're sure this is Aarush?"

"He fits the description. Dennis said he's our age, Indian American, and has a British accent."

Erik pulls the blanket down, cranes his head for a moment, then reports: "I can get to the front if I take out the back seat headrests."

"Too many street cameras and patrol cars out here," Nobody says. "Might as well just walk yourself to the police station."

Bile stings the back of my throat. "Let's stay calm—let's just stay calm. What do we know about this guy?"

Nobody says, "Dennis only knew him online but considers him his best friend."

"Don't tell me he was a *Skullsex* alum?" Erik says, referencing Dennis' old dark web site, which does little to quiet my nerves.

"No, they met doing white-hat hacking competitions," Nobody says. "That's it—that's all I know."

"I know he's Aarush Desai," Erik says. "He looks just like his dad, Sonny Desai. But I'm not sure if that's good news or bad news."

"Sonny Desai?" I whisper. "Seriously?"

"Who is—" Nobody starts, but the car slows, and we all fall silent as the high-powered engine levels to an idle, the car stopping as though for a light. But it stays stopped for far too long. A traffic jam? I look back and forth between Nobody and Erik, who are both listening intently. There's only silence, muffled traffic outside the car. My fingernails dig into my palms, and then there's a whirr, like one of the car windows dropping, and a voice diffused by open air:

"Good evening. May I see your license?"

"Sure. What seems to be the problem, Officer?"

A police officer. A police officer is standing right outside the car, right now. This is it. They're going to send me back to camp, and I'm going to be the next pop quiz.

"Just a checkpoint. It's past curfew. If you were coming through the other direction, they'd send you home."

"Is there a curfew?" I notice Aarush's slight British accent now, as he feigns innocence. "I hadn't heard."

"Everyone under eighteen needs to be off the streets after nine. Just started today. You should get a text alert about it if you haven't already."

"I'll have to check my phone."

"On account of those Class A teen killers," the officer says, his voice closer. "They got them on camera again, somewhere in the city." I hear the click of a flashlight, and through the stitches in the moving blanket register its beam sweeping along the rearview window, just over our feet. In the excruciating pause, I grip Erik's hand, and he brings it against his heart.

"Well. Anyway. You're fine to go ahead, Mr. Desai." The officer's voice floats away from the window. "Drive home safe."

The window rolls up, the engine rises, and the strange thrum of the bridge fills the car.

"We are now crossing the historic Golden Gate Bridge," Erik whispers. His dimples flash as Nobody and I cut him looks. "What? It's a *national landmark*."

"Who is Sonny Desai?" Nobody hisses.

"Founder of Destech, the first name in electronic and cyber security. They make prototype drones and smart security fences. And sometimes Sonny will trend on Twitter for eating a gold-leafed steak or declaring he'll run for mayor or something."

"Smart security fences?" My voice is too high. "Like ones that work with kill switches possibly? Like maybe he works with camp?"

Nobody tenses beside me but says, "Don't get paranoid. He helped Dennis turn them off before, right?"

"And look how that turned out," Erik adds.

Silence fills the trunk as the car bears down a long, winding road. We're out of the start-and-stop grid of the city; I feel certain if we were to throw back the blanket, we'd be in complete darkness.

"I ran into Nobody in Japantown this afternoon," Erik says, running his finger up my arm to get my attention, voice completely unconcerned. "She ordered a ramen and chatted with the shop owner in flawless Japanese."

Nobody barks a laugh. "Flawless? Hardly."

"You can speak Japanese?" I ask, but then the car slows to a crawl, and we all fall silent to hear the tinny beeps of a security gate code being punched in, then the pneumatic shudder of a gate.

The road below is curving and glass smooth. The downhill grade steepens and the air changes, grows colder and denser somehow, an artificial glow suffusing the air around the car that makes our hiding place under the blanket just legible.

Erik's hand slips down to the floor of the trunk and flips open a panel where a tire jack is concealed. He noiselessly removes the handle, then glances up at Nobody, who lifts her jacket to reveal the red lacquered handles of a butterfly knife.

We shudder to a stop, and footsteps rap sharply around the side of the car. Erik disappears the jack handle down his sleeve, and Nobody raises herself on one arm, her other hand inside her jacket as the back door flies open.

"You guys okay?" Aarush asks. A row of race cars gleam behind him.

"Never better." Erik smiles his sheepish, pop idol smile. "Uh . . . where are we?"

"My house," Aarush says. "Come on—I'll take you inside. Leave the bags. I'll have someone bring them up."

Erik rolls his shoulder, letting the handle of the jack drop into his palm, and there are a series of metallic clicks at the end of Nobody's sleeve that make my throat go dry as we follow Aarush into the brushed steel elevator. He goes to stand at the very back, and then once we're in, he leans forward and scans his phone over an inset screen by the open doors.

An expertly modulated machine voice says, "Welcome home, Aarush. What floor?"

"Main."

Only then does the elevator begin to rise. It's operated by voice recognition.

So how the hell do we get out of here if he doesn't want us to?

Nobody cuts a look to Erik. He is staring straight forward, face perfectly relaxed, but the arm holding the jack handle is taut as a pulled-back bowstring. My heart thrashes as we all stand very still in the small space. What's going to be waiting when the doors open? Should we try to get the upper hand now, before we get to wherever he's taking us? While we still have the numbers?

"Why did you bring us here?" Nobody asks through clenched teeth just as the elevator settles. But before Aarush can answer, the doors glide open, revealing a sea of people who turn, see us, and break out in wild applause.

Chapter Seven

The Party

I've never seen so many people in one room. Although this isn't a room exactly—it's more like the lounge of some five-star luxury hotel, a vast open-concept space around a super-modern staircase that bleeds into a balcony looking out onto an infinity pool, and every inch of it is crammed with exceptionally well-dressed, hot people. All cheering.

Why are they all cheering?

Someone yells, *"It's those Cactus Burger Killers, boyee!"*

"Don't worry," Aarush says. "You're among friends. Follow me."

Hunching a little, he silverfishes through his own party, looking vaguely annoyed when various guests stop us for high fives. People keep telling Erik not to forget the fries, and one girl, who I swear is a pop star I recognize from a music video, scans him up and down while tightening her hand on Aarush's arm.

"I need my phone back for just *one picture* with him. I swear I won't post it until—until you say." Her eyes never leave Erik as she speaks in a soft Russian accent, "It's Erik, right?"

Before Erik can reply, another girl throws herself at him from the crowd, scrambling to kiss him; he springs back so fast, she only manages to plant one on his cheek.

"Find me later, okay?" she yells as a guy who's built like a linebacker, and wearing an earpiece, pulls her away. I almost follow her myself, but Erik takes my hand and gently pulls me back, smiling delightedly.

"What a face! Are you *sure* you're not a killer, Signal?"

"I have my limits," I mutter.

Nobody shrinks as much as she can behind me, chin tucked to her chest and her long bang in front of her face. I grab her hand too, so we're linked like three paper dolls as we follow Aarush past the broad marble staircase, past a massive boulder etched with ancient pictographs, and over to another security guard, who nods deferentially to Aarush and lets us down a narrow hall.

This shadowy hall seems to dead-end, but Aarush hits a seemingly random point on the wall, and a panel slides open, revealing another inset screen at shoulder height. Aarush rests his hand on this screen, and a panel in the wall sinks and opens into a darkened room washed with blue light.

"After you," he says, stepping back, and the three of us enter a long, narrow room with a massive conference table and one whole wall looking into the depths of the infinity pool. The lower halves of several people are treading water at the top of the ceiling. The other wall across from the table is paneled floor to ceiling with massive flat screens, the Destech logo rotating slowly in each one.

Aarush pulls out a chunky laptop from under the desk and starts connecting it to an actual dial-up modem. He looks around, holding its plug.

"How can this possibly be considered the 'nerve center,'" he says to himself, his British accent at its thickest, "when it has only one phone jack?" Then, to Nobody, "I presume you have the thumb drive?"

Nobody nods, digs through her pockets.

"I'm sorry," I say, "but should we be concerned about the hundreds of people who just recognized us out there?"

"Phones are strictly prohibited at my parties," Aarush takes a seat at the conference table and gestures for us to do the same. "And you lot will be gone long before anyone can brag about meeting you online."

"Why would they brag about that?" Nobody croaks.

Aarush looks from her to us, a frown flashing across his face, then he taps on his phone, and the wall of flat screens tiles with the results of the Google search "cactus class As": the newest results include security camera stills of me and Erik at the Opera House, our black formal wear cutting us out starkly from the white marble.

"Scroll," Aarush commands his phone, and hundreds of images fly up the wall: Erik's and my mugshots are a meme; there are GIFs of us kissing at Cactus Burger; there's even *fan art.* I'm struck by a chibi-style illustration of a cartoon me blushing and holding a bloody axe behind my back as Erik shakes a finger. But by far the most prevalent image is a GIF made from news footage, when Erik threw the stoned driver out of the car we stole at the Cactus Burger, then turned back to the window and grabbed the fast food before getting in.

Aarush taps his phone, and a news clip of a guy with thinning hair starts playing, the chyron under him reading: "Class A Encounter."

". . . stole my phone *and* tipped the driver twelve hundred dollars, which I can't get back—believe me, I've tried."

The news cuts over to our Uber driver, Dathan, looking thankfully unscathed, a news anchor chasing him across his lawn.

"That's tough about his twelve hundred dollars," Dathan says into an outstretched mic. "I just hope the company reimburses him, 'cause I'm not going to. Let's be real—I earned that tip."

"You've built a following." Aarush stops the video on his phone, then turns back to the chunky laptop. "They'll have forgotten you in another few weeks of course, but right now you're generating the best press Class As have ever received. You're young, you're fit, you're in love." My face goes hot. "And of course, the longer you're at large, the more famous you become." He looks at Erik. "You really weren't aware of this?"

"We knew about the manhunt," Erik says, "but we haven't exactly been following the news. We've been trying to figure out how to get to Ledmonton so we can clear Signal's name. She's innocent. That's what this is all about."

Aarush's eyebrows shoot up, and he looks to me, stricken.

"I was framed," I tell him. "But also Dennis and all our friends back at camp are being trained to kill people. Our hope is that by reopening my case, we can discredit the Wylie-Stanton." I look to Erik, then back to Aarush. "End camp. And save our friends."

"And you have some sort of proof of all this, I hope?"

Erik and I explain about the security deposit key we found in Jaw's room, and how we believe the Ledmonton bank box holds the evidence he blackmailed Janeane with, and our plans to go retrieve it.

"You need the owner of the box and a bank employee to open a safe deposit box," Aarush says, cutting us off. "So that's a nonstarter."

Erik nods. "I know. But I'd hoped maybe we could approach a local authority who knew Signal personally and might be willing to push for a subpoena. Then this manhunt happened."

"As I said, your plan is a total nonstarter."

"Janeane is in Ledmonton?" Nobody asks me, and when I nod: "Have Erik talk to her. Get her to confess on camera and put it online."

My stomach sinks.

"Total nonstarter," Aarush shakes his head, "Her confession would only work if you are able to get her to speak freely and lay out her crimes of her own volition. Which I seriously doubt—"

"He doesn't need to touch her to get a confession. Right?" Nobody looks to Erik.

"Give me enough time"—Erik smiles—"and I can make her roll over and bark."

Aarush shifts uncomfortably in his chair. "If there is even a hint of physical coercion—"

"There won't be," Erik says. "Skye didn't tell you about me? My whole 'apex manipulator' thing?"

Aarush's large, thickly lashed eyes don't blink for a long moment. The Destech logo turns three times on the screen above his head before he nods and says, "I've heard things."

"I just have to be across from her, talking face to face," Erik goes on. "And I don't know how to get up there now with this manhunt going on."

"If you can guarantee me that no one will be harmed, I could help with that." Aarush says. "Not directly. The liability is too high if you're caught at this point. Can't have one of you popping up on a Destech plane manifest, or we'll all go down. But I *could* approach your fans anonymously, vet them, and crowdsource connecting rides for you, up north to Ledmonton."

Our *fans*.

"And if—*if*—you get footage of a confession, I've got a chancer journalist friend I could put you in touch with."

"What's a chancer?" I ask.

He looks stunned again but blinks and explains, "People who think the Wylie-Stanton is a blatant violation of civil liberties. Like myself. And my father."

"Get me in touch with this journalist now," I say. "We can give them an exclusive—whatever they want—if they'll get our side of things out."

Aarush shakes his head. "Any journalist reputable enough to make a difference will also require some sort of evidence. And not just about your case. About this whole training camp even existing."

"You know it exists," Nobody says. "You helped Dennis hack our kill switches before."

Aarush gestures to the code coming up on his small laptop screen. "I believe in camp for the same reason I'm helping you now—because I know and trust Dennis. But all I could prove in a court of law is that some entity has remote tracking devices and fights back aggressively when outsiders attempt to hack them." He puts out his hands. "That proves nothing. So if you're going to count on the public to put pressure on what we're presuming is an *intra-government agency*, you'll need some damn compelling evidence. Something visual. Shareable. And irrefutable."

"Janeane was at camp." I look at Erik. "When we go to get her confession, we could ask her about that too?"

His eyebrows shoot up, his eyes sparking as they meet mine. "Of course."

"Alright." Aarush taps the conference table with one knuckle. "Alright. It's a plan. Now, I'm eager to get into these kill switches. You're all free to enjoy the party." He turns toward the laptop with an air of complete dismissal. After a beat, Nobody and Erik and I stand up from the conference table. I'm almost out the door behind them when Aarush calls, "Signal?"

The door closes in front of me, fitting so precisely into the wall I can barely make out the seam. I turn to face Aarush.

"As you might have gathered, I know Erik's brother, Skye Wylie-Stanton. Silicon Valley is a small town in a lot of ways, and his father was a highly respected programmer whose loss is still felt by the entire tech community." He rubs the back of his neck nervously. "And it's an open secret Erik killed him. Killed his own father and mother. Even if he was never formally charged."

This is not news, not after my visit to the library. But it still makes me sick to hear it.

"If you are innocent," Aarush goes on, rising from his chair, "being associated with Erik only hurts your cause. And frankly, I'm having a hard time being in the same room with him. I'm not sure I'm entirely comfortable sending him off to interrogate someone. I would suggest you let me have security detain him here, and you continue north on your own."

My first instinct is to shoot off some rapid-fire defense, but what can I even say? The only thing I have to counter him is a child's journal and a confession from Erik that only covered eight fingers.

I take a deep breath instead.

"Thank you for the offer," I begin. "I appreciate your concerns—I really do. But I can't get this confession without him."

"You might not be able to get this confession *with* him—not one that will matter." Aarush looks stern. "If it appears she's been forced, nothing she says will matter to my journalist or anyone else."

"I promise you. He won't hurt her. He won't hurt anyone."

He stares at me for a long beat, then sinks into his chair again and taps his phone. The door behind me opens, party music and laughter spilling down the polished hall.

"Enjoy the party then."

* * *

The house seems twice as crowded when I return to the main floor. There are towering pyramids of shot glasses along the bar, and the low couches under the stairs are writhing with sloppy make-out sessions while a DJ in the corner loops bass tracks in an auditory stupor.

I skirt the edge of the crowd and make my way toward the relative quiet of the deck and the still glow of the infinity pool beyond the mesh of dancers. My bare arms erupt in goose bumps once I step outside, but I see Erik across the pool, a red Solo cup in either hand. His tie is loosened, and he's surrounded by women. The Russian pop star grips his upper arm as she throws back her head in a howling laugh.

"*Wow, Signal*"—Rose's voice pierces through the party noise—*"could it be that maybe Erik is way more into you when you're literally the only straight female he has contact with?"*

I squeeze my eyes shut and turn to go back into the house, when his voice rings across the water:

"Signal! Over here!"

He's striding out of the knot of women, holding out a red cup. "Where were you? Talking to Aarush?"

"Yeah, he had a couple more questions about Ledmonton." I wave the cup away. "I don't drink."

"Me neither. It's Sprite."

I take the cup and look back at the circle of young women watching us.

"Seen Nobody?" I ask.

"There were like fifty pizzas in the kitchen. She said she'd finish them."

"I'll go help. You can go back to your conversation." I start to walk off again, but he stops me, hot hand grazing my arm.

"Whoa, whoa, whoa. What's wrong?" He tilts his head, then takes a seat on a lounge chair at the edge of the pool, tapping the cushion beside him. "Come here and tell me about it."

I roll my eyes, but he taps the cushion slower, frowning up at me until I sink beside him.

"Nothing's *wrong*." I try to sound casual. "I just don't want you to feel stuck with me at this party. Or stuck with me in general. Just because I'm the first girl you ever got to talk to. Or whatever." I hide my face with a big swallow from the cup.

"I hate to break it to you, Signal," Erik says, taking off his jacket and draping it around my bare shoulders, "but if you've been plotting to take my virginity, that ship sailed a long time ago."

I almost spit up my Sprite.

"You're not the first girl I've ever talked to. I was *homeschooled*, not sent to a *monastery*."

Alice's face rises in my mind.

"So you've had serious girlfriends before?"

"Nope, no thanks." He laughs.

It's like he's swept me off the chair, the wind is so knocked out of me. But I freeze my face, staring into the bubbles in my red cup, trying to staunch the pain ripping through me.

I think of the line from his diary: *"I need to be more clear with girls I get involved with that I am not available for long-term romantic relationships."* Well, he's being clear. What had I really expected? He told me he's leaving once my conviction is overturned. He'll be my personal ghost, maybe my personal ghost with benefits, even. But never my boyfriend.

"I had friends, they had parties . . ." he's going on, "and I suspect a lot of the Higher Paths hikers are undiagnosed sex addicts." He smiles a mischievous smile, green eyes bright. "Or at least they are when I'm around."

"Wow . . ." I go stiff under his arm and pull away from him. "Gross."

"Gross," he repeats, surprised. There's a long beat, both of us listening miserably to the party music, and then he says, "What do you mean, 'gross'? Me? *I'm* gross? Is that what you mean?"

I shrug: he said it, not me.

"Huh, Signal," he says, voice too light, "it almost sounds like you're judging me for things I did before we even met."

"Maybe I am." The words come out short and flat because I'm trying to keep my voice from breaking. "Maybe I take this kind of thing seriously. What? You thought I would just laugh along with you about all the hook-ups you've had?"

"Yes?" he says. "What's to take seriously here? It was never a big deal with anyone else—that's my whole point." He leans in to examine my expression, and I turn my head away from him. "How are you so worked up about this?"

"How else do you expect me to be when you sit there and brag about sleeping with hundreds of girls?"

"Hundreds?" He laughs. "Whoa, when did I—no. You know what? No." He shakes his head. "I have nothing to apologize for here. I never expected to have serious feelings, so I acted on casual ones. But it wasn't a big deal, to them or to me. And my number is not in the hundreds, but even if it was, that doesn't give you the right to judge me because you've only slept with Javier—"

"Um, *what*?" I gasp. "We never—Javier and I dated for, like, *three days*. What are you talking about?"

"Oh, come on." Erik rolls his eyes. "Two Class As spending three nights in a hotel alone together? We're either highly promiscuous or highly obsessive or both—it's a documented fact."

"Javier and I did *not* 'do it,' okay?" I tell him through clenched teeth, cringing at my own words but simultaneously unable to say the word *sex* to his face. "And that is one hell of an assumption to make, I don't care what Class A psychology you're— Wait. Is this because . . . did you and *Jada*—"

"First of all"—his eyes are wild, and he's almost yelling—"Jada spent every night sobbing about Troy. Secondly, she was *sobbing alone* because I was out, hunting down any internet I could find in a mile-wide radius, to try and stop your little kill switch suicide plot and go find you. That is literally all I cared about, the entire trip—*finding you!*"

"Oh." I remember his pale face when he came into Jaw's room, the dark circles under his eyes from blood loss and exhaustion, though I hadn't realized it then. Once he had convinced Dennis to test his kill switch first, he cut it out of his own neck and then jumped trains and hitchhiked down to Ojai to find me.

And if he hadn't, my body would probably be hidden somewhere in the Star Barn.

I reach for his hand. He lets me take it, though I can tell he's still furious.

"I'm sorry," I tell him. "Obviously, I don't think you're gross. And I don't want to spend this party interrogating you about your body count. It's none of my business. Well, not *that* body count." He cuts me a hard look, and I add, lamely, "Ha ha."

"If you want numbers, I'll give you numbers."

"I *don't*," I say too fast, "except, I guess . . ." I struggle to keep my voice unconcerned. "I *would* like to know how many other girls you've played your 'I bet I can make you fall in love with me' game with."

"Zero." He is disgusted. "Are you kidding? The girls hooking up with me with had no interest in talking. When everyone at the party knows you're going home to an asylum, the less said, the better." His eyes narrow. "How is this making you angrier?"

"Angry? Why would I be angry? It's *so cool* how you treat—doing it—like some daily workout! And girls are like your gym equipment! *Wow,* totally alienating yourself from all human connection, that's sooo awesome." I bury my face in my hands, cringing at my own sarcasm, and try to calm myself down. "I know I'm no expert on this stuff. I don't know what works for other people, or even what works for me, since I'm not—active or whatever. But I know what I *want*"—my face burns—"and I want it to matter when I touch someone. It seems *really* lonely, to me, for that not to matter. But maybe *for you*, it just . . . can't. Matter. So. It's just not a big deal for you. Fine."

My voice twists, and I know if I keep talking, I'll start crying, so I cut myself off. He stares heavily out at the dance floor. The surface of the pool sends ribbons of light and shadow across his profile, like strands of color in marble.

"When you kissed me at the Opera House," he says at last, turning to face me, his eyes glowing in the light of the pool, "that was a very big deal."

The party noise washes over us for a moment as we stare at each other. His face this close makes the moment in the stairway during *Swan Lake* echo through me, like every nerve has been indelibly marked by the memory.

But there's an undertow of embarrassment now, too, at how singular and momentous I had thought it was, when I must have seemed so clumsily naive to him. His phantom partners fill my head, a crowd of model-hot girls with knowing smiles. It makes me nauseous, the thought of anyone using Erik, my Erik, as just a body.

Though obviously *he* didn't mind.

I don't want him to see me tear up, so for a moment I reach down and fix the perfectly tied laces of my black Vans instead.

"Yeah, well, I really should find Nobody and check in," I say as casually as I can. "She's been in solitary the last year, so this party is probably weirding her out."

Erik gets up without another word and walks away.

"Hey—wait—"

He either doesn't hear me or doesn't care. He melts into the crowd, and I turn away from the party lights and wipe desperately at my running eyeliner. I swallow a sob and take several deep breaths until they don't come out shaky, then lift my chin up and move toward the mansion, scanning for Nobody's white hair.

But before I can spot her, my path through the house is blocked by a ring of clapping people. Trying to edge around them, I see a tall, gawky dancer in a tux and makeshift balaclava: she's cut eyeholes into a beanie and pulled it down over her head, and with her face covered, Nobody's confidence is fully restored. Three girls are bopping around her, trying to get her attention, but when she sees me, she reaches out a long burnt hand, crooking one finger. I shake my head, grimacing, but she reaches through the crowd and pulls me into the center of the circle, with a spin that makes several onlookers clap and whistle.

"Can you do Running Man?" she yells over the music, and when I shake my head no: "It's easy—watch!"

Trapped by the circle of drunken onlookers and Nobody's newfound groupies, I give up pretending I don't know the Running Man and fall in step with her, and there are wolf whistles as more girls join the center of the ring. Just the movement of dancing knocks some of the lead out of my chest, and then Nobody gets across from me, challenging, and we go back and forth through every shuffle dance we can remember, bumping into each other the more breathless we get, her groupies fighting to join in. By the third song, I'm not even scanning the crowd for Erik anymore; I'm screaming lyrics I barely know and jumping up and down with everyone else. Maybe he's reunited with the pop star and they've found an unlocked closet—who cares? Okay, I do. I could actually puke at the thought.

When the music begins to transition to something slower, I gesture to Nobody that I'm going to get us some water. But as I make my way across the floor to the bar, someone behind me grabs my hips. A wasted dude starts grinding behind me, cologne and hard liquor steaming off him so strong I gag.

"Hey!" I yell. "No thanks! I don't want to dance—"

I grab at his hands, trying to pull them off. The fingers are thick and hairy and dig deeper in response.

"Get off, seriously!" I scream, throwing an elbow backward, my voice swallowed by the music. *"Let go of me!"*

Then the guy lets go of me so abruptly I almost fall forward, a howl ringing at the back of my head. I turn to see Erik, his thumb through the guy's ear gauge, twisting the lobe back like he's trying take it off, an interested expression on his face.

"Erik, no!"

Erik doesn't look at me, but the corner of his mouth jerks down, and he releases the guy, who cups a hand over his ear, reeling back in pain.

"What the hell, son? You lay hands on me, you better be ready to square up—"

The guy lunges toward Erik, but someone sober enough to recognize us jerks him away, yelling something about Class As.

"I'm not afraid of some punk ass kid. You want trouble?" the drunk guy yells, stabbing the air in front of Erik's face with one finger. "You found it!"

Erik's eyes leave mine, and the corner of his mouth jerks again, upward this time. He reaches out, a casual, almost friendly gesture, catches the guy's finger and wrenches it backward. In another moment, the drunk guy is crumpled to the floor on his knees, screaming so loud the people around us stop dancing and draw back. The guy's finger is breaking in Erik's hand, and in another moment Erik steps over him, curling his arm at an impossible angle, twisting the drunk guy so his head is almost on the ground. His torn earlobe hangs from the side of his head, limp as a gummy worm. His incoherent shrieks drown out the music.

"That Class As about to kill somebody!" a voice yells.

I hurry and grab Erik's shoulder. It's like iron under my hand, but he jerks at the contact.

"Please, Erik . . ." I slide my hand gently down his arm to his wrist. "Let him go—please. We can't do this here. It's not worth it."

Erik stares at the figure in front of us, his face solemn, and at last nods. "Okay," he says with difficultly. "Okay." And he lets him go.

The guy rolls onto his back, flexing his arm like he's trying to get the bone back in place. Erik's fingers, still bloody from the guy's ear, take mine. I don't pull away; I rub his tensed arm and try to lead him away as fast as I can, when footsteps shake the floor below us.

The drunk guy has picked himself up and is charging Erik.

Nobody's scarred hand shoots out, palms his face like a volleyball, and throws him backward.

"You want to dance, asshole?" Nobody says as the music cuts out. "Let's go."

I hear the rattle of her butterfly knife, and Erik must too, because he turns faster than I can stop him.

The drunk guy has got a hand on Nobody's lapel, and her blade is flashing through the air when Erik knocks him back with one precise jab. I swear the whole party hears the guy's nose break, a small hard click of bone that registers in the back of my throat. A roller-coaster scream rises from the crowd as the lights snap on, revealing a thick bead of red creeping between the drunk guy's cupped hands. He pulls his glistening palms away, and a torrent of bright blood soaks the front of his designer T-shirt.

"Security!!" someone yells. *"Someone call Security!"*

"Alright folks," one of the guards calls. "Let's go. Everybody out!"

The crowd that cheered us when we came in starts booing now, half-drunk guests demanding a bathroom stop or a last drink from the bouncers firmly herding them toward the exit. People sneer at us, but they don't flip us off or anything. They'd like to, but they're too afraid.

"The second I get to my phone, I'm calling the police!" my bloody-faced attacker shrieks. "Aarush can sue me—I don't care! They all belong on death row!"

"This way." Another security guard is just behind us, pressing one hand to his ear. Erik leans into me as we follow him down a back hall.

"I had to end it before she stabbed him," he says, his face strained.

I nod and take his hand again, fitting my fingers through his swollen knuckles as we enter the "nerve center."

Aarush is facing the wall of monitors, watching his house empty out. He turns, his arms crossed over his chest, and regards us with cold disapproval.

"Some guy grabbed Signal!" Nobody begins, but Aarush cuts her off:

"I don't care why it happened, or who started it, when you're the ones with the most to lose."

Erik stands rigid, hands in fists.

"This party could have been a way to make contacts and connections. Instead, you confirmed every fear people have about Class As." Aarush stares at Erik, and then his eyes move over to me. "You have got to be more careful than this."

"I'm sorry," Erik says, staring back at Aarush. "You're right. It won't happen again." And then, "Can you still help us with those rides?"

Aarush lets the question hang for a moment, then nods.

"One of the guests at this party will take you three to Oregon. But you'll need to leave immediately in case the guest you assaulted makes good on his threats. Your driver will secure you a burner phone, and you can call me at this number for next steps." He writes out his number on a Post-it Note and holds it out to me. I step forward and take it.

"Any luck with the kill switches?" I ask.

"Bad news and good news on that. The good news is, I can locate all the kill switches Dennis tagged before." His fingers flutter across the laptop. "The bad news is where I found them." He turns the screen to face us. There's a map with three glowing dots on it, a fourth moving to join them.

"Where is that?" Nobody asks, taking off her mask and leaning in to see the screen.

"Ledmonton," I tell her. "They're waiting for us."

Chapter Eight
The Secret Show

"That's right. They're waiting for you," Aarush says. "They know where you're headed, and they're going to try and take you out when you get there."

"They won't hurt us if they don't have to," Nobody says immediately. Not to me, but to Aarush. "Turn off their switches, and they won't be a threat."

"And be personally liable for unleashing several maniacs on the general public?"

"They can testify about camp," Erik says. "If you want something visual and irrefutable, how about six campers cutting the kill switches out of their necks, on camera?"

Aarush looks hard at him a long moment. "Alright. I'll shut down their kill switches once you're up there and can wrangle them back to me. But that's not going to be easy. The manhunt was already ramping up, now with the Opera House footage spreading everywhere—"

"Aren't *you* in the Opera House footage?" I point out.

He holds up the neon-green baseball cap from before. "Not my face. I was careful about that." He throws the hat toward Erik, who catches it easily. "No more fights. Stay out of sight. Keep your heads covered. And not with a ski mask, please." He points at Nobody and keeps pointing until she sheepishly takes off the ski mask and throws it onto the conference table. "And no weapons," he adds.

Nobody makes a sound like she's about to protest, then puts her butterfly knife on top of the mask and folds her arms.

"San Francisco was large enough to give you cover, but if they locate you in a smaller town, it's over. Keep your heads down. Be *discreet.*" The screen of his phone silently lights, and he grabs it and stands. "Ride's here. Let's go."

And just like that we're hurrying after him into the open main floor, back through the space that was a dance hall moments ago and now is empty except for scattered red Solo cups.

"Also, Signal"—Aarush turns to me in the elevator—"I want you to take this. For filming the confession." He hands me what looks like a cuff link. "It's a Destech hidden camera prototype. Wireless satellite connection—it twists on." He shows me how, and in the bubble of its tiny lens, a pinpoint blue light appears. "It'll go red when it's out of charge— charger is here." He fishes a cord from his pocket. "It streams whatever it records to a secure cloud I have access to. So, if you get the evidence and get caught, they can't destroy it."

"Thank you, Aarush," I say. "For everything."

"Dennis said you were a nice person." He tilts his head. "And he's the most brilliant person I've ever met."

I smile, thinking of my baby-faced bunkmate. I'm about to say I hope I see Dennis again. But if I do, he'll have to kill me. I swallow hard instead.

"And any system that would imprison someone like him needs to be utterly destroyed," Aarush goes on. "Until the Wylie-Stanton is excised from our laws, everyone's rights are in danger. This isn't about helping you, Signal. So don't thank me. Just don't fail me."

The elevator doors open, revealing a battered Ford Taurus beside Aarush's glistening BMW. A slim girl with green hair and a blue wool beanie waits nervously by the back bumper. She introduces herself as Sammi Liu before Aarush pulls her into a hushed conversation and we haul our bags from his back seat.

"Are we in the trunk again?" Nobody asks.

"No, there are no checkpoints north of the bridge yet," Aarush says, "but like I said: discretion, at all times, from this point on."

"We should've gotten wigs," Nobody mutters to me.

"We can do that! I'll tell the board!" Sammi says, taking my bag from me, her eyes wide and earnest. "We're all so excited to help you guys, you have no idea!"

"No pictures," Aarush tells her before handing her an envelope. "This should cover food and gas."

We pile in the back, and Aarush stands, hands in his pockets, watching until we've slid out from the sterile light of the garage and back into the night.

* * *

I wake to the sound of giggling, and late afternoon sun washing out my mound of black tulle into a metallic gray. I'm squashed between Nobody and Erik, whose broad shoulder I've been using for a pillow.

"Ramen with macaroni cheese powder," Sammi is saying, like it's a challenge.

"Had it."

"Macaroni cheese kit . . . with ramen powder."

"Had it. *And* sprinkled flaming hot Cheetos on top."

"Baller!" Sammi laughs. "We only dreamed of such brand-name delights."

"Oh, it was *not* brand name. How about . . . Stove Top stuffing sandwich." Nobody grins into the rearview mirror. She's wearing Sam's wool beanie now. "On white bread?"

"*Nooooo!* Oh no no!"

"I've had that"—I yawn—"*many* times before I was vegetarian. You toast the bread and it's like a little Thanksgiving treat."

"She's up!" Nobody says. "How about Romeo?"

I can't help smiling when I look over at him, his head thrown back against the window, lips slightly parted. "Still out like a light."

"Yeah, well, he's not winning the poor kid food showdown anyway," Nobody says.

"What time is it? How long have I been out?" I ask.

"Coming on three," Nobody says.

"You needed it. And Lark has been great company." Sammi grins in the rearview. "It's actually kind of crazy how much we have in common. We both grew up in Tennessee, we both just got undercuts—"

"We're both hot." "Lark" grins, and Sammi turns bright red and after a beat explains she's got to stop for gas. Moments later we're parked at the pumps, and before she goes in to pay, she leans in the back window.

"Anybody need something from the Quik Stop?"

"A gallon of water and donuts," Nobody says, pulling the beanie low over her face.

"And Pop Rocks, if they have them," I add. Sammi nods seriously before going inside.

"And I thought *I* had game." Erik's fully awake voice makes me and Nobody both jump, a grin spreading under his still-closed eyes. "*Lark*, you're such a player."

"Hush your mouth. I told her I have a girlfriend." Nobody reaches over me to shove Erik, who opens his eyes and smiles at her.

"Yeah, about that girlfriend," I say. "She got us the *Swan Lake* tickets, right?"

"Yeah. Didn't tell her I was bringing the famous Burger Lovers, though. I'll be lucky if she ever comps me again."

"But she knew you were in jail?" Erik asks. "For murder?"

Nobody nods.

"Now that's a keeper."

"How'd you meet her?" I ask. "Is she from Tennessee too?" I feel weirdly upset Sammi knows more about Nobody than I do.

"No, she's from New York. We met in Japan."

"You what?"

"I told you," Erik says, "she can speak Japanese."

"I *can't* speak Japanese," Nobody snaps. "I can order shoyu ramen and ask where the nearest train station is, and that's about it."

"Wait." I shake my head. "You've just been sitting on a story about meeting a prima ballerina girlfriend in—"

But Erik brushes my knee with the back of his hand, whispering, "Here she comes, here she comes," just as Sammi opens the driver's side door.

"Hope you guys love super-processed pastries!"

Sammi passes off two stuffed plastic bags to Nobody and gives me a paper tray of sweaty iced coffees to hand out.

"Coffee?" I ask Erik.

"I'd rather sleep."

"Ah," I say, and Sammi puts his in the passenger cupholder before starting the engine back up and merging carefully back onto the freeway. Nobody, halfway through a bear claw, leans over the passenger seat, going through music on Sammi's phone. There's the twang of a slide guitar as the car comes to speed, and then an old country love song starts playing.

"Look, Erik, I'm sorry if I upset you before." I keep my voice low.

"You didn't," Erik says, forearm shielding his face.

"Really? Because you ended our conversation kind of abruptly."

"Maybe try mentally replaying what I said to you, and then what you said to me, but imagine I'm a human being."

"You're seriously going to sit there and act like I hurt your feelings."

He lifts the arm from his face then, revealing a stung expression, as the twang of the slide guitar fills the car again. Nobody's song is restarting. Erik sits up suddenly, calling over the music: "Nobody, did you put that song on single repeat?"

"Yeah, and I'm not taking it off anytime soon."

"See?" He turns his full torn-eyed gaze on me. It's always a little startling, that perfect face with that one piercing asymmetry. "She's a *single repeater. I'm* a single repeater. Class As are, in the majority, single repeaters. That means something—"

"Does it mean you listen to songs on single repeat?" Sammi darts a curious look into the rearview. Erik nods, not looking away from me.

"Exactly, Sammi. One song, for weeks and sometimes months. I could listen to hundreds of new songs every day if I wanted, but one particular song will get stuck in my head, and it's like there's a lock on my brain, and those notes are the combination. Why should one song matter to me so much more than any other?" His face is so close I could count his eyelashes, map the few freckles across his clear skin. "It means something."

"You know, when I want to find new music," Sammi says cheerfully, "there's an app that goes through your most played lists and—"

"I don't want new music, Sammi! I want Signal to understand the truest connection I've had to another human soul is either through headphones or speakers or, once, on a stairwell; and that if music is 'the food of love,' then maybe my real problem is I'm starving."

Sammi darts a concerned look to Nobody, who mutters, "He's on his straight nonsense right now—don't worry about it."

Erik turns back toward his window with a muttered curse, throwing his forearm over his face again. But the cords of his neck stand out, a vein ticking under skin reddened by some inner irritation.

"Well, if you're *starving* . . ." I fish the Pop Rocks out of my bag and set them on his knee.

He freezes. "These are for me?"

"You said they were your favorite," I mumble. "I think."

He inspects the black and pink packet like he's never seen such a thing.

"There are protein bars and pastries too, if you—" I reach for it, embarrassed.

"These are perfect," he says, yanking them away from me. "These are exactly what I need."

"Yeah, well. Thanks for cutting in last night. And I'm sorry"—I look him right in his eyes, so he knows I mean it—"that I hurt your feelings."

"It's cool. No worries." He looks away, tucking the envelope of Pop Rocks into his dress shirt pocket. But when he leans back, there's a slight smile on his face just before his forearm covers his eyes. And in the tight space between us, his hand finds mine. His fingers thread between my fingers, and he tugs my arm just the tiniest bit toward him, once, twice, until I let my head fall against his shoulder, and fit there so perfectly. Every inch along the seam between our arms and legs, side by side on the bench seat, is almost painfully aware.

Nobody shoots me a look as the slide guitar twangs again, and I smile, sheepish.

"This *is* a pretty song."

She rolls her eyes. "Straight *nonsense.*"

* * *

A couple hours later, Sammi pulls into the garage of a shabby, soggy little house at the edge of Medford, Oregon.

"Your next driver is out of work at five, and he's going to bring the burner phone for Signal . . ." She frowns, scrolling through her phone. "You guys are supposed to just hang out here until then."

The air inside the garage smells like old wood and new paint, and a makeshift worktable takes up one entire wall, dotted with screens and sponges and paint bottles. Hanging from shelves that climb across the other two walls are at least fifty drying silkscreen T-shirts, all with band names I don't know.

After we unload our stuff, she hugs each of us. Nobody starts to take her beanie off, but Sammi stops her. "Keep it. You know what? Keep this too." She takes a pen out and writes her number on the tag while Erik and I try not to exchange a knowing look.

Nobody side-eyes us as Sammi's car pulls away, then stomps over to the rusted washer and announces she's going to do a load if we want to throw some stuff in. Erik pulls down the garage door, then starts unbuttoning his shirt. I turn my back and, still tented in Erik's jacket, wriggle out of my black dress, pull on some jeans and wrestle into a huge T-shirt.

When I turn around again, they've laid out the bedrolls in a little makeshift palette and are reclining, propped up on their backpacks, going through our arsenal of Quik Stop snacks.

I can't help but think of the sleepover night at camp, when I woke up from a nightmare to the sound of rain. We'd all pulled our sleeping bags to the floor and split up the trail mix and chips Javier had snuck in from the kitchen. Those same people who stayed up late whispering about the meaning of life are waiting up in Ledmonton, to kill us. My lower lip jerks at the thought, but then Nobody says, "Signal!"

She holds up a small bag of sour cream and onion Ruffles, and I give her my biggest smile. I should really update my theory on the meaning of life. Friends like her and Erik are at least half of it.

When I go sit between them, Erik rolls off his backpack and onto my leg, his head resting right above my knee like it's the most natural thing in the world. When my hand grazes the whorls of his dark blond hair, his eyes fall closed with such a look of satisfaction I have to bite my lip to keep from laughing.

"Real talk," I say to Nobody. "If you don't tell me how you met your ballerina girlfriend in Japan right now, my head will explode."

"There's not much all to tell. I was over there modeling."

Erik starts laughing. "Not much to tell, guys. Just romanced a ballerina against the backdrop of international modeling. Is that, like, interesting or something?"

She swats at him, but she's almost smiling.

"I am not even close to surprised you're a model," I say.

"I'm not and never was." She rolls her eyes. "Some agency rented out the Mall of Memphis a couple years ago. My cousins made us go down and stand in line wearing just bikinis so some creeps could say if we looked right. Like a *dog show* for girls. Well"—she shrugs—"I looked right for Japan, they said." She shrugs again, then stops, like that's all there is to say.

"So you went to Japan?"

"Didn't want to. Didn't want to leave my Gram. But they told my uncle I'd get six thousand for six weeks work if he signed me up. So he did, said he was my parent on the release form, and I was off to Tokyo."

"That's *amazing*."

"No, it was *not.*" Her voice is heavy. "The agency was a scam. They put me and four other girls in an apartment half the size of this garage." She looks around us at the small space. "Charged us a crazy amount for rent and headshots. We all left in debt."

"Tokyo's not cheap," Erik says.

"No sir, it is not," Nobody says, dividing the Quik Stop Danishes into two piles, fruit and cheese. "And my uncle wouldn't send me a dime. The other girls had credit cards. They'd let me finish their food sometimes, but I was always starving. And I stuck out—I always stick out, but it was worse. Felt like I was walking around in a Big Bird suit or something." She yanks nervously at her beanie. "I never liked folks looking at me and that's all modeling is. I wanted to die the whole time, until this one job."

At last, something like a smile creeps into her face. "They wanted pictures of a ballerina doing kicks and jumps. I was cast as the face and arms, but they needed a real ballerina to be the legs. The American Ballet Company was visiting Tokyo at the time, and they sent Amy to the shoot because we were the same height." Her smile deepens. "She comes right up to me and says, 'Guess I'm your other half' . . .'" Her fingers dig into her arms, and she smiles so hard it cuts off her words—that kind of smile you do when you're trying not to cry.

"What, they Photoshopped her feet on you?" Erik asks. "Why not just use her?"

"They said I looked more like a ballerina." She rolls her eyes. "It was just racist, but I didn't get that at the time. All I knew was, we couldn't talk without laughing. We hung out every day after that. She was great with trains, 'cause she grew up in New York. And she wanted to see *everything*, and she took me with her. That's how she ruined my life." She looks at me.

"Oh?"

"What passed for being happy before I met her—well, turned out it wasn't even close." Nobody smiles down at the ground, eyes soft. "Then my visa ran out." She restacks the Danishes then, her head turned away from us.

"So you went home?" I prod.

"Yeah. And I owed money, though not as bad as some. Twelve hundred—that was less than the other girls, but real serious money for where I come from. When I got home, my uncle was mad as hell. Said as far as he could figure, I owed him six grand on top of that." Her eyes glaze over, "My uncle's girlfriend danced at a place in the backwoods called Girlies. And I'm not talking dancing like in *Swan Lake*. She started bringing me along."

"How old were you?" Erik asks quietly.

"Fifteen." Her head is still turned away. "Couple months in, my cousin let me use his phone to call Amy. When she heard what I was up to, she says"—Nobody makes a choking sound, and I can't tell if she's laughing or crying—"she says, 'Lark, I'm buying you a ticket out here, and if you don't get on the plane, I'll come put your long ass in a suitcase.'" She turns her head again, tears sparkling at the edges of her soft flower eyes. "She met me at the airport. Her roommates were waiting with a big dinner for me. I found a job real quick, front desk at a salon. And everything got happy again." She saws her forearm under her nose. "New York is where we became girlfriends." She grins. "Greatest city in the world."

"But then . . ." Erik says after a beat.

"But then"—Nobody leans her head against her arm—"Gram fell, real bad. I took a bus home to see her, but by the time I got there she'd passed. My uncle was just waiting, of course. Got in my face at the wake, said if I'm too good for my own home, I could get out from under his roof. Kicked me out that night." She shakes her head. "His girlfriend told me I could sleep in her car, in the parking lot behind Girlies. Now I know she set it up with him because Gram left me the house. But at the time, I thought she was being nice." Two thick tears roll down her cheeks, and she scrubs them away. "Anyway. I was dumb enough to sleep in her car without checking all the locks first. Driver's side door was busted." Her lip curls. "It was the smell that woke me up. Gas soaking into the seats—it made me choke."

I reach out and take her hand.

"I got out the back door. When he crawled in after me, I slammed it on his face and ran around to the driver's side." Her face is hard now, past tears. "His mistake was, he didn't know I was smoking a pack a day in New York. Always had a lighter on me back then."

I look down at the glossy red hand in mine.

"But I had to hold that busted door shut until he stopped fighting." She shakes her head. "And he took his sweet time."

My stomach flips over at the words.

"Prosecution said I had enough time to change my mind, let him out, call an ambulance. Yeah, right." Her voice is dark. "You strike a cottonmouth, you don't stop until it's still."

There's a long moment, then Erik asks, "And the other five?"

"The roof of Girlies caught while my back was turned. I went in and helped the dancers out the back way. Customers tried to get out the front but couldn't. They were all piled up when help came. And at the trial, the fire marshal testified someone had bolted the front doors from outside." Nobody, still holding my hand, turns blue eyes ringed with red veins on me. "And left traces of 'burnt tissue' behind."

I stare back at her, trying to process what she's saying: that she knowingly killed the five men who'd been in Girlies that night.

"You fastened a door and now there are five fewer pervs in the world." Erik shrugs. "They should've given you a medal."

Nobody gives him a real smile. "I always say, I'm not a murderer. I'm a man-killer. There's a difference."

I cannot find any words.

"So how did you end up in Signal's prison?" Erik asks.

"Class A means automatic death penalty in Tennessee," she says, and I feel a pang of nausea, my hands reflexively gripping hers. "But then Dave came through. Said there was a program I qualified for if I was willing to transfer. I got on the damn bus." She shakes her head. "I know you two are real angry at camp. But it's why I'm alive right now."

The garage door suddenly rumbles, making us all start to our feet, headlights scattering us to the far wall. There's a belch of exhaust as the rusted-out Karmann Ghia shudders to a stop, and then a reedy guy with a struggling mustache and ironic rattail steps out.

"Hey hey"— he grins—"I know who you guys are! I'm Nick Scarpelli, but my friends call me Scraps, and it is a pleasure to make your acquaintances!" He slams the driver's side door closed, "Y'all ready for Portland?"

"Can you drive with that hand?" Erik asks, and I clock the bright yellow cast just visible below the cuff of his red racer jacket. "Scraps" looks at it like he's noticing it for the first time himself, then shrugs and says,

"I'm cool. Here, got some treats for you kids." There's a rustle of plastic as he retrieves two Spirit Halloween bags from the back seat and holds them out to Nobody. Then he pulls a trac phone from his pocket. "And Aarush told me to give this to Ms. Deere, which would be you of course." He gives me a shy nod as he approaches, holding it out like he's afraid he'll scare me away. "He asked that you call him when you can."

"Thanks . . ." I scrounge in my bag for Aarush's number while Nobody pulls a cheap wig from one bag and hands the other to Erik.

"There are sunglasses in there too," Scraps says. "Help you cover up your heads, you know. Go incognito!"

Erik pulls out red heart-shaped sunglasses. "Yeah, these'll really keep us under the radar."

Aarush picks up. "Signal?"

"Yes! Hi, Aarush. We're here with, uh, Scraps. He just gave me the phone, so I wanted to check in."

"Good, good. He's going to take you guys just past Portland, to another garage, and then your last driver will take you the rest of the way to Ledmonton. Everything okay so far?"

"So far so good."

"Excellent." He sounds like he wants to get off the phone. "Let me know if you need anything. And let the others know I'll only talk to you on this phone. Will you do that for me?"

"Okay," I say after a pause, though I have no intention to say anything of the kind. "Later, Aarush." I let him hang up first, uneasy.

Why would he even make a rule like that? What if something bad happened to me, and they needed help?

I guess he thinks they're the most likely bad thing to happen to me.

Erik has put on a white fright wig and is grinning at Nobody, who's pulled on a glam rock black shag that covers most of her face. That leaves me with the last wig in the bag, pastel pink and almost waist length.

"I got some fresh clothes for y'all too!" Scraps hauls down a box of T-shirts from the shelf. He tosses me and Nobody long-sleeved T-shirts with a logo that reads "The Hopeless" across the chest. He throws one to Erik, who immediately throws it back.

"I'm cool, Scraps." Erik smiles, putting on the red heart-shaped sunglasses. "Let's get moving."

* * *

"You could really *do something* with this, is all I'm saying." Scraps is only properly steering with one hand, his cast resting on top of the wheel. "You could make some real money moves. And I mean, let's be real, y'all won't be filling out a W-9 any time soon, so you need to bank up now, get that cash. Which means getting control of your narrative. You ever seen those pictures of Bonnie and Clyde?"

Erik lets his head fall back on the seat behind us. "You mean after they died in a hail of gunfire," he says, "and a crowd swarmed their car and started cutting pieces off their bodies for souvenirs?"

"Nah, I mean like, when they're posing with the guns," Scraps says cheerfully. "There's a reason people loved them so much, you know?"

"Yeah? Why?" Nobody asks, sounding genuinely curious.

But Scraps doesn't seem to have an answer. His brief silence is delightful. We've only been in the car four hours, but somehow Scraps has been giving us career advice for ten. The three of us are crammed into the back seat, leaving the pyramid of camera cases and half-dried band T-shirts in the passenger seat undisturbed.

"My point is, you need to build your mythos," Scraps waxes on. "What's the origin story, huh? How'd you become boyfriend and girlfriend?" Scraps looks over his shoulder at me, car listing slightly as he does. "Huh?"

"Oh, we're not—Erik isn't my boyfriend, we're just . . ."

Erik looks at me, eyebrows up.

"What?" I hiss.

"Smart. That's smart!" Scraps nods. "Let the fans think they have a chance with you. Here, I want you to have this—"

Without looking, he grabs something from the console and holds it behind his head, in front of Erik, who takes it with a gesture of tremendous effort. It's a business card that says "Scarpelli Brand Management."

"Who wouldn't want branding advice," Erik says, "from a man known as Scraps?"

"Just had those cards made, but I've been doing freelance image consulting for over ten months now . . . Geez, wait a second—my engine light is coming on? Not again! She did this to me last week. I need to check something . . ."

He pulls off the dark two-lane highway and down a long purple street of what look like abandoned industrial warehouses, half hidden in the swimming branches of black pines.

"I'm just going to check this out!" he tells us, throwing open his door. "You kids sit tight!"

"What's he doing?" I ask the other two when the door slams shut.

"Putting on some kind of performance," Erik sighs. "But he's not as nervous as I would expect him to be if the police were involved."

"You think it's a sting? Like he's going to turn us in?" I lean forward and scan the street, but Nobody frowns.

"If the manhunt's gone federal, it'll be helicopters. I was in the hills thirty days before they spotted me from the air. I'd still be out there if it wasn't for the damn snow."

Erik and I exchange a look as she cranes her neck to scan the sky. Then she says to Erik, "We should just run for it, huh?"

"Yeah."

"But our bags are in the trunk!" I cry.

"Get what you need now," Erik says quietly. I climb over Nobody and onto the sidewalk. Scraps practically jumps out past the hood when he hears the door.

"Everything okay?" he yells.

"Just getting something from my bag!"

He watches me go around the car, and I rummage frantically through the boot. I still have Jaw's key on my bra strap. I clip Aarush's camera to the other strap, then take Erik's journal and shove it between the small of my back and the snug waistband of my jeans, cram my pockets with cash. I step back onto the sidewalk in time to see Erik and Nobody getting out of both sides of the car.

"Guys?" Scraps has his hands up as he approaches, a jittery smile on his face. "No worries, guys, it's just my radiator. This happened to me last week. I just gotta top up the coolant. It's fine, but the engine will need to cool off for, like, twenty minutes or something? And if you want to stay off the street in the meantime, looks like there's a place open over there."

He points to a doorway down a hill, around the side of an old brick warehouse. A pink plank of light hangs from the doorway and falls across the navy street, a muted bass beat bouncing up the pavement toward us.

"I don't know," I say. "We really shouldn't go somewhere people will recognize us."

"In those wigs? You're fine," he says dismissively, plucking a soft case from the front seat. "I'll pay the door. Come on—let's go."

Erik puts his red-rimmed heart sunglasses back on. He holds out a pair of white-framed oval ones to me, then takes my hand as he walks by. I look over my shoulder at Nobody, who has gold Elvis aviators on under her black synthetic hair. She frowns and links her arm through mine.

"We want to follow this guy?" I whisper to them.

"Easier to get lost in a crowd than an empty street, if he's got friends," Nobody answers.

"Shows have fire exits," Erik nods. "Or at least, they're supposed to."

And we follow Scraps through the glowing pink door.

I'm terrified there will be a big bouncer, like in a movie, demanding our ID and poring over our faces. Instead, there's a thin girl with a bandanna over her face and a shaved head who asks if we have any glass bottles, and when we say no, tells us it'll be five dollars each. Scraps pays, and we walk into a haze of neon red.

The massive open space of the warehouse has been flattened into a red haze by a fog machine. The synthetic mist tastes like sweetened plaster dust, swirling starbursts of white and blue light giving flashes of depth to the air around us. The faces in the crowd are too washed with red to make out clearly, like photographs drying in a dark room, which is comforting, and I start to relax enough to breathe normally. Music throbs from giant speakers posted over an old, raised loading dock that's now a stage for a teenage band.

They're good, really good, and everyone's too absorbed by them to notice us. A scrawny guy on drums and another guy on bass flank a girl coaxing a big sonorous synth sound like a continuous ocean crash. It builds and builds until her vocals pierce through, clear and unaffected, and the three of us all stand, hands linked like paper dolls again, just three friends at a show.

Erik's white wig, bright pink in the light, catches my eye as he turns to smile at me. He turns back to the band, but then looks over at me again. In the red fog, his face is just the perfect symmetry of his dimpled smile and black hearts for eyes.

"What?" I half shout. He mouths something, and I wave him closer, and his deep voice breaks through everything else:

"Second date! Can this be our second date!"

I grab his hand, but it's not enough. I gently pull his face down toward me and rise up on tiptoes to kiss him when bright, blinding light shatters my peripheral vision.

Scraps is holding up an enormous digital camera, which flashes again as Erik grabs for it.

"It's cool, it's cool!" Scraps yells, people in the crowd shooting pissed looks at us. "I'm not going to post these any time soon, okay? Just enjoy the show—it's cool!"

"No, it's not cool!" Nobody grabs his shoulder. "What are you doing?"

The flash goes off in her face, and he grins at us, twitchy. "Look, kids, I got a cute pic of you kissing, and I got another of y'all threatening me. Which one do you want getting out in the world, huh?"

There's a sting of feedback as the lead singer grabs the mic.

"Hello, Portland!" she yells. *"We are . . . the Hopeless!"*

And the music crashes through the room again, too loud this time, bouncing against the cement floors and windowless walls with a ringing I feel inside my teeth.

"You brought us here to promote some *band*?" I scream at Scraps.

"It's just a few pictures—chill! Just keep doing what you're doing! Get your arm around his shoulder maybe—"

Nobody swats the camera to the floor. When Scraps dives down to get it, he almost knocks the big guy in front of us over. The big dude whips around and shoves Scraps hard into Nobody, and I reflexively push him backward, drawing his girlfriend into the scuffle. Erik pulls me away just before her hand connects with my face, and I catch Nobody's sleeve as Erik hauls me along, carving through the crowd with ruthless efficiency, leaving a roiling wake of pissed-off drunks between us and Scraps, who yells, "Come back right now! *This is totally unprofessional!*"

Erik finds the fire door in the back of the warehouse, and we break out into the black and white night, bouncing against a chain link fence close to the side of the building. Nobody throws herself upward and starts climbing. Erik pulls off his hoodie, his wig and sunglasses falling to the ground, and scrambles up too. I follow after them, the chain link singing against itself as I hook my fingers as high as I can reach. Erik gets to the top first, his profile cut out black against the violet sky as he bundles his hoodie over the barbed wire twisted around the top before reaching to help me over, and we hurry down the other side.

Nobody is running ahead of us, her wig melting into the black behind the warehouse, but Erik goes eerily still, staring down at the ground behind us.

And there, where it's fallen from the back of my jeans, is his childhood journal.

Chapter Nine

Maniac Mansion

He picks it up, and the pages of the Armchair.org printout fall loose, the title screaming at us from the pavement:

"WHO KILLED THE WYLIE-STANTONS?"

Erik's face is inscrutable as he takes the printouts and slides them back into the notebook.

"This yours?" He holds it out to me.

I shove it back in my waistband, trying to keep my expression neutral, when we both hear the "Whop-whop!" of a police car pulling up in front of the warehouse, and run for the trees.

* * *

There's a train track behind the warehouses. We follow it north for what seems like an hour, hidden by a thin beard of scraggly pines from the street. We break into a sprint if we hear cars. Erik's face, whenever we pass near enough the streetlights for me to see it, seems deliberately wiped of expression. Like he doesn't want me to see how angry he is? *Is* he angry at me? Why? I have the right to know who I'm traveling with, don't I?

"We're good—I haven't heard sirens in fifteen." Nobody stops abruptly. "Call Aarush."

I hit the "Redial" button, fingers shaking. Erik turns to face the street, his back to me. I watch his shoulders heave as he recovers his breath.

"Aarush?" I say when he picks up, and I recount briefly how Scraps tried to take photos of us at a show, the fight breaking out, and where we are now.

"I have another driver waiting, but she's about two hours away. Will you be alright where you are for two hours?"

"Not really."

"Okay . . . I'm locating your phone—hold on . . ." Aarush says. "Looks like we've got some friends about a quarter mile south. They can't drive, but they offered an overnight earlier, so they should be cool with you guys hanging out for a bit . . . Let me contact them."

I move the phone from my mouth. "He might have a place we can hang out 'til a new ride comes."

Erik keeps his back to me. Nobody looks from him to me, and her eyebrows go up.

"Also, some more good news," Aarush says. "I've been monitoring Janeane's social media. Mike just went on a mission to Costa Rica for several weeks. She'll be in the house alone."

I squeeze my eyes closed. I don't want to think about where we're headed, about what we will have to do in Ledmonton if we can make it there. Just the thought of seeing Janeane face to face makes the back of my throat go sour.

"Kill switches." Nobody taps my shoulder.

"Any luck with the kill switches?" I ask.

"It's a work in progress," Aarush says. "Their security has improved a lot, and I don't want them to know I'm in their system. I've had to sort of start from scratch . . ." His tone relaxes. "Just heard back from our friends! You guys have a safe house."

The directions are simple: we go back the way we came for two blocks, then take a left after the first intersection.

"Aarush says we can go right in, but we'll need to find a door that says 'No Entry,' and we're not supposed to talk to anyone until we're in there," I explain to Nobody as we double back. I'm speaking loudly enough that Erik can hear me, but he still says nothing. He hasn't said a word since he asked me if the journal was mine, and really, what was *that* supposed to mean? Should I try talk to him?

Apologize?

Apologize for *what*?

He's the one who taught me to search under a mattress, and he knows everything about my case. So why would he be angry that I'm looking into his case, unless there's something he's hiding from me?

"Did you hear that?" Nobody stops when we're close to the turnoff point. We step through the pines, peer through the chain link. The traffic lights suspended over the intersection swing slowly in the rising wind. Then I hear it: a wild cackle down the street, from someone out of sight.

On the corner of the intersection, a tall guy in a jumpsuit stands right in front of where we're supposed to go, turning slowly toward the street. Is this . . . our friend?

I'm about to say, "I don't know about this," but the words stick in my throat as he seems to look straight at us. His face is dead white, his eyes just two black holes.

I step back from the chain link, throat closing, heart leaping in my chest.

"Dog Mask." My voice comes out strangled. "It's Dog Mask!"

"No," Erik says. "He's in face paint."

I clutch my chest and blink. He's right. The guy's face is painted, not drowned. As the heartbeat thundering in my ears begins to die down, I see how much narrower he is than Dog Mask, how much younger his hands are. A curvy girl in a short blue dress and red cape runs up to him, and he greets her with a laugh. She is who he was looking for.

The maniacal laughter sounds down the street again, the exact same laugh, cackle for cackle—a recording.

"What day is it?" Erik asks Nobody, drifting away from me again without meeting my eyes. I pull out my phone like I'm the one he asked.

"October thirtieth," I tell him.

Erik starts laughing, then hauls himself up the chain link.

"Hide your heads," Nobody says to me, "from the traffic cameras." She points to the little boxy cameras, perched on the tops of the streetlights and pointing down. We climb up after him and follow him down the empty street toward the safe house.

Erik has his hood down low over his head, the cloth taut over his broad shoulders, hands in his pockets. It is his Normal Guy costume, I guess, except for the little snags down the back from where he laid it over the barbed wire for me. As we get closer to the address of our "safe house," more people appear in costumes. There's a line halfway down the block to get into what a black and orange banner proclaims to be "The Maniac Mansion!"

I look up at the building as we get in line; it's another disused warehouse, but instead of a low hangar, this building is narrow and three stories. Its many windows are boarded over, cheesecloth ghosts with plastic skull faces and light-up eyes twirling from each window ledge. Screams echo from the haunted house entrance ahead, making the line around us giggle nervously. Erik stands facing the front of the line, to hide his face from the people standing behind us—or just from me; I don't know. Nobody hangs her arm around my shoulders and dips her head close, my reflection warping across her aviators.

"You scared of haunted houses?" she asks.

"I don't know. I haven't been in one since I was a kid." I pull my wig forward to cover more of my face. "You?"

She shakes her head.

"Does anything scare you?" I say, trying not to stare at the back of Erik's hoodie.

"Well . . ." Nobody considers. "I'm afraid of what will happen if we run into the others."

I shiver, pulling the cuffs of my thin shirt over my hands. "Like, that they'll hurt us?"

"Nah," she says, "that we'll have to hurt them."

I can't stand the thought, so I push it away. "Aarush will get the switches turned off before we're up there," I insist.

"And if he doesn't?"

Before I can answer, the line moves forward. I feel nothing but dread about the shadowy door waiting beyond the guy in the mad scientist costume counting out guests and inviting them to trickle in. Still, I surrender my ten dollars and plunge through the heavy vinyl flaps into the dark.

* * *

The same wild cackle rings out just overhead, so loud I wince. Erik does not. He is disappearing down a narrow black tunnel lashed with glow-in-the-dark paint, and then his silhouette triples ahead of me as he enters a mirrored corridor. The mirror maze is lit from above by bars of flickering blue neon, and in the pool-colored haze I watch him reach the end of the hallway, and two versions of him turn and hurry in opposite directions. I choose the one I think is the real him and walk straight into glass, cracking my forehead against the mirror.

I turn the other way and hurry down the hall, chasing what looks like three Eriks— now half a dozen—running away from me, then zeroing back to three and disappearing. I'm trying to decide which one to chase when I grow aware of someone behind me and catch a glimpse in the mirror of a tall figure following me.

"Nobody?" But as I turn, the figure steps into some recess in the hall behind me. I pause for a moment and then see what is unmistakably Nobody passing by the entrance to the hall I'm standing in, seeming very small and faraway in the moment it takes her to run past my hallway and disappear. So she is not the tall figure, still hidden, just steps away from me.

I turn and continue down the narrow corridor, flanked by reflections of myself. The tall figure looms in the mirror again, just far enough behind me that I can't make out their face in my peripheral vision. Something tells me I must not turn my head. I must not acknowledge I am being pursued. I do not let myself run. I walk stiffly, my hand trailing the wall closest to me, to feel for when the glass stops; I need to get out of this hallway.

The dots were all in Ledmonton, Aarush said. Except for one, still moving toward the others. Maybe the last one changed course. Maybe we were sighted on the news, and camp sent them down to find us. Maybe Scraps put our picture online when we ran off, and camp deduced our location.

The glass under my fingertips falls away: the exit. I make a sharp left, and the space opens up, the neon lights overhead scattering into blinking fractals. I am encircled by twelve terrified Signals and no way out besides the door behind me, and the tall figure has to duck its head as it follows me inside.

I am not going to die like this.

I turn and charge toward the figure with a scream, pulling one fist back, trying to remember all the things Javier taught me in the hotel room about self-defense. The figure flinches, her painted face distorting, her prosthetic teeth falling with a clatter to the floor. I stop just short of landing a punch.

"S-sorry," I stutter, and she turns and almost knocks into the mirror in her hurry to get away from me. Did she recognize me? Did I blow our cover? I turn back to the mirror and see layers of smeared fingerprints crisscrossing over the heart of the middle reflection. I push the glass and it swings forward so abruptly I almost fall into the red room behind it.

I'm in a dim, narrow hallway, dressed like an old Victorian house. It's all red velvet walls and brass fittings and flickering gas lamps, veiled with nylon spiderwebs—so corny it's almost a relief. And then the smell hits me. Are they piping it in? It's a hideous, visceral smell, like something rotting behind the walls. It's so heavy in the air I'm gagging, when I see the shape of Erik, waiting for me up ahead.

I hurry toward him, when a strobe light catches his face. There's blood running down from his mouth, like right before he killed Angel Childs. I stop short, and when the strobe light pulses again it's not Erik, but another haunted house performer, his lips pulling back to reveal fake fangs as our eyes meet. He lunges at me, and I rush past him, through a jingly beaded curtain, into a darker red room.

A spotlight is trained on a four-poster bed where a girl, all in white, writhes violently. Red blooms and pools from her throat, smearing the white satin sheets as she thrashes, fingers raking across her chest.

"He's inside me!" she moans. "His evil is inside me! Oh, stake me! Stake my heart before I—before I turn! Turn like him! *Like him!*" her eyes open, red with slits like a snake's, some kind of contacts, and yet my heart is hammering as I dart past her and through a creaking door, into a dark, neon-paint-spattered stairway.

The stairwell is empty. Erik must have gone on ahead, and Nobody is still behind me. I pause for a moment, considering waiting for her, then take the steps two at a time to the second story, wanting to just find the No Entry door and be done with this.

The temperature drops as I go through the door on the second story landing. The lighting shifts to something blue and cool and scented with pine. As I walk through hanging black curtains, my feet crunch on dried leaves scattered across the floor, and then a grid of birch surrounds me. Bare white trees have been erected in precise rows, a matrix of forest that fills the entire space, the air cold and shimmering with what I would swear was moonlight. It would be sort of beautiful except for the creepily slowed down version of "Girls Just Want to Have Fun" that hangs in the air. It grows louder as I follow a winding path carved in the scattered leaves through the birches. Up ahead, a small square of orange light flickers between the lacy pale blue branches, and the outline of a shed takes form in the shadows, its roof down at one side like its back is broken.

Is this shed . . . modeled on the one I woke up in, with Rose?

No. That's paranoid.

But prickles break out across the back of my neck as a girl's voice pleads:

"Wake up, Rose! Time to wake up!"

I'm not going in there.

I walk off the cleared path and through the leaves, hurrying straight through the birches until I get to the black concrete wall of the building. I feel along the wall, but there's nothing. No doors, no windows, no exit. I cross the room and check the other wall, hands scraping against the gritty concrete, my own breath rising in my ears. A far-off, desperate knocking sound rises from the shed when I look toward it—or is it just my heart?

But I don't have a choice. The attraction is designed to funnel me into the shed.

I face the orange window, my breath whistling frantically in my ears, the pounding quiet now. The only way forward is through. I walk toward the hulking dark shape, eyes itching with unshed tears. My hand floats out in front of my face to push open its door, and orange light envelops me.

Inside, rough plank walls have been painted with pentagrams and witchy markings in white chalk; a lantern with holes punched in its side spots the floor with light. An actress in a blue wig and sexy goth outfit looks up at me from the corner, rocking a headless mannequin in her lap like it's a baby.

"She won't wake up! She won't wake up!" the blue-wigged girl cries. Then her sob turns into a malicious smile. "I made sure she wouldn't."

I can only stare. They got so much wrong. There was a lot more blood, for one thing. And yet sensory details from the real shed are flooding through me. The sweet floral smell of Rose's shampoo rising from my lap. The way her blood soaked through my jeans and made them stick behind my knees as it dried. The feeling of Rose's long nails against my forehead, pushing back my hair when I couldn't keep my eyes open anymore, mouth going numb from the thermos.

"I'll have to tell you all about it when you wake up."

Tell me what? That you made your boyfriend make out with me when I was passed out? I'm shouting in my head, like I could get an answer from the composite Rose voice buried in my mind. *Why were you such a bad friend to me?! We weren't even friends—not really. You just used me.*

Rose in the shed, laughing so hard, though her eyes were puffy and bloodshot. Trying to get me drunk while watching out the window for Jaw. It seems impossible that I can't actually go back there, to that moment, and save us both. Because I can slide back into it mentally, so fully, so easily, without even trying. All it takes is the right sequence of notes, a smell like her shampoo. The feeling of trying not to cry. That's all it takes to pull me back there, knowing I can never save you.

"Hey—hey!" The blue-wigged girl has dropped character. She's patting my leg to get my attention, her face concerned. "Are you okay?"

I shake my head. I try to ask her how to get out, but I'm not sure if I say it aloud.

"You go through there," she answers, pointing to a hole set low in the ground, a black panel of plywood like a human doggie door. Dumbly, I sink down on my hands and knees. A wood panel springs back on contact, but as I crawl through the ground goes slick and angles sharply down, and I slide and tumble forward into the dark.

Plastic balls crunch around my limp weight, and I fight to stand, hands flailing like I could swim. Dark hair catches between my fingers, dark hair across my face, in my mouth. As I fight to my feet I see mannequin heads bobbing around the pit, beautiful faces and dark scalps crowning through the waves of brightly colored balls. I fall forward onto my hands and knees; I remember Dave throwing pieces of my mannequin at me, the mannequin he had kept aside for me because it looked like Rose. That burnt face staring up from the burn barrel. Rose's eyes looking back at her body in my lap.

No. No.

I keep crawling through the balls and heads.

A human head is nothing like a mannequin's. Real heads have weight, and dead eyes are far more blank. Rose's dead eyes were pieces of outer space that morning. I don't remember screaming, but my throat was raw by the time I got out from under her and into the blue dawn, black with her blood. I was so hoarse I could barely speak when the police found me, staggering through the trees. I kept waiting for the relief to come; rocking back and forth, wrapped up in a blanket at the police station, cupping vending machine cocoa with my hands and waiting for my mom. I knew I was in shock, but I promised myself one day I'd feel normal again, that this was just a nightmare I had escaped from. But the relief never came. The nightmare was the truth. Normal life had been the dream.

"You left me behind," Rose's voice whispers in my mind. *"You really think you can leave something like that behind?"*

No. No I did not, Rose. I have thought of you every day since, I have dreamed of you every night. You have been with me more than anyone alive and I will carry you with me until the day I die. This isn't just my life anymore, Rose. I live it for you too.

I grab the plywood edge of the ball pit and set my teeth against the sob rising in my chest and haul myself up to my feet.

Someone tumbles down the slide behind me, and I turn to see Nobody's shaggy black wig pop up a moment later.

"Signal!" she calls, loud enough I can hear her over the "Girls Just Want to Have Fun" that's still droning overhead, "They did a tribute to— Oh. Well." She sees my face. "You saw. Guess our hosts are fans."

Fans of *what*? Fans of me *murdering Rose*? I reach down to help her up, and realize my hands are still shaking.

"I don't like this," I tell her. "We should just get out of here and call Aarush, see if we can find somewhere else to hide out. We just need to catch up with Erik."

"I think we just did," Nobody says. I follow her gaze to a door to the side of the ball pit, hidden in shadow, edged with black and white caution tape, and a sign that reads: "NO ENTRY."

Chapter Ten
Hometown Villain

We push through the door into a small, stuffy room where two guys in orange "Staff" shirts are duct-taped to ergonomic gaming chairs. Duct tape is also across their mouths, and their eyes are practically bulging out of their heads. Erik sits on top of a bank of small TVs across from them, wearing the duct tape roll around one fist like brass knuckles, veins standing out in his throat as he speaks.

"—what kind of sickos I'm dealing with, exactly. Did you purposefully rig the door above the ball pit so it can't open both ways? I was pounding on it for five minutes—"

"Erik, what is going on?" I cry.

When he turns, his expression is so intense I step back. At my reaction his brow furrows, and he lets out something like a laugh.

"Oh, you're scared of *me*? You're scared of *me* right now?" he half yells. "*That* makes sense. *That makes sense!*" He knocks a stack of folded T-shirts on the counter to the floor, before banging through a door that reads "Staff Only."

The guys—one hefty, one scrawny, both terrified—look from me to Nobody and back again. Nobody leans forward to rip the duct tape off the larger guy, and a red rectangle blooms around his gingery goatee.

"Signal Deere—wow," he blurts. "First, let me say it is our honor to meet you. We meant no disrespect by having a *Girl from Hell*–themed segment. Honestly, we design these haunts like a year in advance, so we'd been planning to do it even before your case got all hot again. I am literally your biggest fan, and Kyle here is second biggest. I swear, we meant no disrespect and really, truly only want to offer you a place to chill until your next ride comes through. I also had a few things for you to sign, if you have a moment—no pressure." He swallows. "Or if you could just untie us, that would be cool."

"Don't," Nobody tells me. "Not 'til our ride gets here. I don't want them calling the police because Erik scared the piss out of them."

I reach down and pick up one of the shirts. It has my face on it, a high-contrast black and white print of my mugshot between lines of blocky text reading: "FEAR NO DEERE."

Nobody drags a heavy chair over alongside the two staff members. She plucks a plastic pumpkin bucket filled with candy from between them and settles down with it in her lap, taking in the security camera footage like it's a movie.

"Did you make this?" I ask the guy, holding up the shirt.

"I wish! Whoever did is making a ton of money. I was just hoping you'd sign it."

I don't know what's worse: the idea of going out and finishing the haunted house or staying in this room.

"I'll babysit them." Nobody nods toward the duct-taped guys. "You go talk to Erik. Please." She rolls her eyes, unwrapping a mini KitKat. "He hasn't been that quiet for that long since you dated Javier."

"I don't think he wants to talk to me."

"He absolutely does," the guy with the gingery beard says. Nobody and I both look at him, surprised. "He only walked out like that to see if you'd follow him. It's *classic* passive-aggressive behavior."

Nobody shrugs and plucks a Milky Way out of the bucket. I set down the T-shirt and head through the "Staff Only" door.

It leads to a narrow hallway strewn with folding chairs and water bottles and Ben Nye makeup kits. At its end is an open window, the night wind rushing me as I walk toward it, the angle of the fire escape just outside it cutting through the distant city lights. The metal fire escape steps ring underfoot as I climb away from the giddy screams and creepy music, onto the silence of the roof.

The wind up here rolls in ceaseless waves, but Erik isn't shivering. He sits staring out at the grid of golden streetlights below; it looks like someone has knocked the stars to the earth and laid them in rows. His shoulders rise as I approach.

"Hey?" I try.

"Hey."

I drop down next to him, on a raised lip of concrete set back from the edge of the roof. We're just out of sight of the people getting out of the haunted house below, whooping and screaming and laughing with relief. I look down to see his hands are in fists, the right one bruised and torn at the knuckles from last night.

"I'm not scared of you anymore," I say awkwardly. He doesn't answer, and I go on. "I haven't been for a while. In fact, it's gotten to the point where I feel safer with you around, weirdly enough."

He gives me a look of utter contempt. "You think I *killed my parents*."

"No, I don't. Because of this." I pull the journal out of the back of my waistband and hand it to him sheepishly. "I'm sorry I took it from your house—"

"You should be." He snatches it away.

"But I'm not sorry I read it," I go on, and his head jerks in my direction, eyebrows flying up in surprise. "Because I know you better now. And that's worth a lot to me."

"I'm sure," he sneers. "There had better be some little pink journal up in Ledmonton I can pop the lock off, because otherwise this is *asymmetrical warfare*."

"I never kept a journal. But I'll tell you anything you want to know."

He squints at me. "Where does the name Signal come from?"

Anything but that.

"Who knows," I say, turning my face to the ground so he can't read my expression. "I think my mom just liked it or something."

"What was the worst thing you ever did as a kid?"

I think for a moment. "I stayed out from school for a week in middle school when I wasn't really sick." That was around the time Rose stopped talking to me.

He laughs.

"I was a good kid. I had to be." I cross my arms over my knees. "My mom was always working, so I had to look after myself. And she was always so tired when she was home, I tried to set things up for her. Tidy up. Fold the laundry." I shrug. "That's where my prime journaling years went. Perfectly squared towels. But I wish I'd kept one, because yours was riveting."

He opens the stiff cover. "You really read all of this?"

"Yes. All of it," I admit. "Are you pissed?"

"Signal, please. Save the sailor talk for the docks," he says, so fake-serious it startles a laugh out of me, and the corner of his mouth twitches in response. Then he looks down, turns the page and sees the lines of Sharpie. "I forgot she wrote such long responses . . ." He pores over the words in the dim light, the little crease returning between his eyebrows. I know there aren't really any soft or encouraging words from her, but he examines the lines so reverently.

"As for the Armchair.org stuff," I say after a moment, plucking the folded-up printouts from where they've slid to the ground, "I found it looking up Dr. Ledrick at the library, and I just—I want to help you. Like you helped me. With your mystery."

"There's no mystery," he says flatly. "Doctor Ledrick killed them."

"You really think so?"

"I know so." He closes the journal and leans forward on his knees. "My parents had just decided to turn down an insane amount of money from the feds for the algorithm. That's why we went up to my grandfather's. My mom wanted to ask him to help her start a private rehabilitation center. She told Dr. Ledrick that was their decision, and a day later my parents were both dead, and Dr. Ledrick had full control of their algorithm, the money, and me."

Erik clears his throat, rolls his neck, turns his face away from me for a moment.

"He's also a fit for the M.O.," he goes on after a beat. "Whoever messed with the brakes had to have dismantled the emergency brake light and possibly even the emergency brake, since my brother was driving. Skye is an excellent driver; I'll give him that. Whoever did this pulled off some 'secret agent man'–level stuff. And that's *literally* what our Director is."

"I could see that," I say gently. "And you were there, so you know what happened better than I do. But from what I read, I couldn't figure out when he had the opportunity. He was only in there at the same time as your grandfather, and then he was up talking with Skye most of the night."

Erik shrugs but doesn't answer.

"Can I ask about Alice?" I say. "In the journal . . . well, you talk about her a lot. I know you've had 'zero girlfriends', but you seem to really—"

"No." He shakes his head quickly. "No, no, no. Her mom was our live-in housekeeper, so Alice grew up with us. She's the closest thing I have to a sister."

"But something happened between her and your brother?"

Erik closes his eyes, kneads his face. "You have to understand," he says, his voice sinking deeper, "everything I know about 'Nice Guys' I learned from Skye."

Skye wasn't just beautiful, Erik explains in a hurried monotone. Skye was the valedictorian, Model UN president, and Prom King. He volunteered at soup kitchens and got straight As. He was perpetually held up as what Erik should be.

"But he's cruel. Crueler than I am," Erik says. "He just knows how to hide it."

When Skye came back home for summer from college, Erik had picked up on a secret excitement in Alice, who was still in high school—a certain eagerness to be in Skye's way when he was around.

But then, all at once, things shifted. Whenever Skye was home, Alice disappeared. And when Erik did see her, she seemed remote. She started wearing much larger clothes but seemed smaller inside them.

It wasn't until Erik walked in on them in the boathouse that he fully understood. It wasn't just the way she was crying or the way her hair was bunched in Skye's fist. It was how Skye wasn't looking at her at all, just the screen of the camera as he filmed her.

"I'd never had a moment I could point to clearly with Skye," Erik says. "He had this trick of doing things you couldn't really explain; like, when I laid out whatever he'd done for someone else, there was always some plausible explanation, some misunderstanding. But *this*." He shakes his head. "There was no excuse for it." His jaw flares. "And when he saw me, he just walked over and shut the door. Didn't even slam it. Like it didn't matter if I knew, because no one would believe me anyway."

"And that's when you tripped his bike?"

"No. That was a couple weeks later," Erik says. "Alice had this Michelangelo book I'd always liked. She never let me take it out of her room. Then one day she's like ‚It's yours.'" He kicks a rock across the roof. "And I knew then she was going to try it, try to kill herself. So I went to Skye and told her he had to leave her alone. And he said, 'Make me.'"

I remember him kicking in the speaker at Jaw's house when he found out Jaw had kissed me while I was passed out. I imagine a smaller, less controlled Erik taking on his towering, athletic big brother, and feel my nails bite the inside of my palms, my fists have gone so tight.

"After the slashing incident, I told my mom about everything. But Alice denied it all, and Skye denied it, of course. Dr. Ledrick had a lot to say about me being jealous of Skye because of my 'deformity,' so that was cool. But Alice's mom quit at least. So Alice got away."

"But then you brought her back to your grandfather's house?"

"After they decided not to sell the algorithm, I thought—I *hoped* my mom and Alice could finally talk through what had happened. But

I didn't know Skye would be coming." He bites at his nails. "He was supposed to be on set that week. Then my parents pulled up in front of his apartment like it was some nice surprise for me. I tried to text Alice and warn her, tell her to go home, but reception on the mountain is terrible, and she didn't get it in time. It was torture from the moment we got there. That whole first lunch Skye kept asking Alice about her mom, about her professors, if this one guy on Instagram was her boyfriend—the subtext was he'd send the video to them if she said anything."

"And then she left in the middle of the night?"

He nods. "The boyfriend drove up to get her. I let him in the gate, but when I went to her room, she wasn't there. I found her at the edge of the lake. She'd swum really far out, but she decided to come back in." He stares out into the distance, into another time and place. "She could barely stand when I got to her. I brought her over to the car, and they drove away, and I haven't heard from her since."

"Why did she care about streetlights?" I ask.

"What?"

"The Armchair.org thing mentioned something about streetlights."

"Probably worried about her boyfriend driving up the mountain at night." He shrugs, and I nod, thinking.

"But even if Alice couldn't speak up . . . couldn't you try and explain to your mom? About Skye holding the video over Alice's head?"

"She'd never have taken my word over Skye's. He's her son—"

"So are you."

"Yeah, but she *loved* him," Erik says: a quick clarification, a simple fact, no bitterness. "When you love someone, you see in them whatever you need to be there." Then, watching my expression, he smiles an unhappy smile. "Just because I can't love doesn't mean I don't know how it works."

"You can love. I know you can."

He leans his head on his arms, waiting for me to say more.

"The thing that really comes through in your journal is how much you loved your mom. You loved her with all your heart."

He buries his face in his arms then, his shoulders so tensed. I put my arm around him, but he jerks away from me.

"Don't," he says roughly. "I don't want that from you."

"What?"

"Your *pity*," he sneers, getting up and walking to the edge of the roof, his motions jerky and stiff. "I don't want to be your poor, sad friend Erik. That—*disgusts* me."

"Then what do you want?"

There's a long pause; he turns toward me and then away again, like a kid running up to the edge of the deep end to jump in, then deciding against it, once, twice, and then:

"Why did you tell Scraps we weren't together?"

"Because we aren't? You told me last night you didn't do girlfriends—"

"What?" he cries, rocking forward with the force of the word.

"When I asked if you'd had a serious girlfriend? And you said no thanks?"

"I meant I'd never had a serious girlfriend *before*. You thought I was telling you to *back off?"* He grabs for long hair that isn't there anymore. "Are you *insane*? Why would I number our dates if I didn't want to date you?"

"I don't—" I lose my words and throw up my hands helplessly to take their place, then say at last: "I thought that was a joke."

"Yeah, wow, great joke: 'Hey Signal I think we're dating!' Hilarious! I mean, the *absurdity*, me and my surreal *tomfoolery*—"

"How could I take it seriously when we both know you have to disappear?"

"I said I'd come back. You said you'd let me in. You think I asked that as your *pal*?"

My stomach twists in a weirdly pleasant way, and sparkles shoot through my bloodstream. I pause to gauge his expression by streetlight: pure frustration.

"Why do you say 'pal' like it's a bad thing?" I ask at last.

"Because it would be a lie, and lies are bad things, Signal. I am not trying to be your buddy or your bodyguard or—*God forbid*—your 'friend.'"

I stand up, clutching the ends of my sleeves, my heartbeat filling my ears with a sound like chasing footsteps.

"I want to be your boyfriend," he says, each word sharp and cutting. "And I am dating you until you accept or reject me as such. Is *that* clear enough? Or should I write it out in black and white? Maybe there's an empty spot somewhere in my journal you could—"

I reach up and pull his head down to mine, and he kisses me—kisses me so the world shrinks down and zeroes out below us, kisses me like I'm his new gravity. I don't open my eyes. I only want to be lost in the dark with him, in this secret oblivion that drowns all my thoughts with the hope I can believe him.

"Okay," I tell him between breaths, "I accept."

"Look at me," he says. "Look at me and say it."

I swallow hard, pull back enough to meet his eyes. "I want you to be my boyfriend, Erik."

"Because you love me."

"Careful." I raise my eyebrows. "I could be making it official just so you'll say the magic words first, and I can win the bet."

"Say it."

I shiver. "Say what?"

"That you're my girlfriend."

I'm a helium balloon again. If he weren't holding me, I'd shoot up into the air.

"Okay . . ." I smile. "I'm Signal Deere, the Girl from Hell, Erik Wylie-Stanton's first real girlfriend."

He laughs, his genuine laugh, my favorite laugh in the world, and he holds me so close you'd think I was made of gold. And when we kiss again, high above the happy screams and fake stars, I allow myself to believe it for one shining moment: he likes me, this is not a trap, this is something true.

Maybe? I have put up such a wall against him, and that's what he was used to with his mom. Maybe that's what love is to him, working for an approval that never comes. Maybe he's glad it never does. Because once you're really loved, the game is through. And all it would take to destroy me now is for him to stop playing. So if I never tell him how I feel, neither of us can lose.

My phone chimes. We both ignore it long enough that it starts to ring.

"Hello?" I answer at last, breathless.

"Signal. It's Aarush. Your ride is here."

* * *

I wake up in the early afternoon, washed in sunlight and slightly too warm from lying tangled up with *my boyfriend*, Erik, on the wayback seat of a soccer van. My head is on his arm, his other arm around my waist. Nobody is stretched out in the middle seat, talking quietly to our driver, a curvy girl with glasses and a puffy ponytail named Hannah. Erik seems to still be asleep, so I keep my eyes closed, basking in the orange-red light behind my eyelids, in the planks of gold sunlight that stream in the window across us, in the steady sound of his breath. I can't remember the last time sunshine felt so appropriate, like finally it's day inside me again.

"Hey!" Nobody leans over the seat, offering up two half-frozen water bottles. "Rise and shine! Hey, what's wrong?"

I rub at my eyes, forcing a yawn. "I'm fine—I'm just waking up. Don't you ever get teary when you first get up?"

"No. That's not a thing." Erik's voice rumbles against me. He sounds wide awake. "You okay?"

I nod, embarrassed, and take a water bottle as Nobody lifts her chin at the wooded town slipping by, dark houses set far back across jewel-green lawns, almost hidden by trees burning with red and yellow leaves.

"Can you guess where we are, Signal?"

I sit up reluctantly, pulling my hair out of my face, and instantly recognize the road. We're one town outside Ledmonton, in Bridgewood. Dread swims up from my gut, past my throat and drowns my brain; I feel a little too slow and heavy and underwater.

When we pull over at an empty rest stop, Nobody and I change into clothes Hannah brought. They're strangely formal and stiff, and all black.

"Her family runs a funeral home," Nobody explains, stepping into some Dickies. "Fits nice, though."

"Maybe if you're six feet tall," I grumble. My only option is a black dress with a white Peter Pan collar and a pack of cheap tights that immediately run when I pull them on. Erik meets us coming out of the boy's side of the pit stop, in a white button up, narrow black tie, and black pants. It all feels very middle school Spring Concert, except of course it's windy and cold on the last day of October. We eat sandwiches out of the cooler sat on the floor of the car, Hannah's police scanner on and the engine idling.

Hannah refuses to enter Ledmonton until sundown, but despite the growing darkness and tinted windows, as soon as we drive down Main Street, I feel exposed.

"Is that your school?" Erik asks as we pass by Ledmonton High, and I slouch lower in my seat. There's a sign out front advertising the Halloween Dance, and a line of people already waiting to get in. I sit up, not quite believing my eyes.

"What the—"

Almost every girl in line is in a blue wig and goth clothes.

"They all dressed as you for Halloween!" Erik laughs. "Hey, some of them are you from last night!" He nods to a girl in a pink wig, and Nobody laughs too.

"Yeah, that picture of you kissing was on CNN," Hannah says, and I feel my chest tighten. "Guess you're a hometown hero now."

"Except the opposite." Nobody grins.

"Hometown villain," Erik says.

They seem to fill the streets then, as we crawl out of the neighborhood and into the rapidly darkening downtown: women wearing black lipstick, leather jackets, and blue wigs. There are also lots of guys wearing "FEAR NO DEERE" shirts in the crowd bunched up around the one street with any claim to nightlife in Ledmonton.

Hot and cold waves chase each other down my spine as I curl forward in my seat. We're really here, this is really happening. Every moment it grows darker brings me closer to standing face to face with the woman who killed my best friend and framed me for it, a woman who has known me almost as long as my own mother. I knew this would be the end of our journey. I know that getting here is a small miracle. Maybe this is what stage fright feels like, stage fright if you were about to star in a show you'd never heard of, across from a stranger. This is my first time facing Janeane when she can't play her loving mom role.

Who will she be?

"Full coverage, that's the important thing," Erik is saying to Hannah as she pulls into the local CVS parking lot. "Doesn't matter who they're of, and zip ties . . ." I press my face to my knees.

"You okay?" Nobody asks.

"Uh-uh."

She jerks her head in my peripheral, and Erik takes the seat next to me, one arm around my shoulders, other hand taking mine, his voice soft.

"You don't have to talk to her if you don't want to, or take off your mask," he says. "You don't even have to be in the same room."

There is a cold excitement in his voice he can't suppress, a terrible anticipation that makes me, for the first time since Ojai, afraid of him. But I clench his hand and shake my head.

"No, I want to be there."

It's not right to ask him to unleash this part of himself and then turn my head away.

"You'll see," he says. "It's going to be fun."

Fun. My stomach turns over, Hannah is back already, offering up three empty latex heads: Erik takes Elvis, Nobody gets the head of Marilyn Monroe. The last one is some kind of Betty Boop rip-off, huge dark eyes and a sad red mouth. I pull it on, my own breath rattling in my ears, but thankfully I can see well. I remove Aarush's camera from my bra strap and put it through one of Nobody's buttonholes so she can be cameraman, and then punch Rose's address into Hannah's GPS.

Families with little kids in fairy wings and groups of schoolboys in plastic capes dot the street as I direct Hannah to the end of Rose's long drive. I set my teeth as we get out of the car, feeling not quite in my own body as we float up the familiar walk to the house. And then, as we climb up to the wraparound porch, my steps making the same hollow sound from all those times I slept over, bile flares at the level of my heart: *this is actually happening, right now.*

I look at the porch swing, half expecting to see Rose's phone on its arm, as we reach the front door and stand under the porch light, a witch-themed welcome mat flanked by two enormous uncarved pumpkins at our feet. Nobody and Erik wait for me to give them some sign I'm ready. But I'm not ready, I never will be ready. I am only here, and the only way out of this moment is forward.

I reach out and knock hard enough to shake the wreath of orange silk leaves on the red door.

"Just a sec!" Janeane calls, and then the door swings open.

Chapter Eleven
Trick

"Happy Halloween!" Janeane smiles at us, holding out a bowl of fun-size candy. I wish I could say she looks diminished, but she actually seems younger-looking than I remembered. Her hair is freshly highlighted, and she wears a sweatshirt with a light-up pumpkin on the front, blinking merrily. "Now, really, aren't you guys a *little old* to be trick or—"

Erik's hands wrap around her shoulders, and he walks her, calmly but forcefully, back into the house. The bowl drops, candy showering across the floor as it circles on its rim faster and faster, like a cymbal crashing. Nobody darts forward to find a chair, I turn and switch off the porch light and shut the door, twisting the lock, then chaining the bolt behind us.

"What is this?" Janeane yells, as Erik pushes her into the dining chair Nobody has dragged into the center of the carpeted living room. "Is this some kind of prank? Let go! Let go of me! What do you think you're doing?"

I lean against the door, afraid I'm going to black out, the familiar smell and details of the house closing in on me. The pearly carpet, the butter-yellow walls, the text art in the foyer: *Gather* and *Family* and *Blessed*.

It's impossible to be here and not expect Rose to look up from the couch, or run down the stairs, or hear her laugh bubble up from the kitchen.

"Who are these people?" Janeane yells to me, as though I'm her best bet for help. Probably because I'm still frozen up against the door while Nobody and Erik finish zip-tying her to the legs and armrests of the heavy wooden dining chair.

The Elvis head turns to me, Erik's eyes connect with mine, and I know what he's thinking. This is the kind of surprise that might get something out of her.

I reach up and take off my mask.

Janeane's jaw drops. She looks from me to Erik, who's also pulling his mask off.

"Wait, I saw you on the news—" She looks at me. "You escaped prison. And—found this person—" She looks warily at Erik. "And you came *here*?" She blinks, genuinely confused. "Well, I don't know what you're after, but Mike will be home any minute—"

"Isn't he in Costa Rica?" Erik sits on the arm of the couch, leaning slightly forward as though he doesn't want to miss a single flicker of her expression. "But if you have some other guy upstairs, please, tell us now."

Janeane twists away from him to see Nobody, her Marilyn Monroe mask still on, grinning red and white.

"We just want to talk to you," Erik goes on calmly. "About Rose. About Jaw. Oh, and camp too. Dave says hi."

Janeane shakes her head, a solitary tear darting down her cheek. "I don't know what you're talking about, okay? I don't know what you're doing here, unless you're—returning to the scene of the crime or something—"

"Scene of the crime?" Erik smiles, his voice so reasonable. "But this isn't where you killed Rose."

Janeane's face freezes. Then pure, righteous fury shoots through her, and when her voice comes, it's cold. "You must be out of your mind to say that to me," she says to Erik, then turns back on me. "I don't know what you've convinced this boy to do, or why, but I won't stop you. Torture me. Kill me. I don't care. Just don't expect me to beg for my life, Signal." Her mouth crumples and her eyes turn to dark stars, the way Rose's used to when she cried. "Because I am done trying to go on without her."

My face burns.

This doesn't feel fake. Is it possible . . . is it possible we were wrong?

We hadn't seen the pictures in Jaw's lockbox. What if Janeane wasn't the killer after all? What did I justify all this with? A really good story from Erik? The rantings of a drugged-out Angel Childs? A couple conversations and a little silver key?

I push away from the front door, the ground tilting around me. Erik walks toward me, but I put up a hand, swerve away from him, then stagger down the hall, fairly running by the time I get to the door next to the laundry room. I fall on my knees on the cool linoleum and heave into the toilet as Janeane's sobs echo down the hall.

And then, the smell hits me.

Not the sour smell of vomit, but an earthy, burning smell that nauseates me all over again, with a chemical sting in its tail that I recognize instantly. It takes me back to camp, to Dennis and our worksheets, and the little paneled kitchen with the pile of rotting meat. I look up at the short counter of the bathroom sink and see all the bottles needed for Kate's proprietary recipe.

Zap Sauce.

I slowly turn to the low tub behind me. There's a ring of beige-pink sludge around the porcelain interior. Below that ring, drying, crackled patterns of red and pink zigzag to the drain, which is choked with dense pink foam.

I'm gagging now, but I have to be sure. I reach over the bottles on the counter for a bright purple toothbrush, then dig its head into the filthy muck clogging the drain. Something catches in the bristles, and I drag it out of the drain and onto the base of the tub with a scraping sound that sets my teeth on edge.

Two irregular, pointy nuggets of gold, smaller than my smallest fingertip, lie now in the flaking red-brown film at the bottom of the tub. I return the brush to the drain and scrape out four more. Six small starbursts of gold. I stare for a moment, uncomprehending, then remember Mike's big laugh, the glint of metal at the back of his throat.

Gold fillings.

These are Mike's gold fillings.

* * *

She's still crying when I stride back into the living room.

"Costa Rica, huh?" I cut a look to Nobody, then her camera. She nods: it's on. "Is that what you call your septic tank?"

Erik looks at me, eyebrows way up.

"She dissolved him in the tub the way Kate showed us. His fillings clogged up the drain."

Janeane looks up at me through her hair, still making crying sounds, but they shift and twist as her smile spreads. It's a long, slow smile that shows each one of her teeth, until she's grinning, and the sobbing is laughter.

"Well," she says at last, "it seemed like the right place for him."

I almost drop onto the couch.

She looks up at Erik, calm now. "Can I have a cigarette?"

"No."

"Aw, come on." She pouts. "I'll share."

Erik looks at me, one eyebrow raised. "May I present"—he waves a hand at her—"a *textbook* 'Nice Guy'."

"And what are you?" Janeane grins. "A textbook hot guy?"

"Okay, you know what—" I start, but Erik puts up a hand: *I got this.*

"You get *one*," Erik says. "Where do you keep them?"

"On the counter, now that Mike can't bitch me out about them." She grins at me. "You remember how he used to get. You even covered for me once. That was so cute of you, Signal. You're a good girl. A little awkward, but that's what camp is for. Isn't it a *ball*?"

I open and close my mouth, unable to begin to answer that question.

"Definitely." Erik laughs, and puts the cigarette filter in her mouth before lighting the end. It flares orange when she sucks it, then he takes it back, cutting a glance to Nobody, who moves to get a clearer angle of Janeane. "I mean, no hot water sucks, but it's nice to be around people who don't get so alarmed when you say what you're really thinking."

"Try 'grieving' for a year." Janeane rolls her head on her shoulders, exhaling the smoke, "The look on Mike's face when I suggested we take a nice cruise, well . . . anyway. Did Dave really say hi?"

"No, but he *definitely* remembers you." Erik's tone is almost flirty.

"Oh, I'm sure. We had a lot of fun at camp. Cigarette again, please."

"Answer a question first." Erik perches on the arm of the couch again, holding the cigarette upright and away from him, like it's a small firework. "Dave was Rose's father, wasn't he?"

"Has Signal told you about *her* father?"

I sense Erik's eyes flash to my face, but I don't look away from Janeane.

"He's the one to blame for that idiotic name of hers," Janeane goes on. "Struggling musician by day, heroin addict . . . also by day. And night. All his adult life." She laughs. "When Signal's mom got pregnant, he said it was his sign to get clean for real this time." Janeane nods for the cigarette again. Erik reaches out, and her lips graze his knuckle before she inhales, peering up at him. "Then he took off six months after she was born!" She exhales. "Didn't so much as call to check in! Whoop! Gone! Bye! *Hilarious.* And of course, it was too late to change the name at that point. At least they didn't *literally* name her Sign. Can you *imagine*?" Janeane looks at me and laughs harder. "Look at her face! Oh, she's just fuming. It's too easy. Like stepping on a kitten's tail."

My hands are in fists at my sides.

"Let's get back to Rose—"

"Let's not." Janeane looks around toward Nobody again, turns back to Erik. "Why do you care? What, is one of you *bugged* or something? Take your shirt off."

"We're not bugged."

"Take your shirt off anyway." She says.

"I just want to know what happened," I cut in. "That's why we're here. We're on our way up to Canada. We're not working with the police; we're being hunted by them. I'm a Class A, they won't listen to any appeal I make. But I didn't want to leave the country forever without knowing what happened, Janeane. You owe me that much."

She raises her eyebrows, gives me a hard look. "Tough titty."

"Of course, we could just leave you tied up, tip off the police and let them find you with Mike's DNA in the bathtub," I say as coolly as I can manage.

Janeane scans me, eyes narrowing. "You've got to be wired. Or you have a microphone or some app or something."

"No wire. Here, I'll turn my phone off." I make a point of turning off the phone; clocking a text from Aarush just before I do:

Switches should be off in two to three hours

My heart leaps, but I don't let myself react. I telegraph a look at Nobody, who smoothly moves Aarush's camera from her buttonhole into her back pocket. Erik turns slightly to take off his shirt, Janeane staring at him the whole time with an expression that makes me want to throw up again. Nobody and I quickly flash our torsos at Janeane, so she sees we're clear of any wires, and satisfied, she tilts her head and regards me with open annoyance.

"So if I talk, you'll leave."

"The sooner you start, the sooner I'm out of here."

She pauses a long time.

"Don't you *want* to brag a little?" Erik smiles, and I look away from him, sickened. But this does the trick, because Janeane turns to me and says:

"What do you want to know?"

I look at Erik. He gives me a slight nod, like I should go for it. And I know the important thing is to get authorities to open the security deposit box, and that means pouring concrete around her connection to Jaw.

"How long were you with Jaw?"

She frowns. "Until I got tired of him. Maybe a year."

"You'd meet him in the shed?"

"No, usually he'd come here, unless Mike was home sick, and he was completely desperate. I'm not a big fan of splinters."

"But you met him there enough to know about his thermos," Erik says.

She turns her head to smile at him. "Teen boys are *very* desperate. It's part of their charm."

Erik smiles back. "But then he dropped you for your daughter."

Her smile vanishes. "He didn't *drop* me. We were no strings. Because that's the way I wanted it. I couldn't drop everything to drink wine coolers in the woods with him, so from time to time he made his own playdates. But I could've called him up at any time, and he would've come *running*. He was *obsessed* with me."

I make a sound like a laugh, just to get her to react. Her head whips toward me, eyes narrowing.

"I can guess who told you he dropped me for Rose, but Signal is extremely inexperienced and quite naive about relationships. Whatever he was telling Rose, believe me, he would've dropped *her* the moment she wanted anything from him that couldn't be snorted."

"So why was he so afraid of you finding out?" Erik asks.

"Because it was *my damn daughter*!" Janeane raps out. "He knew I would protect her from him. And I did." She lifts her chin. "That loser would've ruined her life. Thanks to Mike, I had to sneak around to get my own birth control pills, let alone ones for her."

"Rose was *pregnant*?" The words stick in my throat.

"No, not yet, but it was just a matter of time, I promise you." Janeane scowls. "And then what? She'd have missed graduation—there'd be no college; no career; no rich, handsome son-in-law; nothing for me to look forward to except a horned-up piece of trailer trash calling me 'grandma' while blowing my inheritance on gym socks and online tarot readings. And Rose couldn't keep a *goldfish* alive, so it would be me raising the baby, oh yes. Me, a *grandmother* at thirty-seven! Oh no, no, no. I put a stop to that, alright. In my own way, in a way *I* understand, and have found peace with, I was protecting Rose."

I've slapped her before I realize I've crossed the room. One minute I'm by the couch, the next I'm standing over her, palm stinging, watching the shape of my hand rise across her cheek. Her eyes flash through her dark hair, and she throws herself toward me, but I reflexively kick her chair backward and get on top of her, grabbing the collar of her stupid pumpkin sweatshirt and banging her head against the carpeted ground, again and again, when strong hands pull me away.

"Easy, easy!" Erik leads me firmly down the hall, though I am fighting like hell to get back. He's saying something, trying to get my attention, but all I want is to get around him and back at her. She is evil. She should be taken out like a poisonous snake, like Nobody's cottonmouth, with no hesitation and no mercy.

"Look at me—look at me!" His eyes fill my vision, the round pupil, the torn one; the lacy pattern of gold inside the dark green iris. "Did you know that?" he says. "About your dad?"

I don't want to talk about my dad, not with anybody, but especially not him. My face twists so hard it hurts as I fight not to cry. He pulls me into him, and I press my mouth against his shoulder so they won't hear my sobs in the living room.

"It wasn't really up to him—you know that," Erik says when I've gotten the worst of it out. "He had a disease, Signal."

"I thought there was no chemical form of a soul?" I say sharply, then look away. "That's not what even upset me. I don't even remember him, so it's not like I could miss him or something. It's *embarrassing*." I wipe my face with the back of my wrist. "It's embarrassing, to not be wanted by a parent, but—"

His shoulders drop at the words.

"But I was never *hated*. And *Rose* . . ." I shake my head. "I failed her. She's everywhere I look in this house, and to know she's gone because of such . . . such stupid, senseless hate . . ." I choke back a rising sob. "I don't want to believe in evil. But when we're in that room, it's staring me in the face."

"You don't need to go in there again," he says, dropping his voice. "Nobody has the camera. I'll keep talking with Janeane. You don't have to be there."

"No. Rose was *my* friend, this is to clear *my* name—"

"If you put a mark on Janeane, no one will believe her confession."

My face heats. "I won't touch her again. I can control myself."

"But I can't," Erik says darkly. "She's using Rose to hurt you because she knows you loved her, and she's using you to hurt me because she knows I love—" Erik stops, blinks quickly, and goes on. "Please. Just go get some air or something. Go out in the yard for fifteen minutes and let me work on her."

"Hold on." I tilt my head. "Just hold on. Did you just say . . . the magic words?"

His eyebrows go up, the side of his mouth twitches. "Signal. Please. Enough with your stupid bet. We need to focus right now."

My jaw drops. "You did!"

"No, I did not."

"You totally did."

"Look"—his voice is dead serious—"she saw me react when she made fun of your name. Then she looked right at me when she said it was so easy to hurt you. She knows what she's doing."

"I . . . didn't realize you had such strong feelings about my name."

"Yeah, well, I do," he says quietly. "Your name might be my favorite word in the world."

Heat blooms up my neck and across my face.

A cackle floats down the hall.

"Just give me fifteen minutes, alright?" Erik bows his head over his shirt, buttoning it back up with what seems like his full attention, and yet he still misses a button. "I want to take the zip ties off while we talk about Jaw blackmailing her. That's where our subpoena is."

I nod, stunned, and he walks back toward the living room, the light catching the change in his expression before he goes to deal with

Janeane, still strapped to the chair, still on the floor, screaming at Nobody to pick her back up.

I turn and wander down the hall and out the back door, onto the patio, immediately shivering in the cold but grateful for the clarity it brings. I walk around the patio table and over to the neat lawn Jaw once labored over. Children's laughter washes down the street as I sink onto a low stone bench beside Janeane's rose garden, the blossoms gone, only thorns.

As much as my head is spinning to dissect his motives, to replay his expression, below it all is a simple joy that shines through every other tangled thought, a sunshine-bright happiness like the underlying beat of a dance song: *Erik almost said he loves me.*

We can set him free too. I know we can. We've already gotten footage of Janeane confirming she was with Jaw, and all but confessing to the murder, and we've barely started. Surely there's some way to make her talk about camp, get her talking about the abuses of the Director, maybe even get her to physically describe him.

Tonight, anything we want is possible. Tonight will be where our lives begin again.

And then a step on the patio makes me go very still. Surely I've misheard the echoing night, surely no one could be so close. There's faint laughter down the block, a car up the street playing music loud enough to make its doors buzz, the lilt of wind chimes.

And another step.

"Hello?" I say, turning back toward the house.

The motion light snaps on right behind her, silhouetting her small figure. At first all I see is the blue shoulder-length hair, the leather jacket. Then I register her creeper sneakers and mini skirt from that first makeover day at camp.

"Jada?"

A small, distinct click and a switchblade sends a spark of light dancing across the grass between us.

"Sorry," she says, voice like a sleepwalker's. "This isn't my call, okay?"

I turn and run straight into the thorns.

Chapter Twelve

Halloween Party

Jada's fast, but she doesn't know the neighborhood like I do. I swing around the Jaeger's garage and cut across the Scrofanis' wide backyard, heading for the woods, her footfalls gaining on me. Any moment her hand will close on my hair, but as I pass by the Pletichas' trampoline, I grab the lip of it and crouch down, kicking her legs out from under her so she flies into the tall grass with a startled yelp. I scramble on top of her then, pinning her narrow chest with my knee, and wrestle the knife out of her hand.

"Look at me!" I shout at Jada. *"Look at me!"*

She stares up at me, terrified.

"I'm not hurting you, and you're not hurting me—do you understand?" I say through clenched teeth. "Jada, we have someone turning off the kill switches. He's friends with Dennis, and he helped turn off Erik's and mine before. You won't have a kill switch in a matter of hours. You're safe now, okay? Do you hear me?"

She's still trying to break free, but the choker around her throat bobs like she's swallowing hard.

"You're safe with me. *You will always be safe with me.*"

"Oh, Skipper!" She bursts into tears, and her hands go limp. I shift my weight back cautiously, and she springs upward, throwing her arms around me in a hug. "I'm sorry, I'm sorry, I'm so sorry!"

"It's okay," I tell her, but she still clings, hugging me so long we start to rock a little back and forth, and then she sits back and stares at me.

"Your hair . . . looks so good . . . like that." She sloppy sobs. "You finally . . . figured out . . . your look."

"Finally?" I widen my eyes at her. "What do you mean 'finally'? It wasn't figured out before?"

Jada slowly shakes her head back and forth, a mischievous smile spreading across her face. "No girl, no girl it was not," she gasps at last, and I burst out in outraged laughter, and she cracks up, and we both lose it, kneeling in the grass together with her switchblade beside us.

"Who's your partner?" I ask as we walk down the sleepy street back to Rose's house, dried leaves scurrying up the sidewalk ahead of us. Most of the jack o' lanterns have burnt down; the porch lights are almost all turned off, and the motion lights turned back on. The last of the trick-or-treaters are trudging in packs toward home, clearing the streets before the big kids come out for pranks.

"We didn't do partners for this mission," Jada says. "They just sent all the old campers to this town."

"Old campers? Like, there are new ones now?"

"Oh yeah. When we came back from our mission, they'd fully restocked camp with a new batch of psychopaths. And they told us, if we fail this mission? There's no coming back." She rubs the back of her neck, and even by moonlight I can see how sunken and shadowed her eyes are. "But someone's turning the switches off tonight, for sure? I'm not gonna kill you Signal, promise, but like, if you just said that, please tell me now. 'Cause I can't take the hope."

"It's true." I stop and look her hard in the eyes. "His name's Aarush, and his dad is a tech security CEO, and he's working on it right now. Nobody had a thumb drive from Dennis when she—when she got away from you guys."

Jada cringes. "Yeah. That really—"

"Not your call. I know."

"I should text the boys," Jada says as we climb up the stairs and into the shadow of Rose's wraparound porch. "They're going to want to hear this."

"Hear what?" Javier says, just in front of me, and I almost shriek, except his hand goes over my mouth, and he wraps me in a hug before Jada happily explains to Kurt,

"We don't have to kill them!"

Javier releases me, and I step back a little too far, almost knocking into the thin, bespectacled figure behind me.

"Dennis!" I gasp, throwing my arms around him. "Dennis, it's you!"

"She said they're getting our kill switches turned off!" Jada gushes.

"You got in touch with Aarush?" Dennis' familiar monotone pierces my heart, "Glad to hear it."

The door flies open, and Nobody looks out.

"Did someone say *Dennis*?" she cries and all but picks him up and hauls him inside. Dennis laughs helplessly, and that makes Erik come racing in from the living room with his biggest smile.

Kurt hugs me so hard he lifts me about an inch off the floor, and Erik hugs Jada, who bursts into tears at the sight of Nobody.

"I'm sorry, okay?" She weeps.

Nobody swoops her up in a hug. "Knock that off—we're cool."

Kurt and Erik are punching each other's arms at the end of the hallway, scrapping in a circle until Kurt lunges and deadlifts Erik up on his shoulders, Erik's sneaker striking the *Gather* text art and sending it crashing to the floor, and then the two of them almost collapse through the kitchen door, the rest of us streaming in behind them, all talking at once, the wrapped candies at our feet getting snatched up or spun merrily across the kitchen tile.

"Me and Jada have been up here for days, man. Dennis came yesterday and Javier this morning—"

I know Javier is across the room, looking in the fridge, but I've been trying not to look over at him because I honestly don't know how to be around an ex-boyfriend. Normal, ideally, but that's always been a stretch for me even in the best circumstances. I look at him now as he steps back from the fridge with a bottle of soda, and my smile drops.

Javier's eye is swollen almost closed, his flawless brown skin mottled with vivid purple bruises that break through in bloody tears at his cheekbone and across his nose. I gasp, and he jerks his head away from me, the group falling silent around us.

"What happened?"

"Nothing—don't worry about it," Javier says quietly.

"They questioned him when he got back to camp," Kurt says. "About what really happened to you at the Star Barn or whatever."

I sag against the kitchen island, heat washing up my neck and face.

"They had it mostly figured out," Javier says.

Erik walks over and silently puts his hand on his shoulder, and Javier raises the soda bottle to him.

"Since you two got famous," Javier adds, an edge to his words.

My face burns. I had hoped, if confronted, Javier would confess everything once he got to camp; claim we coerced him, promise to hunt us down. But his loyalty is written across his face in wounds that will scar. I bite my fist to keep the tears back. I don't have the right to cry, and I don't have the right to his kindness, but he looks at me over Erik's shoulder with eyes that are still kind.

"I'm so sorry—" I begin, when a muffled thump from the living room and a strangled wheeze makes Nobody rolls her eyes.

"Janeane's doing the worm again," Erik says. "We tied her back up after we finished talking, but you have to admire her persistence."

"I'll go babysit." Nobody grabs his shoulder. "But someone come tag me out in ten."

I nod, and Erik pulls a knife out of the block on the counter and hands it to her, saying, "Cut the phone line. That's what she's trying for."

Nobody nods and takes the knife, Javier following her out into the hall, mumbling something about finding some Tylenol. Jada pulls another knife from the stand, with a sing of metal. She trots to the kitchen island, plucks an apple from the bowl beside me, and pares it with one flick of her wrist.

"Nice."

"Who's the hostage?" Kurt asks cheerfully, digging through a box of Triscuits from the pantry. Erik looks to me, as though asking if he can tell him, and I nod.

"The woman who killed Signal's one," Erik says smoothly. Kurt pauses, mouth open, mid-bite.

"You didn't kill your one?" Kurt asks. I shake my head, mouth a tight line. He looks from me to Erik. "What the hell, Signal. Why didn't you tell us?"

I open and shut my mouth, unsure what to say.

"So, you're killing her now, or what?" Kurt goes on.

"Gathering evidence," Erik says in a lower voice, and then his eyes slide to mine, crackling with excitement. "We got a full confession."

"Really?"

"Really." He nods. "While she was untied. It's enough. It's more than enough, Signal."

I back against the kitchen cabinet, and cover my mouth with both hands. In another moment tears are slipping from my eyes, and I can feel Erik bob closer to me, like he wants to hug me, but Kurt steps between us, mouth full of cracker.

"Then what?" Kurt says, chewing. "*Then* you kill her?"

"Then we get out of here and anonymously tip off the police. Let them find her in the house with the septic tank full of Mike," Erik says, looking at me.

"And by then, all the kill switches will be off." I wipe at my eyes.

"Speaking of which"—Dennis tugs my sleeve—"how can I talk to Aarush?"

I get out the trac phone and lead Dennis down the hall. Aarush picks up right away, and I tell him I'm putting on Dennis. Dennis takes the trac phone, plugs his other ear with his free hand, and hurries toward the laundry machines as more laughter floats from the kitchen.

"Yeah, Python is definitely the way to go on that module . . ." I hear him say before retreating up the hall.

I stop at the living room door. Janeane's nostrils flare over the broad strip of duct tape over her mouth, and Nobody leaps to her feet.

"Your turn," she says, pushing the knife into my hands.

"Send someone to tag me out soon, okay?"

"Try and leave her head on." Nobody winks.

Janeane tucks her chin almost to her chest and stares up at me from under her eyelashes, her hair matted with sweat from her struggles.

This is not a good idea.

I shouldn't be in a room with her.

I shouldn't be so tempted to rip her duct tape off and make her answer some questions just for me, cameras be damned.

"Hey."

I turn to see Javier, still holding his root beer, leaning against the doorway from the front hall. His dark eyes catch the warm glow of the lamp.

"Hey!" I say, awkward.

Janeane makes a snorting sound behind me, but I'm done looking at her.

"I am so sorry," I say again. "We didn't try to blow up your story. There was an APB on us before we even walked in the Cactus Burger—"

"I don't blame *you*." Javier puts up a hand, then takes a seat on the couch. After a moment I settle at the other end of it, still holding the oversized kitchen knife. "I just don't remember cameras being an issue for Erik on his first mission." Javier is keeping his voice calm, but only just. "He's a smart guy. A smart, sneaky guy." I know we're both thinking of how he saw Erik and me kissing outside the hotel in Ojai right now, and my face burns. "But now the two of you are dancing at an opera, making out at a show—"

He cuts himself off, like he can't go on, and I get it. We were dating just days ago. He took a merciless beating to protect me and then came out of camp to find out Erik and I are the new Bonnie and Clyde. In his position, I'd be a wreck.

"Honestly, to me, it just seems like he's playing into it a little." Javier frowns. "All these people are rallying around your cause now, and that's a good thing because you're innocent. *But Erik's not.* So. Kind of seems like, I don't know . . . like he's using you."

Janeane makes another muffled laughing sound. She really shouldn't be hearing any of this. I walk over to the wood panel entertainment hutch, and though I don't look directly at her, I feel her watching me as I scan the Rowan's ancient CD tower, trying to find something that isn't The Dixie Chicks or World Music to mask our conversation. There's a strange tension in her attitude, like she's crouched and ready to spring, though I know if I were to look at her, she'd still be fastened to her chair.

Javier follows me over to the stereo after a beat, landing so close I can smell the fresh laundry soap of the red sweatshirt stretched across his broad shoulders.

"I'm telling you this because even with everything that happened, I still want what's best for you," he continues, "and Erik is the worst thing that could happen to you."

I set my jaw, putting the first CD my hand lands on into the tray and pressing "Play."

"You're sweet, and innocent, and he's—" He stops himself, but then can't contain the words. "He's a psychopathic *son of a bitch.*" The word breaks through the merry Peruvian flutes that have just filled the air. I stare at him, alarmed, and he goes on, "He's going to use you for whatever he can get and throw you away, Signal. You know that, right?"

"No. I don't know that. In fact, I completely disagree," I say stiffly. "But I don't think a passionate defense of Erik is what you're looking for right now. So I'd rather apologize for how everything happened. Truly, Javier. I'm ashamed of how I acted in Ojai, and I am so angry and sad you were punished for helping me. But all of that was my fault. Not Erik's."

He shakes his head, face sour like he's swallowing down vomit. "I should've dragged you back to camp with me."

"What?"

"I would have, if I'd known he was still alive. You'd be safer there than with him."

"Um, no." My voice wobbles. "*No one* is safe at camp. That's the whole point—" I reach over and turn up the volume knob, anxious that Janeane is listening, and lean in closer to Javier. "We have a plan, alright? I am so sorry for what you've been through, but it wasn't for nothing, I promise—"

"It was for *worse than nothing*!" he interrupts. "You know why I look like this, Signal? Every time they asked a question about what happened with you and I didn't answer, I got hit. And I took it. And took it and took it, because I thought I was buying you time to get away, to *go free*." He is holding my gaze now, like one blink would send tears down his long face. "But I was buying *Erik* time. All the time he needed. Hell, he got started before I even left. How far did he get, Signal?"

"What?"

"Has he banged you yet?"

"Excuse me," I snap, "that's none of your business—"

"Yes, it is. Because if he has, I'll kill him."

I am stunned into silence, when a smell like a pizza parlor fills the air, and Kurt leans against the door.

"Hey guys! There's some *bomb* garlic bread in the kitchen." Kurt grins, looking around. "You two go ahead and get some. I'll hang out with Mrs. Rowan here for a while." Janeane makes a low, muffled sound as I leave, but I don't look back.

Erik, manning four pots on the oven range, smiles up at me when I come in, his dimple flashing. I give him a quick, imperceptible head shake, knowing Javier is right behind me, and veer away from him to join Jada and Nobody.

"Skipper!" Jada cries. "Did you know Nobody can speak Japanese?"

Nobody winks at me.

"Oh, that one's full of surprises."

Javier has left the fridge and is taking the cap off a cream soda over by the sink, so I turn to Erik and ask, "Anything I can do to help?"

"We got spaghetti going, garlic bread just came out." He licks salt off his thumb. "There's a vegetarian lasagna heating up, and I found a bag of buffalo wings in the freezer to heat up too. Can you think of anything else you want to eat?"

"I could make a salad," I offer, pulling open the fridge, eyes bouncing away from the pictures of Rose still stuck to it with magnets.

"I'd *love* some salad. I can help chop!" Jada says as I bundle spinach and lettuce onto the kitchen island beside her. I almost do a double take, seeing her in the bright light of the kitchen. What with the blue wig, torn tights, and mini skirt, she's basically wearing a Sexy Signal Deere Halloween costume. It's almost embarrassing how much better she looks as me.

"Awesome. We got cucumber, we got tomatoes, we got—how do you feel about avocado?" I ask her.

"I need it. But I can't stand—"

"Onions, right?"

She smiles at me, puzzled. "How'd you know that?"

I almost say, "Troy said it once," but catch myself. Troy, the one member of the club who isn't here. His kill switch was set off by the Director the same night he and Jada became a couple. Not even for any real reason. Just to scare us. None of us know where he is now. In pieces in the lake? Burned in the metal barrel back in the woods?

I tear into a head of lettuce with my bare hands, Jada runs a knife around an avocado before turning it out of its peel. I want to be completely in her conversation with Nobody about Tokyo, but some inner barometer is alerting me to an oncoming storm. In my peripheral, Javier has turned to lean against the kitchen sink and is glaring at Erik's back, his crisp dress shirt rolled back at the sleeves, his graceful hands turning knobs and shuffling pots around the range.

Erik, meanwhile, is *whistling*, something I've never heard him do before. A drawling, almost comically atonal whistle that seems calculated to grate on nerves. He turns around slowly, eyebrows up, regarding Javier, and the whistle grows slower and more annoying until his most wicked smile cuts it off completely.

"Yes?" Erik grins. "What's up, Javier?"

Javier lets out a short laugh and shakes his head.

"Need to get something off your chest?"

"I've got *nothing* to say to you, man. But you should have plenty to say to me."

Erik rolls his neck with a crack, shoulders straightening out, hands dropping to his sides. "Like what?"

"Like an apology, to start with."

Jada trails off mid-sentence, her dark eyes going back and forth between the two and then fixing on me.

"What do you expect me to say." Erik smiles. "'Sorry for being alive'?"

Nobody rocks forward and starts clearing her throat so violently, we all turn and look. I hurry to get her a glass of water, and Erik pats her back.

"'Scuse me," she says a moment later. "I'm allergic to testosterone."

Jada laughs too loud, then looks at Javier. "Don't tell me you two are still sore about the Scavenger Hunt fight?"

"Yeah right," Javier says.

I latch onto the change of subject. "The Scavenger Hunt at camp? I don't remember there being a fight."

"Did I never tell you about this?" Jada says. "It was so funny! You remember when we buried your body by those skinny trees, and then Dave called me back before we were done? Well. It was getting dark, and I had one eye out for Dog Mask, when *BAM*!" She claps her hands so loudly I flinch. "Javier comes running out of some bushes and flattens me into the grass. I'm like, *'What the heck?'* And he's like, 'Oh I thought you were *him*. Only the two of us are left for the Sharpie fight, but I haven't seen him in ten minutes.'"

She looks over at Javier, who is scowling down at his bottle, and steps back in front of her cutting board.

"So Javi helps me to my feet, all apologies, always a gentleman." She smiles at him, as though apologizing for what she's about to say. "Then we go like not even three steps and *BAM*!"

She crushes half a head of garlic under the broad side of the knife, and it crinkles into cloves. "Erik just straight up drops out of a tree, right on top of Javier! And the two of them are like squaring up, okay? It was going too far—"

"Yeah, yeah, and then he won," Javier finishes gruffly, "because you know how camp is: it's set up for psychopaths. The more you lie, steal, and cheat—the *sneakier* you are, the more you win." A vein flickers in his neck. "At camp, at least."

"I just wanted to get it over with." Erik shrugs lightly, holding Javier's glare easily. "So I could go find Signal."

"You're so full of it."

"Hey"—Erik lifts his chin slightly, exposing his throat—"any time you want a rematch—"

Dennis' face appears in the kitchen door, and he holds up my phone. "Aarush says it'll be forty-five minutes."

"Forty-five minutes 'til *what*?" Nobody asks.

"Forty-five minutes 'til all our switches are off." Dennis pushes his glasses up his nose, and the kitchen shakes with cheers. Erik and Nobody pick Dennis up and carry him down the hall screaming, "U-S-A! U-S-A!"

Jada grabs my hands and jumps up and down.

"This is officially now a party, ya'll!" she yells. *"Party time!"* Then she leans toward me, confidentially: "What's up with this music? It's been, like, ten minutes of someone tooting a recorder up in here."

"You can change it. There's a stereo in the living room—"

"Next to the devil woman? Cool, be right back!"

Jada sprints out of the room, and a moment later the speakers crackle overhead with radio static, and the end of an upbeat dance song comes on. Kurt runs in and spikes a merlot accent pillow like it's a football in the middle of the tile floor, and Erik and Nobody carry Dennis back into the kitchen, when a radio DJ cuts in, voice smooth and practiced:

"Happy Halloween to all our boos and ghouls from PNW104.7! Next we've got a spooky song request from Hellacious Helen in Bridgewood, for Candyman Andy in Ledmonton . . . Andy, Helen says she wants to be the Signal to your Erik . . . as long as you don't forget the fries!"

Erik looks at me, his whole face flushed, and bursts out laughing as "Call Me Maybe" starts. I can't believe how radiant he is or how clearly I can read him, both of us knowing this moment is ridiculous and wonderful and ours. And then the stool shrieks across the floor as Javier pushes it out of his way in his hurry toward the door. But there, a returning Jada stops him.

Jada slaps a hand on either side of the doorframe, mouthing the words of the song as she dances in a goofily over-the-top provocative way in front of Javier. He laughs, putting his hand up and backing into the kitchen, but she doesn't let him get away with that. She turns and backs into him, then bends forward to touch the ground while comically grinding on him—or at least, it's *meant* comically. Javier seems seriously stunned. Then Nobody gets behind Javier and starts grinding him from the other side, one fist in the air, which makes Jada choke with laughter.

I smile at Erik, expecting him to laugh along, but he's assessing me.

"What's wrong?" he asks.

"Nothing! Are you kidding? High-five!" I hold up my hand. But he doesn't high-five me. He takes my hand, and his fingers lace through mine. A shock of delight travels through me like a radio wave at the contact. He twirls me out like we're back in the Opera House lobby, and I laugh, the last sound before the room goes completely still.

All six of our friends have frozen at the sight of us holding hands. The only sound is awkward silence and Carly Rae Jepsen.

And then Kurt laughs a high, strained laugh.

"Man, that's a relief. Because camp was going to make us do some *messed-up stuff* to you guys."

"Kurt, shut up," Jada says quickly.

"Yeah? Like what?" Erik says, eyes on high alert.

"The deal was, we don't finish this mission, our kill switches get activated, right? So like, I don't see how we would've gotten around it," Kurt says, pointing at Erik. "We were s'posed to bring Erik back alive, to camp, probably to get tortured—let's be real," he says, still smiling. Then his finger moves to me. "And kill Signal. Rip her up completely, the Director said. Make it *sickening*, he said."

The room is completely still as he points back to Erik.

"But make it look like Erik did it."

Chapter Thirteen

Teen Killers Club

"Is this how you get attention at parties," Nobody croaks at last, "when you don't have a guitar?"

"Oh, come on." Kurt laughs, tipping back a cream soda bottle. "Now that it's not going to happen, it's just more to celebrate, right?"

Nobody looks at me. I can feel Javier staring too, and Dennis' neutral gaze. Then there's the piercing stab of the oven timer going off, and I force a smile.

"Food's ready. Let's pass out plates. The forks are over here—"

I turn and get flatware out of the drawer with shaking hands. But my smile hasn't dropped from my face, and my brain is somehow keeping up, keeping me calm, breaking this down in cold, logical terms.

This is the Director's choice, not theirs. I defied our Director, who kills without a second thought—what did I expect? Added to that, as Aarush said, Erik and I were the best press Class As ever had. The longer our manhunt went on, the further our story spread, the more people questioned the narrative around Class As. So *of course* the Director would want to give our story the worst possible ending, to twist us into a cautionary tale. What better way to destroy Bonnie and Clyde then have them turn on each other?

But still. To know my "friends" had been about to go through with it . . . I could accept if they had to execute me quickly to save their own lives. I knew how camp worked. But . . . to make it "sickening"?

I can't keep the smile on. I slip out of the kitchen, through the front door, I don't stop until I'm curled up on the front swing, in the deep shadow beyond the porch light. Muffled talking and laughter leaks through the kitchen window behind me, and I fight down a wave of nausea at the memory of Jada hurrying to text "the boys" to stop them. They'd been just outside the door, surrounding the house, about to close in.

"Signal—"

Javier steps into view, his warped face thrown in sharp relief by the porch light, valleys of swollen flesh filled with dark pools of shadow.

I cringe back as he approaches.

"What Kurt just said—" He leans against the banister across from me. "Dennis and I didn't come here for that, okay? We were tracking Kurt and Jada. We were coming here to stop them."

"Cool." I fold my arms tight across my chest.

"Cool?" Javier shakes his head, shoulders so high. "You think I'm lying?"

"I . . . don't think you had that kind of choice."

His eyes fall closed for a long moment. Then he takes a deep breath and goes on. "I know you're upset—"

"I'm fine."

"Good! Great! Be fine! I *want* you to be fine! No matter who you're with, okay? But if you can say that, you really don't know me." His large eyes fasten on my face. "Or how much I care about you. And if we'd had more time—"

"Sorry, am I interrupting?"

Erik's voice makes us both jump. Javier shifts off the banister, the wall behind his eyes dropping back in place. He stands, his jaw tight.

"I said what I needed to say," Javier says to me, then pushes past Erik as he moves back to the kitchen.

"Careful now, watch your step, buddy!" Erik calls after him, before taking his place on the banister, messy hair haloed by the streetlight. I hear the front door creak open, then hold, and whatever face Javier makes behind me gets a terrifying smile in return from Erik. The door slams, and Erik covers his laugh with his forearm, until my expression registers and he leans forward.

"Kurt freaked you out, didn't he?"

"It wasn't so much Kurt as the whole plan to disembowel me," I say with false bravado, "How do you think they would they have done it? Slit my throat? Then bloody your hands and stamp them on the walls?"

"I don't imagine it would've been death by tickling, Signal, but it's not going to happen. Don't fixate."

I lean my head back on the hard wood of the porch swing. "It doesn't freak you out?"

"Nope. Aarush is turning off their switches, and we got Janeane to confess. You're safer now than you've been in years, and I feel *fantastic*." He considers me for a moment. "Maybe it's because you finally know you're safe, that you can let yourself feel how afraid you *were*."

"Is that what you do?"

"I don't get scared." He sounds actually sorry about this. "Which is a shame. I'd like to be afraid, like, *really* afraid. Just to know what it's like."

"Are you *serious*."

"It seems fun." He shrugs.

A giddy scream up the block from the last of the trick-or-treaters punctuates this baffling statement. His head turns briefly, his perfect profile in sharp relief against the streetlight for a moment, a cloud of breath just visible. Then he turns back to me.

"Why didn't you want to dance with me in front of Javier?"

"I don't want to dance in front of anyone. I'm a terrible dancer."

"I'll rephrase." He frowns. "You are acting like you don't want him to know we're together."

"He knows we're together; he's seen the news."

"Which bothers you."

"He was severely beaten while trying to protect me. So even if *I'm* thrilled we're together, I know *he's* not and I . . . if we know it hurts his feelings to see us all over each other, then the *kind* thing to do is—"

"I have no interest in being kind," Erik says, "if kind means dishonest."

My face goes hot. "I'm *not* trying to be dishonest! I just don't want to turn tonight into some big showdown. Can't we just . . . play it cool? So things don't escalate?"

"I'm not afraid of Javier."

He's not paying attention, then.

"Look," I whisper, "if I tell you something, do you promise not to go in there and start a fight?"

"What did he do?" His voice is ice. I shouldn't have brought it up. *Why did I bring this up?* And I know Erik, he'll never let it go now until I tell him.

"He didn't *do* anything." I squirm. "He just—he said if we'd slept together, he'd kill you."

Erik explodes in laughter. Laughter so genuinely delighted it shocks me, and I lean forward, shushing him, afraid someone will throw open the kitchen window and ask what the joke was.

"How *dare* he tell us what to do!" Erik cries, moving off the banister and settling onto the porch swing beside me. "Are you going to let him control you like that, Signal? Let's show him just what we think of his threats! Right here, right now . . ." The chains creak as he slides closer to me, head dipping toward my face, then he pulls away, sneering. "He's pathetic. He'll *kill me*. Sure, my guy—maybe try tagging me with a Sharpie first—"

"Can't you be a good winner?

Erik's head turns sharply, his expression softens.

"Okay." His arm winds around my shoulders. "If that's what you want, I'll play it cool in the kitchen." I lean into his warmth, and as I fit against him, he reaches out and traces a heart on top of my bent knee, finger moving slowly over the film of my tights, and a shiver runs from the top of my scalp to the back of my heels. "But if I can be a good winner"—I hear his smile, sensing my rapt stillness—"can you finally admit I've won?"

Not if I want you to keep playing.

"Give it up." My voice comes out thick. "I'm never going to say it, alright? It's way too much of an 'L' at this point."

The swing stops rocking, his hand drifts from my knee. He's quiet for long enough that I turn and look: he leans slightly forward, with such a stricken expression I panic.

"What happened? Are you okay?"

"Yeah, I'm fine. That just . . ." Erik's brow furrows, and his hand moves toward his chest as though to correct his still incorrectly buttoned shirt, but then veers to his mouth; he bites viciously at his nails.

"What happened??"

"It like . . . physically hurt. When you said that."

"Yeah, right." I roll my eyes, sagging with relief. "You scared me, I thought something was seriously wrong—"

"Oh, it is," he says distantly. He rises, and the swing jounces below me. "It is," he repeats. And without another look, he turns and strides back into the house. Shoulders hunched, head bowed, moving too fast for me to catch up.

"Erik?"

In another moment I'm trailing after him into the orange heat of the kitchen. Everyone is talking and eating at once, divvying up the lasagna and passing around plates; I smell hot tomato sauce and hear the cold clatter of cutlery, but all I see is the side of Erik's head as he refuses to look at me.

"Who's with Janeane?" Erik asks Nobody.

"We put a stack of plates on her lap." Nobody doesn't look up from the slab of lasagna on her plate. "She moves, we'll know it."

I take one of the two empty stools at the butcher's block, across from Nobody and Jada, assuming Erik will take the other one, but he walks on around me. Okay.

Erik strides past Javier, who's sitting behind me on a dining room chair he must have dragged in, leaned up against the wall next to the fridge. He continues past Dennis, who is standing at the speckled brown counter that runs along the side wall, carefully cutting spaghetti into bite-sized pieces with a knife and fork; and past Kurt, sitting between the paper towels and a big bowl of pomegranates. Finally, Erik hoists himself lightly onto the counter, the furthest spot away from me without leaving the room. Kurt offers him a platter of chicken wings, and he takes the whole thing and starts picking through them with a disinterested expression and a high spot of hot pink in both cheeks.

Look at me, I beg him with my eyes.

But when he does, his gaze passes through me like I'm fog. If I want to talk to him, I'll have to get up in front of everyone and cross the room to do it. Is that what he wants? Is he forcing some grand gesture, to punish me for asking him to play it cool?

Or is he genuinely hurt?

Can someone *be* hurt, who doesn't feel fear?

"Dennis is going to make us all fake IDs and papers and stuff," Jada says, handing me the salad bowl. "We're all picking new names and ages. I'm thinking I'll be Chrystal and age twenty-two."

"Oh?" I try to smile casually as I look over at Dennis, but all my brain is doing right now is trying to decipher the blur of Erik in my peripheral vision.

"Twenty-one is the minimum for renting a car," Dennis explains.

"We have to ditch the ones we have now, which is a shame. I finally programmed all the station buttons the way I like them in the Jeep." Kurt laughs. "You know, we really should go find an ATM and empty out our camp accounts before they freeze them—"

"Not while camp can still track us." Javier's voice rumbles behind me. "They know the minute you take any money out, so they'll know something's wrong if we all cash out at once."

"Exactly," Dennis says. "We'll just have to make do with the money we have on hand."

"How much is that?" Kurt looks around the room, setting down his plate with a clank and digging into his pocket.

"Three twenty-five and eleven cents. But Dennis, feel free to count it again," Jada says, pulling folded bills from inside her boot, which she hands to me to pass on to Dennis. Kurt hops down and hands him a tight roll of twenties, and Javier's chair scrapes behind me. Then he walks past my chair and sets a few crumpled bills by Dennis' plate.

"If we take the current total"—Dennis clears his throat—"and subtract the cost of eight scannable fake IDs, then we've got . . . seventeen dollars and eight cents."

There's a squirmy silence.

"Should I tell them?" Nobody says to Erik, a rare warmth in her voice. He nods, and she turns her radiant smile on the others. "You can add on another five thousand, Dennis."

"Closer to six," Erik says, scowling at a chicken wing.

Dennis' eyebrows go all the way up.

Jada slams her hands on the butcher's block, rises up to her knees and howls, "*Six grand*? *Yes, yes, YES!*" And she breaks out arm dancing so vigorously she almost launches herself off her stool. I reflexively reach out and catch her around the waist, and she grabs me back in a hug, swinging out one arm with a flourish that almost sends us both to the floor: "We're *rich*, baby! Rich, rich, *rich*!"

"I don't know about that, but"—Dennis smiles—"this opens things up quite a bit."

"We need to keep moving," Nobody says. "We should get a camper van. A fixer upper—I can fix it up. Cheap enough we own it outright."

"And we could get a dog!" Kurt adds excitedly, and Jada starts shaking her head.

"Um, I am *not* sleeping with seven other people and a dog in a *camper van*. Are you serious? I love y'all, but I'm *real* sick of the woods. *What if*, instead"—Jada looks around the room with the air of someone making a pitch—"we take our new IDs and our big lump of money to a big city and put a deposit on an apartment? We could all be roommates! And once we have jobs, with six thousand for a deposit? We could get, like, a *nice* place!"

"'A nice place.'" Nobody laughs, mouth full. "What does that mean?"

"Like we each get our own room. And we have a dishwasher, washer dryer, Wi-Fi, and hot water. The opposite of camp, basically."

"I would want an office as I'd most likely be working from home," Dennis says.

"And they have to allow dogs!" Kurt cries, and Jada throws a garlic knot at him, which he catches easily and eats in one bite.

"Cities are tricky." Nobody frowns. "San Francisco was bad. We barely got out." She circles one finger to include me and Erik, and I look up at him hopefully. He continues to stare forward, refusing to acknowledge me.

"Okay, but they knew you were heading North through California, because you got on a bus to Ledmonton," Javier says. "Let's say we pick a random city, throw a dart at a map, and go someplace where none of us have connections—"

"We can't go anywhere together," Erik interrupts. "We have to split up."

"What?" Kurt's big smile falls. "Why?"

"It will take them longer to find us if we split up," Erik says. "And they'll be looking."

"We all split up, except you and Signal, right?" Javier sneers.

"*Especially* me and Signal." Erik stares over my head at Javier, real anger in his voice. "After our little publicity tour? The first place they'll come looking for me is wherever she is. Now we've got what we needed, I have to get as far away from her as I can."

Jada turns to look at me; Nobody is more surreptitious. I stare down at my plate, piled with food I can no longer imagine eating. He doesn't mean it. He's played this trick on me before, after we stumbled into each other at Jaw's house; telling me we'd have to go our separate ways for our own safety. Now he's just doing it . . . in front of everyone.

I look up at Erik. He's staring directly at me, at last.

"That's what you *want*, right?" he says, his meaning clear: *this is what you asked for.* I shrug and jerk my head away, trying to sound as cold as humanly possible when I answer:

"All I want is what's best for everyone."

"Right, of course!" Erik laughs, a ragged laugh. "'Everyone,' of course. What's best for 'everyone.' Awesome—great instincts."

"So wanting what's best for everyone is somehow a bad thing?"

"How is splitting up a good thing?" Kurt interrupts. "We'll all be broke and alone. You think camp can't just track us down one by one?"

"There won't *be* a camp in another couple weeks"—Erik tears a hand over his short hair, breaking off our staring contest—"once Signal's name is cleared."

Dennis leans forward. "Aarush told me about the camera. Did you . . . did you get it?"

"Oh, we got it alright." Nobody nods slowly, then tilts her head back, indicating Janeane across the hall. "More than enough to clear Signal's name."

Jada pulls back to look at me. "Clear your name? How would that work?"

"She didn't kill her one," Kurt answers when I hesitate. Jada looks confused.

"But what about your mission?" Jada looks to Javier. "You guys took out your target, so camp could still charge her with—"

"No. We didn't kill our target," Javier says in a low voice. "Erik did."

A shocked hush extends into an embarrassed silence, and guilt makes my face burn, though I'm not sure why. What do I have to feel guilty about? *Not* killing someone? That's a good thing; yet the room is tense like I've been accused of an unspeakable crime.

But then, maybe I have. Because before I really knew him, I thought Erik was an unrepentant killer. And now I know the last thing he needed was another finger to block out his stars.

"Signal tried to do it herself," Erik says. "She didn't ask me to do anything. She tried to take down the target, and I *chose* to step in."

He's defending me, I know, but my face heats more at the explanation.

"And the fact that she's innocent will save all of us. All Class As." His voice tightens with excitement. "There are hundreds of thousands of people following our manhunt. And we just got a confession that *proves* Signal was wrongfully convicted, then denied the appeal process just because of her Wylie-Stanton classification." He looks around at the others, all now sitting at attention. "Once that's public, all Wylie-Stanton protocols will be called into question. Especially the appeals process. We'll have a chance, at last."

There's a muffled sigh behind me, and I turn to find Javier's glare burning into the back of my head: *See?*

He has a point. Erik is certainly more aware of the value of our celebrity than I've been. Maybe he *has* been playing up to the cameras?

Of course, if that's true, it's not *so* bad, since it could help so many others, and yet . . . the thought of him twirling me around the lobby, imagining how it will look on the news . . . it kills me.

"Geez, Skipper. Innocent the whole time . . ." Jada widens her eyes, the corner of her mouth jerking down. "No wonder you were so jumpy at camp! Your skin must've been *crawling.*"

"No, I *loved* camp," I blurt out. "I mean—not Kate and Dave, and not the hot water situation. And not that *stupid* obstacle course."

Dennis lets out a small laugh of recognition.

"But hanging out with you guys was the best. Our sleepover, our lunches, our cabin . . . I miss it sometimes." I look around the room, embarrassed. "It was the first time I felt like I belonged."

"Yeah, well, it's not like that anymore," Javier says flatly. "Not since the new kids came."

"Jada, you mentioned that before, that there are new kids?" I prompt her.

"A *bunch.*"

"How many?" Nobody asks.

"Eight when we left," Dennis says, knife squeaking against his plate as he cuts more spaghetti.

"Eight?" Erik leans forward. "Already?"

"They're running the Wylie-Stanton on misdemeanors now. Not just felonies," Dennis says, and Erik freezes.

"And they all *suck.*" Jada sighs. "None of the girls sleep. I wake up in the middle of the night, and they're all pacing around and grinding their teeth. Do the boys sleep?" She looks from Javier to Dennis, to Kurt.

"No," Dennis says.

"I don't really sleep." Kurt shrugs. "So it doesn't bother me."

"It's not them, it's the pills," Javier says.

"Pills?" Erik asks, "What kind of pills?"

"Okay. This man is officially a *saint*." Kurt laughs, pointing with a chicken wing at Javier. "The new kids did that to his face, you know." He turns and looks me right in the eyes as he speaks. "The Director picked two of the new kids when they were all pilled up, to be the muscle when he questioned Jav—"

"What kind of pills?" Erik repeats.

"How would we know?" Javier snaps.

"Are they blue and yellow?"

"Yeah," Kurt says. "You know what they are?"

"No. But I know what they do."

"Should we be concerned?" Dennis asks him.

"Yeah." Erik pushes back hair that is no longer there. "Yeah, you should."

"I did a little digging in Kate's files, because *she* didn't seem too happy about it either." Dennis goes on, "The camp budget has spiked. They're getting money from the research and development department of some pharmaceutical company."

"What company?" Erik asks, and I stare at him openly then, struck by the tone in his voice.

Dennis shakes his head. "It was redacted everywhere I looked."

"Hey, more to celebrate, right? We don't have to worry about it now"—Jada waves a fork at Dennis—"because *we* aren't going back to camp! We're going to . . ." she trails off. "We're going to wherever we want to go!" she finishes with a big, uncertain smile.

"How long 'til the switches are off?" Nobody asks Dennis. He moves around the butcher's block and pulls the large digital timer clock from above the oven. He plugs in fifteen minutes.

"The countdown has officially begun," he says and sets it in the middle of the kitchen island to scattered applause.

"Of the last night the Teen Killers Club can be in the same room together," Dennis finishes, and the clapping stops.

"Well, not the *whole* club," Jada says, rising up on her knees, her face solemn. She clears her throat and raises her red cup. "To Troy."

A long silence fills the room as everyone else raises their cups.

We sip together, and she sets her cup down and continues, "The night we all slept out on the obstacle course, he said something like you said, Signal. That camp was the first place he felt normal." A smile flits across her face. "And I said, Troy, you are definitely *not* normal." There's a surprised laugh from the room, and she continues, "Because he was way more funny and hyper and sweet than anyone I've ever met. Normal is awful, compared to him."

Kurt's face darkens, staring down into his drink, but he nods.

"You remember when we cleared the weeds and saplings and stuff off the field, the first day we got to camp?" Javier says then, looking across to Kurt. "I was keeping an eye out for you guys. Like, who are these twins, what're they about? And remember how Dave was going around taking all those pictures?"

"He was doing some kind of land survey or something." Dennis nods.

"Right," Javier says. "Well, at one point his walkie-talkie went off, and he left his phone on top of that camping chair he had while he went off to talk to Kate. And Kurt goes over, real cool and calm, and takes the camera and shoves it down the back of his pants—"

"What!" Jada yelps, clapping a hand over her mouth.

"And a light goes off in the dude's shorts, and I'm just looking at him like . . ." Javier blinks. "And he looks at me and says, 'Just testing the flash.'"

This wins a surprised laugh from Erik.

"Then later that night, at dinner," Javier goes on, "I see Dave going through his phone, and he looks up like this—" Javier pops up his head, eyes wide, nostrils flaring, scanning the room, and this gets a laugh from everyone; Nobody rocks forward and claps.

"Did he get in trouble?" Jada cries through the hand still over her mouth.

Javier shakes his head. "I don't think Dave ever figured out who it was. But he never left his phone out again."

"He used to do that all the time with people at school." Kurt laughs, eyelashes webbed with tears. "Leave your phone unattended around Troy, you *will* find a butt pic."

"Okay, your school friends, but *Dave*?" Jada says.

"That is *bold*," Nobody says with real admiration in her voice.

"One time," Erik says, "Troy tagged me coming into the boys' cabin with his 'mustard slap'—"

"Excuse me?" Jada asks as all the boys groan.

"Troy acquired a stash of mustard packets from the kitchen—expired mustard, I believe. He would squeeze several packets' worth in the palm of his hand, then slap the back of your head if you came in the cabin without checking for him first," Dennis says, and Jada, Nobody, and I trade glances and burst out laughing.

"What?" Nobody grimaces.

"That's *sick*!" I laugh.

"The night the girls moved into the boys' cabin, Troy got me right after dinner; just slapped a handful of mustard all over the back of my head, through my hair." Erik reaches up to his close-cropped scalp. "I was chasing him around the cabin, and he was hollering and throwing things to slow me down, when Kate came in. She takes in the scene—"

Kurt is listening breathlessly, like he hasn't heard this story before.

"I've got mustard all over the back and side of my head, and Troy's hand is just caked with it, and Kate asks, 'Troy, did you put that mustard in Erik's hair?'" Erik's dimple flashes as he suppresses a laugh. "And he looks at her with total outrage and goes, 'Lady, are you high right now?'"

And we lose it. Because we can all hear exactly how Troy would say it in our heads. Jada says it the way we're all imagining it first, and then Kurt says it *exactly* the way Troy would have, and we lose it all over again; the more we repeat it, the funnier it gets, until Jada and I are leaning against each other breathless, and Dennis' unexpected giggle breaks through, and we're all grinning at each other with tears rolling down our faces.

"No one scared Troy," Dennis says once we start to recover, pulling his glasses off and scrubbing his face with the back of his wrist. "Not even the Director."

Jada's face, so close to mine, crumples.

I know she's seeing it again, and at the memory my own eyes grow hot and itchy, and then Kurt slides down from the counter, his face dark, and walks a little too stiffly out of the room. Jada starts to follow, looking awkward, but Javier says softly,

"Let him go—let him have a minute."

"He hasn't been himself since we got back," Jada tells me after a beat, in a half whisper, as Nobody leans over the butcher's block to show Dennis Aarush's camera. "Sometimes I think he's sort of trying to stand in for Troy by making jokes and stuff, but other times . . ." she trails off.

"Maybe he can't help thinking about what Troy would say, in his head"—I think of Rose's remembered voice in my own mind—"and saying it out loud is, like, his way to keep him around."

Jada nods. "Yeah, I'm sure that's part of it. But it's . . . I don't know, like, Troy was funny, but never in a *mean* way, you know? Kurt's like . . . he's all *mean* all of a sudden."

"How did his mission go?"

"He won't talk about it." Jada looks at me significantly. "Not to me, at least—" She looks over my shoulder.

"He told me the target was definitely dead," Javier says without missing a beat. He's been listening to us this whole time. "But that's all he'll say."

"It probably would be good if we could get him to open up about it, talk it through—"

"I know!" Jada smacks the table, then announces to the room: "Truth or Dare time!"

There's a collective groan, but no actual objections.

Jada smiles, carefully pressing a napkin just below her eyeliner, checking for smudges. "Stop, okay? I don't want to hear it! Everybody has to play! We've got ten minutes left, so let's lay it all out there." She twists in her chair and yells across the hall: "Kurt! Get in here! We're playing Truth or Dare!"

There's a groan from the living room.

"*Javi*, I'm starting with you." Jada whips around. "Truth or dare?"

Javier shakes his head.

"Truth or dare," Jada repeats, leaning with one hand on the back of my stool to get more in his face. I can't see his expression, but I feel the silence stretch between them, as though he's gauging the least dangerous response: truth, or dare, or no I'm not playing.

"Truth," Javier says at last.

"Oh *good*," Jada says, "because I *have* to ask. Neither of you get mad, okay?" She looks at me, and my stomach twists. "I'm not trying to stir up drama—I swear I'm not. I just think it'll help clear the air. Okay?" She puts her hand on her hip. "What happened between you and Signal in Ojai, Javier? Because last we heard, you all were dating, and now no one knows what the hell's going on."

Dennis' eyebrows go way, way up, and Nobody reaches up and covers her face with one hand, probably so she doesn't cross eyes with me and burst out laughing.

Javier shrugs. "Signal had the opportunity to leave camp behind. Get her life back. I wasn't going to get in the way of that, so we broke up. With no hard feelings on either side."

"So it's over, but you two are totally cool, everything's fine?" Jada smiles at me knowingly, like she's doing me a favor.

"Yes. We're fine. I'm over it," Javier says, and then, "Who's next? Nobody, you playing?"

"Sure," she croaks, slapping the table. "Dare."

"Alright. I dare you to drink the rest of the Italian dressing."

She picks up the bottle without blinking, unscrews the top, throws back her head and swallows what must be two inches of oil and vinegar. It immediately comes back up and she lets it fly across the floor, Dennis jumping back with a horrified cry.

"Gross!" Jada shrieks.

"What's gross? What'd I miss?" Kurt comes back in, red circles around his eyes.

"Nobody just did a shot of Italian dressing, then sprayed it everywhere!"

"Too zesty." Nobody chokes. "Kurt, truth or dare?"

"Dare. Wait! I don't want to eat anything gross. Truth."

"What happened on your mission?" she asks flatly.

"Same thing that happened on all our missions." He shrugs. "I killed some idiot."

"Did it go okay?"

"Yeah." I don't like the way he smiles. "It went *great*. Signal!"

My shoulders go tense, I can feel myself clenching up, but I give him a smile.

"Truth or dare?"

"Um . . . dare?"

"I dare you to go slap the lady across the hall."

Everyone is looking at me. I roll my eyes. "Truth then."

"What, you can't even *slap someone*? Won't dirty your hands, huh? One slap. Real quick, just across her cheek."

"She said truth," Erik says.

"Why would I ask her the truth?" Kurt brays. "She cheated on Nobody, she cheated on Javi, and she's been lying to us since we met her, so—"

In another moment Kurt is sprawled across the floor, scrapping with Erik in a slick of Italian dressing. Kurt's face is purple, but he grins as Erik twists him in a headlock, laughter bubbling up in a wheeze. I don't think I could speak if I knew what to say. I hear Javier's chair creak and turn to see him rocking back with his hand over his mouth in silent laughter, enjoying my embarrassment.

"Uncle!" Kurt cries just as Erik starts to twist his arm behind his back. Erik lets him go, and the alarm goes off, so shrill we all wince. Dennis fumbles to turn it off as Erik returns to the counter, his eyes cutting to me, then bouncing away, cheeks flushing again. Kurt picks himself up off the floor, still grinning.

"We should check in with Aarush," Dennis says to me.

"I'll call him now." I hop off the barstool, eager to get out of the room. I hurry out into the dim hall, the trac phone's dial tone running and running in my ear. I hang up and call again, hang up and call again, pacing down by the laundry machines, refusing to cry.

Kurt clearly thinks the way to score points with Javier is by picking on me. And if Erik jumped him to defend me, he's a hypocrite, because he's hurt me more than Kurt ever could.

Aarush picks up.

"Hey! It's me! I wanted to check in on the—"

"I can't talk right now," Aarush cuts in. "The kill switches aren't done yet. I'll call when they're done, alright? Have you recorded the confession from Janeane yet?"

"Yes, it should be on the cloud."

He curses under his breath.

"What's wrong?"

I hear him frantically typing. "I got an alert that footage was streaming, but nothing was saved—a stream was received, but it didn't log it properly. There must be some glitch in the settings—"

"Nothing saved?" Pins and needles of anxiety pour down the back of my neck and somehow collect in my stomach. "Nothing at all? You're sure?"

"Yes, I'm sure!" he says impatiently. "Now I have to go. All sorts of firewalls are popping up. It's defensive maneuvering from whoever's monitoring the kill switches, they know I'm trying to get in. I have to deal with this. You just rally Erik and Nobody and focus on getting Janeane to confess again."

Getting Janeane to confess again. Is that even possible?

The phone goes dead against my ear, and it takes me a moment to pull it away, stomach churning. They're laughing in the kitchen again, and I hear them call my name.

"Well?" Kurt yells. "What's the news?"

I walk down the hall, phone in my fist, trying to figure out how to tell them camp knows Aarush is trying to hack in, how to break it to

Nobody and Erik we'll have to talk to Janeane again. I glance into the living room, wondering if she's been able to hear us all this time.

But the living room is empty.

There's just a chair with a stack of plates on its seat.

Janeane has escaped.

Chapter Fourteen
Hide and Seek

And then the lights go out. There are startled sounds from the kitchen and nervous laughter; then everything in me seizes up at once, my vision narrowing as though my body is about to shut down. I shake off the panic and sprint for the kitchen, shouting, *"She's loose!"* My Vans squeak on the tile as I round the doorway. *"Janeane got loose!"*

"Lock the doors and windows," Erik says, his blue shape springing down from the counter and crossing directly to the kitchen block. The metal sings as he pulls out a knife, and the others hurry over and follow suit, Jada letting loose a giddy laugh.

"Man! Everything left is serrated!" Kurt cries. "Jada, let me borrow your switch?"

I hurry to the front door. It's still bolted, the chain in place. I stop by the utility closet next to the bathroom and grab some flashlights, racing into the living room with my arms full and handing them out to everyone. Blue stripes of moonlight cut across the wall from between the blinds, across the empty chair and neat stack of plates.

"The neighbor's lights are all on," Dennis says. "Do you know where the circuit breaker is?"

"Upstairs, I think."

"Then that's where we'll find her." Dennis looks up, and we all follow his gaze up the carpeted stairs from the living room to the black hole of the second-story entrance, shadowy portraits of Rose and Mike smiling down at us through the blue air.

"Why didn't she just leave?" Jada snorts. "What is this bitch up to?"

"She went to camp," I tell Jada.

"What?"

I nod. "She was in the middle of getting rid of a body with Zap Sauce when we got here. My guess is she's trying to get us to come find her so she can pick us off one by one."

"Sounds like this party's finally getting started!" Jada laughs and turns on her flashlight, spots of color jumping to life across the carpet and wall as everyone else turns theirs on too. I've stupidly given them all away without keeping one for myself.

Nobody approaches me and drops Aarush's camera in my palm.

"Hold onto this," Nobody says. "I don't want to spatter it up too much before we give it back to Aarush."

"What did Aarush say about the switches?" Dennis asks.

"He's still working on it. Camp was throwing up some firewalls."

"They know he's hacking in?" Dennis says, loud enough that a look flies from Kurt to Javier, to Jada.

"They must," I say awkwardly. Dennis' face, always serious, becomes grim. "Here, if you want to talk to him—" I hand Dennis the phone, and it practically leaps out of my shaking hand as he takes it. But he doesn't dial Aarush; he just stares at me.

"I'm just surprised we're not dead, if they know someone's hacking in," Dennis says. "But maybe, since they can see the switches are all at the same location, they think we're in the middle of our mission."

Killing me, he means. Making it "sickening."

"Which is good," Dennis goes on. "That gives us some time. But if Aarush hasn't finished in another couple hours—"

He cuts himself off, like he doesn't want to finish the thought. I stare at his glasses, trying to see through the scratched reflections to his eyes.

If Aarush can't disable the switches, and camp will set them off if they don't go through with their mission, and their mission is to kill me . . .

Erik's tall figure cuts through the moonlight. A raised river delta of veins stands out sharply along the inside of the arm holding his knife. His free hand takes mine, and then he wheels around to confront everyone else in the room with a hard stare, the gesture large enough to be read in the dark: *you want her, you go through me.*

And I understand why he laughed about me wanting the best for everyone. Because he would choose me over everyone, he would take my side against the rest of them. He always has.

"Where's your flashlight?" he asks.

"I don't have one, or a weapon, or anything."

"That's okay." Erik picks his flashlight off the couch and hands it to me. "I'll be your knife, and you be my light."

I lean forward and kiss his cheek then, and a stripe of moonlight catches his eye, wide and surprised. I lean into him until my mouth finds his. There's a small jerk of surprise, then the arm without the knife wraps around my waist, his hand pressing against the curve at the small of my back as I tilt forward, kissing him like we're alone. There's a gasp, then a long wolf whistle, and the inside of my eyelids goes hot orange as flashlights sweep over us. Jada yells, "Damn you two, just damn!" and I feel Erik's smile against my mouth. By the time we pull apart, every flashlight is on us, and I burst out laughing, half drunk with relief. The relief that we've made up, that we've let everyone know we really are together, the relief on *his* face: like he can hardly believe what I just did either.

"Just damn," Jada says. "Well, you're going to have to press 'pause' on the Seven Minutes in Heaven because we're about to play some Hide and Seek." And she steps forward, cups her hands around her mouth and shouts up to the second floor: "And you better hope I'm not the one that finds you, bitch! One! Two! Three! . . ."

Nobody is already crawling silently up the stairs.

". . . Four! Five! Six!"

Erik and I, arms linked, move toward the stairs. I turn on our flashlight, and a dim moon of light ripples up the carpeted stairs ahead of us.

". . . Seven! Eight! Nine! *Ten!*"

Javier slides ahead of us as we gain the second story. Nobody has already merged into the shadows of the hall; I hear her moving around in the master bedroom as we pass its door.

"Ready or not, here we come!"

Kurt tears ahead with deliberate violence, banging open the linen cupboard, ripping a woodblock piece of text art off the wall and throwing it through the first door he sees. It knocks the thin door open with a sharp bang. He stomps in after it and tips Janeane's Peloton to the floor, and there's the crash of a mirror shattering.

Erik opens Rose's bedroom door, and for just a moment I hesitate, then force myself after him.

The room is just as I left it. I sense the shape of the canopy bed even before my flashlight slides over its Tiffany-blue ruffled underskirt. The air still carries traces of her floral shampoo and beachy body spray, and tears heat the back of my eyes at the familiar smell.

"Is there a shower?" he asks, indicating the narrow door to the en suite bathroom.

"Yeah."

"I'll clear that alone—it's a small space," he says, and I hand him the flashlight. He steps ahead of me, through the grid of light thrown by the window facing the lawn, but pauses at Rose's vanity, the beam catching something that he plucks from between the mirror and its wooden frame.

"Here," he says, handing me a strip of paper the size of a bookmark, before disappearing into the bathroom. There's not enough light to see it, so I fold it up and put it in my pocket and stand at the foot of the bed, shivering, feeling exposed without him.

I don't like to be alone in this room, even with Erik just a few steps away. I can't stop imagining Janeane working her raw wrists out of her zip ties, Janeane creeping up the stairs to the circuit breaker as we all talked in the kitchen. She turned off the lights to give herself an advantage. She knows the house and we don't. But still, she's a free woman. Why take on seven other killers when she could just run to the police?

I feel someone staring at me.

I whip around to face the bed, but there's nothing, just the four-poster and climbing roses of the wallpaper. But my nerves are jangling in alarm, and something primal and very loud tells me I should not have turned my back, even for a moment, to the closet.

I turn back to it now, straining my eyes to see more clearly in the dark without stepping closer. It stands slightly open, the lone slash of black in a room otherwise purple with night, a vinyl shoe rack hanging down the outside. On the inside, I know from memory, is a full-length mirror with smeared-off lipstick kiss prints at Rose's height. Are my eyes playing tricks, or did it just sway a little more open?

"She always liked to snoop around in here," Rose says in my head.

Hands in fists, I hold my breath to listen, chest tight as my pulse rises in my ears. And there it is, a sound just beyond the muffled blood thudding in my ears.

An excited, ragged breath that is not my own, just audible in the dark.

Erik. My mouth moves, but my voice won't come.

"Erik!" I wheeze as Erik strides out of the bathroom and lands across from me, in front of the closet.

"All clear. But the flashlight is running out of—"

The black wound of the closet door swells behind him, some crazed glint fixing on us.

"No!" I get in front of him, kicking open the door and staring, wide-eyed and chest heaving, at a rack of empty hangers.

"What the hell are you doing?" he laughs.

"I thought I heard breathing." I collapse onto the foot of the canopy bed. "I thought she was in there."

"So you were going to *protect me*?"

"I guess."

He stares down at me for a long beat. "Thank you," he says, then sits down beside me and takes my hand. And as our fingers wind together in the dark, I don't just hear breathing, I feel it. Hot breath tickles the back of my ankle, and then her teeth sink into the thin skin of my Achilles' tendon.

Erik's flashlight throws the grotesque moment into full color: a grown woman with her jaw clamped around the end of my leg, perfect white teeth and pink gums and one red-veined eye rolling up to meet mine through hanks of dark hair. Her pale hands, purple at the knuckles, are splayed out on either side of my feet, muscles standing out along her rigid jaw as she shakes her head back and forth, like a dog trying to snap the neck of a squirrel. It takes forever to just rise to my feet, time freezing around me, and she responds by digging deeper; teeth scraping against the lump of my ankle bone. I lunge forward, ladders racing up the black tights, the nylon caught in her teeth, stretching between us fine as spider web until it finally snaps to reveal a red half-moon of broken skin, and the walls of Rose's room ring with her laugh.

Erik kicks at her head, but she spiders backward before it connects, disappearing through the ruffled underskirt of the bed, and we hear the frantic thump of her crawling fast under the bedframe. In another moment she's scuttled out, moving with uncanny speed on all fours before leaping up and hurtling through the door.

"Hall! She's in the hall!" Erik yells, bounding over the bed, knife blade catching the light. At the door, he looks back to me. I hobble forward.

"I'm okay, I'm okay!"

There's a creak, then the metallic screech of a ladder falling down the hall.

"The attic!" I race past the confused faces emerging from the doors on either side of me, "She's going up to the attic!"

The metal ladder shrieks again from so many of us racing up there at once, we sprint to the top of the steps but then slow almost to a crawl. The attic's windows are blocked out, it's blackout dark and crowded with old furniture and stacked storage boxes. Our flashlights paint the labyrinth of junk in disorienting streaks of stark light: bags of suffocated teddy bears rear up to block our path; pyramids of cardboard boxes shrouded in spiderwebs lean over us; folded-up camp cot frames form a rusted corral that forces us further and further into the dark.

"Everyone *stop*!" Erik calls from beside me, and all my friends go still. Sharp steps ring out ahead—Janeane's heeled shoes. Erik squeezes my hand, then chases after her.

A moment later, the steps turn back toward us, and there's a screech as the trap door slams.

"Did she get out?" Erik yells.

"She pulled the ladder up," Javier answers.

"But she didn't go down. We would've heard," Dennis calls from somewhere in the dark.

She *wants* to trap us in here with her. Why? Why would she possibly want to corner herself in an attic? What's her plan? My dimming flashlight flickers and goes out in my hand. I step backward, and the moment I do a switchblade presses into my throat.

"It's me!" I choke.

"Oh, my bad!" Jada cries, the blade flitting away. "Sorry, girl."

I hear Janeane's sharp steps again, faster, at the edge of the attic, then the groan of old wood shifting its weight; shattering glass. Jada grabs my arm and pulls me forward just as a stack of boxes comes down behind us. I'm choking on dust, and Jada keeps pulling me forward as another stack comes down with a crash that makes the thin beams of the floor shudder, blocking off the whole west side of the attic and forcing us to turn and run the other way, coughing and choking, when suddenly the dark seems to open up. The air is thin but moving back here, whistling in the eaves above us. Then just ahead there's a stiff flap, a sound like a sail unfurling, and a gust of stale air.

"She's here—she's back here!" I yell to the rest of them.

A sharp click, a sputter, and the gold flame of a cigarette lighter throws Janeane into existence, tall and still in the blackness. She stands between a headless dressmaker's dummy and an old crib, flame painting her face orange as she lights her cigarette.

"You know, I'm actually jealous of you kids." Janeane exhales coolly. Then she reaches up and yanks a dangling beaded chain. A bare lightbulb comes on with a jounce, swinging back and forth overhead, shadows shifting along the wood beams of the room and tilting across her face at extreme angles, back and forth, back and forth, until it seems like the room itself is listing, like a ship in a storm. One moment she looks too old, the next too young, back and forth. We fan into a loose circle around her, everyone with a knife and ready to go. But Janeane seems strangely relaxed. She just smiles around the circle at us, her expression soft. There's dark red in the corner of her mouth, and when she speaks, I realize her teeth are glazed with blood.

My blood.

"I would give anything to be where you are right now. Just starting camp. No parents, no school, no responsibilities. Just hanging out with your friends and road-tripping to missions." She shakes her head. "But from the poor attitudes you have displayed this evening, it's clear none of you understand the opportunity before you. You're not thinking about your future, you're not setting goals. If you fail to plan, kids, you plan to fail."

Erik, just behind her, shifts his weight like he's about to spring, but I make a motion with my hand that catches his eye. I open my fingers enough that he can see Aarush's camera in my hand. He nods, puzzled but trusting me. We need her to keep talking. I activate, then angle the camera as best I can on Janeane. I just hope this time it's recording.

"I'm one of the only people in the world who's been *exactly* where you are," Janeane continues. "I went to camp after a murder conviction. I got 'pardoned' when I got pregnant and thrown out of camp with nowhere to go. My family cut me off. But at least my murder conviction was wiped from my record." She blows out smoke. "You kids won't even have that. You'll be fugitives. No education. No money. No friends. You'll be working cash-under-the-table jobs for people who can report you at any moment. Living in trailer parks and spending your weekends at laundromats, like I had to before I married my idiot husband. But the girls have that at least. They can find a sugar daddy—"

"Shut up," Jada says through gritted teeth. Nobody, on the other side of Jada, looks like she's ready to puke.

"It's you boys I really worry about." Janeane locks on Javier, who stands at my right, and scans him appreciatively before turning to wink at Kurt, who hovers behind Erik. "Signing on for days and weeks and *years* of hard labor. For what?"

"To live past thirty-five?" I snap. "All our targets, in our first mission, were the previous generation of campers. That's why she's one of the only people in the world who's been to camp." I look seriously from Kurt to Jada, to Dennis. "We killed off the rest of them! That's why Dog Mask tried to stop us ever leaving camp. They kill you off when you retire, at, like, thirty-five—"

"Thirty-five is forever away when you're sixteen," Janeane scoffs, ashing onto the stump of the dressmaker's dummy. "And what do you think your life expectancy will be when you're a fugitive who can't step inside a hospital? You'll be lucky to see *twenty*."

Jada bites her lip. Kurt's expression is stone.

"Signal is fine with this, of course. Trading your lives for hers. *She* hasn't done anything wrong, so if her naughty Class A friends have to spend the rest of their lives in abject misery, well . . . it's just what they deserve."

"We won't be Class As," Erik interrupts. "Once everyone finds out you murdered Rose and framed Signal, the whole concept of being Class A will be over—"

"Oh *honey*"—Janeane's blood-tinged smile is cold—"how have you not figured this out? There's a *very obvious* reason Signal is unlike any Class A you've met before. *She's not a Class A at all.*"

Erik's eyes meet mine. The others don't know our counselor, Dave, was a camper at the same time as Janeane and that he'd kept a stack of clippings on my case, as though investigating me. But Erik does. And I can see the tumblers falling in his head before she even explains.

"Dave faked her Wylie-Stanton score so he could bring her to camp. And I know this because *I told him to*."

His gaze falls from mine like a plug from a socket. His expression goes dark, his fingers go slack around his knife.

"She's *lying*, Erik. She'll say anything right now—"

"I'm telling the truth, and he knows it," Janeane snaps. "You're not going to clear all Class As—you have nothing to do with us! You're not good or pure or special. The only thing you're proof of, Signal, is the importance of birth control. And if I were *you guys*"—Janeane addresses the rest of the group—"I wouldn't throw your lives away because this impostor is jealous you can do what she can't. Finish your mission and go home to camp." She drops the cigarette, steps on it, and I realize what the sound was, that stiff flapping like a sail: a tarp. She's standing in the middle of a heavy-grade blue tarp.

"Kill her right now, and I'll even clean her up for you."

I can feel them all staring at me now, the still-swaying lightbulb making their expressions shift from pitying to gleeful, and back again. All except Erik's. His eyes are going through me, seeing some distant place where I don't stand.

"Well," Kurt says, "I'm convinced."

And then he takes Erik's knife from his hand, strides over to Janeane, and plunges it straight in her chest.

Chapter Fifteen

The Altar

"Kurt!" Jada gasps. "Savage!"

Janeane's hands spasm toward the handle still quivering in her chest. The knife has set off whatever little electronic device turns her sweatshirt on, the pumpkin flashing as deep red blood soaks through its smiling face.

"That's why I let her out of the chair." Kurt jerks the knife back out of her chest, and she makes a sound like the last of the dishwater down the drain before falling to her knees.

"You *what*?" Javier chokes.

"Did you not hear her?" Kurt yells. "You want to be broke and alone out there? Because I don't! Hey, guess what, Signal?" He says my name, but he's watching everyone else around the circle. "I never killed anyone either before I got to camp. And no one helped *me* out."

"What?" Nobody says.

"Yeah." Kurt nods. "I covered for Troy because I didn't want to lose him. So I looked guilty, I got convicted, and I made my peace with that. Because at least we were *together*." His eyes start streaming. "And now he's *gone*. And if the rest of you go, I don't have anyone left who even remembers him, okay?"

"What are you doing." Dennis shakes his head slowly. "What are you even doing, Kurt?"

"We can just go back to camp!" Kurt yells, tears fully streaming now. "Dennis, you know those switches aren't getting turned off. And even if they were, where would we go?" Kurt shakes his head. "The Director said we could come back if we had Erik and Signal was dead, and we tied up the loose ends." He points down at Janeane without looking at her. "Half the work is done. So let's just finish the mission and go home." He turns to Jada. "You take care of Signal. Javier, help me with Erik—"

"I'll go," Erik says. So lightly. "I want to. I belong at camp."

What is he doing? This must be strategic. He's going to talk Kurt down. Or distract him enough to get the knife. Kurt's relief is playing out in every line of his body.

"If"—Erik's eyes go huge in the harsh light, his pale face cut out against the dark—"*if* you let Javier take care of Signal."

Kurt's eyes narrow. "You're only saying that because you think he won't hurt her."

"Well, he's wrong." Javier laughs. "I told you, Kurt, the bitch cheated on me. And she just made out with this fool, right in front of my face. Let me take care of her real quick. And then we'll all be cool again."

Kurt looks at Javier for a long beat, then nods. "Get to it, bro."

Javier strides over, grabs the back of my dress collar and drags me then, my feet scraping across the floor as I try to get away. He picks me up and I kick and howl while they all just watch. Jada, Dennis, Nobody—none of them do anything. Kurt goes over to the nearest window and starts pulling the boards away.

And Erik turns and helps.

"Erik!"

The back of his neck flushes, but he doesn't turn around.

Janeane's eyes roll up to meet mine, the side of her mouth twitches, and then Javier pulls me back into the black maze of the attic.

"Erik! *Please!*"

"Shut up already!" Javier yells, but once we're out of sight his hand slides from the back of my neck to my wrist. He half lifts, half pulls me over the pile of fallen boxes, the shattered mirror and broken armoire, the two of us sliding and scrambling in the dark, running like we're being chased. The moment his hold flickers, I try to run back, but he spins me around and shoves me forward.

"Get down there, damn it!" Javier yells, throwing open the trap door with a crack, the ladder falling heavy as a guillotine. He hurries me down ahead of him, drags me through the trashed second story and practically pushes me down the stairs. He herds me past the chair with the plates still stacked in the living room, through the kitchen with the empty lasagna tray and the drinks we'd raised to Troy, all the way to the back door. He unbolts it and throws it open, leaning back to retrieve my Halloween mask from the butcher's block. He shoves it into my hands.

"Run," Javier says. "Run as fast as you can."

"You don't understand." I shake my head. "Erik's going to talk Kurt down and get the knife back. He's got some kind of plan—"

"His plan is to go back to camp."

"He wouldn't leave me—"

"Maybe not when you were a Class A. When you were *useful*. But the second you can't benefit him? He's through."

A jolt goes through me like I've missed a step going down the stairs. Erik protected me when I was his proof. But if I'm not, if there's no proof of goodness in him anymore, what's the point in trying to be good? If he can't use me to reopen his case, and this manhunt can only end with him in prison, why not go back to camp?

"You're not safe here." Javier moves toward me, and I back up until I bounce against the door. "You're barely safe with *me*. You know what's going to happen to me if they find out I let you go again?"

He punches the door right beside my head, leaning in, only the swollen half of his face visible in the dim light, and grabs the door knob next to my waist with his other hand.

"Get out of here. And if you see one of us ever again, you *run*, do you hear me? Even if it's me. You understand?"

He opens the door so it swings out behind me, and I almost fall backward onto the deck, just managing to stay upright as he slams the door in my face. The bolt slides home, and I turn, hardly believing what has just happened, and stumble down the side stairs.

Headlights flash at the end of the street—the blue Jeep SUV Kurt took on his first mission. Three figures cut diagonally across the road toward it, a block ahead. Kurt is laughing, Erik is behind him, someone tall and lanky has their arm over Erik's shoulders, Nobody? It is Nobody. What's she doing?

Kurt gets in the drivers' seat. Nobody guides Erik's head into the back and leans in for a moment.

Now's your chance guys. You hijacked Dathan—you can't hijack Kurt? Take his keys. Reverse the car. Come back.

Come back for me.

But Nobody steps away from the car, slams the back door, and jogs across the road, disappearing around the opposite side of the house. I limp across the lawn as the headlights come on, the taillights go red, and pounding music starts mid-beat as the engine revs up.

I run after them, heart racing my legs as I throw myself forward, burning every shred of muscle and bit of my will trying to close the space between me and the accelerating car. But it slips around the corner just before blue and red lights bounce down the oncoming lane, and my breath sticks in my throat.

Police. The police are coming.

Did Janeane call them? We cut the landline, but she must have had a cell somewhere. I swallow a scream and hobble into the bank of backyards across the street, hauling myself over a splintering wood fence, sprinting past a covered-up aboveground-pool and across a hollow, damp deck, tired Labradors and startled terriers barking from behind their windows and patio doors as I pass. Their barks are lost in the sirens that seem to come from all directions now, closing in.

The thud of helicopter blades rises in the distance, and I scramble under the nearest deck, squatting between a toddler trike and stack of folded-up lawn chairs. I clip Aarush's camera on the inside of my dress. No phone, no money, no car keys. It's virtually the only thing I have now, and I don't even know if it works. The helicopter thrums directly overhead, so loud I can feel it in my burning chest. Its searchlight cuts out the green grass and yellow house across the yard in noon-day color before it glides up the street toward Janeane's house. The dogs are howling and barking now, and the deck quivers as someone runs overhead. When I'm sure they've gone back inside, I pull on my mask, crawl back out onto the lawn, and run for the shadows.

* * *

I keep to the quietest streets of my hometown, the cul-de-sacs and dead ends, the places the asphalt crumbles back into dirt, so I'm close enough to the protection of the trees without losing my bearings.

My face is frozen under my mask, and I can't really feel my fingers anymore, but I just keep running. Running and staggering, running and crying, until I'm stopped by a line of white that rises straight up into the sky, catching the glow of the lone streetlight ahead of me. The thin ribbon of white pauses, then tumbles back to earth. I hear laughter up ahead and drop my pace, afraid to draw attention. I stay in the shadows, half-hidden by the trees as I approach a small crowd gathered in the middle of the street.

Thousands of white paper ribbons stream from the reaching branches of an old oak. High schoolers surround the tree, throwing rolls of toilet paper back and forth over its limbs. This is a local tradition I never got to participate in: seniors would TP the big tree in front of the principal's house every Halloween. I've never seen it done before, a starburst of people gathered around the trunk, throwing the rolls as high as they can. It's lovely, the way the paper seems to stick momentarily to the sky before coming back down, a flowing white tail tracing its fall. A laughing girl in a blue bob wig and black hoodie goes skipping around the tree and lobs her roll over a branch to her friend, a brunette with a line of red paint across her neck.

I turn my head and see a couple sitting on the hood of a nearby car, making out in the streetlight. The girl is in a pink wig and has "The Hopeless" written on her long-sleeved T-shirt, the boy wears a white wig and red heart-shaped sunglasses, their hands grip each other so tight, like they're both afraid to fall. Before Erik, I didn't understand how people could do that, act like there was no one else in the world. Because of Erik, I know there is a place between two people that fades reality to nothing. But was I alone then too? Alone in that feeling, the whole time?

I thought *heartbreak* was a poetic term, but it's stupidly literal. That's what it feels like, standing there alone in the crowd. Like the meat of my heart is ripping deeper with every beat. I should taste blood and be on my knees. But I'm still standing. How can you hurt this much and still be standing.

"Skiiipper!"

A matte black lowrider prowls half a block behind me, hanging just outside of the hazy yellow streetlight. The driver's side door opens and Jada gets out. From a distance she looks how I wished I did in high school.

Jada stares through the crowd at me, the only person on the street who knows who I am, and smiles. Smiles and holds out her hand. Just like she did the first day we met.

I turn from her and break into a run down the street. A ravine is not far from here that opens out into a creek; I can follow it through the woods. There's only one trail I know by heart, even in the dark, and the only way out of here is through it.

* * *

I fear, from my first step down the trail, the moment the shed will rise before me. I don't want to see it—I never wanted to see it again. So it's a relief when I find it's been razed to its foundation, the cracked cement rectangle like a vast grave marker in the black earth. But razing the shed hasn't stopped people from leaving a tribute: burning tea lights spell out "ROSE" across the cement, and an upturned log has been dragged in from the woods as the base of a makeshift altar.

In front of it is heaped a mound of cellophane-wrapped flowers and stuffed animals. There are wooden crosses with "REMEMBER ALWAYS" and "LOVE NEVER DIES" written on them. There are several tightly folded notes on blue-lined paper, blurred from rain and time, and laminated cards with poems and Bible verses. And above it all, on top of the log, sits Rose's yearbook portrait in a gold frame, smiling at me through the flickering candlelight as I kneel down in front of her.

I pull my mask off, wringing it in my hands. I can't believe I'm here again. This place that has lived in my nightmares for so long, the place where Rose died. And I know it's in my head, I know it's not her, I know it's only what I think she would've said. But I swear I can hear her saying the words.

"See?" Rose's voice rings in my head. *"I told you my mom was a psycho-bitch."*

And I laugh.

"Ho, you're a mess. What happened? Where are your friends?"

I start sobbing.

"You pushed them away, didn't you?"

I shake my head.

"Signal. Look at me. You push people away. That's your whole thing."

I look up at her portrait. The tea lights flicker in the wind, making her expression seem to change.

"Remember after I moved?"

I never—

"Are you seriously going to kneel there and act like I didn't invite you to church socials? You said no every single time. And it was basically all I was allowed to do!"

You stopped talking to me at school.

"Um, you stopped talking to me too. A couple days of not being at the same lunch table and you wouldn't even look at me in the halls!"

I have my pride.

"And now I'm dead," Rose snaps. *"But you still have your pride, so good for you. Look at that thing your boy stole from my room."*

I remember the bookmark Erik handed me before. I pull it out of my back pocket and tilt it until it catches the wavering glow of the burned-down tea lights. It's not a bookmark; it's a photobooth film strip. From when our moms took Rose and me to the Grand Reopening of the Bridgewood Mall.

There were free samples everywhere that day, balloons and T-shirt giveaways, and a sun-warmed jolly jump we decided we were too old for. But we'd begged our moms for two dollars to take photos in the photobooth. Mom and Janeane had come up one quarter shy and told us it was time to get home anyway. Then, like we'd willed it into existence, we spotted a shining silver coin just a few feet from the car. We'd raced back to the mall, hand in hand, our moms screaming to come back, and piled into the photobooth. We'd meant to do our model poses, but every picture caught us laughing uncontrollably.

Why did you have this up on your mirror?

"Because you were my first best friend, idiot."

It makes me very happy you held onto this.

"That's probably why he gave it to you."

And then he left me. He left me, Rose. I didn't push him. He just left.

"Oh yeah? And all those times he asked if you loved him, what did you say back?"

I stare at the picture of Rose, startled. I know it's just the shadow of the flowers cast by the tea lights, but I'd swear she's laughing at me. It looks so much like she's laughing, I look away, afraid what I'm seeing is evidence of a mental breakdown.

"Push, push, push." She laughs in my head.

What do you care? You thought he was bad for me—everyone thought he was bad for me. And all of you were right.

"This isn't about him. This is about you. About why you won't even try for something you want with all your heart."

Try for what? He left me! He wants to go back to camp!

"He wants to go back to camp? Really? He knows he's going to be tortured, again. Drugged, again. Only this time, he won't be able to blame it all on Dr. Ledrick. Maybe that's why he wants to go back. He needs to know."

Know what?

I stare at her picture, not really seeing her, but remembering Dennis in the kitchen, how Erik reacted when he spoke about the pills.

Something had thrown Erik, bad, when Dennis mentioned R&D for a pharmaceutical company.

Erik's grandfather had a pharmaceutical company. That was on Armchair.org—it was a company called CurtPro. I'd gone over and over the time line, trying to figure out who'd had access to Curtis's office to get the keys to the garage, and it had never occurred to me that one person *always* had access to those keys, and that was Curtis himself. Curtis knew about cars, alright. And Dr. Ledrick and Curtis had been in the garage for so long together. Were they just discussing his collection?

Or making some kind of deal?

I shake my head. A deal to kill his own daughter, his own *grandsons*, to close some government contract? Is it possible?

"Yes," Rose says, *"it's possible."*

But then to test those drugs on Erik? Why?

"He was the prototype Class A. If you want to figure out how to better control Class As with drugs, then he's an irreplaceable test subject. Maybe the larger question is, why was Erik even in the lab in the first place? Who made that call?"

His brother, who hated him.

"His brother wouldn't make custody decisions. *His grandfather would have ultimate say. Erik* wanted *to live with his grandfather, he made that clear. So if his grandfather signed him over to Dr. Ledrick, it's likely he knew exactly what Dr. Ledrick was doing."*

But Erik would have thought of that.

"Maybe he did. But maybe he needed to believe there was one person in that family on his side." Rose's voice is sad. *"When you love someone, you see in them whatever you need to be there."*

Is that why Erik went back with Kurt? To find out for himself if his grandfather had been in on it?

"And to protect you, dumbass. Because he loves you."

No, he doesn't. Not really.

"Honestly, I don't really care if he likes you or not. I care about how you *feel about* him. *Do you? Care about your own feelings, at all?*

Because you don't act like it. You act like you need permission from a guy to like him. What the hell is that about? You're not good enough until he explicitly tells you so, is that it? Or is it easier to never win than to try and lose?"

I've already lost.

"That's the spirit!" Rose says sarcastically. *"Would you listen to yourself? Look. I'm not going to lie. Odds of a happy ever after are slim, bitch, but they're zero if you don't fight for what you want. You love him and that's the truth. If you don't pursue what you truly love, what will you pursue? What will your life even mean?"*

But I'm . . . he's . . . we're both too messed up.

"Signal, if someone doesn't seem messed up, you don't know them yet. People are, always and everywhere, weird and messy. Especially you two freaks. But you get each other completely. How many times do you think that's going to happen? How many times has it happened before?"

I look down at the photo strip in my hand, the two little girls hugging each other and laughing so hard. What had it cost me, pretending I was okay with losing her? What had it cost her?

"You keep that." Rose says. *"Remember I wasn't always such a bad friend, okay?"*

I get to my feet, still staring at her portrait, all alone in the dark.

"I love you, Rose," I say out loud, then turn down the path out of the woods.

* * *

When I get to the edge of the woods and stare into the park, I almost don't recognize our trailer because the goose isn't up. The wood goose with the windmill feet, who's stood over my mother's garden of sweet peas since before I can remember. It's gone, and the garden is trampled into the empty gravel driveway. Where is my mom's car? It's almost morning. She should be home. I walk fast, mask on, past our neighbors' trailers to our home and tiptoe up the shivery metal stairs. I knock until the thin door rattles in its frame, even after I've read the sign on the door: "GO AWAY." I step back, chest heaving and read the smaller but all-caps print:

"NO INTERVIEWS, NO PICTURES, NO COMMENT!
SUPPORT FEARNODEERE.COM"

"Mom?" I say weakly, afraid someone else will hear, then my hand lands on the padlock on the doorhandle. It's the kind with punch code buttons and keys inside, like when they're showing a trailer for rent.

Did she . . . move?

A dog barks across the narrow lane between our trailer and the neighbors, I hear a car approaching and slip over the railing and down under the deck. Jada and the others, come to find me? No. A compact yellow car pulls into our gravel drive, and there's a crunch of heels as a girl in a blue wig steps out, giggling. A guy with a ring light clipped on his phone follows after her, and their footsteps clip up the steps to our front door. The driver's side door slams and I hear a third girl hiss,

"Nooo! Get off the porch! What if someone's home?"

The deck creaks just over my head, by our living room window.

"Nah, didn't you see on Twitter?" the guy says. "The mom moved out. Sick of all the people yelling on her lawn."

"Yeah, and the cops were just *letting them*," says a tipsy voice just overhead. Boards creak under her heels as the girl dressed up as me restlessly shifts her weight. "Meanwhile they won't let news trucks even down the street where that *bitch* Rose lived."

"Fine. Just—take the pictures and let's go." The driver comes up the stairs, her steps halting.

"Signal Deere did nothing wrong!" the girl in the wig and heels screams to the entire trailer park: *"Kill the cool kids! Kill them all!"*

"Is that . . .?" The guy sounds excited. "Do you see that hair tie?"

"What?"

I hear them around our front window.

"It's half pink, half purple—from blue dye," The guy says excitedly. "That is Signal Deere's hair tie! Get the door open. Get a rock, we're breaking the window, I'm not leaving without that hair tie—"

I'm able to haul myself up the struts below the deck so quietly that they don't turn around until I've got one leg over the railing. And I don't blame the girl in the wig for screaming when they do. With my funeral dress, and mask, and bloodied ankle, I'd scare me too. But they don't really freak out until I've taken the mask off. They recognize me alright, the guy almost breaks his neck flying down the stairs.

"You're—you're—" The blue wig girl can't finish.

"The Girl from Hell." I take a step toward the two girls, and they back away. Another step, and the tipsy girl turns and stumbles down the stairs, her heel folding under her so she manages the lower five on her butt. Then she leaps up and breaks into a full-tilt run. The driver is the only one left, and she's the one I want. I get between her and the top of the stairs. She fumbles getting her phone out of her pocket and points it at me, her hand shaking. The camera flash goes off in my face.

"I'll post it," she whispers, voice shaking. "I swear, I'll post it and tag the location."

I step forward and pull the phone easily from her hand. She shrinks back, throws herself against the door like she thinks I'm about to sink fangs into her neck. Unable to help playing into this, I lean forward, then whisper, *"Give me your car keys."*

She pulls them out of her pocket, and they jingle wildly in the space between us before she drops into my hands.

"Thanks." I clamber back down over the side rail and sprint to the car, pull open the driver's side door, then stop and call back:

"I'll leave it somewhere you can find it later. Fear no Deere, okay?"

I don't wait for her response. I start the tiny yellow car and wheel around with a screech, then go flying down the road out of the park. As soon as I'm on the emptied main road, I dial Aarush's number from memory. He picks up on the first ring.

"*Signal!* You're alive!" He sounds like he was actually worried about me. "I couldn't disable the switches. I'm so sorry, Signal."

"Are they—"

"They're all moving East out of Ledmonton, so they're still alive, but I couldn't break through. You're alright?"

"I'm fine."

"I saw the stream with Janeane—"

"Did it record?"

"I hadn't fixed the glitch when you started, so I captured a screen recording on my computer. So we have an MP4, at least. And it—it was the craziest thing I've ever seen, if I'm honest. It certainly convinced *me* she did it, but Signal . . . she doesn't actually mention Rose or Jaw or anything that has to do with clearing your name—"

"Forget clearing my name," I tell him. "I've got a new plan."

I pull onto the highway and point my car toward the first light of dawn.

Chapter Sixteen

Sunshine

"Sunshine?"

Even after a week, it takes a moment for the name to register. I look up at Lupin. She tilts her head to one side, her expression one of practiced patience. The seven people around her stare at me or down at their own crossed legs, or they pluck at the grass. The only sound is the birds in the trees overhead and the wind in the pines.

"Do you have anything to bring to this Share Circle?"

I shake my head.

"Everyone here at Higher Paths is given the space to share in their own time. And I know you joined our journey a little later in the session, so you're still finding your feet. But I ask that you consider how open your fellow hikers have been with you." She sweeps her hands to indicate the circle around me, silver bangles clinking at her wrists, every word measured. "You've heard a lot of our stories. Stories that were difficult to tell and, I'm sure, difficult to hear. You've listened without judgment to everything from Fox's phone addiction to Lady Bug's compulsion to dip her fingers in hot candle wax. And for that we thank you. But I think it's time you gave *us* the opportunity to hold space for *you*."

"I'm cool."

"You can share *anything* here, Sunshine." She knits her fingers together. "A memory. A fear. A dream."

She's not going to let this drop. Well. A dream won't give anything away, and I know the rest of the group wants to get started making dinner before it gets dark. We did several miles today, and we're all tired, so I start rattling off the dream I had last night.

"Last night I dreamt I was burying a dead girl who looked just like me. Maybe she was me, just a couple years younger. Anyway, the hole was too small. I had to break her legs and arms to make her fit. It was one of those dreams that happens in real time, so for hours and hours in my sleep, I was stomping her down and snapping her limbs. But it didn't work. No matter how much I broke her, she wouldn't fit."

Every person in the circle stares at me. Lupin stares at me. The birds seem to have stopped chirping to stare at me.

"And then I woke up," I finish.

One of the girls, Fox, bursts out in muffled laughter, and the guy sitting next to her says under his breath, "Thank you, Sunshine."

"Okay!" Lupin looks around at the rest of the group. "On to dinner! I'm going to gather some kindling. Sunshine, could you help me with that?"

I guess I've messed up again. Whatever. Lupin leads me over to a grove of thin birches far enough from camp that no one will hear us, and for a while we just pick up small dry branches. Then she says,

"Thank you for sharing at the Share Circle, Sunshine. I don't want to discourage you from contributing, but I wonder if you understand that some people may have found that dream almost aggressively disturbing . . ."

She goes on and on, turning back to me every ten seconds or so to make sustained eye contact. I go out of my way to meet her gaze and nod like I'm listening, because she seems pissed. Still, all she's going to do is talk. She's the type of person where just the idea of hitting me would probably make her burst into tears, and I like that about her. But now her tone is slipping into something urgent and confidential that seems off track for one of her usual "course corrections", and as I try to actually listen, something gets through worth hearing:

". . . a lot of issues with getting your parents on the phone to voice my concerns, I don't understand why they're so hard to get a hold of."

"I thought there were no cell phones on the hike?"

"For the hikers, yes, that's non-negotiable. For counselors, we have satellite phones in case there's an emergency. And I've considered the last couple days of this hike something of an emergency for you, Sunshine. An *internal* emergency."

"You're not sending me home?"

"No, no of course not." Lupin sighs. "I'm just concerned that I can't contact your parents."

"They travel a lot," I improvise. "I don't know what time zone they're in, but it's probably not this one."

Her lips press into a line. "A lot of our parents have very demanding jobs that absorb their time and attention. I find it especially important to keep these parents in the loop as we hike, to actively remind them they're part of the healing process, and Higher Paths is the first step of a much longer journey." The skin between Lupin's warm brown eyes gathers together like someone's pulled a thread through fine fabric. "But for your parents to be so completely out of touch, when, for all they know, their daughter could've broken her leg or—" She stops herself, and forces her face into a neutral expression. "They need to be more available."

It's actually quite sweet that she's so angry at my imaginary jetsetting parents. The reality is, Aarush will only email with her, so she won't hear how young and British he is over the phone. He paid something like twice the normal fee so I could join Higher Paths halfway through their session, after I pitched him my plan the morning after Halloween. I explained traveling through the Cascades wilderness to Camp Naramauke with a bunch of people who hadn't seen the internet in two weeks was my only chance of getting there, and after he agreed, he got together the paperwork and fee money with impressive speed.

And so far, so good: this Higher Paths hike-in group started on their trail before the manhunt started, so no one here has heard of Signal Deere and Erik Doe. But they move so slowly. Every two hours there's a trust fall or relationship relay, and it's all I can do not to grab the counselors by the shoulders and yell that we're running out of time.

"Your parents said your catalyst event was falling in with a toxic friend group," Lupin continues.

Thanks, Aarush.

"And I keep hoping you'll share about that. If not in the circle, then with me, or Raven, or Quercus. I hope you know that whatever you choose to tell us will be kept in the strictest confidence." She gives me a look. "Even from your parents."

"Thank you," I say awkwardly. "This is as much kindling as I can hold. Can I take it back to the fire?"

Lupin sighs and nods, and I hurry over to the clearing, where a couple of hikers are digging a firepit in dirt as rich and moist as chocolate cake. They avoid my eyes as I walk past, but in a way I recognize from prison as fear, not disrespect, so that's fine. It saves me the trouble of learning their names.

When the last driver met me in the wilderness station ten miles outside of Ledmonton, they'd brought a printed-out map Aarush had marked with the approximate location of Naramauke. We're one day out from the point where Higher Paths' trail comes closest to camp, which is when I'll finally sneak off and go face Dr. Ledrick.

But I'll still have to find my way through five miles of wilderness first, and the trail so far has taught me this is no small matter. Even with a clear path and counselors to follow, I often feel disoriented in the deep woods, the sky barely breaking through the dense moss-covered trees, streams and other trail markers often hidden by banks of Jurassic ferns. It's hard to translate the chaotic terrain into the faint lines of the black and white map, harder still to orient myself when a newly fallen tree or swollen stream forces a detour. And if I get lost, no one will know when I left or where I've headed. Not even Aarush, because my phone—aside from not being charged—is completely out of range.

I need to find those satellite phones.

In a small clearing set back from the firepit, the other hikers are setting up their tents, laughing and pelting each other with bits of grass. It's maybe my favorite thing about Higher Paths, that everyone gets to sleep separately, so I'm able to study my maps and prepare my breakaway kit long into the night. To avoid the small talk, I chop the kindling until the others have finished, and then go set up my own tent.

All the company I need these days is in my head. I imagine Erik, a lot. I imagine what he was like on these hikes, what he would've said during Share Circles, and what corny hike name he would have given himself. I imagine him here, happy, because I cannot bear the thought of where he really is. Or what they could be doing to him. I stop before turning my back to the woods, to secure my rain canopy, a shiver going up my spine.

I'm not alone in the clearing.

I scan around me, breath rising, peering through the golden-edged moss that covers the dark tree trunks. Is it him?

Why do I feel like he can somehow always find me?

"Stupid! Stupid! Stupid!"

The voice is halfway to tears, and I know its Feather even before I step past the green and red bubbles of standing tents and see her. She's kneeling heavily beside a deflated gray tent, telescoping tent poles fisted in her hands. She should really stop trying. One is hopelessly bent, and the other has been broken cleanly in the middle. As I watch, she smacks the side of her close-cropped head and mutters, "Stupid, stupid, stupid!"

The dinner bell claps, and Feather throws the tent poles down and buries her head in her hands. It's not like she'll get in trouble. What's she so afraid of?

"What's wrong?" I ask.

She startles and looks up at me, her mouth a small "o." She pushes herself to her feet and hurries away without answering. Okay. I finish securing my rain canopy and head up after her to the firepit, where everyone's circled on damp logs to eat dinner.

I settle at the end of the emptiest log, with a steel bowl of lentils, going over how to stage my tent tomorrow night (door facing forest, sleeping bag and leave-behinds piled into a body-like silhouette in the corner), when I see our counselor, Raven, has her hands on her hips. Her usually smiling face is serious as she repeats,

"This is the *third time* her tent poles have broken! We're only halfway up the trail and out of spares, and I find it hard to believe this is a coincidence, guys!"

Feather's shoulders are hunched almost to her ears, her round face downcast, arms crossed tight like she's trying to shrink into nothingness.

"I'll see if I can cobble together something out of the spares. Feather, if that doesn't work, well, you can always join the counselor's tent—"

"You can stay with me," I tell Feather. The entire circle turns to me for the second time today. I'm not sure if they're shocked at the offer or just at the fact that I spoke at all, and I'm sure I'm the last hiker Feather wants to stay with, but I'm still way, way ahead of the counselor's tent.

"You really think she'd fit?" Fox asks innocently, and suppressed snickers vibrate through the other hikers.

"You really think you can say crap like that and I won't cut out your asshole and make you wear it like a headband?" I ask Fox.

In Naramauke this would pass as light banter, but the Higher Paths hikers react as though I've broken a bottle and waved it at her, everyone gasping and sucking in their breath as Fox cries something about verbal assault, and Raven claps as loud as she can, which is the crunchy counselor equivalent of yelling.

But Feather laughs. I smile at her across the fire.

"Sunshine!" Raven cries. "Threats of violence will not be tolerated on this hike!"

"I'm not going to hurt her, and she knows it. She's perfectly safe and having a *great* time flirting with Bear or Oak or whoever this guy is." I wave a hand at the athletic black guy next to me, whose eyebrows shoot up, "It's not my fault she can't be happy without making someone else miserable. It's not my fault she's a sick sadistic freak—"

"Okay, enough!" Raven actually yells this time, but I can't stop.

"Feather's just the easiest target. She's a keypad with three of the numbers worn down. The fact the rest of you let 'Fox' get away with it is a lot scarier than anything I've said, acting like I would actually cut out her a—"

"Sunshine!" Raven hurries through the circle and tries to pull me to my feet. I yank my arm away from her.

"Don't touch me. I'll go to the Reflection Tree or whatever."

"You are not going to the Reflection Tree!" Raven's voice shakes. "You are going to go gather kindling for our Fire Song, which you will *not* be attending tonight!"

I shrug, swallow down the rest of my lentils, and head out into the trees without protest. I go a lot further than I should, because I want to test my bearings a little. If I go far enough and wait until the stars come out, I can try and spot Cygnus, like Erik did during our night hike after the Color War, and then I'll have at least one anchor to guide me.

Part of me, the happiest part of me, keeps listening for him to step through the trees. I imagine him telling me he got away from camp, got in touch with Aarush somehow, came and found me.

Another part of me knows I will never see him again.

A twig snaps.

And then another, and my heart sinks. Definitely not him. He'd never step on two twigs.

"What." I sigh, not turning around, hoping against hope it's not Lupin.

"I just wanted to see if you needed any help?" Feather asks, her voice a little too high.

"Oh." I turn to her. "No, I'm fine. You can go back to Fire Song."

But she's already started picking up kindling. She keeps glancing back at me, as I pull out my map and examine the route I have planned.

"What're you doing?" Feather asks, voice closer than I expect, peering over my arm.

"Oh, just, um, plotting out tomorrow's hike to Big Pass."

"Didn't you hear?" She scrunches up her nose, squinting at me. "We're doing a detour to Starfoot Ranch."

"What? That's not on the itinerary."

"Raven said usually they do it on the way back, but they think the group could use some extra cohesion right now. It's, like, equine therapy and stuff. Which is cool, like, if you like horses. And I do. Do you like horses?"

"Where is this ranch?!" The white paper is a blur of pale blue in the retreating light. Feather shakes her head, she doesn't know. But of course, it's going to be West, because ranches tend to be on flat land, taking us further away from Camp Naramauke. And bringing me in range of people who have watched TV or get the newspaper.

I'll have to head out tonight. Get my pack, my water, and get going East until I recognize something.

"S-Sunshine . . ." Feather's voice comes out like someone is squeezing her throat. She tugs on my sleeve, her eyes fixed on a spot far behind us. "There's someone . . . there's someone there, staring—"

My heart leaps. I turn and peer through the darkening forest, map fluttering in my hands, until I see it: the lanky, too-tall figure watching us through the trees, through the eyeholes of a black ski mask.

"NOBODY!" I cry out, and race through the woods toward her.

Chapter Seventeen

Back to Camp

We meet in a long hug. She's real, she's here; then she pushes me away, one hand gripping my shoulder as she pulls up her mask to reveal a beautiful and furious face.

"What the hell, Signal?" Nobody says, "Why'd you ditch me on Halloween?"

"*I* ditched *you*? Javier threw me out into the street, and then the police came! And I saw you, I saw you walk Erik out to Kurt's car—"

"He asked me to walk with him. What'd you think I was doing?"

I blink at her, "I figured you wanted to go back to camp like everyone else—"

"Hell no," she sneers. "No one wanted to go back. Kurt had a nervous breakdown, and the switches were still on. Erik had me walk him out because he figured I was his best bet getting a message to you."

"What message?"

"To forget him." Nobody looks sad. "We couldn't talk much with Kurt right there. But we both thought the confession he got from Janeane would be enough. We didn't know it hadn't logged."

"You talked to Aarush?"

"Yeah. Dennis got him to talk to me, and left me the phone." She pats absently at her hip, "And it's a real shame nothing logged, because we *had her*. We thought you were all set."

"But Erik wanted me to forget him?"

"Yeah. And camp. And all of it. He said to clear your name and get on with your life."

"Yeah, well, I'm not going to do that."

"I know." She gives me a grim smile. "But he meant it. Otherwise I wouldn't be trying to help save his ass. I don't think he's a psychopath, Signal. What he did that night is just about the kindest thing he could have done."

"Or he just figured he couldn't use me anymore," I say, "since I'm not his proof."

"Proof?" She frowns. "Yeah, he said something about proof. I thought maybe I heard wrong 'cause it didn't make sense to say, not after the confession we got—"

"What? What did he say?"

"Last thing before the car drives off, he goes, 'Proof or not, at least I set her free.'"

I burst into tears.

"Well," she says, patting my back, "maybe I did hear it right."

There's a whinny not thirty feet away, and I whip around to see the long nose of a white stallion glowing through the dark trees ahead.

"What on earth?" I clutch my chest. I've never seen a horse in real life before, never understood how huge they are. The one staring at us looks like it could leap over a car easily, and there's another one behind it, black with a white star on her nose and strangely wise eyes.

"Easy, boy." Nobody shoves past me toward the clearing where they're tied, and pats his broad neck reverently. "This one's Star and the other one's Foot."

"Because you stole them from the Starfoot Ranch?"

Nobody winks at me, then, off my expression says, "Borrowed them. We'll bring them back when we get out of camp."

"I'm going alone."

She lets out an angry laugh. "Yeah, Aarush said you were trying to kill yourself again."

"I've got the prototype camera." I begin calmly. "It's set up to stream correctly now, Aarush has checked and double-checked. I'm going into camp to confront the Director. About Troy, about the kill switches, about everything. Get that journalist enough evidence to take camp down—"

"You'll be dead before you say howdy."

"What can he do? I don't have a kill switch."

"Signal." Nobody grips my shoulders and lowers her eyes to mine. *"He will kill you."*

"Even if he does, the evidence will be out."

"Or we could sneak in the back way, pass off the camera to our friends, get Erik, and get out."

I go very still. But then I shake my head.

"Why not?"

"Pass off the camera to one of 'our friends'? Is that a joke? The first one of them that sees me, it's over. They'll turn me and the camera into Dave for brownie points—" Nobody crosses her arms, and my voice rises. "You were there! When Kurt said you were all better off at camp, no one contradicted him, no one did anything to stop him—"

"What should we have done? Killed Kurt?" Nobody says coldly. "He was out of line, sure, but he's had a tough couple weeks, in case you forgot—"

"So you let him take Erik?" I say, tears spilling over. "You all just stood there and let Javier drag me away—"

"Erik *volunteered*, ma'am. Because everyone in that attic knew those kill switches weren't getting turned off. You forget what it's like having one of them in your neck? Our friends were s'posed to kill you and bring back Erik. If they didn't at least bring him back, they were as good as dead. *Our friends* risked their lives just letting Javier get you out of the house."

"Is that why Jada hunted me all the way across town?"

Nobody points a long, scarred finger in my face. "I will tell you one thing I know for certain, Signal Deere. If Jada had you in her sights and you're still standing across from me, then she let you get away."

"So I'm supposed to just assume this was all some big misunderstanding?" I shake my head. "I have *one* chance to get the Director on camera. And you want me to just hand it over to the same people who were chasing me around last week with switchblades?"

"Yes." Nobody flings her arms out in exasperation. "Yes, I do. Because you need them. You can't do it alone. No one can."

"Says the girl who hid out in the woods for thirty days."

"I wasn't alone. I've never been alone. I was just between friends. That's all you are right now. Between friends." Nobody points toward the mountain. "But they're right over that ridge, and they'll have your back if you give them the chance."

I glance up at the ridge. Then I look back through the trees to Feather.

"I have to get back."

"Well, come back when you're ready."

I nod noncommittally and turn back to the clearing.

"Who was that?" Feather asks, hurrying after me as I stride toward camp.

"My girlfriend."

"What?" Feather's face goes from terrified to delighted. "Like—like she followed you out here?"

"She's a romantic."

"That *is* romantic." Feather sighs.

"Don't tell anyone?" I cut her a look as we climb toward camp, a streamer of smoke from the firepit rising above the purpling globes of the tents.

"Of course not!" Feather says loyally. We drop the wood beside the fire before she hauls her stuff over to my tent, talking briskly the whole time, about what I don't know. I can't hear her over the knot in my stomach.

I have to leave tonight, and I could really use Nobody's help getting through the woods, but the idea of facing Javier, Jada, and the rest after Halloween is scarier than confronting the Director. The Director can only kill me; they could break my heart.

But . . . if we *did* pass off the camera, they could get tons of footage of Dr. Ledrick interacting with campers while Nobody and I sneak

Erik out. Camp would still get shut down, we'd get the Director red-handed, and the three of us could still be together.

But no, that's delusional. There's still a manhunt on for me and Erik. There always will be, now that Janeane is dead. Even if Aarush has a recording of her rant in the attic, it would make no sense to an outsider and ends with her being stabbed. There's no way we're getting a subpoena anytime soon. And why would Javier and Jada and Dennis and Kurt help me? Where do they go once camp is shut down? I have nothing to offer them, and without something to offer them I'm better off dead, apparently.

But whether I go off tonight with Nobody or on my own, I need to tell Aarush, because I'll be streaming twenty-four hours sooner than planned. Which means I need to find those satellite phones.

"What you said about me being a safe target," Feather says, huddled up in the corner of my tent, "I just don't get it. I try so hard to be nice and likable—"

"Don't." I tell her sharply. "If you're really nice, you don't have to *act* like it. In fact, you're better off acting *not* nice every so often, just to throw people like Fox off."

She blinks at me, alarmed.

"You're going to be late to Fire Song." I sigh.

Once she's left, I creep out of the tent and peer across the campsite, the difference between the trees and air and people blurring as the sky darkens, red fire throwing everything around it in sharp relief but casting everything past it in deeper shadow. Including the counselor's tent.

I have the prototype camera and Jaw's key on my bra strap, and the map is in my back pocket in case I need to run. I put on my heaviest jacket, pull a wool cap low on my forehead, and sling my canteen around my shoulder. Then I slide carefully down the small incline into the ravine that rings the campsite. If I keep low and step quietly, I might be able to circle all the way around to the back entrance of the counselor's tent without them seeing me.

"Ooh Lo-ord, koom-bay-yaaaah!" Raven ends the first song, and the hikers snap in applause as Quercus strikes up his banjo, nodding

for everyone to join him in singing "Someone's in the Kitchen With Dinah." Their voices ring though the trees, putting any roosting birds to flight and masking my footsteps as I scramble along the ravine and around to the back entrance of the counselors' five-person tent.

And there they are, all the way across from me, by the front flap: three thick satellite phones hooked into a cube-shaped, solar-powered generator on a low, metal fold-out table. I thread through the cots and hanging LED lanterns, I'm right over the table when Lupin walks in the front entrance of the tent, bathroom kit in one hand, her locs wrapped up in a scarf.

"Sunshine!" Lupin cries, "What are you doing in here?"

"I was, uh . . ." *Think fast, ho, think fast.* "I wanted to talk to you."

Lupin moves to a cot with a mandala blanket near one of the net windows, tucks her bathroom kit below its frame, and sits. She folds her hands, bangles clinking; takes a deep breath with her eyes closed; and then smiles at me.

"Well, here I am. What did you want to tell me?"

"I, um, . . ." *Come on, come on, come on! What was she going on about in the birch grove before?* "I wanted to talk about my friends from home, I guess?"

"I am very glad to hear that," Lupin says sincerely, gesturing for me to sit on the cot across from her. I perch on its edge, miserably, mind racing. She's doing her freakishly sustained eye contact again, which I can't maintain as I try to concoct some story. Then, as though sensing my discomfort, she plucks a wooden puzzle from under her cot and hands it to me without comment. I stare down at three circles and a long piece of yellow string, interlinked.

"Well. My 'toxic friend group,' um, kind of pushed me out of the group anyway, so. I don't think it should really be an issue anymore. You can tell my parents when they call. I'm out of the club or whatever. So. They don't have to be worried."

"Do you mean like a *gang* or—"

"Oh no. Nothing like that. We're just people who like hanging out together, I guess. Or did." I shift around the wooden rings, trying to wrestle them apart, "We were all kind of the bad kids at our different schools, but when we were together, that kind of got canceled out. So we were just ourselves. Or something."

"And this is your primary friend group?"

"They're my only friends. I don't . . . I'm not good at making friends."

"I've noticed," she says quietly. "But that seems to be very much a choice, Sunshine. You have lots of walls up."

"Fair enough." The rings are hopelessly tangled. "But it wasn't like that with them. It was easy. Until . . ."

I remember Erik's voice: *"I'll go."*

"Until I got dumped. In front of everyone. And this other guy I sort of dated for a while, he told me no one wanted me around anymore . . ." The wood rings knock against each other. The harder I pull, the worse it gets. "So it turns out none of them thought of me the way I thought of them. As, like, an actual friend, so . . ." I give her a wide-eyed smile. "Now I know."

"Things can get complicated when you date multiple people in a friend group. It can shift loyalties in ways you don't expect—in ways the group doesn't expect either. Before, it was your group versus the world," Lupin says, "Now it's not that easy. So you're retreating."

"I'm not *retreating*. I'm not doing anything!" It comes out too loud. "*They* made it clear they don't want me around!"

"I spend a lot of time in groups, leading these hikes, Sunshine. Each group has its own unique energy, but generally, when something is off in the group, I find it's time for one-on-ones. Did you try connecting with your friends, one-on-one, and telling them how you felt? That you were hurt?"

I shake my head. "They were there. They know."

"So, this rejection was not a cumulative distancing over time, but sort of one big event."

I nod.

"And you're relying on your ex-boyfriend's reading of it, when his feelings about wanting you around have to be very complicated?"

I nod again.

"Well. It's possible to outgrow a group, and sometimes that's for the best. But it's also possible to misread a situation. I understand you want to protect yourself by pulling away. But you could be interpreting what happened as being much more final and black-and-white than it was. What you assume to protect yourself from being hurt could be much more hurtful than what you're protecting yourself from."

Push, push, push.

"Did any of your friends reach out to you after the breakup?" Lupin asks.

"Yeah"—my voice breaks—"my best friend. She wants me to go see them again. But I don't see the point."

"You're rejecting them before they can reject you again."

"No, I just know when I'm not wanted."

"Do you *know*, or does it just feel familiar?"

The puzzle drops to the soft tent floor, and I cover my face with my hands.

Lupin sighs. "Well, I don't know what your parents' objections are to this group, but if these are real friends, then you should be able to share these feelings on an individual level, and they will support you when the group comes together again. And if they don't, then you can walk away, to find people who *will*."

"That sounds nice, but it's really not that simple."

"It really *is* though, Sunshine," Lupin says knowingly. "It *really* is. I know that at your age, fitting in with your 'group' feels like life or death, but one day you'll look back on how dramatic this all felt and just laugh."

I almost laugh now, but I'm crying too hard for the sound to come out. Lupin moves over to the cot beside me and gives me a long hug. She smells like cocoa butter and apple cider vinegar.

"Can I have a minute?" I ask her. "To kind of get it together before I go outside again?"

"Of course." Lupin gets up, ducking under the flap and slipping on her Birkenstocks at the entrance. "I'll be at Fire Song if you need me."

Once her footsteps have retreated into the dark, I pick up the satellite phone and dial Aarush. It takes me a few times before I figure out there's a code to connect to the satellite first, on a sticker on the side of the generator, but at last it goes through, and he picks up.

"It's 'Sunshine,'" I whisper. "I can't talk long, but I'm going to start out for camp tonight."

"I reckon Nobody caught up with you, then," he says. "What do you think of her plan?"

"I think . . ." I squeeze my eyes closed. "I think it's worth a shot."

"Well, it's your neck. You can stick it out for whoever you like. I've already set an alert for the stream. As soon as it starts, it will record."

"Could you share it with the 'Fear No Deere' people live? Or the people on the boards or something? Just in case . . ."

"I understand your reticence, but I promise you, I fixed the bug."

"Just in case, though." I think of the sign on my mom's trailer door. "So I know someone sees it if I don't come out."

There's a long pause on his end. "Very well. I'll put it on the boards and post mirror links for any site that wants to watch along."

"Thank you, Aarush." I sigh with relief, when I hear steps at the mouth of the tent and look up to see Fox's angry smile.

"Lupin!" Fox yells. *"Sunshine's on the phone!"*

I knock her backward onto the cot, then kick the middle leg from under it so the cot collapses, and sprint out through the flap. The banjo cuts off with a sour twang as the entire fire circle looks up at me, open-mouthed. I hurry past them, Quercus on his feet and Raven screaming: *"Sunshine! Get back to your tent!"*

And as though on cue, Fox's red tent goes sailing past me, unmoored from its pegs and rolling like a half-deflated beach ball, the wind sweeping it straight into the fire. There's a rush of flames along its side as it continues merrily into the trees, and Quercus and Raven scurry after it. Fox, who's just managed to stagger out of the counselor's tent, starts shrieking as more unpegged tents sail toward the group. I look over at the clearing as I run past, and see Feather racing from tent to tent, pulling out the pegs, and I almost laugh out loud at the grin on her face. She waves to me and I wave back before sliding down the ravine and sprinting for where Nobody is waiting.

* * *

"Finally." Nobody hops up from a small fire dug between the trees. There's something on a forked branch in her hand, which I fear is a squirrel skeleton.

"We should go. Now."

She stomps the fire out and throws the blankets off the dozing horses tied to a nearby stump, without another question.

"I've never ridden a horse before," I warn her.

"Oh, I figured," she says, one eyebrow up. "You can take Foot—she's a sweet one. Up we go."

She boosts me up, and I throw myself into the saddle like I'm going over the top of a chain link fence. She gives me directions on steering that are immediately useless: Foot can sense my inexperience the same way I can sense her disdain, but she's happy to follow after the white stallion, which Nobody commands effortlessly, a headlamp on her forehead carving a trail through the trees ahead.

* * *

The horses carefully pick their way through the dark. I'm sure any moment I'll hear Raven shrieking through the woods, or chasing footsteps, but the only sounds are nightbirds above and the steady feet of the horses below. I mostly try not to annoy Foot and keep warm. After about two hours, we come to the top of a ridge, and Nobody stops and raises one long arm.

"See?

Through a far break in the trees, the windows of an apartment building stare back at me.

"The obstacle course." I shiver seeing it again, though part of me is a little relieved it wasn't all some dream.

"Let's give the horses a break and get some sleep," Nobody says. "We'll get over there at dawn, when they're running drills."

I don't think I'll be able to sleep, but I nod off almost instantly when first watch is done, and wake to Nobody gently shaking my shoulder. She gives me a pack of peanut butter crackers, left over from our Quik Stop breakfast, and I make her drink half my canteen before she helps me into my saddle again. Up and down my legs, muscles I didn't know I had scream in protest, but my adrenaline overrides them, and as we start off on the trail again, I feel strangely electric knowing how close we are to camp.

The closer we get, the more intense the feeling grows. My knuckles around the reins are white, my teeth clenched as we pass through the grove of birches where Jada and I buried my mannequin. Here Nobody descends from Star and helps me down. We find a clear rivulet and tie the horses close enough that they can drink, before continuing on foot to the thin band of trees between us and the obstacle course.

I pluck Aarush's camera from my buttonhole and try to turn it on, but my hands shake so hard, it falls into the leaves at our feet.

"Here." Nobody retrieves it, turns it on, hands it back to me. "Lights. Camera. Action."

I stare it in its beady lens.

"I am Signal Deere," I say, just a little louder than the morning birds overhead. "If anyone is watching, thank you so much. Please stay with me, and please tell your friends to watch this stream. We need witnesses. I am just outside Camp Naramauke"—I turn the camera around to scan the woods—"in the Cascade region of the Pacific Northwest. It's a camp where teenage Class As are being trained to kill people."

"I think your face was probably upside down, the way you did that," Nobody points out, pulling her ski mask under her chin.

"Whoops," I say, turning the camera right-side up before threading it in my buttonhole. "Alright, let's go."

The obstacle course is audible long before we can see it through the trees. The clanging steps down the fire escape at the back of the apartment facade, the shiver of chain link at the start, the creak of ropes in between—it all grinds along so much louder than I remember, and all at once. And there's no laughter, no whoops, no angry yells from Dave.

Nobody and I get as close as we dare, peering through the leaves, and watch twenty teenagers we've never seen before make their way through the obstacle course at breakneck speed. They're all in white T-shirts and black sweatpants, and as soon as they get off the fire escape at the end, they sprint to the start again. Having collapsed with exhaustion from going through the obstacle course twice, this seems almost superhuman to me.

As I watch, a girl about my height falls from the climbing ropes and hits the mud with a sound that makes me queasy. The other campers keep moving, closing to fill the space she left, without looking down. I expect Dave to come help, or at least yell at her to get up, but as I scan the field, I realize there're no counselors up here.

They're running the drill on their own?

"They're not here," Nobody says, jerking her head away like she can't stand to watch anymore. "Cabins. Let's go."

I angle the camera to catch what's happening on the obstacle course for a beat longer, then follow her through the woods that ring the field, sprinting through the forgotten playground and threading through the pines, keeping the lake just in sight to orient ourselves as we make our way to the cabins.

Nobody signals for me to go to the girls' cabin, the first place we lived when we came to camp, and she moves toward a further one. Between them is the burnt foundation of the boys' cabin. You'd never guess a cabin once stood there that smelled like gardenia soap inside. A cabin where Javier slipped me a drawing under my pillow, where I asked Erik to help me get the clippings from the pantry, where Nobody killed Dog Mask. It's just blasted cement now.

With a lump in my throat, I scan the field, then sprint across the open grass until I can press my back against the rough planks between the windows at the far side of the girls' cabin. As I catch my breath, I hear a voice I recognize instantly:

"You have to take them."

Kate. I detach my camera and raise it over the windowsill, hoping it catches something, anything.

"No." Jada's voice breaks, and the lump in my throat rises. "Erik said they'll mess us up."

"If you're taking orders from Erik," Kate says, "then maybe you'd like to join him?"

Join him? Join him where? I turn and rise high enough to peer through the torn screen that drifts from the window. Jada is on the bottom bunk in the corner, curled up like it would hurt to straighten out. New bruises warp her face. Kate kneels beside her, first aid supplies piled on the bed between them, a gloved hand extended.

"Can't you just tell me what they are first?" Jada asks in a small voice.

"They're what all the other campers are taking, Jada. He's going to be back soon, and if you haven't taken them yet, I don't know how I'm going to—"

A heavy hand jerks me backward, spins me around, cold fingers clamping over my mouth.

Dave stares down at me.

Chapter Eighteen

Seeing Things

For a moment, Dave looks almost as shocked as I am, going pale behind his tan, his lips tightening over his too-white teeth. Then, hand still clamped over my mouth, he practically lifts me off my feet, hauling me toward the main cabin. I kick at him, claw at him as he hauls me effortlessly under the covered porch, through the kitchen, and into the dusty air of the pantry. There he pushes me up against a shelf.

"Easy!" he hisses. "Easy, alright? *I'm on your side.* Now if you'll just calm down already, we can have a little chat. Can you calm down, Signal?"

I nod, and his shoulders drop. Then I bring up my knee and get him in the groin as hard as I can. But apparently not hard enough; he recovers almost instantly and palms my head into the shelf behind me so hard the pain rings through my teeth. His hand stays wrapped around my face, one fingertip digging into my eye with just a fraction less pressure than it would take to pop it open.

"Stop. Wasting. Time," Dave says. "I have maybe five minutes before he comes looking for me. And then he'll find you too. Why are you here, Signal?"

He moves his hand enough that I can talk.

"I came to take this place down," I gasp.

He laughs, stepping back from me.

"Alright. How can I help?"

"Why would you help me?" I knead my eye, black snow swimming before my vision.

"We want the same thing. To nail the bitch that killed my daughter."

"I'm surprised you haven't heard, but Kurt killed Janeane."

"I'm surprised *you* haven't heard, Signal." Dave reaches past me, to the shelf behind my head, and pulls out a newspaper, pushing it toward me. "Go on. See for yourself."

Warily, I unfold the front page. Janeane's grim face glares up at me from beside three-inch-tall letters spelling out the headline:

"GIRL FROM HELL CAN'T FINISH ME!"

And smaller: *"Viral Teens Leave Mother Clinging to Life."*

"Janeane's still alive?" I say after a beat.

"And thriving," Dave says grimly. "She held a press conference while she was still in her hospital bed. Claiming you and Erik killed Mike and left her for dead."

"What? We didn't! *She* killed Mike and—"

"I don't care who didn't kill her." Dave cuts me off. "I just want the job done."

"*Don't.* Please. I want her tried and convicted for what she did to Rose. Don't you?"

Dave looks at me, some calculation going on behind his eyes. "How?"

The prototype camera is still in my fist. I place it gently on the shelf just behind my hand as I talk, afraid if he recognizes what it is, he'll take it from me.

"That's why I'm here. To gather evidence of camp to give to a journalist," I tell him. "Files and other hard proof this place exists and that Janeane was a part of it, and she used her training to frame me for Rose's murder. I'm going to take it all public and get camp shut down."

"You'll find what you need in the Nurse's Office." He reaches over my head and coolly pockets a couple water bottles. "Kate's footlocker, by the generator. Code to the combination lock is M-U-T-T." He plucks a travel first aid kit and a couple Clif Bars from the shelf behind me. "But you'll never get it out of here without an airtight extraction plan"—he waves a Clif Bar in my face—"and the way you were goofing off out there, I seriously doubt you have one."

He turns to go; I grab his arm.

"Where's Erik?"

"No." Dave shakes his head, "Forget it. *I* couldn't make it out of here with Erik at this point."

He goes for the door, but I get in front of it, blocking his path, bracing myself to try and knee him again if I have to. "Tell me where Erik is, Dave."

Dave looks at me a long moment, almost with pity. "Were you at camp long enough to visit the cellar?"

I shake my head.

"It's across camp, up past the Arts and Crafts table. There's a traffic cone on the doors so people don't trip over the handles sticking out of the ground. If he's still alive, he's in there." He pushes easily past me to the door, then digs around in his jacket pocket until he pulls out his kill switch fob, the one that used to hold the power of life and death over my head. He tosses it to me.

"Those new kids come at you, don't hesitate," he says. "Line it up with their neck and press the button hard. It only does one at a time, so if they rush you, click fast."

"Where are *you* going?"

"The hell out of here." He cracks the door, peers down the hall.

"Wait. Dave."

It takes him a moment to hear me. He's already thinking far past this moment, to the next leg of his plan. And I'm almost afraid to ask, but I have to know.

"Janeane said I wasn't a Class A . . . that she told you to fake my score."

No reaction registers on his face.

"Well? Am I? Am I a Class A?"

"Of course not, Signal," he says. "I thought you'd killed my daughter. So yes, I took some liberties with your Wylie-Stanton report." He opens the door again, scans, then nods to me. "But I always respected how hard you tried to keep up."

And like that, he's gone.

I shut the door after him, then lean against it, mouth dry. I was so sure Janeane was lying. Because if I'm not a Class A . . . what even am I?

If I hadn't been a Class A, I could have appealed my sentence once the cloud of grief and medication had cleared. Maybe I wouldn't ever have gone to prison at all. I could be home and safe, and *graduating* soon. I would never have *heard* of this place!

"And me?" Rose's voice says in my head.

The smell of blood rises in the back of my throat. That is where my life split, where normal stopped and the nightmare began: losing her. I might have been able to maneuver my way out of prison, but I would have been seen as guilty all the same, and over time I might have convinced myself I was capable of such a thing . . . just like I started to at camp. Because I never, ever would have suspected Janeane. Not without Erik pushing me back into my memories, not without him finding the proof in Jaw's room.

Proof. I'm not his proof.

I picture Erik in his kitchen, the rosy morning light turning his green eyes to sea glass when he said I proved there was good in him. And then the blankness of his face when Janeane said it was a lie. What he'd told Nobody made me hope he still believes in me. But if he does, he's wrong. I don't prove anything about him. I'm not the angel only he can see. I'm not his better nature or higher self. I'm just a weirdo with terrible luck.

Well. Maybe that will change things for him, but it doesn't change anything for me. He's my Erik, and he needs help, and that's why I'm here. Weirdoes can be heroes.

I hope.

I take the camera from the shelf, stick it back in my buttonhole. I scan the room for something I can defend myself with that will not present immediately as a weapon, and grab an old mop handle from the corner.

I crack the door, scan the hall, then pad softly toward the Nurse's Office, hearing the clatter of keys rise and fall as I approach. My foot hits a squeaky board, and Dennis calls:

"Kate?"

I move into the doorway, and his eyebrows go all the way up.

"What are you doing here?" he says in his usual monotone, but his hands slip from the keys and clutch his chair's armrests.

I point to the camera in my buttonhole. "Getting some evidence to close this place down."

He leans back, scans out the window, then waves me over. "Feel free to catch some of the coding I'm doing currently, then," and he fans a hand toward his screen.

"Hacking pacemakers?" I angle the camera on his screen.

"No, hacking small aircraft engines, turning them off in midair. A refresher course." Then, his voice neutral, "Why did you run away on Halloween?"

"I thought I had to."

"You didn't." He looks hard at me over his scratched lenses. "And then you ran from me and Jada when we came to get you."

"Because I knew you wanted to go back to camp."

"Oh, right. How could I give up all of this?" He waves at the stripped-bare cell he's in, with such a dry expression I almost laugh. "No, Signal. We drove out to bring you your phone. So that you and Aarush could keep trying. And you ran away." He frowns. "Like you were scared of us."

I think of Jada in the streetlight, her hand extended toward me. The gesture had rattled me so much, I hadn't noticed if she was holding something.

"You told me you guys couldn't go back without killing me."

"Before we drove out, I called the Director and told him you'd gotten away, but we had Erik. And trust me, that was not a fun phone call to make." Dennis looks at me steadily. "Even as a Class A, with a low capacity for fear, I was terrified, Signal. But I made that call when we still could have caught up with you."

“Thank you,” I say honestly, then add, “What did the Director say about me . . . getting loose?”

“He said if we brought Erik back, Janeane could take care of you. He didn’t know she’d been stabbed at the time.” He adjusts his glasses. “Jada convinced him to let her go off her route to find you. She told him she would kill you, but she wanted to get you the trac phone. But you turned your back on us. And when we returned without you, she paid the price.”

I think of her bruised face and want to puke.

“Why did they put Erik in the cellar?”

He looks away then. “They’re testing something new on him.”

“Testing what?”

“Something like the pills, I think. I don’t know.” Dennis frowns. “They don’t give me anything. Kate says they need my head clear. I just code in here all day.”

“SIGNAL!” Kate’s voice booms. I turn to see her round face in the doorway, eyes blown open with shock. Then Nobody’s burnt hand closes over her mouth, and they tumble forward into the room. I hop over their thrashing legs and slam the door shut, bolt it, then help Nobody bundle Kate into a chair. Nobody only has three zip ties, so we use a long spare ethernet cable to finish trussing her up in the heavy office chair, gagging her with her own cheerful red bandanna. Her cat eyeglasses are badly askew as she glares from me to Nobody, to Dennis.

“You seen Dave?” Nobody asks me.

“Yeah, he left.”

“What?”

“Left camp. Like, he’s *out.* He’s done. Look.” I hold up his fob and feel Kate react.

Dennis leaps from his chair and darts down the hall.

“Where is he going?” Nobody steps out into the hall just as he comes running back. The laptop in his hands must be Kate’s, because she immediately starts bouncing around in the chair, hard enough I put the mop handle against her temple, like her head’s the T-ball and her neck is the stand.

"Calm. Down," I tell her. "Nobody, get her fob."

"Already ahead of you," Nobody says, holding it up.

"I'm DM-ing Aarush," Dennis' fingers are flying over the keyboard. "He says the stream is up, and recording, but so far there's no real handle on what the camp is *doing*, and we need more hard evidence . . ."

"Dennis, you work on disabling the kill switches." I move toward the footlocker in the corner. "I got this under control."

Kate's heavy metal chair actually hops across the room toward me. Nobody takes the mop handle then, and Kate stops moving, but her face is so distressed Nobody and I exchange a look, and Nobody loosens the gag a bit.

"If you disable the kill switches," Kate gasps, "we won't be able to stop the new recruits. This camp will be a blood bath!"

"Why?" I turn the camera on her. "What's going on with the new recruits? What have you been giving them?"

Kate glares at me.

"You can help us, Kate. Don't you want to help? Don't you want people to see you helping?"

"Five hundred thousand people," Dennis adds, "to be exact."

"What?"

Dennis toggles between a streaming site with jittery footage of the room we're in, and a screen of code, his tapping accelerating.

"Excuse me. Seven hundred and fifty thousand people currently watching. Seven hundred and ninety, now—"

Kate ducks her head, trying to hide her face.

"Nobody," I say, "Go to the footlocker by the generator on the floor. The combination is M-U-T-T—"

"It's an experimental drug." Kate gasps, chin still tucked, "I don't know what's in it. It heightens focus, suppresses inhibitions, and increases aggression. We were told it was reconfigured Adderall, but the side effects seem inconsistent with that framing."

"What side effects?"

Kate keeps her head bowed and stays silent.

Nobody takes the footlocker of files and spills them onto the ground, and I see a manila file with "R&D" on the tab. I fall on my knees, spread the papers out, and run the camera across them. The name of the pharmaceutical company has been thoroughly redacted, but there might be something here that could link it to someone.

"Dennis, is this reading on camera? Or is it all just a blur?"

Dennis taps wildly then answers, "Someone on the board is making stills and posting them . . . they said do another scan, but slower." I move the camera carefully over the papers again, as steadily as I can, gripping my wrist with my other hand to keep it from shaking.

"Aarush's coding team wants to help with disabling the kill switches." Dennis' voice is approaching excited. "That will make things go a lot faster—"

"Did you not hear me?" Kate shrieks. "You set the new kids loose, no one is getting out of here! Why do you think Dave gave you the fob, Signal? To protect you!"

Ignoring her, I open a file marked "TRIALS." Photos of two teenagers that I don't recognize, in orange T-shirts, are clipped to a piece of paper marked "AUTOPSY."

"You've *lost campers*?" I look up at Kate, holding up the photos. "These pills are killing people"—she turns her head away again—*"and you gave them to Jada?"*

Nobody pulls me away from Kate before I realize I'm clutching her collar. I turn the camera on the photos, scanning the faces of the two teenagers as slowly as I can, eyes hot and itchy.

"Gray Johnson, sixteen. Maite Gomez, seventeen," I whisper to the camera. "Pronounced dead at Naramauke, three days ago, because of the pills they were forced to take, pills provided to camp by an unnamed pharmaceutical company."

I scrounge through the files, almost afraid of what I'll see next. "What about Erik?" I ask Kate. "What are you giving him?"

Kate mutters something, but her chin is still tucked to her chest.

"What have you been giving him?"

"I don't know!" Kate cries. "I don't get paperwork on Erik anymore!"

Nobody's hand lands on my arm. "Go check on Jada. I'll keep things under control in here."

"Tell her we'll have her kill switch off in thirty minutes!" Dennis yells after me as I throw myself down the hall and into the pink light of sunrise blooming across the lake.

* * *

When I open the back door into the girls' cabin, the shriek of its hinges sends footsteps flying across the floor and up a bunk ladder across the room, so fast. Too fast.

"Jada?" My voice echoes in the bathroom, my hand on the door, "It's Skipper. Me and Nobody are here to help. Jada? You hear me?"

I pull the door back, my heart in my throat.

"Jada?" I call. "Jada, answer me."

There's a low groan from the far corner of the cabin. I walk through row after row of bunk beds crammed into the space. There was one bunkbed in each corner when I was here. Now there are four bunkbeds lined up in a row on either side, bunks ratcheted so they each fit three mattresses instead of two.

I scan through the hanging towels and sweatshirts until I see her, on the top bunk in the far-left corner, huddled with her face against the wall, her medical gown falling open to reveal a back scattered with bruises, curly hair trembling.

"Jada . . .?" I climb up the bunk toward her. I put my hand on her back, and she turns to me, eyes slightly glazed.

"You're really here?" she says. After I nod, she asks, "So is he here too?"

"Who?"

She looks down at the aisle between the crammed-in bunkbeds in the center of the cabin, tracking some point in the air back and forth like she's watching a pacing ghost.

"Him," she whispers, "Don't you see him? My stepbrother. He came back. I don't know how, but he came back. All the pieces."

"Look at me." I cup her face in my hands, trying to avoid the tender bruise that's swollen her cheek and eye. "I'm here Jada. He is not. You took those pills, right? The ones Kate had?"

She nods, still watching the ghost below us.

"What you're seeing is a side effect from the pills Kate gave you."

She shakes her head, eyes tearing. "No, no, no . . ."

"That's why I walked right by him. Because he is not here, he's just in your head. But I'm real, and so is Nobody, and we're getting you guys out."

Her fingers dig into my arm like little hooks, breath shaking in my ear as she whispers, *"He can hear you."*

"Okay," I say gently. "Okay. Come on. Let's get out of here, Jada. Straight through that front door, alright? We'll move fast, and I'll get you to the main cabin with Dennis and Nobody—"

I'm cut off by the high screech of the door flying open, and two lines of five girls race inside the bunkhouse.

"Jada!" One of them yells, pulling back a comforter.

"Where is that sneaky little rat?"

"Jaaaada! Oh Jaaaada! We get to play with you some more!" one of them yells. We hear them throwing blankets to the floor, sweeping bottles off a windowsill. Jada curls into me, hiding her face against my neck.

"*They're* real?" she whispers.

"Yes."

There's a creak from just below us as someone climbs up the bunk, then a ropy forearm and a hand with nails bitten down to the quick clutches at the mattress for leverage, and a head pops up just beside us. A freckled girl with hugely dilated eyes stares back at me.

"Found her!" the freckled girl yells, her mouth twitching into a toothy grin. "And who is *this*?"

I pull the fob from my pocket, and her smile disappears.

"Drag her down here!" another girl calls from below. But the freckled girl doesn't so much as blink, doesn't move her dilated eyes from the fob.

"I don't want to hurt you," I say slowly. "I just want to leave the cabin with my friend. Can you help us with that?"

The freckled girl turns and shouts for the others to back away, and they fall silent, sensing from her tone something is very wrong. The air crackles as I move into view and start down the ladder, the fob extended so they can all see.

"I don't want to hurt anyone," I announce, trying to keep my voice calm. "Just let us through, and then we'll all be out of here soon."

There's no sound but breath. As I pass by the girls, their body heat seems almost unnaturally high. They all stare at me, not blinking.

"Come on down," I call to Jada, my eyes flitting around the group fanned out in front of me, not wanting to miss the flinch or spasm that will tell me they're about to pounce.

A few sharp creaks, and then Jada lands behind me, huddling against me. Once her arm is through mine, we start backing toward the door, me lining up my fob with any person who so much as blinks. It's an empty threat. There is nothing they can do that will make me press the button. But I can't let them know that.

"Thank you," I tell them, as we edge closer to the door. "It's going to be okay. We're all getting out of here. Just"—the eyes staring back at me are so hollow—"just don't take any more pills, okay?"

Someone in the back bursts into laughter as the hinges of the front door screech open and we back onto the porch. The moment the door falls closed, we turn to sprint down the steps to the field, but stop short. Jada's sob catches in her throat so hard she chokes on it. If she asks if this is real, I won't know what to say.

Because standing right in front of the cabin are ten more new recruits, fresh from the obstacle course.

And in front of them is the Director.

Chapter Nineteen

The New Recruits

"Signal Deere," the Director says, his face expressionless.

"Dr. Ledrick."

His head moves just the slightest fraction, whether because I used his real name or because I've got Dave's kill switch fob, I don't know. When he turns to the boys behind him, I swiftly reach up and make sure my camera is angled to catch him, my flannel well out of its way.

"What are you doing back at camp, Signal?" Dr. Ledrick asks, swinging his arm so the fob tethered to his wrist lands in his hand.

"I came here to talk to you, Dr. Ledrick, about the testing you're doing on your teenage inmates. And the murder of Mr. and Mrs. Wylie-Stanton. And how you started this camp in the first place."

He stares at me, stony-faced.

"Because you did start this camp, didn't you? What do teens come here to learn, Dr. Ledrick?"

He smiles, an entirely muscular exercise. No spark of human emotion animates the flat pink face as it twists to bare his teeth.

"Drop that fob, and I'll tell you."

"I'm sure."

"I could kill her right now," he says, nodding toward Jada. She shrinks beside me.

"And I could take out all your new recruits." I wave my hand around, hoping the motion hides its fluttering. "Or we can go somewhere else and talk, just the two of us?" He'll try to kill me once we're alone, of course, but I need to buy Dennis time. Or none of us gets out alive.

For a long moment Dr. Ledrick stares at me, considering. The sky has gone from pink to white behind him, the rising sun sending silver ripples across the lake.

"I don't want to have to hurt anyone," I say in my hardest voice.

"I know," he says.

And he points the fob straight at Jada and clicks.

A shriek tears from the bottom of my heart as Jada cringes back, her eyes squeezing closed. I wrap my arms around her, screaming incoherently. But her heart beats under my arm, her dark eyes open. They're dilated, but clear; no broken blood vessels.

"I'm alive?" she asks me.

"You're alive!" I clutch her shoulders, "Dennis did it! He turned off the kill switches!"

Jada bursts into sobs as she falls against me. I have to struggle to keep her from collapsing to the ground, and a hissing sound fills the air, the shift of bodies in grass as the crowd of young men around Dr. Ledrick move out of formation. One of the guys in back, the tallest, steps out of line and I realize it's Javier. Javier, with a new crew cut and his hands in tight fists, strides toward Dr. Ledrick. Scattered whistles and whoops break out as Javier marches right up to the Director, who is clicking his fob wildly, pointing it straight at his neck right up until Javier knocks it out of his hands. It bounces harmlessly into the deep, dewy grass.

But Javier doesn't throw the first punch. It's another kid who kicks the Director's legs out from under him, but I see Javier's arm go back and his eyes go dark, and I sprint through the grass and grab his elbow.

"Javier, no!"

He turns on me, teeth bared, his scarred fist twitching, his eyes so empty. But when I flinch, he blinks, his eyes connect with mine, and before I can jerk away, he's pulled me against him and he's kissing me, bending me backward with the force of it. The intensity that would have dealt a killing blow to the Director is channeled instead into a rageful passion completely unlike the few kisses we shared before. It's a kiss that's half hatred, but whether he hates me or hates himself, I don't know.

I'm pushing away the whole time, and break it off as soon as I can, shaking my head angrily, when blood spatters across his shirt from the ground below and we both turn back to the crowd roiling around the Director, muffled shrieks rising from the grass.

Jada stands just above him, hands in fists, leg recoiling from a kick.

"That was for *Troy*!" she yells.

"Jada, no! Come on, honey, let's go find the others—" I try to pull her away and Javier has to help. He lifts her up and, throwing her over his shoulder in a fireman carry, sweeps her away.

"Where?" he gasps, not looking in my eyes.

"Nobody and Dennis are in the main cabin."

SCREEEECH!

The door to the girls' cabin flies open, and the new recruit girls come streaming out, filling the porch and looking down on the field with expressionless faces.

"Who you got?" the freckled one calls to the boys in the field. They don't answer her, they're so intent on the howling Director at their feet.

I start to call up to her that the switches are off, but Javier grabs my shoulder so hard it hurts, the muscles standing out in his arm, his hugely dilated eyes locking onto mine with mesmerizing force.

"Don't."

It's too late, the freckled girl has seen us. Her eyes are strangely cat-like, jumping between us and the knot of boys stomping the Director, like she can't decide where to pounce first. Javier steps closer to me, glaring at her.

Then another arc of blood spatter makes her head jerk back toward the grass, and the Director lets out a strangled moan.

"Help!" he howls. "Someone help!"

"Here we come!" The freckled girl laughs, and the girls pour down the steps toward the melee in the field.

"Let's go." Javier pulls me away. "Now! Come on!"

I nod and run after him, watching Jada hang almost lifelessly over his shoulder, all the way across the glowing green field, around the side of the cabin, and under the covered porch, where Javier gently sets Jada down on a picnic bench and kneels in front of her, scanning her face.

"You took the pills?" he says, voice ragged.

"I had to, okay? What do you care?" She won't look at him. "It's done now, so whatever."

"You could've died!" Javier grips her arms; I don't think he realizes how hard. "How do you feel? Have you seen things?"

Jada's head falls forward. Then she covers her face and starts crying into her hands.

"She has," I answer for her. "Why, is that bad?"

But before he can respond, Nobody comes running out through the dark door of the kitchen, Dennis right behind her.

"Dennis did it. The switches are all off!" she announces.

Javier turns to Dennis. "She's seeing things."

Dennis staggers back. "For how long?"

"What does it mean?!" I cry, looking between them. "What does it mean that she's seeing things?"

"The last two kids who started seeing things went to the Nurse's Office and never came back." Javier says.

My chest tightens, and Nobody and I look at each other, picturing the photos clipped to the autopsy reports.

"How long do we have?" I ask.

"Hours," Dennis says quietly.

"Maybe there's a radio or something?" I start, throat tightening, "Or maybe Aarush could send somebody?"

"Or one of our two million viewers?" Dennis reaches out and grabs my shoulders, leaning into the camera wedged in my shirt, putting on an almost-comical newscaster affect in his effort to be clear. "Can someone in the viewing audience alert emergency services that we need a medical evacuation? I'll write out the coordinates—"

He turns and runs back into the main cabin. Nobody gets a water bottle for Jada, hissing at the sight of her bruises.

"If you can watch her," I tell Nobody, "I need to go up by Arts and Crafts."

"No. No, you don't." Javier says, on his feet with uncanny speed. "You can't go near the new recruits. They'll take you down."

"I have to get to the cellar."

"There's no point." Javier shouts, "Erik is not here."

"What?"

"Kurt and Erik were sent out on a special assignment by the Director. Kurt packed up his bunk last night. They're supposed to leave today. That's what they've been getting Erik all geeked up for."

The vertigo comes in a rush, like when the tide pulls the sand out from under your feet, cold and sick and dizzy.

"Did you see Erik pack up? Or just Kurt?" Nobody asks.

"Erik was never in the cabin. They haven't let him out of the cellar since he got here."

"So you don't know if they actually went," Nobody points out.

"Look, I'm trying to help you." He looks to me, then says, "Kurt took me down there to visit him, after they started shooting him up. You don't want to be around him like this."

I shake my head. "Enough. I'm going—"

But Jada's hand flashes out, catches my arm.

"He's trying to help you, Skipper. You don't know what these pills are like. And Erik's on more than pills." Jada peers up at me through her hair, face glistening with sweat. "They mess with your head."

"Even if you get past the recruits," Javier goes on, "if you open up the cellar and walk in on him like he is, there's no telling what he'll do to you—"

"I'm not leaving without him. You don't have to go, but you can't stop me."

"Oh, can't I?" Javier says, moving toward me, but Nobody's arm flies out and catches him across his chest, stopping him short.

"No, you can't," Nobody says, and as his lip curls back further, her brow furrows. "How many of those pills have *you* had?"

"He started yesterday," Jada says, not looking at either of us. "To get them to stop hitting me."

"I'm not saying we leave him here, because I don't think he's here." Javier brushes Nobody's arm aside. "But if he was, he'd be safer in the cellar than we are out here with the new recruits running around. And he could use a day or so to cool down. So let's stop wasting time, get in one of the Jeeps, and get Jada to a hospital."

"Medevac would be faster!" Dennis darts in front of me, brandishing a piece of lined notebook paper. The edge is ragged from where he tore it from the metal spiral, the coordinates blocked out in thick letters. "This location is pinned in the chat on our stream as well. Help us out, viewers! We need a medevac sent to these coordinates as soon as humanly possible. It's a life-or-death emergency," he shouts at my buttonhole, then sets a gallon water jug by Jada.

"You need to be hydrated," he tells her, more gently than I've heard him say anything since I've known him. Jada uncaps the jug and starts chugging. Dennis stops then, hearing something I can't, and turns his back to us, staring up at the sky, one hand shielding his face from the growing morning light.

"Dennis, Signal thinks she's going to the cellar to free Erik." Javier says, "Would you please explain to her why that's a bad idea?"

But Dennis doesn't turn from where he stands, frozen eerily still.

"Dennis?"

The moans of the Director across the field have rattled to a close. There is only the roll of the lake, the birdsong, and something very distant, something like circling thunder. My stomach turns over as I follow Dennis' gaze to a black dot at the edge of the horizon, growing slightly larger every moment, like a falling asteroid.

"Is that the medevac you wanted?" I squint into the bright sky. But I know, even as I say it, there's no way that's a medevac; there's no way they'd get to us that fast.

Dennis turns to us, his face perfectly calm. "That will be headquarters. Coming to shut down the stream. We're out of time."

Javier curses and Jada blinks from me to Dennis, stunned.

"Stop the stream?" Her voice wavers. "How?"

I know, but I don't want to say. I step past the covered porch, out of her earshot, holding out the camera in the direction the helicopter hangs, its hornet buzz more and more audible.

"That helicopter is from headquarters," I say, though my throat is constricting. "The last time they came, our friend Troy died. This time they'll be after all of us." I clip the camera back in place and return to the covered porch. Dennis is staring at me, eyes steady behind his smeared glasses.

"I can take it down." Dennis tells me. "I've been hacking into small flight craft since I got here. Helicopters included. With Kate's laptop, I can access the server headquarters uses, maybe even find the exact vehicles headed toward us." His inflection is flat, but his cadence has never been so fast. "But I have to start now."

"Go," Nobody says hoarsely. "You can do this."

He turns, lips twitching a little with unspoken ideas of how to attack the helicopter churning toward us, then turns back again, brow furrowed. "But just in case I can't pull it off, you should *all* try and get to the cellar."

"The cellar?" Javier says.

"They don't need to land to shoot." Dennis tells him. "You'll all be safer below ground."

"And what about you?"

"If I can't bring it down, we're dead anyway." He glances again at the growing black spot in the sky, straightening his shoulders and lifting his jaw. "I've got to code. The rest of you get to the cellar and stay there. Until you hear me bring it down. It will sound like an explosion. Hopefully." He leans into my buttonhole again: "And if anyone out there wants to jump in on this epic hack, my links are all pinned at the top of the Twitch chat."

I hug Dennis hard before he sprints back into the cabin, and then Nobody and I haul Jada up to her feet.

"I can run. I can, really guys. I *want to*," she insists. Nobody and I exchange a look: we'll stay close. Javier starts to object, shaking his head, but Jada slips loose from us and starts running out from under the covered porch and into the sunshine with manic speed. He falls in beside us, and we all hurry to catch up with her.

* * *

We move through the trees behind the cabins, hidden from the new recruits in the field. The fastest way to the Arts and Crafts table would be straight through the tall, cool grass alongside the lake, the reverse of the race Javier and I had on my first day here, when we saw each other across the field and started running toward Dave's air horn.

But that field is blocked by a knot of bloodied campers fighting over what is left of the Director, grunting and laughing like a field day game of tug-of-war. Luckily, I can only hear them and not see them on the path we're taking, running along the woods just behind the cabins, but a break in our cover is coming. The burnt foundation of the boys' cabin looms ahead, the morning sunlight pouring into the grass beyond it, the ghoulish shouts and the snaps of the Director's remains growing louder and closer.

"Woods, we need to get up higher in the woods," I pant to Nobody, and she catches Jada by the wrist before she can cross into the square of daylight that will expose her to the field. Jada blinks, her face feverish, and we gesture silently uphill. She follows after us, dripping with sweat. We're maybe four feet up the incline when Jada goes down hard beside me. She's stepped into some ravine buried in fallen leaves, I clamp my hand over her mouth before her scream comes out. We can't pull their attention.

"My ankle," she whispers as we crouch down to help her up. "I heard it pop. Just leave me." Jada shakes her head as we pull her up to her feet. "Just go."

"Stop it," I pull her arm around my shoulder. Nobody crouches down a little and gets Jada's other arm around her neck, and we start hauling her forward. But the way Jada limps along, there's no question of going further up into the trees. Nobody shares a look with me, face hardening: *Alright then.*

Javier doubles back from halfway up the hill to see where we are. He takes in the situation and sprints back down to us, moving to the very outside of our huddle, as if to block us from the field as we pass by the burnt foundation. I am too afraid to even glance over at the bright green field that opens up beside us as we shuffle past the foundation of the boys' cabin, but what registers in my peripheral is enough. Red ropes and strings of flesh hanging from red hands and red teeth, the splintering sound of bone breaking free from bone amid shrieks of laughter.

Jada bites her lips, trying to hold in her screams as we limp past the agonizing length of open field. I can feel them noticing us. My breath comes shorter as one of them goes still and stands. She staggers a few steps through the grass toward us, like a sleepwalker. As she gains speed, more heads flash up from the remains. The hairs on the back of my neck rise as I feel them go still, watching us, like hunting dogs catching a scent in the air.

Before we've reached the shelter of the further cabin, three of them are moving toward us across the sunny grass, reaching out with red hands.

"Run." Nobody says.

Chapter Twenty
The Cellar

Nobody and I pivot into the trees, Jada's head dropping between our shoulders. We don't have to look back to know more of them are coming. Their cries sound closer every moment.

"Playground," Nobody hisses, and we shift direction, lifting Jada over fallen logs and stumbling down the overgrown trail that leads to the forgotten playground. Javier moves effortlessly, clearing stumps and holding back branches for us. I'm still half winded from our ride out and slowed down even by Jada's slight weight. Jada's head rolls between us deliriously, and when she looks up, she winces at every tree branch, like they're jumping out at her. The thrum of helicopter blades rings clearly through the sky now, but it's not as close as the excited laughter of the new recruits, echoing through the woods around us.

"I see the slide!" I cry when the silver handles of the old playground slide glint through the trees, half-buried in orange-red bittersweet berries and dark vines. We hurl ourselves toward the swing set, the same swings where Erik and I sat when he'd made the offer that broke my heart and saved my life:

"I was hoping you'd let me help."

"Help what?"

"Help figure out who killed your best friend."

"Come on!" Nobody yells desperately, but Jada's face has gone gray, and she drops between the swings and covers her head with her hands.

When Nobody and I scramble to haul her back up, her arms flail out at us, eyes not really focusing, hands moving like she can't tell how far away we are.

"Just go, okay? Just go. I can't—"

"I know, I know, but please," I beg her, "it's just a little bit further."

"*I see Jaaada!*" A mocking voice rises through the trees. The freckled girl from the cabin slips between the nearest pines. Everything from her upper lip to the top of her waistband is bright red, thin lines of scarlet tracing the folds of skin around her grinning mouth. I'm cringing back at the sight of her when there's a seagull cry of rusty chains just past my head. And then one of the thick plastic swings goes flying between me and Nobody, arcing up perfectly to connect hard with the freckled girl's jaw, sending her sprawling backward onto the ground. Her cries gurgle with blood as Javier shoulders me and Nobody out of the way and catches Jada up over his shoulder again. Then he turns and sprints toward the open field.

"They're coming for us anyway," Nobody rasps. "Might as well face them," and when she runs into the sunshine after him, and I follow without hesitation.

But just as I break out from the shadow of the forest, someone grabs my hair and yanks me backward. I lunge down and forward, dropping to one knee, sending them tumbling over me. Then I bring my foot down hard on the body below me, not sure what I'm stepping on, just stomping blindly, screams I don't recognize coming out of me. Another recruit barrels up the field toward us. I hold his gaze like I'm scared, but drop low at the last moment and clothesline his leg with mine like I did with Jada. On the way back to my feet someone punches me hard in the back, knocking the breath out of me, and then breaks out in a howl. I turn to see Nobody dragging my attacker backward by his ear and wonder if she picked that up from Erik before she dashes him to the ground. I spin, world tilting queasily around me, to handle the guy I clotheslined, who's back on his feet, but he's not looking at me. His eyes are fixed upward, the thrum of the helicopter blocking out the rest of the world.

The trees are billowing like it's a storm in the middle of the sunny morning, leaves scattering in the wind forced down by the helicopter blades. The helicopter itself is just past the row of canoes, swaying and bobbing as it drops lower and lower toward the field. How can something so huge and metal stay in the air? The few recruits still toying with the Director stop and stare. We're all struck by this utterly impossible thing, a surreal special effect from a movie, inserted into real life.

Two of the new recruits who are fully in the helicopter's shadow turn to stare, their hair and clothes streaming back, squinting against the wind. One waves his arms over his head, jumping up to get the pilot's attention, but then he freezes in midair. His arms go limp, his head falls to the side, and he comes down all at once, like a puppet whose strings have been cut. His friend turns to see what's wrong and then instantly drops beside him, and only then does the firecracker sound truly register.

They're shooting from the helicopter.

"Come on!" Nobody grabs my wrist and pulls me forward. *"Cellar!"* Ahead of us is the sycamore, its leaves gone golden-yellow; below it is the Arts and Crafts table. The first place I saw them, that sunny afternoon Kate marched me and Nobody from the prison bus to the Arts and Crafts table, where Jada and Dennis and Kurt and Troy were all waiting. I had been so rattled at how peaceful it was.

The staccato blast of automatic fire rings out again, cutting through even the thrum of the helicopter blades. The brightly lit grass rolls ahead of us in shimmering waves of green, and I know when I see the shadow, that will be the end. So I stare at the sycamore, at the way its leaves magnify the daylight, as I run hand in hand with Nobody. Javier, Jada still on his shoulder, slides to his knees in front of a bright orange traffic cone, far past the tree ahead, and sets her down gently before throwing open the doors in the ground.

The shadow of the helicopter darkens the world around me, the force of the blades so powerful they shake my heart out of sync with its own beat.

Not before I see him—please, please let me see him one more time.

Every muscle in my body knows the shot is coming. Nobody pulls me as fast as she can, we're almost under the tree, I squeeze her hand so hard: at least we won't be alone when it happens.

"You're never alone," Rose says. *"You're just between friends."*

And then the thunder of the rotary blade stops, leaving a ringing silence, a high repeating internal tone in my head cut by the sigh of the blades going still.

Dennis did it. The glorious genius did it.

Shots go off, but they go wide of us, hitting the ground as the angle of the helicopter abruptly changes. Pure joy fills me at the frantic scream of whoever is inside the helicopter falling behind us. But then it hits.

The ground flies up to meet us, the impact of the crash sending a wave of rolling earth across the field that bucks us off our feet. Nobody and I hurtle forward, the landing knocks my breath out of me. In the endless moment before I can breathe again, clods of dirt and grass scatter around us with a sound like heavy spring rain. Nobody turns to me, her white hair brown from the wash of dirt, rises on one elbow, and starts to laugh. I'm laughing, too, as I watch tear tracks of laughter carve down her dirty cheeks, and then I look up and see Javier standing halfway out of the ground, waving his arms. I smile, getting to my feet, when the field turns red and gold in front of me, an eagle scream explosion like the last round of firecrackers on the Fourth of July right behind my head.

Heat rips up my side, a lightning strike that pins me back to the ground, sweet grass and dirty-penny blood mixing in my mouth. All feeling on my left side cuts out. I reach with my hand and feel split flesh. I cannot turn my head to see, cannot send the message to my body. Colors I've never seen before bloom before my open eyes.

"Signal!" Nobody screams. She must turn me over, because the gold leaves of the sycamore tree against the blue sky fill my vision. Everything is slick and sticky, like when I woke up in the shed. It smells like that too, except there's so much sunshine. It's so weird there's sunshine. I never thought I would die in broad daylight.

"You're okay, you're okay, you're okay." But Nobody's voice is shaking. Nobody, who isn't scared of anything. Then she screams: "I can't move her! *I can't move her!*"

A moment later, Jada's face hovers over me. She's got a T-shirt—it must be Javier's—and as she presses it to my side, it turns red, like a magic trick.

"That's not good," I say, my voice far off somehow. But that's not the only concern. "The new recruits—"

"Javier and Nobody are holding them off," Jada says.

"There are too many—"

"We're good. You're safe here—you're safe with me."

"Erik, is he . . .?"

Jada shakes her head, "No, honey. I'm sorry. He wasn't in the cellar."

"Where is he?"

"We don't know yet," Jada says, "but we'll find him."

But they won't. The only person who knows where he went is the Director, and the Director is dead. Without proof he could be good, he gave up. Gave up on himself and gave up on me.

I turn my head so she won't see me cry.

I see Javier and Nobody, circling around us protectively as the new recruits gather at the edge of the trees. They want to come for me, but something is making them hesitate. Jada's head bobs at the edge of my vision, her dilated eyes falling closed momentarily.

"How are you holding up?" I wheeze.

"Better than you," she says, tears at the edge of her voice.

"Jada, listen. I'm sorry I didn't—"

"No. Don't start up with that." Jada shakes her head. "Neither of us is dying in this damn place. We're almost out. We get through the next hour, we're home free. The rest of our lives, okay? That's what we've got if we get through the next hour. We're going to go dancing—you, me, and Nobody. We're going to get matching tattoos and be bridesmaids at each other's weddings, and it's going to be Barbie and Skipper for real, do you hear me? Promise me. Promise me!"

The sycamore's golden leaves glitter in the wind, its broad branches waving to welcome the clouds coming over the lake. Such beautiful clouds, rolling white mountains tinged with pink and gold, framing Jada's angelic black curls. I can hear the flames from the burning helicopter snapping close by, the smell of burning gasoline stings the back of my throat. Jada is sobbing now, but it's alright—she'll see. Everything is going to be alright, I can feel it, and the comfort is like a heavy drowsiness washing over me, blanking out all the pain. I love it. I love everything.

"Jada, you have to tell Erik—"

"No! No! You'll tell him yourself, alright?"

And she's right. But not the way she means.

A low droning sound in the corner of the sky. Another helicopter. Jada looks up, frozen like a prey animal.

"Over here!" Javier yells to the sky, waving his arms over his head.

"No, go to the cellar!" I sob, screaming with the last of my strength, "They'll kill you! Go to the cellar!" But it's like they don't hear me. What are they staying for? I'm already dead. "All of you! Please!"

"It's red, Signal!" Nobody screams. *"It's red!"*

I don't know what that means, but Jada gets up and moves away from me. Good, go, go; I have to say a few things. It's embarrassing. Can you be embarrassed when you're dead? If anyone could, it would be me.

My hand floats to my shirt buttonhole; it's so wet, it feels like warm wet sand, but I dig through and find the little camera. I bring it right across from my face. The light has started blinking red, but that's alright. I don't have long either. I stare into its beady little eye.

"Erik, wherever you are, I need you to listen to me," I tell the camera. "I know you. Better than anyone else, I know what you're capable of."

I have to talk louder now, as the helicopter sinks to the ground beside the lake, just past the trees.

"I know I'm not a Class A"—my words are slurring—"but I don't need to be. You've got so much good in you, Erik. I've seen it. You never needed fixing. Don't let them tell you who you are or what you can be. Because I know you better than them, and you win, okay? I—"

The red light dies out. The lens goes dark.

The camera slips from my hand, and my eyes fall closed. But I can still see the sycamore tree, only now Erik is sitting astride the branch staring down at me, his long hair falling around his distant face. What kindness to see him one last time, even if only as a memory.

". . . I love you." I finish. And if these are my last words, at least they're true.

Chapter Twenty-One

The Guests

The footage cuts from a freeze frame of my bleary face, too close to the camera, to news footage from a highway traffic copter that had been diverted to camp during the stream. Though it's grainy and distant, the footage clearly shows me passed out on the grass, with Nobody, Javier and Jada circled around me as the medics approach from the lower field, where the medevac helicopter had landed.

Sonny Desai pauses the footage and looks around the conference table of the nerve center. It's still strange to be in the same room with a person I'd only ever seen before on the news, but I'm starting to get used to it. Especially after the last two days, cooped up together with him, Aarush, and their lawyer as I gave a statement on everything that had happened. Everything from waking up with Rose in the shed, to camp, to my mission, to falling down in the grass after the shrapnel from the helicopter's exploding fuel tank hit me.

Now we sit back from a conference table scattered with LaCroix cans and brown paper boxes full of fancy wilted salads, all of us wrung out from watching the whole stream. The room seems very still as I blot my wet face with a napkin. This is my second time seeing it, but watching my friends surround me protectively and stay by my side to the end will never not make me cry.

"So"—Sonny looks at the lawyer—"can we submit it as evidence?"

The lawyer, a sixty-something black woman with an ever-present bottle of kombucha, considers, daylight refracting through the pool water behind her and scattering blue lines across her dark tailored suit. Far above her head, Jada's legs circle in the water, then Nobody cannonballs into the deep end, a blonde asteroid of bubbles that sinks almost down to the conference table but then shoots back up. I'm the only one who has to sit in on these meetings. Nobody, Javier, Jada, and Dennis can enjoy the heated pool once they finish tutoring. Not that I could go swimming yet, with my stitches still bandaged; it took fourteen of them to close my shrapnel wound.

"It depends on the judge." The lawyer sighs at last. "My concern with the footage is that when Signal scanned the files in the footlocker with her camera, that could land us in fruit-of-the-poisonous-tree territory if we submit those papers for evidence."

"Even if we can't submit the stream, everybody's seen it anyway." Aarush doesn't look up from his phone. "It's been viewed enough times for each person in this country to have watched it twice by now."

"Which is going to make jury selection fun," the lawyer says dryly. "But my greatest concern is nailing whatever pharmaceutical company is behind this. The government was *funding* neurochemical testing on minors to benefit a private company—"

"Run by Erik's grandfather," I point out.

"That's speculation." Sonny Desai frowns. "And Curtis retired ten years ago."

"The point is," the lawyer goes on, "I'll take any lead I can get. If this Erik person took a prototype of the drug at Ledrick's facility, then I want his statement."

"Which brings us back to my idea," I add, but Aarush, still frowning at his phone, shakes his head:

"Your idea is terrible."

Sonny gives me an apologetic smile. "Aarush is concerned about your plan, Signal, because he feels strongly that the risk is not worth the reward."

"I would argue it's absolutely worth the risk," the lawyer says coolly, "because without the pharmaceutical angle, the stream is just footage of a prison riot."

"They opened fire on minors!" I cry.

"*Class A* minors," she says wearily, "who'd just ripped a man to pieces on camera."

Aarush's phone chirps. His thumbs fly over the screen, and his frown deepens. "Update from our friend at the hospital . . . Janeane has been discharged, and she was picked up and driven out by a round white woman in her mid-thirties, wearing red cat eyeglasses."

"Kate!" I sit up in my chair.

"Where are we with the Janeane of it all?" Sonny asks the lawyer.

"I'm in talks with Ledmonton police and the Ledmonton bank to get a warrant on the security deposit box," she says. "Meanwhile, Janeane is doubling down in press conferences about Erik and Signal breaking in and torturing her and Mike. For now, we let her. Let her incriminate herself as much as possible before we drop the attic rant. It'll be a bombshell."

"Especially alongside Erik's testimony about what happened that night, which, if we go through with my plan—"

"It's not happening, Signal!" Aarush cuts me off. But then he looks to his dad, who's staring at me with a detached assessment exactly like his son's.

"It would take some gumption," Sonny says, "but Signal has plenty of that. Aarush, I completely understand your reservations about Erik. But I need you to remember what we are doing here: preparing to challenge the U.S. government in court over the Wylie-Stanton. This is about more than the people in this room. This is about preserving human dignity in the face of technology for generations to come. And if we are to have even a hope of getting full transparency on that algorithm, we will need Erik's testimony. No matter how despicable we might find him personally." He clears his throat and looks to me. "So, Signal, I've taken the liberty of reaching out to the property holders. They're willing to rent the house out if we're willing to take it as-is. And if the authorities are nearby—"

"No authorities." I shake my head quickly. "He won't walk into a trap. Don't underestimate him."

"You're the one underestimating him," Aarush snaps, his ergonomic chair flying upright as he leans toward me. "Have you read *any* of the articles I sent you? Three mutilated bodies now, all found less than ten miles out from camp. You said yourself, Kurt and Erik were drugged up and sent out to kill people. There's video evidence of a young man matching Kurt's description two blocks away from the latest crime scenes. And you want to meet with Erik in private?"

"There's no evidence that Erik is with Kurt," I counter. "We have no way of contacting him at all—that's the whole problem. But if we set this up, he will come. I *know* he will!"

"I'm not worried he won't come," Aarush says. "I'm worried about what happens when he does!" He looks past me to the lawyer. "If we lose her, what do we have? A couple random juvenile delinquents? We lose our public pressure, we lose our star witness, and we lose our chance at the Wylie-Stanton—"

"He's not going to hurt me," I interrupt.

"He doesn't have to kill you to make you disappear," Aarush says. Then, to the lawyer: "He just has to convince her to run off with him."

"Enough!" I'm on my feet, pounding the table before I can stop myself. "I know you don't trust Erik, but you need to trust me. Clearing my name matters to me. Helping my friends matters to me. Ending the Wylie-Stanton matters to me! And we need Erik to do any of those things. Just give me one week. That's all I'm asking. Give me one week, and we'll have everything we need."

Sonny Desai looks at me over his son's head for a long beat.

"Let's start with three days," he says.

* * *

I leave the conference room moments later to pack, and almost run into Javier, still damp from the pool. Jada and Nobody are at the long white bar, mixing virgin cocktails. Dennis is on the couch, happily tapping away on a high-power laptop. They would look like any group of kids hanging out, except for the ankle bracelets required by their house arrest.

I'm the only one without a bracelet because my sentence was overturned, thanks to Dave's recorded confession that he fudged my Wylie-Stanton score. Strangely, this single clip of our viral stream, proving someone might erroneously be labeled a Class A, has alarmed the public far more than unarmed teenagers being shot down by a helicopter. The public outcry was so intense Sonny's lawyer was able to push through an appeal on my conviction before I was out of the hospital, and hopefully, if the subpoena goes through, we'll finally see what's in Jaw's security deposit box.

"Signal can settle this," Javier smiles at me, rubbing his head with a beach towel, "What're we watching tonight? *The Mummy* or *Bladerunner 2049*?"

Since Sonny moved us all into his house, leading up to our wrongful imprisonment suit against camp, we've had a standing routine: one of us screens our favorite movie to the rest of the group each night in the Desai's luxurious home theater. Now that we've all had a turn, debating what to watch for movie o'clock is the best way to distract each other from the Zoom tutoring and endless homework packets. Sonny, who seems to be as much of an altruist as he is a chancer, has insisted our way of repaying him for standing bail and hosting our house arrest is to finish our GEDs.

"I won't be here." I smile apologetically. "I'm heading out on a secret mission. But I'll be back tomorrow."

"Yessss!" Jada says, because I've been telling her and Nobody about this "secret mission" plan for days. She hugs me so a band of pool water sinks through my sweater, and whispers, "*Finally.* Go get him!"

Dennis looks up at me. "You sent the email to the address I gave you?"

"Yeah."

"Has he replied?"

I shake my head.

"He hasn't replied to any of my emails either," Dennis says, "but that doesn't mean he's not reading them."

Nobody smiles hugely at me and sticks her hand out to begin our elaborate secret handshake: classic shake into fist bump, into two snaps, double high five; then we both say "Ridin'!" while pretending to ride a horse and swing a lasso over our heads, lick our fingers, touch our shoulders, and hiss.

"Bring that bald asshole home," she says, close to my ear, before heading back behind the bar.

Javier waits until I come up to him; then we do a stiff, one-armed hug. It's weird living together again, and not just because of the kiss when he was on pills. My nurse at St. Joseph's, where my side was stitched up, asked why the "cute boyfriend" who had watched over me all night after surgery left just before I woke up. And I highly doubt she means Dennis or Aarush. But I don't know what to do with that. So I don't bring it up.

* * *

A tide of people with news cameras surges toward the car when the driver gets past the heavy gate at the edge of the property. I know I'm protected by the tinted windows, but my mouth still goes sour when I hear a news helicopter circling. But the Desai's professional driver makes good use of overpasses once we're past the Golden Gate Bridge, and by the time we're against the coast, I can take my hat and sunglasses off and roll down the window to see the real color of the water. Our construction site flashes by, and my heart starts racing.

Just a little further.

We pull in the driveway of the abandoned Wylie-Stanton house. The gate has been left open, the keys are in a padlock attached to the front handle. Never mind that all the street-facing windows are broken.

The driver insists on carrying my backpack and bedroll into the front foyer. He looks around the dim marble hall, wary. "Sure is cold in here."

"Is it?" My blood is surging. When he leaves, I walk down the marble hall into the kitchen. There are still a few pieces of broken mug on the floor from our kiss on the table. I grab a flashlight off the table and go down the basement stairs to Erik's room, heart pounding nonsensically hard as I open the door, like I expect him be waiting.

But it's empty. I look again, longer now, at the family pictures, poring over them with my flashlight since the electricity is still off. I inspect the photo of him and Curtis, and a shot I didn't notice before: Erik, arm-in-arm with his mom. He's beaming at her, and she's looking at the camera.

I collect the pillows and comforter I slept in weeks before and haul them up to the room on the second story, to augment my bedroll. I open the windows that look out onto the ocean, unlatch one, and swing it wide. The sunset turns the waves into flames.

Then I take out my laptop and lose myself in my tutoring homework. I didn't like homework back when I took going to school for granted, but now it's genuinely fascinating, particularly AP biology. By the time I finish my assignment, it's completely dark. Now I have no idea what to do with myself. I brought a bagged dinner, but I can't eat it. I brought books and a reading light, but the words refuse to become more than letters. The only thing I want to do is refresh my email. It comes up with nothing every time.

I give up trying to distract myself from his absence, curl up on the window seat in my sleeping bag, and find *Swan Lake* on YouTube. As beautiful as the dancing is, I find myself closing my eyes and picturing the Opera House lobby instead.

* * *

I wake with a start to rain on my face and scramble to pull the window closed, overgrown branches lashing at the glass like they want in. I'm half soaked by the time I've figured out how to bolt the old-fashioned casement windows, and that's when I hear the knocking. Someone is out here at night, in the rain, pounding on the door.

Could it be . . .?

I run down the stairs, sneakers squeaking on the marble, heart in my throat as I throw the door open to someone I've never seen before. A tall, twenty-something guy, face shadowed by an expensive-looking umbrella, a cord of grocery-store firewood under his arm.

"Hi!" he says loudly, so I can hear him over the pounding rain. "Aarush asked me to come check on you."

"Who are you?" I ask, moving the door slightly more closed between us.

"Sorry—of course. I'm the owner, Skye." He puts his hand, a graceful hand with perfectly manicured nails, into the spotlight of the solar-powered motion light above us. I shake quickly, his palm hot and dry. "I live in Pacifica, close by. Aarush was very insistent I come in person and check on you ahead of the storm. And I wanted to get ahead of some leaky areas in the roof before the rain gets much worse."

"Oh . . . okay," I stammer, opening the door but feeling annoyed. He owns the house so I can't exactly refuse him entry. Knowing Aarush, he'd probably come back with him and drag this out even further. And there is a certain morbid curiosity about Erik's older brother, a weird compulsion to see his scars. Skye turns his back on me and shakes his umbrella over the porch.

"I could make a fire in the living room," he offers, hand shading his face as he knocks the rain from his slicked-back blond hair.

"Um, sure."

He starts down the dark marble hall, his athletic stride shortened by a jerking limp. I pad after him, through the towering pillars and into the living room. I don't sit down; I don't intend for this to be a long visit. I hover by the door as Skye crouches beside the fireplace, blond hair catching the light of a small flame, his face hidden by his shoulder as he coaxes it larger. Once its leaping and bright, he sits back on his heels and turns to me, almost but not quite smiling.

Don't look away. Don't you dare look away. Erik did that. You look at that face. That is what Erik did. That is what he is capable of.

The angelic blond boy from the family portrait is hardly recognizable in the stiff mask that stares at me now, marbled with pearly scar tissue from the corners of his mouth to the edges of his eyes. He drops my gaze immediately, then rises painfully and settles onto the drop cloth–covered couch. The light isn't as harsh at that distance, and he's had some good surgery; in the glow he could pass for a Botox addict. But there's no question: he was mangled. He politely stares at the fire until I've gotten over my shock enough to look away.

"So did Aarush want a picture of me with today's newspaper before you leave, or . . ."

He laughs. "To be fair, I've been bugging him about getting us in a room together since I learned you were staying with Sonny. You're the girl from the manhunt."

"Signal Deere."

He nods, leaning forward, elbows on his knees. The gesture reminds me so much of Erik, without him actually being Erik, my heart skips a beat. "Well, Signal, it's nice to finally make your acquaintance and have a chance to talk."

"Talk about what?"

"My brother, of course."

The fire snaps, wood tumbles.

"I saw your stream. I heard what you told him, and I . . ." Skye stops, recalculates. "Erik is an extremely charming and charismatic person. He could be anything he wanted, do anything he set his mind to, except . . ." Skye's thumb digs between his eyes. "Except he also happens to be a homicidal maniac."

I nod slowly. "Well. Thank you for the fire, but it's getting late and—"

"I don't think I've said anything you don't know," Skye goes on. He carefully lifts one leg over the other with both hands, the way a much older person might. "Can I ask what he told you about our parents?"

"I know that shortly after the funeral you committed him to a facility where he was psychologically tortured."

Skye's mouth jerks down at one corner.

"Dr. Ledrick, who ran that facility, also ran a camp where I was tortured, so." I tilt my head. "Not as badly as Erik, of course. But enough that I have some idea of what he went through."

"Dr. Ledrick was a depraved individual." Skye looks me in the eyes, an apology in his voice. "I was shocked and horrified when I saw the stream, when I saw those— What he did, to the children at that camp, is unforgivable. I've had to really confront the idea that my family, like so many others in the behavioral psychiatry community, were at one time taken in by that man. But Erik was never tortured. I went to his facility as soon as I got out of traction."

I shrug. "And?"

"And it was utterly banal. Erik took meds, did homework, and attended group therapy. He was surrounded by kids his age and the best therapists west of the Rockies, Signal. Erik was bored, I don't doubt it. But that hardly qualifies as *torture*."

"What about the drugs tested on him?"

"Erik didn't want to take antipsychotics. He felt they dulled him. And maybe they did. Actually, you know what? I'm *sure* they did. But they were necessary for the safety of the staff and patients. Because without them, Erik would manipulate anyone he came into contact with, into acts of violence against themselves and others, just for his own amusement. It got to the point where he couldn't have roommates or visitors. The one nurse who had regular contact with him committed suicide. After that tragedy, I was told he was going to be moved to a federal detention center. Which, I realize now, was Ledrick's way of bringing his 'talents' to camp."

My stomach twists at his words, but I don't let the discomfort reach my face.

"Miss Deere, I am telling you these hard truths about Erik because you seem to have real feelings for him." He clasps his hands, "And it seems like a shame that such a brave and kind person would have those feelings for Erik when he is *incapable* of returning them." His face flushes, as though he's embarrassed for both of us. "Erik gets . . . fixations. But they are about mental and sexual possession. Nothing more."

"What about your own 'fixations'?" I ask. "What about Alice?"

"My high school girlfriend?" He blinks at me, "What about her?"

"*She* was in high school." I cross my arms. "You were in college."

"She was a grade behind me, yes . . ." He nods. "I don't know if it was smart of us to continue dating after I went off to school, but we were hardly the first couple who've tried it."

I try to remember what Erik said before. He made it sound like a serious age gap between Alice and Skye, but I can't remember any specific numbers. Skye is lying to me, of course. About all of it. I know he is. It's just the truth is so fantastic, and his lies are so mundane, they sound more convincing.

"I know this isn't my business," Skye goes on, "but Aarush told me you're trying to get my brother to come meet you here. I told Aarush there was no way Erik would come, but he told me you would be here for days, and frankly I don't know if I can in good conscience let you freeze to death while acting as bait—"

"I'm not *bait*." I cut him off. "I just need to talk to him."

"Even if he did come, you really think all he'd want is to *talk*?" Skye says.

The fire spits and hisses.

"He's been off his medication for who knows how long. Ledrick had him on some kind of steroid or stimulant and then sent him out on a killing spree—"

"There's no proof Erik has hurt anyone."

"I'm sitting right here," Skye says wryly. "He's tried to take my life twice now."

"Look, it was nice to meet you, Skye"—I sweep an arm toward the doorway—"but I'd like the house back to myself now."

"Alright." He lets out a heavy sigh. "I'll call an Uber and get out of your hair." He slides to the arm of the couch then, pressing himself upward. "But I do need to look in on the ceilings on the third story. We had some water damage the last time it rained."

"Sure, that's fine."

His hand fumbles on the arm of the couch, and he jounces back onto the seat awkwardly. I hurry over to help him up, and he leans on me hard, though clearly embarrassed, as I guide him back out into the hall.

"I really hate to ask you this," Skye says, "but would you mind helping me up the stairs? When it rains, I get . . ." He gestures to his hip. "It's harder when it rains."

"Of course."

"I appreciate it," he says, relieved, hand gripping my shoulder. "Aarush is going to be furious when he finds out you're still staying here tonight. You're sure you don't want a ride back to his house?"

"Positive."

His long, slick blond hair falls in front of his face with the effort it takes to make our way up the winding gallery of stairs that encircle the sloop sail; it hangs like a giant silver knife blade in the dark. We at last gain the third story and he stops, gripping the banister, and looks around breathlessly.

"Sorry—" he pulls his long hair back from his face. "It's been a while since I've been back here."

"I thought you lived close by?"

"I don't usually come onto the property," he says softly. "I don't like to see it like this."

He drifts toward the "SWS" door and disappears inside the dim room. The drumming of the rain is louder up here, closer to the roof. I hear the window slam.

"It's coming down sideways!" he announces.

I duck a little, trying to see past the sail, its point cutting across my view of the door to his room, which is across the stairwell from Erik's. Heavy paper crinkles, then hits the floor. Skye stands framed in the doorway, reaching into his pocket, a pale rectangle on the wall where his poster had hung only moments before.

"Done with Gran Turismo?"

"It was all wet. Ruined." He smiles, limping heavily into the hall: *step, clomp; step, clomp*. "I play a lot more of it these days, actually. Since I can't work an accelerator anymore."

He limps around the gallery toward me, pulling something leather from his pocket. *Step, clomp; step, clomp.*

"I'm sorry," I say awkwardly, to fill the conspicuous silence.

"Don't be. I'm grateful for my accident. If Erik hadn't cut those brakes, it might've been years before I started my real career."

"What do you work in now?"

"Oh, you know," Skye says absently. "Joined the family business."

CurtPro Pharmaceuticals, of course. With Erik under a conservatorship, Skye was the sole heir to CurtPro *and* the Wylie-Stanton algorithm. I watch him move painfully through the shafts of blue light that fall from the skylight overhead, worrying with whatever he just pulled from his pocket, the clomp of his limp faster once he gets between me and the stairs; *Step, clomp! Step, clomp! Step, clomp!*

He's working his fingers through tight black leather gloves. Driving gloves.

If Skye can't drive, why would he carry driving gloves?

Chapter Twenty-Two

Third Date

I back into Erik's old room, the rain louder here than the hall, drumming against the windows that face the ocean, bits of Owen Heo's time line swimming in my head as I scan the floor for my phone, lost somewhere in the dark and blankets.

Skye hadn't had the opportunity to mess with the car. And why would he dismantle the brakes of a car he was driving? Unless . . .

"You did stunt-driving before," I call, frantically kicking through the blankets. "Pretty dangerous stuff, right? You like—get into accidents on purpose?"

I look up, and he's in the doorway. He got there so quickly after struggling down the hall while I was watching.

Almost like he dropped the limp after I backed in the room.

"If that's what the shot calls for. Sometimes they film you doing the stunt slowly, then speed it up. Or sometimes they just let you go for it." He grins. "Mom said I was born without the fear gene."

"But your stunt-driving skills didn't help when the brakes went out."

"Or maybe they did. I don't remember much from the crash."

And it's a wild theory from an anonymous armchair detective, but I state it as confidently as I can: "Then why did you pay that mechanic not to make a statement to the police about the brake lines?"

He looks at me a long moment.

"Because I realized Erik must have cut them. My mother didn't press charges when he mutilated me. So why send him to prison for killing *her*?" He seems to catch himself then, shadows of sliding raindrops distorting his face as it cycles through a few different expressions, as though trying them on, before landing on a frown. "Of course, now he's out in the world, carving folks up, I regret that choice. Terribly. But at the time, I felt I'd lost enough family."

"You didn't want to lose him. So you and your grandfather signed him over to Dr. Ledrick?" I crouch down beside the blankets on the floor, feeling quickly under my pillow, sliding my hands across the nylon bedroll. "That doesn't make sense."

"Signal, I know you don't want to believe that Erik could have killed our parents, but logically it's the only conclusion." Skye still wears his frown. "Unless you think it makes more sense for the car to just go spinning into a cliff?"

If Skye was driving? Yes. Yes, that did make more sense.

The mechanic had announced one night at a bar that the brake lines of the Wylie-Stantons' car had been tampered with. But he'd refused to swear the same thing to the police and had ended up moving out of town when they pressured him. But what if there was nothing to swear to? What if he was paid not for keeping his silence, but for starting the rumor?

A couple drunken insinuations in a bar weren't perjury. That couldn't get him arrested, and the car had been destroyed, so no one could check up on whether he was lying or not. One tall tale at a bar, and all his money problems had been solved.

But if, then, the brake lines had never been cut—which by several accounts was almost impossible, even with enough time and knowledge to pull that off—then the only logical explanation was the car had been spun purposefully into the side of the cliff.

What if Skye had thought he was a good enough driver that he could pilot such a crash and walk away from the wreck? Walk away as the heir to the Wylie-Stanton family fortune, with total control over a brother he hated, a brother who was trying to bring his sexual misdeeds to light?

Wouldn't that be worth the risk for someone 'missing his fear gene'?

"You look so worried. What's wrong?" Skye asks. "Maybe I can help."

I grab the corners of the duvet and snap it, sending the blanket flying up between us, hoping my phone will tumble out. It does, clattering heavily to the ground and spinning to a stop just at Skye's feet. He steps over it lightly, a half smile on his face, pulling the door shut behind him. The bolt catches with a click I feel in my throat. If I want the phone, I have to get past him, and every instinct screams not to go in reach of his gloved hands.

He bites the inside of his lip, jittering eyes landing on the computer near me. "What's this? A video?" He lunges forward, and I step back. *"Swan Lake!"* He brandishes the laptop at me as I keep edging away from him. "A classic. The last act—the best part!"

"You like the music?" I scan around for something, anything I can use as a weapon.

"Not particularly. I'm not a big music fan." He swallows a giddy laugh. He can no longer keep from smiling. "Maybe I just hate swans!"

He brings the volume all the way up, the music ringing through the room, violins swirling madly, loud enough to mask my screams.

The flashlight. The flashlight is on the window seat. That's my best weapon. I step toward the window. He sets the laptop down with a crack and strides after me, the limp completely gone.

He will tell Aarush he came here and warned me, and I didn't leave. And tomorrow they will find my body, and the window open, and they will assume Erik came after all. Came and killed me. And there will be no star witness against CurtPro. No one fighting to end the Wylie-Stanton. And no one in the world who believes Erik.

I catch up the flashlight, its heft comforting, as he steps closer.

"Well, thanks again for checking in," I say as casually as I can, my whole body shaking. "But I really do need to sleep."

"Of course, of course." He grins, stepping closer, my heart jerking painfully hard now. Even the rain seems to be beating against the glass faster. "But I'd feel a lot better if I knew that window was bolted. Could you check?" His hand flits out sharply, pointing just above my shoulder, and he smiles broadly as I flinch. "Right behind you! Right there, Signal. There's a great big brass bolt, right in the middle. Sometimes, it sticks! Could you just check it and make sure it's closed?"

"It is." I will not turn my back on him for anything. The moment I do those gloves will close around my throat.

"Just check?" He smiles, so reasonably. "Then I'll go. Just check for me."

I wring the flashlight with both hands. If he comes one step closer, I will crack it across the bridge of his nose, then his temple, going the other way. He's about to spring: we both know it. The understanding hangs in the air. He's high on the anticipation of my first scream. I try and remember everything Javier and Jada have said in the couple self-defense sessions we've had over the last week. They'd insisted on it after seeing how Dave had manhandled me in the stream. I should strike out at his knee and shin rather than the groin—they're larger targets. Connect as hard as I can just under the kneecap. If you do it right, your attacker won't be able to follow you so fast.

"I told you to *go*." I turn the flashlight on, training it on his eyes, bringing every pucker and seam in his reconstituted face into sharp relief.

"This is *my house*, Signal." His eyes are almost transparent in the light, the rain crashing down on the glass behind me. "You don't get to tell me anything."

But then his eyes move over me, up and through the window. Trying to get me to turn around? I glare at him, teeth clenched, refusing to blink, bracing myself for his next step closer.

But he steps back.

"No way. . ."

And then I turn.

Glass explodes from the windows above us, shards cast by the howling wind to the far corners of the room, Skye shrieking in fear as something comes in from the night in an animal rush, something dark and elemental that pulls him out of the room and into the hall, the door slamming behind them.

I am too stunned to react at first, bits of glass sliding down the back of my shirt and rain pelting my hair. Then I rush forward and throw open the door to see Skye bent backward over the stair banister, a knife at his throat.

"Erik, *NO!*"

Erik's back is to me. His shirt seems too tight, his muscles swollen yet his figure cruelly defined, like everything that's not for fighting has been wrung out of him.

"Erik, please—"

He turns his head just a fraction, and Skye throws a weak punch and runs for the stairs. He's in full flight when Erik breaks the top of a newel post off the railing beside him and sends it flying toward the back of his brother's head. There is the crack of wood against skull, and Skye slips down a flight of steps with an incoherent shriek. Erik lunges toward the sound, but I grab his arm. He looks at me full on then, his beautiful face so twisted in rage I almost back away. But instead, I make myself grab the knife handle in his hand and shake my head.

"Erik. Please. You're better than this—"

"No." His voice has teeth, the words sounds like they hurt coming out of him: "I *am* this. Do you understand?"

He jerks his arm away, leaving me the knife, and stalks toward the stairs, rolling his neck and swinging his arms as Skye moans on the landing below. Erik grabs the railing and slings himself easily onto the second-floor gallery. It's not a superhuman gesture, but a jarringly animal one, the unconcerned way he throws himself over the rail. As though anyone could move through space like this, if they truly don't care if they fall.

Skye has managed to pull himself up the banister and hobble halfway down the second flight of steps. Erik stalks slowly behind him, as though enjoying watching his brother stumble, watching the back of his head go dark with blood. He can close the distance whenever he wants. Skye doesn't have a chance. As soon as he's in the open of the atrium, Erik will leap for him unless—

I sprint around the hall, to just under the place on the wall where the top of the sloop sail is anchored; its taut tether of nylon strap secured by a steel bolt. I put one foot up on the railing, then the other, and reach my hands over my head, only just balancing over the three-story drop behind me. My fingers close around the nylon tether of the sail, my bandage straining against my stitches as I reach. I take the tether in one hand, raise Erik's knife above my head with the other, and start sawing frantically. Every stroke makes my stitches burn hotter, the surgical thread straining at my skin, the brothers' voices echoing up from far below.

"You should be *thanking* me, freak," Skye says. "You finally look like you lift. Maybe I'll try some. Though I hear the side effects are pretty intense—"

"When does it wear off?"

"Who knows. But any time you want to turn it off, all you have to do is ask."

Erik lets out a sob and rushes him just as my knife breaks through the last of the nylon fibers. The sudden release of the tether makes me wobble on the banister, panic surges through me, but I pitch myself forward and fall hard on the landing as the top of the sail goes billowing down, down, down. I drag myself to the edge of the gallery, the wood banister pressing against my cheek, the air too knocked out of me to try and stand. The sail billows like a tidal wave, a mass of blue and white plummeting three stories to the atrium floor with a sound like rushing wind. Erik, standing just below where the two bottom points of the sail are anchored, is buried in a sea of tensile fabric. He curses, fighting to get out from under it, and Skye looks up and yells:

"Thank you, Erik's girlfriend!"

And then his running steps echo down the marble hall.

I twist myself upright, grimacing with pain, fresh blood soaking into my bandage. Below me, Erik rips through the fabric, tendons standing out on his wrists and neck, face incandescent with rage. A moment later he's climbing up the stairs, and I do not mean taking the steps. In the time it takes me to get back to my feet, Erik has hauled himself up the banisters of all three stories to land beside me. He grips my shoulders, and his eyes seem to make a sound, like the high whine of a dental drill, as they bore into me.

"Why? Why would you save him?"

"I don't care about him. I'm saving *you*!" And something inside me snaps. I push Erik into the wall. He's so surprised by my anger, he lets me. I bear down on him, his shirt in my fists, hot tears flooding my eyes. "I will *kill him myself* before I let you do that, do you hear me? You're this—fine! But you're my Erik too. *And I will not let you destroy my Erik.* Do *you* understand?"

He blinks at me, amazed, then slides down against the wall to the floor, hands over his head like the house is crashing down around him. I sink down across from him, trying to see his face through his hands, but there's only darkness.

I touch his shoulder, but he flinches away, muscles jumping along the side of his neck.

"I get it, okay," he says finally, though his voice is furious, hands falling away so I can see his face at last. Too handsome as always, but with dark circles carved under his eyes, and a vein standing out at the edge of his temple I don't remember from before. "It's *sweet* of you." He pulls himself to his feet. "Well. I should go."

"Go? What?"

Erik hurries into his old bedroom, moving like he's desperate to get away from me. I follow him, glass crunching underfoot, the hardwood floor beaded with rain. The shattered window casement bangs against its frame in the wind, but the last movement of *Swan Lak*e still soars under the low rumble of the ocean tide, building to its climax. He stops and holds still, listening. Then he goes straight to the computer, tapping it back to life, a hulking gargoyle shape in the bluish light.

"Erik, you need to come back with me to the Desai's. We need you to testify in court. They'll pay your legal fees, alright, and once you explain—"

I reach for his shoulder again, but he jerks away again, puts up a hand: *Don't touch me.*

"No, they won't, Signal. That thing that just cornered you? It owns me. Sonny will smile and nod at whatever I say and hand me straight back to Skye. And there will be more drugs and more facilities and no escape. Ever."

"You can't just talk to him? He'll hear you out. Why do you assume—"

"Who told my brother you were here, Signal?" Erik rises to his feet.

"I mean, Aarush did, but—"

"There is *zero* possibility of Sonny Desai siding with me against Skye and his own son." He shakes his head. "Especially not the way I am now."

He staggers over to the wall then, presses his forehead against it like he's desperate for its clammy cold, like it's a hundred degrees in this freezing room, although the fine November rain glitters in the air between us. I move toward him slowly.

"But you can't just leave—"

"Yes, I can. I don't want to be around you right now."

I freeze. "Because I kept you from killing your brother?"

"Because my current brain chemistry was engineered by Satan himself before he got stomped by the new kids, alright?"

So he *has* seen the stream. He saw my teary, desperate confession. And he's not acknowledging it and won't let me touch him and won't return my emails.

Awkward.

"There is very little distance," Erik says then, "between what I want and what I do right now."

I step away until my back touches the opposite wall, the rumpled blankets and sleeping roll sparkling with shattered glass between us. He leans back against his side of the room, facing me now, but his feverish eyes still won't meet mine. Even though I stare at him, trying to read his strained expression.

"You want to hurt me?"

"No. The opposite." He swallows hard. "The things I want to do to you are . . . affectionate in the extreme."

His eyes meet mine at last, a look that's a physical sensation. Shivering heat cascades down my back. Even pressed against the cold wall I'm suddenly burning inside. He jerks his head down, and the song grows loud enough that I can recognize it; the waltz from *Swan Lake*, the song that was playing when we kissed at the Opera House. Hot tears edge my eyes, and I am almost sickened by how desperately I want to return to that place, my favorite in the world, that place I go when we touch.

"I don't—I don't really have a filter on what I say or what I do right now," he says gruffly, "so I need to keep some distance between us until I figure out what the hell is happening to me."

"Then why even come here?"

"Kurt. I need your help with him. I think I know what he's doing, or maybe I'm just making too many associations, I don't know. It's all—it's hard to think right now—and it always helps to talk to you. But I can't email you or call you while you're with Sonny. He's monitoring everything—"

"Wait. So Kurt *is* behind those murders?" I blink at Erik. "The ones near camp?"

"Yes. But he's going off script. None of them are related to our mission—"

"Our?"

He nods slowly. Bile rises in the back of my throat. I look away first, and he goes on, "Ledrick told me my first night back, about Dave faking your score. So yeah. You were never proof of anything. I was an idiot to think you could be."

I close my eyes.

"Then they started shooting me up with whatever the hell I'm on," he continues, "and the cellar got . . . a lot smaller. They said I could go out if I went with Kurt."

"To go kill people."

"What else am I for?" he says. Then: "But I didn't get to after all."

"No?"

"You stopped me."

I look up at him.

"When we got to the first hotel, your stream was all over the news. You, lying in the grass, all bloody—" He looks down at his hands; I realize they're trembling. "And I was so afraid, Signal. I was finally afraid and it wasn't fun, okay?" He looks up at me, eyes shining. "It felt like . . . I swear, I felt my heart rip open, but it kept going"—he clutches at his shirt, face sick—"and there was this panic, like right before you throw up, but for *days*, worse and worse and worse until I got to St. Joseph's—"

"You came to the hospital?"

"I had to make sure you were alright."

"You went inside?"

"I had a hat. No one saw. I took a visitor sticker off a guy sleeping in the hall."

It's like the moment I almost fell off the banister all over again: the dizzy fear at what could have been. The hospital they airlifted me and Jada to was crawling with police and reporters. And in the middle of all that, *Erik* had been the "cute boyfriend" who watched beside me all night?

"What were you—you could have been—are you out of your mind?"

"I thought you were going to die!" There's fear in his voice even now. "You almost got yourself killed, Signal! And for what? For a bunch of random Class As—"

"I came back for you."

"Don't say that! Don't say that! I can't take it." He slides down the wall, his head in his hands. He wasn't kidding about not having much of a filter, and there's a guilty thrill in questioning him with his mental guard down. I can't help myself from stepping closer and asking:

"Take what, Erik?"

"You. You make everything hurt. Even before I went back to camp. You don't even know. It's almost *beautiful* how much you can hurt me." He looks away, shaking his head like he wants to stop himself, but blurts, "My mom always said, 'Erik, you were born with a broken heart. You'll never know the highs, but you'll never have the hurt.' And she was right. I was nice and numb. Until you made my heart a living hell."

I kneel a few feet from him.

"When I left, I thought I was setting us both free. You'd clear your name, and I could get over this. But your voice calling for me kept ringing in my head. And then, that stream—" His face twists. "And you were so still in the hospital bed. I'd squeeze your hand and you wouldn't even blink. I hate when your eyes are shut, okay? I hate it more than anything. Finally, right at dawn, your fingers closed around mine . . . And I broke down, Signal. I was so happy I *cried*." He shakes his head like he still can't believe it. "I'm not good. I can't be fixed. But my heart works. You prove that alright."

I've closed the distance now, on my knees on the floor across from him, in arm's reach. It's like I'm seeing him for the first time, this strange and complicated person who is incapable of hiding from me any part of himself.

"Sorry," I say at last, and he laughs. "Erik, can I touch you?"

He holds very still, then nods.

I take his hand. He stares down at my fingers like they're live wires, tension building up his arm and along the muscles of his neck, chest rising and falling fast. The cold wind lashes us with rain through the open window, but it barely registers over the heat of his face as I press my other hand to his burning cheek. His shoulders drop at the contact, the crease between his eyebrows going smooth.

"I love you," I tell him, looking him right in his eyes, the torn one and the sad one. "I love you, Erik." His head sinks heavily into my hand. "I love you. I love you, I love you . . ."

I will keep saying it until he knows it's true, until it's the only thing my voice in his head ever says again. Because I was right about only one thing, back on the bus to Ledmonton. An unconfessed crush *is* nothing. It is an airless void that will suffocate your heart quite comfortably.

That's tempting when your heart is trying to ruin your life. But sometimes your life needs ruining. Sometimes what you thought was living isn't even close. And like a crush, that is a secret only your heart knows.

A low wail of sirens moves south down the highway toward us. But the whistle of the northbound train cuts through the rain, closer and closer. He can catch it if he goes now, runs down the steps to the beach.

"Sirens, Erik. Time to go."

I have to shake him like a sleepwalker to get him to his feet, but his gaze is clearer now. He moves through the window and into the tree, slipping a little on the wet bark, then catching himself with a wild laugh. He turns back to me, smiling his most beautiful smile, my own beam of daylight.

"We need to go on our third date, Signal," he says. "I'm going to plan it all out—you'll see. I don't know how or where yet, but look out for a sign from me in the next couple days—"

"I will, I will, now *go*! Right now!" I am all but pushing him out the window.

"Wait, one more thing—"

Blue and red lights bounce through the fog, down the long highway. Still, he hangs half in the window, refusing to look away from me, holding my wrists like he can't bear to let me go. He presses the back of my hand to his burning mouth.

"I love you too," Erik says.

And then he's gone, and I'm alone in the ruined room, soaked with rain and scattered with broken glass. But I can't stop smiling because our song has started up again.

He has it on single repeat.

Acknowledgments

It has meant so much to me to continue this story, and this series would not exist without the enthusiasm and effort of my literary agent, Stacia Decker. My sincere thanks to Matt Martz and the team at Crooked Lane Books; especially my editor Melissa Rechter, whose excitement and insight has so elevated Teen Killers in Love, and the conscientious eye of Rebecca Nelson.

I could not write without the world's most dedicated father, my husband Ryan, making sure I have the time to do so. I am forever grateful to my sisters Cinnamon and Allison, both for their love of this series and their endless flexibility as baby-sitters during a pandemic. Thank you to my parents, Richard and Barbara, for showing me the dedication and mental resilience required to create something. And thank you to my little poet Lovey, who keeps me, in her words, "hungry for tomorrow."

A book is not truly alive until it's read by someone who loves it. To everyone who loved the first book, Teen Killers Club, and recommended or shared it in any way, thank you forever.